MEDIE

In Shadows of Kings

K. M. ASHMAN

CANELO

First published in the United Kingdom in 2013 by K. M. Ashman

This edition published in the United Kingdom in 2022 by

Canelo
Unit 9, 5th Floor
Cargo Works, 1-2 Hatfields
London, SE1 9PG
United Kingdom

A CIP catalogue record for this book is available from the British Library.

Print ISBN 978 1 80032 445 9
Ebook ISBN 978 1 80032 444 2

Look for more great books at www.canelo.co

Printed and bound in Great Britain by Clays Ltd, Elcograf S.p.A.

1

Foreword

Medieval II – In Shadows of Kings is the second book in the Medieval Series and though it can be read as a standalone novel, it is recommended that you read, *Medieval I – Blood of the Cross* first to get a feel for the background story of the main characters.

The storyline is obviously a work of fiction but like all my books, it is set against the backdrop of real events at the time.

However, this novel takes a direction you will not expect. It follows the story of something reputed to have happened in the twelfth century and whilst there are those who claim it didn't happen, there is growing evidence that some of the things you are about to read are a historical reality. Further justification can be found at the back of the book but I would strongly suggest you read the novel first so the storyline isn't compromised.

So sit back, relax, suspend reality for a while and be prepared to go somewhere you would never expect a medieval book to take you.

Chapter One

Wales, 1274

Deep in the hills of mid-Wales, a cloaked rider approached a sprawling village spread around the base of a hill. Perched high above, a castle loomed menacingly against the darkening sky and the rider waited until the daylight was almost gone before gently urging his horse forward through the claustrophobic streets. The candle-light escaping from the slats of the shutters cast shimmering shadows as his horse plodded through the stinking mud and sounds of merriment filtered from a distant tavern in one of the back lanes. His attention was briefly caught by a young man pulling a giggling woman into a side alley to claim the pleasure his hard-earned coins had bought him. As the peasant's hands lifted the whore's skirts, he scowled up at the rider.

'What are you staring at, stranger? This is no business of yours.'

'Oh, I don't know,' said the girl looking up at the rider with a hopeful gleam in her eye. 'He looks like he may have a heavy purse about him. Perhaps he is a nobleman who fancies a bit of commoner. Is that it, stranger? Fancy a bit of real woman instead of those lace-covered cadavers that chill the beds of nobles?'

She cackled at her own joke before being pulled further into the shadows by the needy farm worker and as the rider continued on his way, the sounds of her laughter echoed through the narrow streets around him.

A few minutes later he approached the castle at the top of the winding path and stopped before the draw-bridge covering the defensive ditch. It was unusual that any drawbridge was down at this time of night but he knew he was expected, as indeed were several others of equal importance. A yeoman with lowered pike stepped forward out of the darkness.

'Make yourself known, stranger,' he said quietly.

'My name is of no consequence,' said the rider. 'Be it known I am expected by the master of this house.'

'Let me see your seal,' said the yeoman.

The rider took off his ring and handed it down. The yeoman walked over to the light of a burning brazier and compared the ring to a vellum document showing the twelve seals of the expected guests. Though he could not read the words alongside each mark, the picture of a thrice-speared boar was clearly visible.

'There,' said his comrade, pointing at the matching design. 'The seal is true.'

The yeoman walked to the rider and returned the ring.

'Proceed, my lord,' he said. 'Once inside the castle you will be met by a page who will see to your further needs.' He looked down the hill. 'Do you not have courtiers?'

'I travel alone,' said the man.

'A risk in these troubled times,' said the yeoman.

'A business for me to worry about, not you,' said the rider replacing the ring. 'Now stand aside for I have been detained long enough.'

The yeoman turned and called across the drawbridge.

'Raise the gate, we have another.'

'Aye,' came a muffled reply and within moments the clank of chains signalled the portcullis was being raised within the deep castle walls.

The rider entered the castle and handed his horse to a boy. Outside the two guards returned to the warmth of the brazier.

'Who was that one?' asked the first soldier.

'I know not,' came the reply. 'Again he kept his name to himself, one of seven so far this evening. Whatever is going on, they seem desperate to keep their identities secret.'

'A strange business, but not something for us to fret over.'

'Really?' answered the first soldier. 'When men of means make plans in secret, you can wager it is men at arms who pay the price. No, whatever they are up to, no good will come of it; that much is certain.' A cough from further down the hill echoed through the darkness, returning their attention to the task in hand. 'Back to it, comrade,' said the soldier. 'It seems another approaches. This could be a long night.'

—

Fifty miles away in the hills above Brycheniog, the abbey kitchens were a frenzy of activity. Usually the buildings were silent as night fell with only the quiet echoes of evening prayers whispering through the stark passages between the chapels. Tonight however, a rider had arrived with momentous news. A caravan approached which had been on the road for two days without rest. The occupants were hungry and desperately looking forward to the sanctuary the abbey would afford. Brother John issued his instructions quietly, knowing full well they would be carried out efficiently and with minimum fuss.

'Is everything ready?' he asked.

'There is cold meat laid out with warmed wine and loaves of bread,' said one of the other monks. 'It is the best we could do with such short notice.'

'It will be enough,' said Brother John. 'I'm sure he will want to give thanks for his safe journey first so we have some time. Prepare his rooms and place a clean cover at his disposal. Stoke the ovens and warm a pot of water so he can wash the dust of the road from his skin.'

'Immediately,' said the second monk and disappeared to his duties. Brother John summoned the rest of the monks and lined them up on either side of the corridor leading into the cloisters.

'They are here,' said a voice and Brother John walked toward the door, subconsciously straightening his habit as he went. The sound of voices outside the walls mingled with the unmistakeable clatter of a tailgate falling open from the back of a wagon. Moments later the gate opened and a man ducked under the low lintel before straightening up to face the two rows of monks. As one, each lowered himself to his knees, folding his hands in prayer at the unexpected arrival of the man wrapped within a warm travelling cloak. Brother John stepped forward and took the hands of the abbot.

'Father, it is good to see you again,' he said.

'Thank you, Brother,' said Father Williams, 'it is good to be back.'

Chapter Two

Dolwyddelan Castle

Sir Robert of Shrewsbury stood at the far end of the hall, admiring the tapestries showing hunting scenes from across the centuries. In his hand he held a silver goblet of warmed ale. The last of the summer days were clinging on desperately, and the chill in the evening air meant the harvests had been collected and many beasts slaughtered and salted ready for the coming winter months.

Overall it had been a fair summer and though colder months always claimed their victims, there seemed no need for anyone to go unduly hungry this winter, always assuming they had made sensible provision. Those peasants who had frittered away the few coins they had earned tilling the manor's fields would find stern faces and often be on the end of a beating stick should they beg as a result of their poor planning. At such times many would turn to family and friends but those who were alone in the world often found only death's deadly sickle at the end of a cold night.

Luckily these were not issues Sir Robert need worry himself about for as a landed knight, he had ample provision for all his family and indeed the many servants in his fortified manor house in the Welsh Marches. He even maintained a small corps of men at arms within the manor as a security measure, an expensive necessity yet so needed in these turbulent times.

'Sir Robert,' said a voice behind him, 'good to see you could make it.'

Sir Robert turned and saw Lord Idwal of Ruthin standing a few paces away.

'Idwal,' he said holding out his arm, 'it has been a long time. Well met.'

Idwal took the arm in friendship and summoned a page to refill Sir Robert's goblet.

'Too long,' he replied. 'How is that wonderful wife of yours?'

'Just as beautiful,' said Sir Robert, 'and I am now the proud father of a two-year-old son.'

'So I heard,' said Idwal, 'allow me to drink to his health.' He lifted his goblet and sipped at the wine though never taking his eyes from those of the knight before him.

'So,' he said eventually looking around, 'why do you think we have been summoned here?'

'I think summoned is too strong a word,' said Sir Robert. 'There are many in this room who would respond to no summons except from Llewellyn himself.'

'I agree,' laughed Idwal. 'Pride is a severe master and many in here bow to its demands. Let's use the word invited, far more congenial to gentlemen such as these.'

The conversation was interrupted by the sound of doors crashing open and people striding purposely into the room. Sir Robert turned to see the Castellan head straight to a side table, pushing a page out of the way to access an ale jug. Rather than fill one of the many goblets he drank straight from the jug before wiping the foam from his beard. Letting out a belch he turned to face the gathered men before him.

'Gentlemen,' he said, as he removed his leather gauntlets, 'apologies for the lateness of my arrival but there was a situation that needed my personal attention. It took a little longer than I thought, but suffice to say, the matter has been resolved to my complete satisfaction.' He threw the gauntlets toward a waiting page, who dropped one in his nervousness. Sir Robert bent and picked it up, noticing the stains across the studded knuckles, still sticky from the blood of some unfortunate recipient. Sir Robert handed the glove to the page and looked over to the man who had administered the justice.

Rhodri ap Gruffydd was a man of immense stature. He was at least a head taller than any man present and his barrel of a chest was complemented with muscular arms, the result of constant sword practice since he was a boy, twenty-five years earlier.

Overall his appearance was one of a brawler and his manners certainly didn't reflect his ancestry from one of the greatest Princes of Wales but despite this, he held the respect of every man present. He was a strict master to all who lived on his lands and administered swift justice to any brigand, cheat or varlet who carried out their less than honest trade within his jurisdiction. However, it was also said that those who worked hard and showed fealty to his name were rewarded by his protection, and nobody went cold or hungry when times were hard. By doing this he had amassed many informants throughout the country and every man present had benefitted from his wealth at some time or another. Eventually he had been given the name that he now bore as proudly as his coat of arms: Tarian, shield of the poor.

'Tarian,' called a voice, 'I see age has not been kind. You are even fatter than I remember.'

The man glared toward the rear of the room and focused on the speaker.

'Idwal, my friend,' he said loudly. 'Alas you speak the truth. My girth does indeed expand beyond my sword belt but it is only because every time I bed your wife, she feeds me sweet pastries.'

The room erupted into laughter at the riposte and Idwal crossed the hall to grasp Tarian's sword arm in friendship.

'Good to see you, friend,' he said.

'And you, Idwal. Come, be seated for though there are matters to be discussed, I would see you fed first.'

The twelve men each took a seat around the long oaken table and waited as the servants filled their tankards with frothing ale.

'Gentlemen,' said Tarian standing up, 'thank you for coming tonight. I am sure you all have a thousand questions and all will be revealed in the fullness of the evening but before I fill your heads with words, I will fill your bellies with food.' A side door opened and a column of serving girls carried trays of roasted pork into the room along with bowls of stewed pheasant in red wine. Loaves of bread were spread down the table and the ale jugs topped up. As soon as the servants had gone, he turned to the table and lifted his tankard.

'First, a toast,' he said, 'to the recently deceased King Henry of England,' he paused and looked at the expectant faces around the table. 'May his corpse rot in the fires of hell.' He lifted his tankard and drained the contents to the supportive cheers of his guests. He slammed his tankard down on the table and clapped his hands for the entertainment to begin. A jovial tune floated through the air and a troop of flute players entered the room followed by an old man beating out the rhythm on a handheld tabor.

–

Sir Robert enjoyed the entertainment provided by his host and the company of similarly minded folk; however, despite the light-hearted mood, he noted that like him, all present were careful how many times their tankards were refilled, knowing full well that serious matters were afoot. He looked around, mentally naming each of the men around the table and realized the deceased King would have paid a handsome price for the heads of most present. These were the minor lords of South Wales and the Marches, the men who gave the crown many sleepless nights with their constant problems and demands.

Even though their notoriety was common knowledge, Sir Robert took comfort in their presence for these were men of similar ilk, fellow nobles who could be trusted to share his extreme political views without fear of contradiction. Over the years many men such as he had become disillusioned with the monarchy holding court from London and whilst this in itself was no great shock, the dangerous undercurrent of all men present was that they were also disrespectful about their own monarch, Prince Llewellyn of Wales.

Once the meal was over, the talk dwindled as the servants cleared the tables and once the last of the musicians had left, Tarian himself went to the three doors of the hall and barred them from the inside. At this the room fell silent for it was obvious the business of the evening was about to start and the Castellan had ensured they would not be overheard or interrupted.

He regained his seat and took another draft of ale before slowly looking around the table, pausing to stare each man in the eyes for several seconds. When they alighted on him, Sir Robert felt his head had been pierced with blazing pokers.

'Gentlemen,' said Tarian at last, 'to business. I have asked you to come here tonight not as lords or knights, but as trusted friends whose love for this country is as passionate as my own. I know that every man around this table bears a heart that aches for the times of our grandfathers when our country stood proud alongside the English, strong in its own identity, and honoured its own heritage.'

A couple of mugs were tapped gently on the table in acknowledgement.

'As you know,' continued Tarian, 'Henry is long dead and we await the return of Longshanks from the Holy Land with trepidation, for make no mistake, no matter what you thought of Henry, Longshanks will make his father's brutality seem like a mere shepherd's scolding.'

Again there were murmurs of agreement around the room. Prince Edward was famed for his brutality, and his hatred of the Welsh was well known.

'When will he return?' asked a voice.

'I know not for sure but it is said he could be back within months. Until then the country is still led by a coalition of favoured nobles and is nothing but a ship without a rudder. You would think, would you not, that a strong prince of equal nobility would seize the chance of kingship?'

'You talk of Llewellyn?' suggested Idwal.

'I do, but we all know he is a man of hesitation and fails to see the opportunity which begs for attention at his feet.'

'Llewellyn would never attack London,' said another voice. 'His army is too weak.'

'And his treasuries too full of the King's gold,' sneered another. 'He has been in Henry's pay since the treaty of Montgomery. Why would he attack the very system that fills his coffers?'

'I have heard a different account,' interceded Sir Robert. 'They say he struggles to pay tribute to the Crown each year and since the King's death, has neglected to send the three thousand marks the treaty demands.'

'If that is so,' said Idwal, 'why does his tax collector still cast his shadow across my gates? He still collects his taxes from the likes of us, and I fear we have a man who has lost his way and kneels to the English Crown at the slightest whim.'

'You do him a disservice, sir,' said Sir Robert. 'Forget not it was he who defeated the English at Cadfan and singlehandedly united Wales under his rule.'

'That's as may be but was over twenty years ago. Since then he signed terms at Montgomery and his rule has been as diluted as the wine in a cheap tavern.'

'Gentlemen,' interrupted Tarian, 'we squabble like washerwomen yet the facts are these: the Crown of England is weak, and Longshanks' return is imminent. The future is unknown and a veil of uncertainty clouds our vision. As a squire, I carried a knight's shield onto the battlefield at Cadfan and yes, Llewellyn was as impressive as the bards' songs suggest, but he is that man no more. His time is done. What we need is a new torch to light the way, a guiding light to take us through the darkness of uncertain times and unite the country under a common banner. If that means facing Longshanks across the battlefield of a misty morning, then so be it.'

A gasp rushed around the table for though they hated the Crown with a passion, another uprising could cause an all-out war between countries.

'Calm yourselves,' said Tarian, noticing the angst amongst them, 'I have not brought you here to plan rebellion, at least not yet. I have a different idea. A path not considered by any man here nor any other I know. It is different and dangerous, yet could provide an answer to all the uncertainty that tears our country apart. This is why I have brought you here, to hear my plans and hopefully pledge your support. All I ask is you hear me out and if you think I speak as a fool, then you are free to leave with our friendship intact.'

The noise died down as everyone waited for him to continue.

'What I am about to suggest,' said Tarian, 'will stretch your minds to the limit. It will ask you to suspend belief and entrust your faith not only in the Lord but in my ancestry and limited evidence. Yet, if what I am about to propose comes to pass, it will enable this country to be united once more under a common banner recognised by all. However, should this scheme fall upon the ears of the court of either Longshanks or indeed Llewellyn, then I fear all our heads will be set upon pikes above the Tower of London within a month. For this reason I ask that any man not willing to contemplate treason leaves now before it is too late. Absent yourself without fear of retribution for nothing we have said so far is evidence of anything except the drunken ramblings of old men. However, if it is your choice to stay and hear my vision, then there is no going back and if I have any suspicion of even a rumour leaving this tower then my wrath will fall upon you like a rabid bear.' He looked around the room at the silent men. 'So,' he continued, 'let it be known which side of these walls you stand, inside or out.'

For a moment nobody moved until an old man at the back of the hall pulled himself to his feet.

'Tarian,' he said. 'I have been honoured to call you friend for many years. Before that, I fought alongside your father at Cadfan and consider myself your family's most loyal comrade. However, my bones are weary and I find more comfort before the burning logs of my hearth than hunting deer on my courser. My heart craves the adventure of youth but my head overrules such foolish whims. I fear my days of campaign are over, so for that reason, I will decline involvement and respectfully withdraw from your presence.'

'Sir Bevan,' answered Tarian, 'go with head held high for there is not one amongst us who doubts your courage, and I know you will keep your silence in these matters. Go forth with my gratitude and respect.'

Sir Bevan nodded silently and turned to leave the hall. When he had gone Tarian turned to the remaining nobles.

'Is there anyone else?'

Nobody moved, so Tarian walked over and secured the door once again before returning to the head of the table.

'So this is it,' he said. 'Brothers united in a noble cause. Prepare yourselves for astonishment, my friends, for the tale I am about to relate has the power to change our world.'

Chapter Three

The Benedictine Abbey, Brycheniog

Father Williams walked around the cloisters taking in the morning air. His journey from the Holy Land had been arduous and had taken much longer than he had anticipated. Longshanks had decreed he would travel via Rome and he had been escorted on his journey by a unit of Hospitaller knights. As instructed, they had sailed via Cyprus before landing at Venice, and travelling overland to surrender the relic recently discovered in Syria.

The sea voyage had been rough and in his weakened state he had caught a fever, coming close to death but the prayers of the pious knights seem to have been answered, and the fever broke before they reached the mainland. As soon as he was strong enough, the Hospitallers bought a covered wagon and they continued their journey to Rome to deliver his sacred package.

That had taken the best part of two years and though he was now back within the familiar walls of his own abbey, he was exhausted from travelling and he drank in the familiarity of his surroundings with silent gratitude. He looked up at the familiar pre-dawn stars visible in the navy sky. This had always been his favourite part of the day, the time between morning prayers and breaking his fast.

A noise behind him made him turn and he saw the silhouette of a hooded man standing quietly in the shadows.

'Brother Maynard,' he said quietly, 'I didn't see you there.'

'Father, forgive me,' said the monk. 'I know you favour this place and since you have been away, I too have taken the opportunity to wonder at God's majesty during this quiet time. I intended being gone before you came out but alas was slow in my execution.'

'Worry not, brother,' said Father Williams, 'God's majesty is big enough for both of us. Come, join me under His splendour.'

The two monks walked quietly around the cloisters, talking quietly about the business of the abbey. Finally Brother Maynard broached the subject everyone was desperate to hear more about.

'Father,' he said, 'would it be remiss of me to enquire about Rome?'

'I don't see why,' said Father Williams, 'knowledge is good for all men and as such we have a duty to share. What do you want to know?'

'Everything,' said Father Maynard, 'I have heard it is a beautiful city.'

'It is indeed,' said the abbot. 'The cathedrals are a sight to behold and all the holy palaces are lined with the finest marble.'

'Is it true that artisans roam the streets in search of commissions?'

'Indeed they do,' said the abbot, 'and many are given tasks to decorate the walls of the churches. Personally I prefer something a little more austere but there is no denying their work is remarkable. Pictures the size of ten men atop one another illustrate passages from the bible and the gaze of our Lord peers down from every corner.'

'It sounds wonderful,' said Brother Maynard. 'You must have been immersed in the glory of Christ but it does make me wonder why you have returned so soon. Surely it was an opportunity to bask in our Lord's glory, especially as you were the bearer of Christ's cross?'

The abbot turned to stare at the monk.

'You know about the cross?'

'A little,' said the monk. 'Apparently the taverns are rife with rumours and the tales are repeated here by the traders who supply the kitchens.'

'What do you know exactly?'

'Only that Garyn ap Thomas, the blacksmith's son, rescued the artefact from the possession of the heathen and delivered it unto Prince Edward. Subsequently you were tasked with delivering the relic to the Pope himself. Is this true, Father, for surely the fact that two people of this manor played such an important part in the tale is something to be celebrated? We are truly blessed.'

'The tale is true to an extent,' said the abbot, 'but unfortunately falls short of the conclusion.'

'There is more?' asked the monk.

'There is and I will share it with you soon but first there is business to attend. After we have broken our fast attend me in my rooms, for I have a task I would have you undertake on my behalf.'

'Of course,' said Brother Maynard and together they re-entered the corridors to make their way to the eating hall. Outside, the first birdsong heralded the approach of the dawn.

–

The day passed warm and sunny and down near the village, Garyn ap Thomas stood atop of a wooden scaffold passing up bales of packed straw. The sun was hot on his naked back and sweat dripped off his chin as he laboured to replace the roof that had been destroyed by fire four years earlier. The thatcher placed the bales in place ready to be pinned to the lower layer, keen to get them all up before it got dark.

'One more day, Master Garyn, and all the hard work will be done. The rest will be trimming and dressing.'

'A welcome thought indeed,' said Garyn. 'I never realised it was such hard work.'

'Lucky we have the weather,' said the thatcher. 'At least the house will be habitable again before the autumn sets in.'

'Garyn,' called a voice, 'I have ale and cheese.'

'A few minutes more, Elspeth,' answered Garyn. 'We'll get these last few bales up and then take a break.'

Elspeth was Garyn's young wife and was the daughter of the village fletcher. They had been wed soon after Garyn had returned from the Holy Land two years earlier. He lifted the last bale onto the rafters and climbed down the ladder to face the girl.

'I can't stay long,' said Elspeth. 'My father needs more goose feathers from the manor. By the time you return home I'll be back and we can eat together. Father has caught a couple of hares and mother is cleaning the turnips as we speak.'

'Soon this will be our home,' said Garyn, glancing at the smoke-blackened walls. 'Another week, two at most, and we will be sat at our own hearth making our own hare broth.'

'It has been a hard few years, Garyn; I can hardly wait. What about the shutters?'

'Geraint is making them. By the time the roof is finished the walls will be weathertight and a new door will keep wolves and brigands at bay.'

'Don't even jest about such things,' said Elspeth. 'It is said a wolf took a child from the outskirts of Senni just a few weeks ago.'

'A mere tale to frighten children,' said Garyn with a smile.

'Possibly, but you can't deny they are getting braver. Anyway, how is Geraint? I haven't seen him for many weeks.'

'He is much better,' said Garyn, 'and has regained much of the muscle he lost in the dungeons of Sir John. He still refuses to speak about what happened down there but at least he is regaining his health.'

'And Misha?'

'She has settled in well, though many heads turn to stare when they walk into Brycheniog.'

'To be fair, not many have seen anyone with such skin colour before,' said Elspeth. 'It has been likened to a seasoned hazelnut. Does Geraint intend to take her as his wife?'

'They have got very close,' said Garyn, 'but marriage between Christian and Muslim is forbidden by the Church. Until recently he was too sick for such things to be an issue but as he regains his strength his thoughts turn to the future and I feel there may be upset to come.'

'In what way?'

'At the moment, Misha shares the rooms of the serving girls at the manor while Geraint helps with the stock and sleeps above the stables, but soon he will want to make

18

his own way and as far as I can see, whatever future he pursues, it will include Misha.'

'But surely there will be a place alongside you at the forge?'

'I had hoped so but he has never taken much interest in the ways of iron. He seeks a more adventurous life and talks of making his fortune overseas.'

'God will decide his path,' sighed Elspeth. 'Anyway, take this cheese for now and we will eat a meal fit for kings when you get home.'

Garyn kissed her goodbye and watched as she made her way to the track that would lead her to the manor a few miles away.

'A fine-looking woman,' said the thatcher joining Garyn on the ground.

'She is,' said Garyn. 'Sometimes I feel I don't deserve her.'

'It is said she waited for you while you were on Crusade,' said the thatcher.

'It is true she waited,' said Garyn, 'but I never took the way of the cross. I simply travelled to the Holy Land to ensure my brother was safe.'

'But wasn't there a little matter about a holy relic?'

Garyn looked at the thatcher and laughed.

'Gossiping in the tavern again, Tom?'

'I wouldn't say gossiping,' said Tom, 'for such things are for the likes of washerwomen, but you have to agree, it is not often a man as young as you travels to the Holy Land and returns alive within two years. Either you are extremely lucky or blessed by Christ himself.'

'I suspect the former,' said Garyn, finishing his ale. 'Now, I reckon there is an hour of light left. Shall we get those last bales fastened while we can?'

'Sounds good to me,' said Tom and climbed the ladder once more.

–

The following morning Garyn lay exhausted in his bed. Elspeth lay next to him and smiled as she saw him stir.

'Good morning, husband,' whispered Elspeth, kissing Garyn on the cheek. 'Do you intend waking up today or do you hope to sleep the day through?'

Garyn opened his eyes and stretched his arms above his head.

'I think I slept the sleep of the dead,' he said between yawns. 'It seems that roofing wears out the body more than the severest beating.'

'A few more days,' said Elspeth, 'and it will be done. Here, I have brought you milk and fruit.'

Garyn lifted himself up onto one elbow, pushing the woollen cover to one side. Elspeth was already dressed in her linen kirtle, a one-piece dress with long sleeves, and though her hair fell loose about her shoulders now, he knew it would be tied up and covered with a loose wimple prior to going out in public.

'Have you eaten?' he asked.

'I have had some cheese,' she said.

'Are your parents here?'

'Why?' she asked slowly, recognising the gleam in his eye.

'I thought you could come back beneath the covers,' he said with a smile.

'No time for that,' she laughed, 'besides, my father is loading the cart with feathered arrows. We have to take a delivery this morning to the manor.'

'I'll come with you,' said Garyn, draining the tankard. 'Tom Thatcher has some business in Brycheniog this morning and won't be here until noon.' He threw back the blanket and stood up.

'Garyn,' shrieked Elspeth with a laugh, 'cover yourself up. My mother could come in at any moment and she would surely die of shame if she saw your naked body.'

'Don't fret so, Elspeth,' answered Garyn pulling on his braies. 'She shouldn't be looking.'

Elspeth laughed and walked around the wicker screen. Her parents slept on a platform above, while the newly-weds had been given one end of the long room normally used to store the unfletched arrow shafts that provided the family with their living. She picked up the bucket used for the night-time toilet and made her way out of the door.

'I'll be back in a few minutes,' she called and made her way up the path to the ditch they used for the latrine waste.

Garyn donned his woollen stockings and pulled a tunic over his head before adding a belt around his middle. Fully dressed he put on his shoes and left the house to find Elspeth.

'Ah, you have arisen' said Elspeth's father.

'The height of the sun shames me,' said Garyn, 'but I have no work until noon.'

'There is always work, boy,' said Fletcher securing the last bundles of ash arrows in the small cart. 'You would do well to remember that.'

'I will, sir,' said Garyn before adding. 'If you like I could take this load for you. I have a few hours to spare.'

Fletcher paused.

'That sounds like a good idea,' he said. 'Unlike you I have plenty of work to do and could do with the extra time. Are you sure?'

'Yes, sir,' said Garyn. 'I intended to go and see my brother anyway so I can do both at the same time.'

'So be it,' said Fletcher. 'Give me ten more minutes and I will have this done.'

Garyn nodded and walked toward the returning Elspeth.

'Good news,' he said. 'We have the morning together. I am coming with you; your father is staying here.'

Elspeth grinned and held his hand.

'Good news indeed,' she said before adding a little more quietly, 'and if you are lucky, we may just stop off in the woods for a while.'

'My thoughts exactly,' laughed Garyn and watched her go back into the house to get ready. For a few moments he reflected on his life so far and realized that at last, he was getting over the death of his family in the fire and though he had suffered badly in the Holy Land, that was now behind him and his life was getting back to normal. He was with the woman he loved, his brother was safe and the family forge where he intended to make his living was almost repaired. Life was good and all he could see before him was a future as a blacksmith surrounded by strong sons. Little did he know that fate was about to intervene and an old adversary would force him into an uncertain future he could never have imagined in a thousand lifetimes.

-

Several hours later, Garyn and Elspeth delivered their cargo of arrows to the manor but as they drove the cart up to the courtyard, they could see a crowd gathered before the doors, many holding their heads in their hands as wails of anguish filled the air.

'Oh Lord,' gasped Elspeth, 'what's happened?'

'I'll find out,' said Garyn and leapt from the cart to approach the crowd.

'Garyn,' called a voice and he turned to see his brother running toward him.

'Geraint, what's happening?' he asked. 'Has there been an accident?'

'Worse,' said Geraint. 'There is news about Cadwallader, he has fallen whilst serving Longshanks.'

Garyn's face fell for he knew the man well, having travelled to the Holy Land with him a few years earlier, and though he had been a hard master he had also been very fair.

'Is he badly injured?' he asked, dreading the response.

'He is dead,' said Geraint. 'A messenger arrived this very morn with the terrible news. The letter is from Longshanks himself and in it he says Cadwallader fell in a skirmish on the outskirts of Acre many months ago. He instructs the family to make ready a tomb, for his body is being returned for burial.'

Garyn looked around the gathered people.

'Are all these his workers?'

'They are,' said Geraint.

'There is much grief; they must have thought a lot of him.'

'Perhaps,' said Geraint, 'but they also grieve for the certainty that is now lost. With Cadwallader, they knew what to expect. He was hard but fair and everyone knew their place. His wife is ill and as he has no sons; his land falls to his eldest daughter. Already there is talk that

Cadwallader's brother will arrange for her to be married to an English noble with a view to securing peace on the borders of his own lands. If this happens, the estate will be sold off to the highest bidder or gifted to a Longshanks loyalist.'

'It is a sad day,' said Garyn eventually, 'but no amount of fretting will change what has happened. All we can do is keep working and carve out our place amongst the people of the village.' He turned to face his brother. 'Geraint, this news has dragged us down but we need to focus on ourselves. You are getting stronger by the day and now the forge is almost done, you can come home with us, back to the place where we grew up together.'

'I don't know, Garyn,' said Geraint. 'A lot has happened since I last set foot in that place and I'm not sure I can face the memories.'

'The only memories will be happy ones,' said Garyn. 'Besides, you said yourself there is no way of knowing what will happen to this place now Cadwallader is dead. Many of these people have no other option but to accept whatever fate throws at them but you have a choice. Come home with me and Elspeth. Make your place at our side and help me rebuild that which was lost. There is room enough for you and Misha and you can stay as long as you want. It is as much your place as mine.'

Geraint thought for a while as he watched Cadwallader's tearful daughters come out to calm the people.

'We will come,' he said at last, 'but only until I know my own mind. I feel there is no place for me in farming or indeed at the forge, but for now I will need to earn our bread.'

Garyn smiled and walked back to the wagon to share the news with Elspeth while Geraint went in search of

Misha. Misha was a member of the Muslim Hashashin, people who had helped him in the Holy Land. For that she had been condemned and had fled for her life, joining the brothers on the journey back to England and nursing Geraint back to health in the process. Both had been taken in by Cadwallader's family as farm workers when they returned as recognition of Geraint's service to the family, but this news cast doubt upon their future.

Garyn and Elspeth paid their respects to the family and delivered the arrows to the overseer of the manor. Geraint and Misha finally reappeared, and by the time nightfall came they were all back at the forge with what meagre possessions Geraint and Misha owned. Elspeth helped Misha make up a temporary bed in the driest corner of the building.

'It seems the lure of the tavern was too much for Tom Thatcher,' said Garyn. 'He didn't turn up today.'

'It matters not,' said Geraint. 'Now I am here perhaps we can finish it together.'

'That would be good,' said Garyn. 'I have to get Elspeth home. Will you be all right here tonight?'

'It is more comfortable than the stable he has been sleeping in,' said Misha. 'We will be fine.'

'Until the morrow then,' said Garyn and left the unlikely pair alone in the part-finished forge with only a candle for company. As they rode back to the village and the house of the fletcher, they talked quietly of the day's events and the implications they may have.

'If he really is dead,' said Elspeth, 'what will become of his men who are still out there?'

'Some will return,' said Garyn, 'but some will stay and join the ranks of a new master. I expect many will come under the sway of Longshanks himself.'

'But they are Welshmen,' she said. 'Surely they would balk at serving an English Prince.'

'There are no such divisions on Crusade,' said Garyn, 'and the petty arguments of back home are for politicians not brothers in arms. Besides, Edward is no longer a prince; he is now the King of England and the treaty between Llewellyn and the Crown, no matter how precarious, means their loyalty falls under his banner.'

'You say his body will be returned for burial, but surely it will rot long before it reaches the manor?'

'His corpse will be disembowelled and his bones stripped of all flesh within days of his death,' explained Garyn. 'All soft tissue will be burned or buried but his bones will be packed in salt and returned home to be buried in the land of his birth.'

'That's awful,' said Elspeth.

'Yet preferable to being buried in a land which does not share our beliefs. How could a soul rest in unconsecrated ground?'

'I suppose you're right,' she sighed, 'but it is so sad.'

'Shed no tears, Elspeth,' said Garyn, 'for it is no sadder than any other man who falls in service away from home. Unless they have enough coin saved for their return, many ordinary men are doomed to have their bodies burned where they fall or even left to become carrion for the buzzards. Cadwallader is lucky to have been a man of privilege, for at least his family can tend his grave.'

'I suppose so,' said Elspeth. 'What do you think will happen now?'

'There is no way of telling but one thing is sure, it won't be long before there is a new lord of the manor in place. Some things never change, Elspeth, and though names may be different, fealty will still be expected by whosoever takes over Cadwallader's mantle. All we can do is continue what we do and let the world take care of itself. More than that is beyond us and it is not worth worrying about that we cannot influence.'

—

For the next few weeks they all worked hard finishing the forge. Tom Thatcher eventually turned up and the roof was finished in plenty of time for the winter. Shutters were added and all the walls scrubbed to remove any signs of the blaze. While the two women plugged any gaps in the walls with a mixture of horsehair and clay to block out any drafts, Garyn and Geraint cut down an aged oak in the nearby forest and though the whole tree would be used to fuel the fires for much of the winter, the main reason was to obtain a base for an anvil.

Eventually they cut a piece of the lower trunk the height of a man's waist and dragged it back to the house, placing it on the flat edge like a low table near to the actual forge itself. Geraint removed the bark and fashioned a skirt of iron to enclose the trunk, before casting a solid block of steel two feet long by one foot wide and as thick as his fist. This was the working surface and he cut an inch-deep trench into the oaken surface to hold the steel slab in place.

With the anvil done, they spent the last of the money on provisions for the winter and told the merchants that they were in the market for iron ore. Finally they went from house to house in all the local villages passing word that the forge was back up and running.

Business was slow but with the dried stores they had bought and the occasional job received from passers-by, they managed to get through the mild winter without too much trouble. By day the young men worked the forge or hunted for whatever they could find in the forests, while the women baked bread or prepared potage for their meals. All four shared the forge together and formed private sleeping areas separated by willow screens. The worst of the cold was held at bay by the thick stone walls and the embers of the overnight fires, but even then, the warmest place during the hours of darkness was beneath the heavy woollen bed covers. The nights were long and the two young men spent many hours sat at the table talking across a solitary candle as they recalled the past and discussed the future.

Occasionally Geraint went into the tavern in the village, often not returning until the dawn and when the few coins he may have saved ran out, he had his ale bought by those who wanted to hear tales from the Crusades. Often Garyn worried for him but it seemed his brother still suffered from nightmares and often needed the company of men of a certain ilk, fellow soldiers who had suffered as had he. The bond made by such men was unbreakable and Garyn knew any attempt at reining him in would be futile. One morning he came back from such a trip and Garyn came out to find him dipping his head in the horse trough.

Geraint threw back his head and tied his wet hair back with a leather thong before turning to see his brother staring at him.

'Garyn,' he said, 'I am sorry I am late but I have news.'

'Geraint, we have a commission to deliver to the mill,' said Garyn. 'It has to be there by noon and it isn't even loaded yet.'

'I know,' said Geraint, 'but the tavern was awash with tales of a coming venture. We need to talk.'

'There will be time to talk later. First, we need to get these chains delivered. I'll get the horse harnessed; you get yourself some food.'

'But Garyn...'

'Later,' snapped Garyn and left his brother standing outside the forge while he went to the shed where they kept the horses. He had intended to ride alongside his brother on the cart but was so angry at Geraint's lateness, he decided to ride Silverlight instead, the charger he had brought back from the Holy Land.

An hour later they were on their way, and while Geraint drove the cart Garyn rode on in front, happy to keep his distance. Eventually they delivered the chains and were on the way back when they pulled up at a crossroads to eat some food.

Garyn unwrapped some salted cheese from his pack and breaking it in half, shared it with his brother. The two young men ate hungrily before Garyn broke the awkward silence.

'Misha was worried about you last night. She wanted to come and find you.'

'I know,' said Geraint, breaking some bread. 'I don't mean to hurt her; it's just that sometimes I need to share ale with others who have known the burden.'

'You can talk with me,' said Garyn.

Geraint looked over and smiled.

'Garyn, you are my brother and I love you dearly but your time in Acre bore no resemblance to the life of a paid man in the King's army.'

'I served as a lancer while travelling through France,' said Garyn.

'It's not the same,' said Geraint. 'When you reached Acre you were released from service and never saw battle.'

'You know why that was,' said Garyn, 'but those months in the saddle were no less service.'

'I do not mean to diminish your time,' said Geraint, 'but as paid men we lived alongside each other, trained together and fought for the man alongside us as brother. Many I called friend have been long buried and those who still live, serve in Palestine. But location is just a place, for all men at arms carry the same burden and when I meet someone who has taken the king's coin, there is a need to share the tales. I am not the only one to feel the need; many feel the same.'

'What is it you miss so much?' asked Garyn quietly.

'I don't know,' said Geraint. 'It was hard; we were often cold and hungry and men fell all around us. Yet there is something about that life that aches when it is absent. Perhaps it is the not knowing how long you have left, but whatever it is, I have a gnawing hunger to feel the camaraderie again.'

'You intend re-enlisting?' asked Garyn quietly.

'I do,' said Geraint. 'I am grateful for what you did, brother but now the forge is finished, I see no future for us there. I have to move on.'

'But where?' asked Garyn. 'Even you have said the Holy Land is all but lost. Why go out there to die when there is so much here?'

'That's just it,' said Geraint. 'I admit I considered taking the cross again but last night I met someone who has offered me a new life. One which meets the burning ache inside, yet gives a new purpose.'

'And who is this man?'

'He didn't say his name, only that he was enlisting experienced men at arms for a voyage across the sea.'

'To where?'

'He would not say more except the ships would sail from Caerleon six weeks from now.'

'Does that not cause concern in your mind?'

'No. The thing is, I have an opportunity to do something for myself, a chance to make my own fortune. He said that they are going to seek a great treasure and those who return will do so as wealthy men with enough gold to buy their own land.'

'You already have land, Geraint. Our father bought the land upon which the forge is built.'

'Yes, but it is not mine.'

'Of course it is,' snapped Garyn. 'It belongs to both of us and we can work it together.'

'It's not the same,' said Geraint. 'I want something I have earned by my own hand, not fallen at my feet due to the murder of my father.'

'He would have wanted it so.'

'It matters not. I will never be at peace until I have earned my place.'

'And what about Misha?'

'I am doing this for her as well as me. She will understand.'

A silence fell between them until Garyn spoke quietly.

'Your mind is set?'

'It is, brother. I have to do this.'

'How long will you be gone?'

'Two years, no more.'

'I cannot come to your aid if your fate is ill, Geraint. My place is here at Elspeth's side.'

'I understand, Garyn,' said Geraint, 'and nor would I expect you to. If my fate is to fall in a foreign land then so be it. All I ask is that you look after Misha and should opportunity arise, help her with passage back to her home.'

'Let us pray that day will never come,' said Garyn.

The two young men stared at each other in silence.

'Then we are agreed?' asked Geraint eventually.

'It gives me no happiness, Geraint, but a blind man could see you are not happy. I will not stand in your way.'

Chapter Four

The Port of Caerleon

Geraint sat alongside Tom Thatcher as he drove the cart along the busy wharf on the edge of the tidal river. Misha sat in the back alongside a barrel of dried fruit and a sack of salted meat, provisions they had accumulated for Geraint's journey.

The river water was high and amongst the myriad of smaller trading vessels, four huge ships lay tied to metal rings embedded into the ground of the dock. Each ship had two masts situated equidistantly along the deck and on each end, a small castellated tower had been incorporated into the design. Along the edge he could see the row of openings for oars, and toward the rear a mini drawbridge had been lowered from the side to allow the loading of stores and horses straight into the holds.

'Look at that,' said Tom Thatcher, reining in the horse. 'I have never seen such a thing. Surely those doors will leak when at sea and send them to the bottom as sure as lead.'

'On the contrary,' said a voice, 'they will be nailed shut and recaulked with pitch before they set sail. They won't open again until they reach landfall.'

Geraint and Tom looked at the man who had appeared alongside the cart with a ledger of names.

'And where would that be?' asked Geraint.

'Who's asking?' said the man.

'My name is Geraint ap Thomas and I have enlisted on one of these cogs though I know not which one.'

The man checked the list and nodded.

'From Brycheniog?' he asked.

'Yes.'

'Then you are expected.' said the man, 'and are designated as deckhand to the *Coronet*, the flagship of this fleet. I am the harbour master. Your journey is to the east but I know not where for it is a journey of exploration. Your ship's master will no doubt know more but that is a task for him, not me. Now, unload your cart over for I need to record your goods for taxation.'

Geraint, Misha and Tom unloaded the cart and watched as a team of workers carried the goods onto the ships. Eventually a man approached and Geraint recognised him from the tavern weeks earlier. All those on the dock gathered around him as he called their names and allocated them a ship.

'I see many faces I recognise,' said the man, 'as well as some new to me. Those who will travel on this voyage do so of their own free will, and for the duration, will be subject to the captain's justice without question. If you are not willing to heed this proclamation, even unto death, then return from whence you came now. Those who still seek the riches this quest promises, then step forward and make your mark.'

Geraint turned to face Misha.

'This is it,' he said. 'After this, there is no turning back.'

'You must do what you have to do,' said Misha.

Geraint nodded.

'I will return, Misha, I promise, and when I do, we will seek a way to be together. Whether that is in this land, or one we have not yet trod, we will find a place whose people will not judge.'

'Then I will wait with undoubting patience,' said Misha, 'or until age leads me to my grave.'

'You there, make your choice,' shouted the man.

'I must go,' said Geraint and kissed her on the cheek before turning to join the last of the men boarding the ship. Within minutes he was on the gently moving deck and looked down at Misha on the wharf.

'Until next we meet,' he shouted and received a wave in return.

'Clear the wharf,' shouted the harbour master and the crowd still ashore manoeuvred carts and horses as they jostled to return to their villages.

Geraint watched as Tom Thatcher drove the cart out of the gates and within minutes, they disappeared from sight.

'Everyone gather together,' shouted a voice and Geraint joined forty other men before the forecastle. 'You have made your choice of your own free will,' he continued, 'and whilst you are on this ship you will answer to me on a daily basis. My name, as far as you are concerned is Logger, and I act on behalf of the captain.'

'What's his name?' asked a voice.

'That is of no consequence to you and if you should have cause to talk to him, you will address him only as captain. The forecastle here,' he pointed behind him, 'is out of bounds to everyone except the captain and his staff. The castle at the stern is where the food will be distributed while at sea. There will be one meal a day of hot broth, weather permitting, and an issue of dry oats for every man. Use it sparingly as on occasion, the oven will not be fired and you may have to go without hot food for many days. Oats and water make an adequate meal when times are hard.'

'But what of our own food?' asked Geraint. 'We each brought stores for three months.'

'It is no longer yours,' said Logger, 'but adds to the communal pot. We have a long voyage before us and only by sharing everything can we hope to reach our destination.'

'Where do we sleep?' asked another voice.

'You will soon be allowed into the hold. Below deck you will find three levels. The top level is where the food and equipment is stored. Find what space you can but know this: any man found cutting into any container seeking unissued rations will be thrown overboard without hesitation. This is not up for discussion, so don't even think about it. On the next level down, you will see a platform on either side for the permanent crew aboard this ship, the mariners. Upset them at your peril for though their task is menial, they are highly thought of and good fighting men. When we disembark, they will stand alongside you as pikemen in any conflict. There may be times when you too will take turns at the oars if need be but when we make landfall, you will revert to the skills each has brought with you.

'Finally,' he continued, 'there is the lower hold but there is nothing down there for you as it's where the horses are kept as well as the barrels of water.' He looked down at the river. 'The tide is about to turn. We will be leaving within the hour and will anchor off the coast while the ship is made ready, so I suggest you try and find yourself somewhere comfortable to lay your packs. This will be your home for many months so choose well. Once out to sea, you will be addressed by the leader of this quest and it is he who will answer any questions you still have. Now, get yourselves sorted out and muster again at the sound of the bell.'

'Months?' said a man beside Geraint as they dispersed. 'What journey east takes more than a month?'

'Perhaps the intention is to seek a sea route to the lands of the Mongols,' said Geraint. 'It is said they know the source of silks, spices and precious stones.'

'To what end?' asked the man. 'They are a warlike people and can turn as fast as a rabid dog. There are already merchants who travel those routes; let them have the risk of losing their heads.'

'We haven't yet left port and already you criticize the reasoning,' laughed Geraint.

'On the contrary,' said the man. 'I embrace the ultimate adventure but the lack of knowledge frustrates me.' He held out his arm. 'My name is Marcus and I am an archer from Builth.'

'I too am an archer,' said Geraint, taking the man's arm as a sign of comradeship, 'but hail from Brycheniog.'

The men dispersed to find themselves a space and Geraint found himself below deck, struggling to see in the dark hold. Candlelight seeped from holes in the clay pots hanging from overhead beams and it seemed that every spare inch of space was taken up by the huge number of stores. Many men made their bed space on top of the stores, using sacks of grain as a mattress whilst others burrowed between caskets or barrels, relishing the privacy the temporary walls would bring. Geraint struggled to find any room and made his way down to the lower level, passing the side staging where the rowers would bend their backs to their tasks. The seats were empty at the moment but he could see the horsehair mattresses beneath the benches where each man would sleep between shifts.

The hold got darker as he reached the lower level and the smell of animals was heavy in the air. As his eyes adjusted to the gloom, he could see a row of horses, each tethered to a rail fixed to the ship's side. At the far end there were sacks of grain and bales of hay filling every inch of space. He made his way forward and looked hopefully at the huge stack of hay.

'What do you think you are looking at?' said a voice from the darkness.

Geraint spun around and faced the man coming out of the shadows.

'I'm looking for somewhere to sleep,' said Geraint, 'and I thought…'

'You thought wrong,' said the man. 'Get yourself topside.'

'There's no space up there.'

'Then set up on deck, plenty of room there.'

'What about the weather?'

'Not my problem.'

'But why can't I sleep down here? I won't take much space.'

The wizened old man drew closer and squinted up at Geraint before snarling through rotten teeth.

'Coz this is reserved for the special guests. See, me and them.' He gestured his thumb over his shoulder toward the horses. 'They is more important than either of us, see, and if anything happens to any of 'em, it's my hide that will get flayed. Wivout the beasts, we stands no chance where we are going, see, and the master would throw every damned one of us overboard before he lost even one of 'em. Now,

38

take your stuff and get back up that ramp.' He turned to walk back into the gloom.

'Wait,' said Geraint, 'what if I help?'

The man stopped and turned.

'What do you know about beasts?' he asked.

'My family own two horses,' said Geraint, 'one cart horse and one destrier.'

'A destrier you say. How comes a knave such as you owns a charger?'

'I am no knave,' said Geraint. 'I am a trained archer who has served in the Crusades. The destrier belongs to my brother and my father was a secular knight.'

'And you expects me to believe that?'

'Believe what you want,' said Geraint.

'So why are you on this damned ship and not in some distant castle fighting the heathen?'

'That is a story for another day,' said Geraint, 'but I will say that my father is now dead and my brother runs the family blacksmiths.'

The old man's eyes widened slightly, reflecting the flickering candlelight.

'You are a blacksmith?'

'No, my brother is.'

'But you were brought up around blacksmiths?'

'All my life.'

The old man rubbed his chin and walked around the hold mumbling to himself before returning to face Geraint.

'Perhaps there can be an arrangement after all,' he said. 'I'll let you stay down here away from that lot and in return, you can help me wiv the beasts. How does that suit?'

'What will I have to do?'

'Feed and water 'em, twice a day; brush 'em once a week and clean up their shit and piss as needs be. When the weather is good, take half of 'em up each day to walk around the deck. Keeps 'em strong, see.'

'And what do I get in return?'

'A bed of hay and the company of beasts better than any man I ever met.'

Though the hold stank, Geraint had made a short sea voyage once before and knew how uncomfortable the journey could be, especially when men were packed as tight as apples in a barrel.

'Agreed,' he said and held out his hand. 'My name is Geraint ap Thomas.'

The old man ignored the gesture and turned to shuffle away.

'What do I call you?' asked Geraint, walking after the man. 'Surely you have a name.'

The old man turned and stared into space.

'I had a name once,' he said, 'but the crew, they calls me Spider.'

'Good to meet you, Spider,' said Geraint. 'So where shall I put this?' He took his kit bag off his shoulder.

'You can doss over there,' said Spider, pointing to a corner. 'Take a bale of hay for a bed but don't piss your breeches in the night. I don't want my beasts eating pissy hay, see.'

'No problem,' said Geraint and walked over to the corner. Within a few minutes he had made a small living space and unrolled his blanket over the hay. 'So,' he said, turning around, 'where exactly do you think we are going?' But there was no reply. Spider was nowhere to be seen and before Geraint could look for him, the sound of a bell rang out from above.

He walked up the ramp, past the rowers now taking their place on the benches, and joined the rest of the enlisted men on deck watching as the ships eased away from the wharf. Up on the forecastle, a weather-beaten man wearing a heavy coat gave orders to Logger who shouted them across the deck to all who needed to hear. Geraint rightly assumed he was the captain and watched with interest as the man went quietly about his business.

For an hour they were powered downstream by the steady strokes of the oarsmen and behind them, three more ships followed in their wake. Gradually the river widened and eventually the estuary opened up to the sea allowing the ships to spread out. Orders echoed around the ship and the men got out of the way as the mariners raised the sails to take advantage of the strong breeze.

Two men carried a box between them and passed it up to the forecastle where the captain and Logger spent several minutes securing it down to a fixed table. Finally Logger climbed down and joined the men on deck. Another man climbed up the ladder to join the captain. This man was far larger and Geraint could see he wore a dark green tabard beneath his heavy black cloak. A chainmail coif lay loose about his neck and his hand rested naturally on the hilt of a heavy sword. He was obvious a man of nobility and held himself with a self-confidence that demanded respect. He stepped toward the rail overlooking the deck and looked down at the men before addressing them loudly.

'Fellow travellers,' he said, 'men at arms, my name is Tarian and I am the master of this quest. I am sure you have many questions about our destination and I make no apology for keeping the secret amongst a few trusted men, but the reason will soon become clear.' He paused and looked down at the expectant faces before continuing.

'As you know, our beloved country is fractured, its inner borders disputed by many men each claiming title to their neighbour's lands. Brother kills brother whilst above us, Prince Llewellyn argues politics with the court of a king who has lain dead for over a year. That king's heir, Edward Longshanks, makes his way from the Holy Land as we speak, and instead of strengthening our walls against his armies, we quarrel like children at play. Make no mistake for though Henry was a tyrant, Longshanks will make him look lenient and his treasuries will already be making space for Welsh gold.

'Yet amongst us there are a few who are not willing to let that happen. Together we have identified a way of uniting all Welshmen under one banner, of brushing aside every claim without argument and forging our fellow countrymen into an alliance with an unbreakable cause.

'For over a year we have made our plans and put together this fleet to seek what it is that will ignite that flame of nationalism. This ship and those you see around you have been paid for by the treasuries of patriots and they expect no return. Their names will be kept from you for they are nobles of great renown and should we return successful, as I fully intend to do, then and only then will their names be made public as the heroes they truly are.

'Today we set out on a voyage that few have made before, certainly not within our lifetimes. The journey before us is virtually unknown, but with fair winds and God's grace we will reach our destination with strong hearts and iron resolve. Be of good heart and bend your backs into any task set before you, for only by sharing our strength will we succeed in aiding the weak.

'Some amongst you will have doubts and we will not shy from open and honest debate, but know this. From this day forth there is no turning back. We will sail into the face of every storm, suffer the greatest calms and ride the highest seas without any thought of falling short. Only with this mindset do we have any chance of success and when we make landfall, as we surely will, you men will cast eyes upon what few have witnessed before, the richness and bounty of a new land.

'So, I say this. Set to your tasks with vigour and look forward to returning as rich men, not measured by the weight of gold in your purse but by the freedom in your hearts as liberators of a united homeland.'

He pointed to the box on the forecastle.

'Behind me is an instrument used by the seamen from the east. It is capable of telling us which direction to sail, even when the stars are covered by cloud. With this box, we will sail across seas unimagined and find treasures undreamed of, knowing that even in the darkest of nights we know where we are under God's sky.

'Yes, there will be earthly rewards but do not let greed cloud your vision, for they will be but mere trinkets compared to the greater treasure, that which will bind us once more and free us from the yoke of Henry. Fellow countrymen, your wait is over and I can now reveal we sail not east to the Holy Land, but west across the great ocean to find a strange land once trodden by our ancestors. Once there, we will bring back not only hope and renewed belief but a burning flame to light the path against the English. Comrades, rejoice! For today we set forth to seek the legacy of one of the greatest sons of Wales and in the process, become the anvil upon which the unity of our country will be forged.'

Chapter Five

The hills of Gwent

Tom Thatcher and Misha rode the cart back to Brycheniog but were only halfway when the night closed in. Tom led the horse off the track and found a small clearing where they could bed down for the night. He fed the horse and set up a small shelter made from oiled calf skin for Misha.

'Where will you sleep?' asked Misha.

'Well, eventually I will sleep under the cart,' said Tom, 'but there is a village at the bottom of the valley and I thought I would make a visit to the tavern.'

'I will come with you,' she said.

'No, Misha,' he said, 'taverns are not places for ladies such as you.'

'Why not?'

'They are places of ruffians and murderers,' he said, 'and you may get hurt.'

'If they are so bad, why are you going?'

'I crave the ale they serve, Misha, and besides, there is other entertainment that I may partake of.'

'You talk of whores?'

'Err, you could call them that I suppose.'

'They are either whores or they are not.'

'Well, yes, then I suppose they are.'

'I will still come with you,' she said. 'I will watch your back while you seek relief.'

'No,' gasped Tom. 'I don't know what you do where you come from but over here it is a private business.'

Misha shrugged.

'I would not watch the act itself but guard the door.'

'I will be perfectly fine without you.'

'But you said it is a dangerous place. What is to stop a brigand cutting your throat while you are distracted?'

'I can look after myself,' he said and threw his cloak about his shoulders. 'No, you stay here and get some sleep. Light no fire and you will attract no attention. We are far enough off the track to avoid the eyes of passers-by.'

'When will you return?'

'Before dawn, I promise.'

'Then let it be so,' said Misha and watched him walk out of the wood.

–

Half an hour later, Tom Thatcher walked into a tavern already busy with aching farm workers and travelling troubadours. Monks mixed with labourers, and serving wenches dipped wooden tankards into casks of frothing ale, struggling to meet demand as thirsty men demanded attention. Men sat in groups talking the politics of the day while others played games of chance to increase the weight of their purses. Dice seemed to be the favourite in this tavern but Tom had long learned the outcome was down to nothing but chance and avoided the small group huddled around the upturned cask used as a dice table. He made his way through the throng to a table with an empty bench before beckoning one of the serving wenches.

'A tankard of ale,' he shouted over the noise, 'and make sure it is full. I will not part with good coin for half a mug of froth.'

'We are honest folk, stranger,' answered the wench, 'and you will find fair measure for fair coin. Do you want something to eat? We have good cawl for another coin.'

'That would be good,' said Tom. 'Add a hand of bread as well. I have travelled long today and my stomach aches from hunger.'

'And do you have any other hungers, stranger?'

'We will see,' laughed Tom. 'Let me eat first and we can barter for your other wares later.'

'So be it,' said the wench and went to get the ale.

'You will have your hands full with that one,' said a voice and Tom turned to face the man sitting alongside him.

'You speak from experience?' asked Tom.

'I do,' said the man, 'and still have the scars to prove it.' Tom laughed.

'Then I will choose carefully,' he said. 'What is your name, stranger?'

'I am Jonas,' said the man, 'and I earn my bread by digging graves.'

'A service needed by every man, eventually,' said Tom.

'A truer word was never said,' answered Jonas.

'I am Tom Thatcher of Brycheniog,' said Tom, 'returning from taking a friend to a ship in Caerleon.'

'Keep your business to yourself, friend, for there are as many brigands as tankards. You are a new face and already eyes are cast in your direction. Do yourself favour and wash your meal down quickly before ale strengthens their resolve and you become more than a curiosity.'

'Thank you for your concern, Jonas, but I can look after myself and am in no hurry. Besides, your story of that wench's ferocity has whetted my appetite. I may seek her company.'

'Then I wish you well,' said Jonas draining his tankard. 'Don't say I didn't warn you.' He stood and left the tavern without another word.

A few minutes later, the wench returned with a wooden bowl of meaty stew and a tankard of dark ale.

'Two coins,' she said, holding out her hand.

Tom retrieved his purse and paid the price.

'Bring me another,' he said.

'You haven't started that one yet.'

'By the time you return it will be empty. I have the thirst of the devil himself.'

The girl nodded and turned to walk away.

'Wait,' said Tom, 'what is your name?'

'I am called Sian Buckley and I am the daughter of the landlord.'

'It's a lovely name,' said Tom. 'Tell me, Sian, I hear there are other wares to be sampled here.'

'There may be, if you have enough money.'

'How much?'

'It depends on what you want. You can get a quick one out the back with one of the whores for a farthing but if you want something classier, it can cost you a bit more.'

'What do I get for a silver penny?'

'One of the cleaner girls. Freshly washed each time and a room for an hour.'

'What cost for your company?'

'Me? I am not for sale, sir.'

'At any price?'

Sian paused.

'Every girl has her price, sir, but I fear I am beyond your means.'

'How much?' he asked again.

'Four silver pennies,' she answered.

'Four silver pennies? No woman is worth that.'

'I am,' she said, 'but I suppose you will never know?'

She walked away but glanced over her shoulder as she went, throwing him a wicked smile.

Tom got stuck into his meal and over the next hour, sank four more tankards. He ordered a fifth but was disappointed to find a different wench bringing his ale.

'Where is Sian Buckley?' he asked.

'She is getting ready for her first customer,' said the wench.

'What customer?' snapped Tom, beginning to feel the effect of the beer.

'Guy Lambourne,' she said, 'the man with the scar.'

Tom looked over at a man sat alone near the door. His jacket was black leather and a fierce red scar ran down his face.

'Why is she going with him?' asked Tom. 'He looks like trouble.'

'He is,' said the wench. 'He is the overseer at the manor farm and is too free with his fists. But he offered three pennies and business is business. Do you want another tankard?'

'No,' snapped Tom, 'I want you to pass a message to Sian Buckley. I will pay five pennies for her company but I want her now, before that animal gets his hands on her.'

'Five silver pennies,' said the girl. 'Do you have such an amount?'

'I do, but that is not your business. Tell your mistress they are hers if she will agree to a liaison with me.'

'I will pass your message,' said the girl and disappeared through a side door.

A few minutes later the girl reappeared and beckoned him to the door.

'My mistress accepts your offer, sir, but will only accept four pennies as she can spare only half an hour. Take it or leave it.'

'I accept,' he said.

'Then come with me' she said and led him to a room at the rear of the tavern.

The room was bare except for a large bed with a sheepskin cover, a table holding a mirror and a flask of wine next to two goblets. A jug of water and a washing bowl sat discreetly behind the door alongside a neatly folded pile of linen towels. Sian Buckley sat before the table, brushing her long hair before the mirror.

'Hello again, Tom Thatcher of Brycheniog,' she said, smiling at him through the mirror.

'How do you know my name?' he asked.

'I make it my business to know the name of every man who frequents my tavern.'

'I thought it belonged to your father?'

'It did, but he was killed in a brawl. I run it now. So you have had a change of mind?'

'I have,' said Tom.

'Do you have the money?'

Tom retrieved his purse and poured a pile of silver pennies onto the table, counting out four before replacing the rest back in the purse. 'You had better be worth it, Sian Buckley.'

'Oh I am,' she said standing up and walking to the bed. 'Come and join me, Tom Thatcher. Let me make your dreams come true.'

Half an hour later, Sian Buckley was once more sitting at the table having washed with the water in the bowl. Tom Thatcher sat naked on the edge of the bed watching her brushing her hair.

'Come back to bed,' he said quietly. 'I want to spend the night alongside you.'

'I can't,' she said, brushing her hair briskly. 'I have others to entertain. Get yourself dressed.'

'Sian, I have never met anyone like you. Allow me to stay, I pray.'

'Master Thatcher,' she said turning to face him, 'don't lose sight of the reason you are here. I am a whore, nothing more. I see men such as you every night and I have learned my skills from repetition. I offer a brief respite from the rigours of daily life but when done they move on, as must you. Now, get dressed for there is another waiting.'

'Tell him to go away,' begged Tom. 'I will give you all the coin I have, I swear, but I will not share you with another man this night.'

'That is not your choice,' snapped Sian. 'Your time is done, Tom Thatcher. Now get dressed and get out or I will have you thrown out.'

'I will not,' he said.

Sian got up and walked toward the door but Tom jumped up and grabbed her arm.

'Let go of me,' she shouted.

'Stay with me,' he pleaded, 'just until dawn. I will pay whatever you want, I swear.'

'*Help*,' shouted Sian and pulled from him.

'Stop it,' said Tom, 'there's no need to shout, I don't want to hurt you.'

The door burst open and one of the wenches ran in along with a large man carrying a knife.

'What's happening?' asked the girl.

'This man here is about to leave,' said Sian, staring into Tom Thatcher's eyes, 'aren't you, sir?'

Tom didn't answer.

'Get dressed,' said the man with the knife.

'Sian, please…' started Tom.

'Get dressed and get out of my tavern,' she snarled, 'and if you come back any time soon, I will have you beaten like a dog.'

Tom shook his head but walked to the bed and retrieved his clothes. A few minutes later he walked through the door but paused and looked back at her.

'I am truly sorry,' he said, 'I never meant to hurt you.'

'Get out,' she answered.

Tom walked through the tavern, closely followed by the man. Many jeered and ridiculed him as he passed but before he could leave, Guy Lambourne stood before him, blocking his way.

'You have kept me waiting, stranger,' he said, 'and I don't like that.'

'I care not,' answered Tom. 'Now get out of my way.'

'I can't do that, stranger. You see, I have a certain standing around here and wait for no man.'

'The decision was hers,' answered Tom, 'and my coins are as good as yours.'

'I will deal with her later,' said the man, 'but first I will deal with you. My honour is slighted, stranger, and I seek redress.'

'I will fight over no whore,' said Tom and barged past the man into the muddy street. Surprisingly no one followed him and he walked back through the village toward the hill where he had left Misha, but back in the tavern Guy Lambourne was whispering to two of his henchmen.

Ten minutes later, Tom paused to catch his breath. The moon was high in a cloudless sky and the path was easy to follow. His mind was still fuzzy from the effects of the ale so he failed to hear the snap of twigs in the forest before him. Finally he started again but stopped dead in his tracks as a man stepped out in front of him.

'Hello again, stranger,' he said.

'Who are you?' asked Tom.

'You may not remember me,' said the man, 'but I was in the tavern a while back when you insulted my friend.'

'As was I,' said another man, stepping from the trees.

'I insulted no man,' said Tom. 'Now let me pass.'

'To where?' asked the first man. 'You are heading into nowhere or do you have a comely wench of your own hidden away back there? Perhaps we should take a look and have some fun of our own.'

'I have paid you no insult,' said Tom, 'so I say again, let me pass in peace.'

'Can't do that,' said the man, 'you see, that lovely miss Sian Buckley tells us you have a heavy purse about you and we wouldn't want you to wear yourself out carrying all that weight.'

'If I give you my purse, will you let me pass?'

'Nah, not really,' said the man drawing a knife. 'You see, our friend wants redress and that means your purse and your life. Your life is done, stranger, so I suggest you think of your time with the whore so your last thought will be a good one.'

'There is no need for this,' said Tom.

'There is every need,' said the man. He lunged forward but Tom had not frequented so many taverns without learning how to defend himself and knocked aside the knife before punching the man across the face, knocking him to the floor. The other man immediately pounced on Tom's back, throwing his arm around his throat and squeezing the breath from him. Tom threw his head backward to smash his assailant's nose and the pressure released momentarily allowing him to breathe but the man clung on. The first man stood up and punched Tom across in the jaw and both men fell to the ground. Quickly Tom was overpowered and the first man sat on his chest, holding a knife to his throat.

'You fight well, stranger,' he said, 'but enough is enough.'

'What are you waiting for?' asked Tom through his bleeding mouth. 'Get on with it.'

'I said you was going to die,' said the man, 'but I never said by whose hand.'

A third, previously unseen man stepped from amongst the trees and stood above him.

'Lambourne,' said Tom. 'I should have known.'

'Shut your mouth,' said Lambourne. 'You insult me in my own village and expect to get away without redress. That was never going to happen.' He knelt at Tom's head and grabbed his chin, pulling it back to stretch his neck, before laying the flat of his blade against Tom's throat and rubbing it gently back and forth.

'Embrace the sensation of cold steel, stranger,' he said, 'for it will be the last thing you feel before it carves through your flesh and you choke on your own blood.'

'Go to hell,' spat Tom through gritted teeth and braced himself for the searing pain that would end his life but as

Lambourne braced to drag the blade, a shout echoed from the darkness and Lambourne spun his head to see a shape running toward him from the treeline.

'Who's that?' he started but before anyone could speak, a knife span through the air and embedded deep in his throat. For a second, nobody moved but as Lambourne's confusion turned to panic, Tom seized his chance and pushed the other man from his chest.

'It's a trap,' shouted the first attacker and turned to face the oncoming stranger. The rescuer didn't change their speed but threw another knife embedding it deep into the man's chest. Tom got to his feet and grabbed Lambourne's own knife before turning to face the last man.

Seeing his chances were now limited, the third man turned and crashed into the undergrowth, desperate to save his own skin. As soon as he had gone, Tom spun around to face his rescuer and was shocked to see Misha crouching over the kneeling man with the knife in his chest.

'Misha,' called Tom, 'what are you doing?'

'Saving your life,' said Misha and before he could stop her, she slit the assassin's throat.

'Misha no,' shouted Tom but it was too late, the stricken man fell forward into the foliage, his body shuddering as the blood gurgled in his throat.

Lambourne struggled to his feet and managed to stagger a few steps before falling to the ground, still clutching at the blade in his neck. Tom was astonished and watched in horror as Misha retrieved both her knives and wiped them on her victims' clothing before coming over to face him.

'Are you wounded?' she asked.

'No.'

'Good. You stay here, I will be back soon.' She turned to go but Tom stopped her with a shout.

'Wait, where are you going?'

'To catch the one who escaped. He crashes through the forest like a wounded bear and is easily followed.'

'But why?'

'He will tell his comrades of this night and we will be hunted down. I must kill him.'

'No,' shouted Tom. 'There has been too much killing already. Where did you learn how to throw a knife like that?'

'I am Hashashin,' said Misha, 'and my people are well versed in the ways of killing.'

'But why?'

'You have not heard of my people?'

'No, I have never left the shores of this country.'

'I believe your people refer to anyone who is capable of inflicting death as assassins, is this correct?'

'Yes, but it is a general term like murderer or brigand.'

'You are wrong, Tom Thatcher, the word is taken from the name of my tribe, the Hashashin. We are honoured amongst the tribes of the east as inflictors of death and learn the many ways from the time we are able to walk. My throws were poor and could have been bettered by any Hashashin child. I am embarrassed.'

'I don't believe it,' said Tom. 'You just killed two men, one of them in cold blood.'

Misha looked at the man with the slit throat.

'My first blade found his lung,' said Misha. 'He would have died a horrible death so I helped him on his journey.' She turned to face Tom again. 'I should go after the third man before it is too late.'

'No,' said Tom, 'we have to get out of here.'

'What about these?' asked Misha, looking toward the bodies.

'Leave them,' said Tom. 'With any luck the wolves will get rid of them before morning.'

'But the third man will raise the alarm.'

'There is nothing we can do about that, and anyway, he may not want anyone to know he was up here with murderous intent.'

'Then we should go.'

Misha walked back into the forest watched by Tom. After a moment's pause he followed her into the darkness, his mind spinning at the events of the evening and not knowing what the future may hold.

Chapter Six

The Coronet

'Wake up,' said a voice in the dark. 'The beasts need doing.'

Geraint groaned. It seemed he had been sleeping only a few moments. The past few days had been a nightmare and although the weather had been relatively fair, the swell meant the cogs pitched like untrained horses and the experienced mariners laughed with delight as the enlisted men were ill to a man.

Geraint groaned again and pulled himself up. His body ached from the constant retching and his clothes stank of puke and diarrhoea. The ship had been at sea for six weeks without sign of land and though the captain was happy with their progress, the higher swells meant many men were constantly ill from the motion. On top of that, one of the broths prepared by the ship's cook had contained bad meat and many men, including Geraint, suffered from crippling stomach cramps and rampant diarrhoea. Those who suffered often failed to make it to the rope sling overhanging the stern or even the buckets tied in strategic places around the ship and the result was the ship stank of illness.

Teams of men took it in turns to hoist buckets of sea water onto the deck and washed the filth away through the seep holes in the sides but seepage to the lower decks was unavoidable and in the enclosed darkness the effect was ten times worse.

'Come on,' said Spider again. 'The floors need cleaning and the beasts need walking.'

'The ship is too unsteady to take them on deck, you said so yourself.'

'Then we will walk them around the hold,' said Spider. 'They need to walk, Geraint, or their legs will stiffen up. Come on, get yourself up or I will chuck your stuff on deck and you can sleep amongst the puke.'

'At least there's fresh air up there,' groaned Geraint.

'Nothing keeping you down here,' said Spider. 'Feel free to go topside with your stuff whenever you likes.'

'No,' sighed Geraint. 'I have lasted this long, I may as well stay for the rest of the journey, and besides I have become attached to the animals if truth be told.'

'They are better than most men I know' said Spider. 'So, come on, there's work to do.'

For the next few hours they cleaned the hold, carrying buckets of horse shit and sodden straw up to the deck and throwing them overboard. Next, they walked each horse around the hold many times before brushing and rubbing them down with a hessian glove. Finally, they hung up nets of hay between each horse and topped up the buckets with fresh water.

'Those animals get treated better than the crew,' growled a voice.

Geraint looked over and saw the ship's carpenter standing in the gloom. The man was aggressive and always in trouble but his essential skills meant he got away with things that would have got other men flogged.

'That's because they are,' said Spider.

'How come they get full buckets when we are rationed to two tankards a day?'

'They get just enough as they need,' said Spider, 'and we collect the rainwater in the empty barrels.'

'I say kill one of them and let the men have a feast,' said the carpenter. 'I am fed up with broth and dried lamb.'

Spider bent over and picked up one of the pitchforks used to handle the hay. Before Geraint could stop him, he ran toward the carpenter and forced him back against the wall with one of the two points against his chest.

'Spider, stop!' shouted Geraint.

'You listen to me,' hissed Spider to the carpenter. 'You even think about coming anywhere near my beasts and I will cut your throat as you speak, do you understand?'

'Relax, old man,' said the carpenter, 'it was a joke. And anyway, it's only a matter of time before the captain sees sense and gives the men a break. All this time at sea is not natural and the men need something to take their minds off it. You'll see, you mad old man. A couple more weeks and it'll be horse steaks all round.'

'No,' shouted Spider and made to push the pitchfork into the carpenter's chest but Geraint pulled him away.

'Get out,' screamed Spider. 'Get out.'

The carpenter laughed and walked up the ramp, all the while taunting the old man about tasty, juicy horse meat.

'Leave it,' said Geraint quietly to Spider. 'He is deliberately trying to upset you.'

'One day, I will kill him,' said Spider.

'Come,' said Geraint, 'sit down. Such men are not worth countenance.'

'If it wasn't for his trade the captain would not suffer him aboard,' said Spider. 'He is as poisonous as a snake.'

Geraint poured a mug of water from his own ration.

'Here,' he said, 'take a drink.' He gave Spider the mug and sat alongside him.

'Have you sailed these vessels long?' asked Geraint eventually.

'Not this one but many others,' answered Spider. 'I am known as being able to look after beasts when they are on the ships, see. It's not natural for them and it takes a special skill to keep 'em calm.'

'Then all this is nothing new to you?'

'Nah, it's how I earn a crust. I have lived half my life on cogs such as this and one day I expect I will go to my death on one.'

'Why do you say that?'

'God made the sea for the fishes, not man. We just gets away with it but eventually, every ship sinks. It's just the way it is.'

'So why do you do it?'

'I know no other way,' said Spider, 'and anyways, I do it for the beasts. As afraid as I gets, they are more scared than me.'

'What do you make of this voyage?'

'It's not natural,' said Spider. 'I have forgotten how many voyages I have made through my life and twice I have sailed all the way around to the Holy Land but nothing compares with what we are trying to do now.'

'Do you think we are doomed to failure?'

'Not if God is with us,' said, Spider. 'The ocean is bigger than any of us can imagine but with favourable winds we just might make landfall.'

'But surely there is no land to the west. If there is, I have certainly not heard of it.'

'Oh there is land alright,' said Spider, 'and it has been done before but not in our lifetime.'

60

'What do you mean?' asked Geraint but before the man could answer the bell sounded up on deck.

'Shit,' cursed Geraint, 'what now?'

The two men walked up the ramp and out onto the deck where the rest of the men were gathering. Upon the forecastle two of the rowers stood alongside one of the men who had boarded at Caerleon. He had his hands bound before him and his face was creased in fear. Eventually the captain climbed the ladder along with Tarian, the expedition leader. Logger stood alongside them.

'Silence,' shouted Logger.

'Men of the *Coronet*,' shouted the captain, 'we have come a long way together, further than most mariners sail in their entire lives. So far we have been fortunate, for the weather has been as fair as we can have hoped and our estimates are that we are over halfway done. However, there is still a distance to go and discipline is essential if we are to set foot on solid ground again.'

'I know your empty bellies ache,' he continued, 'and rest assured, I feel your hunger pangs for on this ship we are equal and no man gets more than his share, not even my lord, Tarian; however, when you boarded this ship, you agreed to certain rules, rules that mariners live by every day of their lives. Only by enforcing these rules do we have any hope of reaching our destination.' He turned to stare at the shaking prisoner. 'This man, however, sees himself as above his comrades and while our bellies ached from hunger, his ached from gluttony.'

A murmur of anger rippled from the gathered men.

'It came to my attention,' continued the captain, 'that he had cut into a sack of dried meat in the hold and has been helping himself as he saw fit.'

'Traitor,' shouted a voice and the men joined in the condemnation.

The captain held up a hand and the noise dropped.

'I made it perfectly clear at the start such action would not be tolerated but it grieves me to have my hand forced to make a point. It also worries me that he may not have acted alone though he swears there was no accomplice. Whatever the truth, I cannot ignore his crime and justice will be done.'

He turned to the guards.

'Seize him,' he said.

The two men grabbed hold of the prisoner.

'You, sir, are a knave,' said the captain, 'and don't deserve to share breath with good men.' He paused. 'Your crime is grievous and I will not tolerate such brigandry amongst comrades.'

'Forgive me, my lord,' begged the man, 'I was starving. I didn't take much, I swear. I will work twice as hard to pay my debt. Please, give me a chance.'

'Logger,' said the Captain, 'how much food has gone?'

'Half a bag, my lord.'

'And how long would a man last on those rations.'

'Four weeks or so.'

'Twenty-eight days' worth of food,' said the captain and turned to face the captive again. 'Tell me,' he said, 'which twenty-eight men should go without food tomorrow because of your treachery. Select those if you will, or better still, select one man to starve to death over the next month as the food stocks catch up.'

'I don't understand…' said the man.

'Look at your crewmates,' snapped the captain. 'You were brave enough to steal the food, yet I don't believe you did so without the knowledge of others. Point out your conspirators.'

'My lord...'

'*Do it,*' screamed Logger and the two guards dragged him to the rail above the deck.

The men looked up in confusion at the man who held their lives in their hands.

'But...'

Logger cut him short by punching him in the face, knocking out two of his teeth.

'Point them out,' shouted Logger again.

'Him,' gasped the man, pointing down at John of Wye, a man he was known to be friendly with.

'Come up here,' ordered the captain.

'But I have done no wrong, my lord,' answered John but two more rowers stepped forward, forcing him to the foot of the ladder.

'Get up there,' growled one and John reluctantly climbed up to join the captain in the forecastle.

'I'm sorry,' whimpered the first condemned man, his spittle oozing frothy red.

'What have I ever done to you?' growled John.

'I had no choice,' sobbed the man. 'I don't want to die.'

'Neither do I,' said John, 'but you chose your path. I have no such choice.'

'John of Wye,' said the captain, 'your comrade has accused you. Speak true before God. Did you share this man's crime?'

'I did not, I swear before Christ.'

The captain turned to the condemned man.

'He says you are lying. Did he or did he not aid your crime.'

'He told me to do it,' sobbed the condemned man. 'It wasn't my fault. He threatened to hurt me.'

'He speaks false,' shouted John of Wye. 'I told him not to do it. I warned him many times.'

'Silence,' shouted the captain, 'I have heard enough. Logger, deal with the thief.'

Logger stepped forward and produced a knife as the gathered men gasped at the unfolding events.

'No, please,' begged the man. 'I am sorry; don't cut me.'

'I have no intention of cutting you,' said Logger quietly and placed the blade between the captive man's hands to cut his binds.

As the rope fell to the deck the man looked over to the captain with renewed hope.

'Thank you, captain,' he said, 'you won't regret this, I promise.'

'You are right,' said the captain, 'I won't.' He glanced at Logger and nodded almost imperceptibly.

Without another word, Logger and the two guards dragged the captive to the deck rail before throwing him screaming to the water below. Many of the men below ran to catch sight of the condemned man, their combined weight causing the cog to list.

'Hold your ground,' screamed Logger, 'and listen to the captain.'

The shocked men returned to their places and stared up at the captain who now gazed down at them. In the background the screams of the struggling man were rapidly receding, replaced by the groans of the rigging and creaks of the straining ship. Within minutes, only the sound of the rolling cog could be heard and every man's thoughts lay with the poor wretch now sinking beneath the waves of the ever-hungry sea. Finally the captain addressed them.

'Waste no further thought for him,' he said, 'as he had no thought for you.' He turned to face John of Wye.

'You may or may not have been part of this brigandry,' he said, 'but by virtue of a dying man's accusation, you have been implicated. You will be issued no food for fourteen days, your share of what has been taken. If at that time you still live, you will be pardoned. Such is my justice.'

'Wait,' said Tarian stepping forward, 'by your leave, captain. I respect your authority on this vessel but I have a question for this man.'

'Please, my lord, feel free to proceed,' answered the captain.

'John of Wye, I accept that we do not know the true extent of your involvement and indeed you may be the recipient of a grave injustice by a man desperate to save his own skin, but I would ask you this: did you or did you not try to stop him from undertaking this path?'

'I did, my lord, on several occasions.'

Tarian stared at him coldly before answering.

'Then by your own words you admit knowledge of his wrongdoings. You and you alone had the power to stop his crimes and by failing to do so you are just as guilty as he, if not more so. You sat back and stayed silent whilst knowing others would go hungry. You are no innocent, John of Wye, you are guilty by association.'

'But...'

'John of Wye,' shouted Tarian, 'we made it clear at the beginning we would countenance no such activity. Your actions condemn you and as such, your fate is sealed. As you shared your comrade's crime, you will share his fate.

Captain, this man is no good to me and a traitor to his comrades. I have no more use of him on this quest and submit him to your jurisdiction. Deal with him as you will.'

'Guards, seize him,' shouted the Captain. 'Logger, send him the way of all such traitors.'

'My lord, please, don't do this,' shouted John but before he could say any more the guards grabbed him and dragged him to the rail. Within seconds, he too plunged into the sea below and once again the crew were forced to listen to a man's dying screams.

'Let this be a reminder to all,' shouted Tarian. 'The guilt lies not only on the hands that do the deed but on the hands of those who allow it to happen. This journey will be hard enough to complete as it is but if we cheat on each other, then we have no chance. I need us all working together as comrades. If one thirsts, we all thirst. Each man eats the same as the next and each man will die to protect the brother alongside him. If we can reach that state, then we will have a chance.'

'My lord,' shouted a voice. 'We support your leadership and accept your justice but beg a question.'

'Continue.'

'We are two months in with no sign of land. It is being said that there will be no landfall and any talk of this new world is but hearsay. Surely, we should turn back, if only to seek bigger ships and more stores.'

Tarian turned to the captain.

'Perhaps you can answer this,' he said.

'There can be no turning back,' said the captain. 'We have stores enough for three weeks only and the journey back is two months. We can only go forward or die of thirst in the middle of this cursed ocean. The wind is still favourable and with God's will, we can yet make it. Tighten your belts and double your prayers. We are not lost yet and I swear I will do everything in my power to set your feet on solid ground once more.'

'Does that answer your question?' asked Tarian.

The gathered men mumbled in acceptance but were quietly shocked at the finality of the captain's explanation. The only way was forward, and live or die there was no way back.

Chapter Seven

Brycheniog

'Riders are approaching,' shouted the page running toward the house. All eyes turned to see the column of armed men riding across the field as one of the servants ran in to forewarn the lady of the manor. Five minutes later, a handful of workers lined up in the courtyard waiting to receive the horses of the expected guests. To the fore was Master Reynolds, the stockman who had taken on extra responsibilities since the lord of the house, Sir Robert Cadwallader, had marched out on Crusade and ultimately lost his life.

'Good day, my lord,' said Reynolds as the horses pulled up in a cloud of steam.

'Greetings,' said the lead rider, pulling back the chain-mail coif from his sweating head. 'I am Owen Cadwallader, brother of the deceased lord of this manor. We are expected, I believe?'

'Indeed you are, my lord, and all preparations are in place. You will be accommodated in the house, as will your seconds. Your men will be barracked amongst the outbuildings. They are dry and warm so comfort will not be wanting.'

'It will suffice,' said the rider, 'though I will need an extra room within the manor for my guest, Sir Gerald of Essex.' He indicated the man next to him who stared down at the stockman without acknowledgement. 'He will be treated as an honoured guest and denied no privilege. Is that clear?'

'Of course, my lord,' said Reynolds, 'I will see to it immediately.'

'So, how fares my brother's wife? I hear she is frail.'

'She is indeed weak but rallies with the warmth of each sunrise. Once you are settled, she will receive you in the hall.'

'Good' said the man. 'On the morrow, I would also visit my brother's grave. Where has he been interred?'

'In the abbey of Brycheniog, as befits a man of his stature.'

'That is satisfactory,' said Cadwallader and slipped from the saddle, as did Sir Gerald. A page ran forward to take the reins but was cuffed away by the second knight.

'Keep your station, boy,' snapped Gerald. 'My steed will be cared for by my own squire.'

An older boy rode forward and took the reins of the charger before leading the party through into the courtyard. Once gone, Cadwallader removed his riding gauntlets and turned to Reynolds.

'Show us to our quarters,' he said, 'and inform the Lady Elisabeth we are here.'

'Of course, my lord,' said Reynolds and though he was seething at the unnecessary treatment of the young page, he knew better than to express such emotion. 'Please follow me.'

Cadwallader and twelve other knights were led into the manor house and shown to the guest wing. Water and towels were provided to wash away the dust of the road and a message sent that a meal was to be served in their honour.

An hour later they assembled in the hall where seats were arranged around two long tables. At the far end, a large solid chair emblazoned with the coat of arms of the Cadwalladers was flanked by two lesser chairs. The knights sat talking quietly and sipping ale as they waited for their host to arrive. Finally the doors opened and three women walked into the room.

The first to enter was Lady Elisabeth, widow of Robert Cadwallader. Her head was covered with a simple linen wimple though her long scarlet dress had been carefully selected to demonstrate wealth and power, for though she was now indeed a widow it was important to always present an image of strength and assuredness in meetings such as these. Her poise was elegant and though she was still relatively young at thirty-two, her eyes peered through a gaunt face ravaged by illness.

Elisabeth was followed in by her two daughters, one of thirteen years and the other, two years older. Both girls kept their eyes lowered as they entered and took their place alongside their mother at the head of the table. All the knights stood until the ladies were seated, and then waited as Owen started the formalities.

'My Lady Elisabeth,' he announced, 'first of all, my condolences for the loss of your husband and indeed my beloved brother.'

'Thank you, Owen,' said Elisabeth quietly, 'I expect your pain is no less than mine.'

'Indeed,' said Owen. 'Secondly, please allow me to express our gratitude in receiving us this evening, so soon after the tragedy. I appreciate the wounds are still raw but there are things that must be arranged as soon as possible in order to protect the family's affairs.'

'I understand,' said Elisabeth, 'and of course you are right but first, please allow me to discharge my obligations as a hostess and provide respite from your long journey. Please, be seated.'

With the formalities over, all the knights sat down and conversation resumed as the food was brought in. The fare was simple yet elegant, consisting of rabbit stew and thick slices of roast swan accompanied by roasted vegetables and small loaves of bread. The food was washed down with flagons of mead and wine before the tables were cleared and conversation turned to the politics of the day.

Throughout the evening, Gerald of Essex went out of his way to engage the elder of the two girls in polite conversation, and indeed the Lady Suzette found his attentions more than flattering, finding herself very attracted to the handsome young man. The Lady Elisabeth talked at length with Owen Cadwallader until finally they came to the subject that both knew was the real reason for Cadwallader's visit.

'Owen,' said Elisabeth, 'I know you mean well but I have my concerns.'

'And what possible concerns can there be?' asked Owen. 'It is for the best.'

'Perhaps we could discuss this more privately?' asked Elisabeth as heads looked up at the raised voices.

'Of course,' said Owen. 'I forget myself.' He turned to his knights.

'Gentlemen, I think you will join me in thanking our gracious hostess for excellent fare and agree that it has been a long time since we have eaten so well in such pleasant company.'

Shouts of drunken approval echoed around the hall accompanied by the banging of tankards on tables.

'But alas,' continued Owen, 'the time has come to break up this gathering for I have business to discuss and request you retire to your quarters to continue your merrymaking. I will arrange wine to be brought.'

'Thank you, my lord, my lady,' came a chorus of voices and eventually they filed out with Gerald of Essex being the last to leave. Before he closed the door, he turned to smile at Suzette and was gratified to receive a wave in return, a gesture not lost on her mother.

'Girls, you too should retire,' she said.

'Of course, mother,' said Suzette and after kissing her on the cheek, both girls disappeared through a different door, leaving Owen Cadwallader and the Lady Elisabeth alone in the hall.

Elisabeth poured herself a goblet of wine and stared at her brother in law.

'You cannot blame me for being worried, Owen,' she said. 'I fear I am not long for this world and my daughters have no father or husband to guide them.'

'Then consider my proposal,' said Owen. 'Gerald of Essex is a man of standing and a union between our families can only bring good.'

'To whom?' asked Elisabeth. 'You or him?'

'To both,' said Owen. 'A union of families will strengthen both names at court and will glean favour from Longshanks himself.'

'Our allegiance has always lain with Llewellyn,' said Elisabeth.

'I know,' said Owen, 'but times are changing. Llewellyn is but a prince and a weak one at that. Under Henry, England has become strong and grows annoyed with the Welsh Prince as a horse does with a fly. He was patient due to the treaty of Montgomery but now Henry is dead, the treaty holds no water and the houses of England and Wales manoeuvre to decide allegiances.'

'Why would his son annul the treaty?'

'Edward is an ambitious man, Elisabeth, and such things are of trivial importance. Yes, the ripping up of the treaty would be seen as an act of aggression but what could Llewellyn do about it? Declare war on England? I think not. Longshanks is of a single mind. He is focused on the unification of all these lands, and those who do not declare for him sets themselves in the opposite camp.'

'But our family is Welsh.'

'There is a time for national pride, Elisabeth, but this is not it. Our family name is at risk of being wiped out within years should we not ally ourselves with the King. Your daughters could be sent to a convent to see out their lives in isolation or even worse, find themselves at the end of an English Pike should war arrive on our doorstep.'

'But why this man, Owen? What made you choose a man of such dubious reputation?'

'Gerald is young, Elisabeth, and yes, he has been known to fall short of the chivalric code but what man hasn't? He will mature and I have no doubt become a fine man in time, but the facts are these: his father has the ear of many influential men at court and marriage into their family will secure our place for as long as a Plantagenet occupies the throne.'

'And my daughter's happiness?'

'I am sure she will be fine. Did you not see the way they laughed together this evening? They are obviously attracted and will make a fine couple.'

'A skin-deep attraction, no more,' said Elisabeth. 'Suzette knows little of men and is easily swayed. I fear she sees only the fair face, not his black heart.'

'That is unfair,' said Owen, his voice rising. 'You have known him hours only and already cast doubt on his honour. If you were a man you would be obliged to settle the insult.'

'But I am not a man, Owen. I am a dying mother with the best interests of her girls at heart. Allow me this one discretion for it is all I have.'

Owen paused and took a deep breath.

'Of course,' he said. 'I forget myself and beg forgiveness.'

'And what of little Margaret?' continued Elisabeth. 'What will become of her?'

'I will take her into my house,' said Owen, 'and see that she marries well. Your daughters will be well cared for, Elisabeth, I swear. All I ask is that you see the sense in this arrangement. I am sorry it has come to this but had my brother been here, I assure you he would see the eminent sense in this matter.'

'And if I say no?'

'I will be honest with you, Elisabeth. I will wait for your death and as their protector will make the arrangements anyway. It means waiting a while but the result will be the same.'

'I could have her married off elsewhere before I die.'

'You have no time to find a suitor of adequate standing, Elisabeth, and anyway, do you not wish them to marry into nobility?'

'I just want them to be happy.'

'She will find no happiness in being married beneath her station. She has been brought up in this noble family and knows no other way of life. Surely you want what is best for her?'

Elisabeth paused and stared at her wine. Finally she spoke again without taking her eyes from the goblet.

'I have no choice in the matter, do I?' she asked. 'You have me cornered like a frightened deer.'

'Elisabeth, I mean you no distress but the politics must be addressed. Trust me on this. The joining of our house with that of Essex will forge a place in history for our family name. Your grandchildren will be seen around the courts of kings and your memory blessed as a woman of vision. Do this for us, for your family, but most importantly, do it for your daughters.'

Elisabeth looked up.

'I have heard enough,' she said. 'Thank you for your concern, Owen. I feel very weak and will now retire but you will have my answer on the morrow. Now, if you will excuse me.'

'Of course,' said Owen and stood up from his chair. 'Sleep well, Lady Elisabeth.'

Elisabeth disappeared through the same door as her daughters, and Owen Cadwallader sat back to finish the jug of wine. A few minutes later the door at the opposite end of the hall opened and Gerald of Essex entered carrying his own flask of wine. He sat opposite Owen and stared at him with amusement.

'Well,' said Gerald, 'Did you make representation?'

'I did.'

'And how did it go?'

'As well as can be expected,' said Owen. 'These things are delicate matters.'

'I see no need for delicacy, sir. These women now answer to you and as such, should bend to your decree.'

75

'I accept this, Sir Gerald, but they are still the family of my dead brother. I will respect Elisabeth's doubts, but worry not, she will see sense in my argument.'

'Let's hope she does,' said Sir Gerald. 'Having now cast eyes on the prize I find myself much more agreeable to the arrangement.'

'I told you the estate was impressive,' said Owen, 'and easily outweighs my debt to you.'

'It is indeed an impressive place,' said Gerald, 'but I speak of the Lady Suzette. The quicker she warms my bed the better.'

'She is still a child, Gerald. Harness your ardour and let these things take their course.'

'I am not known as a man of patience, Cadwallader,' said Gerald. 'You of all people should know this.'

'I am trying my best, Gerald. At least respect my brother's memory and allow me to do this my way.'

'Do it whatever way you wish, sir knight, but I want this situation resolved within days. The addition of these lands to my estate will go a long way to repairing the relationship with my father and the thought of that pretty thing in my bed only sweetens the deal.'

'Do not press me, Gerald,' growled Cadwallader. 'It pains me enough to have to do this. At least have the courtesy of allowing me some saving grace.'

'You should have thought of that before gambling away your fortune, Owen.' He stood up. 'Continue as you will, sir knight. You have until the end of this month and no more. Deliver your promise and all debts will be cancelled, but fail and I will ensure every noble family in the country knows the extent of your disgrace and you will be hung as a brigand.'

'I will deliver my debt, Gerald, and after that I hope for your sake our paths never cross again.'

'Brave words from a poor man,' said Gerald. 'I will leave you now with your thoughts.' He walked across the hall but stopped before the far door and turned around. 'I believe you are going up to the abbey in the morning to pay respects to your brother?'

'I am.'

'I will accompany you,' said Gerald. 'After all, he was a fellow knight and we are a brotherhood, are we not?'

Before Owen could answer, Gerald left the room, slamming the door behind him. Owen threw his wine tankard across the hall to break against the door but despite his frustration, he knew he had no option but to do as Gerald demanded. His fate was in the other man's hands and there was nothing he could do about it.

—

The following morning saw a group of riders approach the abbey through the morning mist. Owen Cadwallader led the group along with all his knights. Elisabeth had been too weak to ride but her two daughters went in her place. Margaret rode alongside her uncle while Suzette rode alongside Gerald of Essex.

'Your father was a great man, Suzette,' said Gerald.

'Thank you,' said Suzette. 'He was also very kind.'

'I'm sure he was. His chivalry was well known and it is said Longshanks valued his alliance above all others.'

'Once his word was given it was unbreakable,' said Suzette, 'and when he took the cross, he swore allegiance to Longshanks for the duration of the Crusade. Alas, we will never see him again.'

'Let his memory be your light, sweet lady. It can be a beacon for you.'

'Thank you,' said Suzette. 'So what of you, sir knight. I hear you are making a name for yourself around the tournaments?'

'Jousting is indeed my passion,' said Gerald, 'and I have won many a prize, though I would give them all up for just one kiss from you.'

'Sir Gerald,' gasped Suzette in feigned shock. 'You are very forward.'

'I only speak the truth,' said Gerald. 'God frowns on falsehoods.'

'He may do,' said Suzette with a blush, 'but I expect he also raises an eyebrow at such brazen nerve.'

'Well, I will beg forgiveness when we get to the abbey,' laughed Gerald, 'but until then, I will settle for a simple smile.'

'A smile is something I will willingly share,' said Suzette and followed up her comment with the prettiest smile he had ever seen.

'Suzette, if I fall from this horse and end my days right now, I will die a blessed man.'

'Your words are like honey, sir,' laughed Suzette, 'but I am well pleased.'

'Then my life is complete,' said Gerald but before Suzette could continue the conversation, the abbey loomed before them and the column clattered into the courtyard. Within ten minutes they had discarded their riding cloaks and entered accompanied by a dozen monks carrying candles to illuminate the darkened interior. In the background hidden voices recited psalms as they walked up the nave to face the abbot waiting before the cross of Christ. All the travellers got to their knees and crossed themselves as Father Williams blessed them and said a prayer. Finally he stepped forward to greet them.

'Suzette, Margaret, how lovely to see you again. How is your mother?'

'She is as well as can be expected, father,' answered Suzette, 'but sends her apologies. She hopes to be able to attend in a day or so.'

'There is plenty of time,' said Father Williams. 'The good Lord places no deadlines on faith.'

'Has father's tomb been finished?'

'It has had the relief added,' said the abbot, 'and we will have a blessing ceremony as soon as your mother is well enough to attend. Are you ready to pay your respects?'

Suzette and Margaret nodded silently and followed the abbot over to the family chapel. Owen Cadwallader joined them as the abbot pulled aside the curtains. Margaret stifled a sob as she saw the magnificence of the carved knight atop the stone tomb and both girls held onto their uncle's arms as they approached the final resting place of their father. The abbot withdrew quietly and closed the curtains for privacy. As he turned away, he saw Gerald of Essex staring at him from the central nave.

'Sir Gerald,' he said. 'Good to see you again.'

'And you, father,' said Gerald. 'It seems our paths are destined to cross many times in this life.'

'It seems so,' said Father Williams, 'and if I remember, the last time we met there was mutual beneficial outcome.'

'Indeed there was,' said Sir Gerald. He looked around the impressive abbey.

'So this place is yours?' he asked in admiration.

'It is the house of God,' said Father Williams, 'and you would do well to remember that.'

'Oh I know my place,' said the knight, 'it just surprises me to see you in your alternate guise.'

'My holy life and my personal life are two separate things,' said Father Williams.

'Is that normal for a monk?'

'Perhaps not, but I will seek my own redemption at another time.'

Sir Gerald smirked.

'You and I are men alike,' he said, 'and truth be told, I enjoyed our last business venture. Perhaps we can work together again sometime soon.'

'Actually, now you come to mention it, there may be something you can do for me,' said Father Williams.

'And the benefit?'

'Huge,' said the abbot.

'Then I am intrigued. What conspiracy is swirling around that dark mind of yours?'

'Not here,' said Father Williams looking around. 'Let the family see out this day, and return after dark. I believe I have an offer you cannot refuse.'

'Then how can I say nay?' said Sir Gerald. 'Perhaps you can arrange some refreshment.'

'I will have wine and ale waiting as well as good food.'

'And entertainment?'

It was Father Williams' turn to smirk.

'You have the same appetites, I see.'

'I am a young man with healthy needs, father, and if I recall, you were not averse to carnal pleasures the last time we met or have you forgotten that night in the tavern?'

'A moment of weakness and the subject of much prayer since,' laughed the abbot. He paused before continuing. 'Bring yourself back later, Gerald, for I feel this meeting is most opportune.'

'Until later,' said the knight and stepped past the abbot to approach the Cadwallader family chapel, closely followed by the rest of the knights.

–

Down in the valley Garyn and his wife were paying respects of their own in the village graveyard. Garyn leaned against a tree and watched as Elspeth placed a posy of holly on his family's grave before joining him.

'They would have been proud of you,' she said quietly.

'Really? I couldn't save them from a killer's knife.'

'That wasn't your fault, Garyn.'

'I should have been there.'

'If you had, then you too would be lying in that grave and I would be without a husband.'

'Still, I miss them every day.'

'And so you should,' said Elspeth, 'but use that emotion in a positive way. You have already done them proud by rebuilding the forge; now take that further and rebuild the family name. We will do it together, Garyn. You will become a successful blacksmith and I will give you many sons.'

'And Geraint?'

'He will make his own way, Garyn. When he returns, I expect him to have purged his demons and settle down with Misha.'

'If he returns,' corrected Garyn.

'That is in the hands of the Lord,' said Elspeth. 'Anyway, come on, those hares have hung long enough. You skin them and I will make a stew for tonight's meal.'

'Sounds good,' said Garyn and after a quick backward glance at the grave followed Elspeth out of the graveyard and back toward the forge. As they approached, they saw Tom Thatcher leaving the house and disappearing up the path. Misha stood in the doorway watching him go.

'Misha,' said Garyn as he approached. 'What did Tom want?'

'Nothing,' she said, 'just to talk. He asked how you were.'

'I haven't spoken to him properly since you both took Geraint to Caerleon. Have I offended him in any way?'

'No,' said Misha, 'but we share a burden.'

'What burden?'

'I cannot tell you, Garyn, I swore I would not, but the burden weighs him down and he seeks my company to lighten the load.'

'I respect your oath, Misha,' said Garyn, 'but if you need to talk, then at least take Elspeth into your confidence. Nobody should struggle alone.'

'I will remember that,' said Misha. 'Anyway, come in for I have prepared the meat but there are still turnips to boil. Tonight I will regale you with tales of my people.'

'Sounds lovely,' said Elspeth clapping her hands. 'I can't wait.'

Chapter Eight

The Coronet

Geraint stood at the rear of the ship, looking back at the wake left behind as the vessel continued its journey south west. The cog was quiet except for the creaking of the rigging and the stars shone brightly above. A few crewmen manned their stations around the deck, many dozing where they sat but would be awake in an instant should they be required.

'Can't you sleep soldier?'

Geraint turned to see a large man sitting in the shadows.

'Sleep has evaded me for many nights,' said Geraint straining to see who it was.

The man leaned forward and Geraint was shocked to see it was Tarian, the expedition leader.

'Sleep is overrated,' said Tarian. 'A couple of hours are plenty.'

'My lord,' stuttered Geraint, 'I never meant to disturb you.'

'Be calm, soldier,' said Tarian. 'I have watched you closely these past few weeks and have been meaning to talk to you. This is as good a time as any. I hear you saw action in England as well as the Holy Land.'

'I did, my lord.'

'And you were released from service?'

'I was. I did no wrong but my brother bought my release as part of an oath to my family.'

'And how do you feel about that?'

'I respect his motives and would never dishonour him by voicing my regret but truth be told, I miss the calling of shared campaign.'

'Spoken as a true soldier,' said Tarian. 'To the uninitiated, war is a brutal state of affairs but those who have experienced its demands find it difficult to settle back into normality.'

'I know what you mean,' said Geraint. 'My mind is eased only amongst those who have shared similar experiences.'

'Sit,' said Tarian, indicating a pile of coiled rope. 'It does me good to talk to my men sometimes. It reminds me of my time on campaign.'

'Have you fought in many battles?' asked Geraint.

'Too many,' said Tarian, 'though this expedition is by far the most important.'

'Why?' asked Geraint.

'Because it is the opportunity to change our world,' said Tarian.

'My lord,' said Geraint. 'I am honoured you share your time with me but I have many questions. Are you at liberty to share your thoughts with a common man?'

'Indeed,' said Tarian. 'The night is yet long and there is nothing better than sharing tales with comrades. Ask your questions, young man, for you are the first to show mettle amongst the men.'

'Do you really believe we will reach this strange land we seek?'

'I do,' said Tarian. 'The captain is the best money can buy. His reputation is second to none and he has always come through. If he thought there was a risk of failure, he wouldn't have set out.'

'Has he been there before?'

'No man alive has been this way before, at least none that have travelled and returned to tell the tale.'

'So how does he know we are going the right way?'

Tarian stared at Geraint for a while before standing up.

'Come with me,' he said and walked over to the aft castle to climb the ladder. Geraint hesitated as it had been declared out of bounds but Tarian put his mind at rest.

'Come,' said Tarian, 'there will be no retribution.'

Geraint followed him up the ladder and within seconds was on the highest part of the ship bar the masts. The area was similar to any castellated tower except that it was much smaller and made of wood. Around the castellations, many boxes were lashed to the timber walls and tied securely with heavy ropes. In the middle of the floor stood a pedestal covered with a waxed cloth. Two mariners manned the large arm controlling the steering rudder while a guard armed with a pike stood to one side. As they approached, he lowered the pike to the challenge position.

'State your business,' he said quietly.

'Stand down, soldier,' said Tarian. 'He is with me.'

The man returned to his station but watched closely as they walked slowly around the wooden fortification.

'It is right that no man alive has been this way,' said Tarian, 'nor has there been any since before the time of our grandfathers but men have travelled this way before and left us directions.'

'How can that be?' said Geraint. 'There is nothing but open sea for reference. For all we know we could be sailing in circles.'

'You may be no sailor' said Tarian 'but surely even you know how to navigate by the stars.'

'Alas no,' said Geraint. 'I went the direction I was ordered and paid no heed to such sciences.'

'But you must have seen the heavens circle around one point.'

Geraint looked up and found the North Star.

'I have,' he said, 'and know that star is the only one that maintains its position.'

'Exactly, and that is the secret. By using that star as a reference, we can ensure this ship is always pointing in the right direction.' He walked toward the rear of the ship and pointed at a piece of flat wood fixed on top of the rail. In the board were two wooden dowels spaced about an arrow's length apart.

'By lining up these two dowels with the star, we know the ship sails true. There are always two men on duty as well as the guard. The guard's job is to ensure those on navigation duty stay awake. All three are on pain of death should any fall asleep. Every few minutes they take it in turn to check the alignment and adjust the rudder if needs be. During the day we can do similar alterations using the sun as a reference though that is more complicated due to its travel across the heavens.'

'I understand,' said Geraint, 'but often clouds fill the sky. How do you keep the course true on such days?'

'That is where it gets clever,' said Tarian, 'and we have an instrument from the east to help us.' He stepped toward the pedestal, removing the cover to reveal the box that had been brought aboard at Caerleon. 'This is called a compass,' he said casting aside the lid of the box to reveal a round instrument the size of an open palm. 'That needle always points north so the same rules apply. By keeping the direction of the ship relative to north, we maintain our course so as long as we have this, we know we sail true.'

'Nothing short of witchcraft if you ask me,' said Geraint.

'No witchcraft, boy, just eastern science. The oceans have opened up since the discovery of such things and the world has become a different place.'

'But surely you have to know where you are going before you can set a course,' said Geraint. 'How do you know which way to go?'

'Because we have maps from the time of Prince Madoc,' said Tarian. 'He sailed this way a hundred years ago and kept detailed logs of the journey. He eventually made landfall and was so taken by the bountiful land, he returned to Wales a few years later to recruit more settlers before making the journey once more, never to return. What he did do however, is leave a copy of his first logs and it is those that the captain uses to follow his passage.'

'I don't know much about Madoc,' said Geraint, 'but remember you used his name at the beginning of this quest. I assume it his treasure we seek?'

Tarian paused before answering.

'What is your name, boy?' he asked.

'Geraint ap Thomas. I hail from Brycheniog.'

'Well, Geraint ap Thomas from Brycheniog, to answer that question, first I must give you a lesson in history. What do you know of your heritage?'

'I am well versed in our ancestry,' said Geraint, 'as are all men of my village.'

'In that case, tell me, who was the last King of Wales?'

'Iago ap Idwal,' said Geraint without hesitation. 'He reigned over two hundred years ago and was the ancestor of our current Prince, Llewellyn ap Gruffydd.'

'And what makes you say Iago?'

'It is well known.' said Geraint, 'and tales are told of his rule in every tavern across our land.'

'And like all laymen, the tales of poets and minstrels become the truth to your ears,' said Tarian.

'Why wouldn't they be?' asked Geraint. 'It is the way our place in the world is remembered.'

'It is the way certain people want you to remember,' said Tarian, 'but is far from the truth.'

'You surprise me, my lord,' said Geraint, 'for I know no other version.'

'History is written by the victors, Geraint,' said Tarian. 'Always remember that and do not fear searching deeper for any truth. Iago was indeed a King of Wales and it is his lineage that has ruled most of our land in some way over the last two hundred years, especially through his grandson Owain Gwynedd and Owain's grandson, Llewellyn ap Iorwerth.'

'They were great leaders,' said Geraint, 'especially Llewellyn the Great.'

'Indeed they were and if our current Prince displayed the same mettle as the forebear who shared his name, I would have no argument with his leadership. However, the truth is this: the courts of Llewellyn ap Gruffydd are rotten with petty squabbles as nobles jostle for position. Many such as I doubt his ability to lead, especially as he is known to sign treaties with Henry's court at less than preferential terms. The houses of Wales are fragmented,

Geraint, and whilst we argue amongst ourselves, Longshanks looks toward Wales with conquest on his mind. However, I get ahead of myself. The line of Iago is undisputed but there is another line originating at the same time, that of Gruffydd ap Llewellyn.'

'Gruffydd, the Usurper,' said Geraint.

'Some called him that but he is recognised as a great leader and while Iago's son was in exile in Ireland, Gruffydd earned the title King of Wales through conquest and political manoeuvring. He was a strong king and his lineage would have had lasting claim to the throne, however their fortunes died out through dissolution and petty squabbles. His line was closely linked to the English kings and their blood became so diluted, their claim became weaker until any realistic chance of true kingship was lost and Iago's ancestors eventually regained that which had been lost to them.'

'Through Llewellyn,' said Geraint.

'Yes, however, it is Gruffydd's kingship that many see as the true lineage and though his line is fragmented, many have claimed his blood as a sign of royal pedigree and garnered support to their claim to authority.'

'That is ridiculous,' said Geraint.

'I agree,' said Tarian. 'Even if a true heir was proved, it would set brother against brother, and Longshanks would just sit back and watch with glee as we tear each other apart.'

'Why would he do that?'

'Longshanks is known for his love of conquest and his hatred of Wales. His love of drinking is also common knowledge and during the times his tongue has been loosened by wine he has oft stated his intention of one day conquering our country. Subsequently, I and others like me fear that with the death of his father, that drunken boast has now become a certainty and Wales lies at the mercy of Longshanks' experienced army. It is for that reason that I and a band of close comrades seek to unify Wales under a single banner, an attempt to join every family in common cause to guard our borders and, if necessary, march on to London to unseat the incumbent ruler.'

'Surely Llewellyn would balk at such ambition?'

'Indeed he would,' said Tarian, 'and that is why he is not included in our plans.'

Geraint stared at the knight in astonishment.

'My lord, I fear we are talking treason.'

'There is a thin line between a patriot and a traitor, Geraint, depending on the outcome.'

'But I don't understand,' said Geraint. 'If we are in so much danger, why don't the nobles just unite under Llewellyn's banner?'

'Because each has his own argument as to who should lead us and each is equally stubborn in his view.'

'So how do you intend to unite the houses?'

'By installing a figurehead to whom all can relate. A king with credentials so clear that nobody can deny his lineage.'

'Is there such a man?'

'I hope so,' said Tarian, 'otherwise, this quest has sailed in vain.'

'We seek a man?' gasped Geraint.

'We do.'

'I thought we sought a great treasure?'

'Is not freedom from tyranny the greatest treasure of all?'

'Yes, but how do you know such a man exists?'

'Because history tells us he does,' said Tarian. 'Cast your mind back to Owain Gwynedd, the grandson of Iago. Have we not agreed that he was a great and respected ruler?'

'We have.'

'He had many children, Geraint, each of which has played a part in our history but he also had another son, Madoc ap Gruffydd. Madoc was born out of wedlock to one of Owain's many mistresses and though he had a place in Owain's household, he played no great part in his father's kingdom. When Owain died, Madoc could see he had no chance of succession and fearing for his safety, assembled a fleet of ships to find a new world across the sea.'

'I fail to see the link,' said Geraint.

'Madoc's mother was Anne Fitzroy, daughter of Henry Fitzroy. Are you aware of him?'

'No, my lord.'

'Henry Fitzroy was the son of Nesta, Princess of Wales and King Henry I, and of course, you know who Henry's father was?'

'William the Conqueror.'

'Correct, which means by direct lineage, Madoc has a true claim to the throne of England, should the current court fall but not only this, as his father was Owain Gwynedd, he also has a claim to the Welsh throne according to our own people.'

'Thus making Madoc a potential ruler that would satisfy both camps in Wales,' said Geraint.

'Exactly,' said Tarian, 'and therein lies the nature of our quest.'

'But he must have died many years ago.'

'Obviously,' said Tarian, 'but hopefully he would have surviving heirs and as they have been isolated all this time they would not have been married off to other houses and thus diluting the lineage.'

'How do you know that anybody has survived?'

'We don't but we know that Madoc found the place so acceptable he returned and took many hundreds more settlers with him. To me that says the land lends itself to easy living and there is no reason to believe they have died out.'

'It is a fantastic story,' said Geraint, 'and indeed a worthy quest but leaves much to chance.'

'Some things I can control,' said Tarian, 'the rest lays in the hands of God.'

Geraint nodded.

'My lord, I thank you for your frank explanation.'

'You will find me a fair and honest man, Geraint of Brycheniog, but as you have seen I will not suffer treachery off any man. The reason much of this has been kept private is that if we had to return without finding the new world, then such conversations have the power to lose people their heads. Now there is no chance of returning alive unless we find land, the risk is no longer there.' He paused. 'The captain reports you are a good worker with sense above most men, Geraint. I could use such a man when we reach land.'

'To what end.'

'There are over five hundred men on this quest,' said Tarian. 'Many have not met before embarking and need to be led. I also have fifty lancers and ten knights. These men will need direction.'

'I am no knight, my lord.'

'I will lead the titled men as well as the lancers,' said Tarian, 'but seek men with clear values to lead the foot soldiers. You saw service in the ranks of Henry in England and again on Crusade in the Holy Land. That is experience I cannot teach. What say you? Are you up to the task?'

Geraint hesitated only momentarily before answering.

'I believe I am, my lord, though would beg patience to fit the role.'

'Time will be limited,' said Tarian, 'though I accept it will be strange to you. When we land you will be given a unit of fifty archers and fifty men at arms. Do well and you will rise to your true potential.'

'An honour indeed,' said Geraint. 'I will try to meet your expectations.'

'I'm sure you will,' said Tarian. 'Now I suggest you get some sleep before Spider has you mucking out the horses again.'

Geraint climbed down the ladder as the sun was rising in the east. He headed down to the hold but as he did, a solitary voice echoed through the decks causing men to stir from their sleep in confusion and excitement.

'What was that?' asked a rower, looking over at Geraint. 'What did he say?'

'I'm not sure,' said Geraint, 'but I think it was land ho.'

Before he could say anymore the bell rang out summoning all off-duty men to deck and Geraint knew he had heard correctly. After months at sea, the *Coronet* had finally reached land.

-

A few days later, all four cogs were anchored in a bay, rocking gently in the swell. They had sailed as close into the shore as they dared and had all the side panels to the lower hold removed, leaving a gaping hole in each ship. The captain gathered the men on deck.

'Fellow journeymen,' he started, 'God has seen fit to deliver us safely to dry land, however, count not your blessings just yet for this is but the first stage in our journey. According to our predecessors, our destination lies many weeks south at the mouth of a mighty river. It is said that so big is the river that the clear sea is brown for many miles as the river water churns the bottom. However, we need water and fresh food so will be sending hunting parties ashore. We will stay here for three days only before heading south and you will all get a chance to walk on solid ground before we leave.'

'Captain,' said a voice, 'we notice the holds are opened for the horses. Are they to go ashore?'

'They are. They are weakened from inactivity and need to feed on fresh grass to strengthen their limbs. All will be swum ashore and allowed to graze on the hills. We know not if these lands are inhabited so a guarding force will be required to ensure their security.'

'But how will they get back aboard?' asked the voice. 'The hatches are above the waterline and there is no dock.'

'Once ashore they will stay on land and travel south the same time as the fleet. This will enable them to regain the strength in their legs. The ships will shadow them and an armed force has already been selected. Now, those of you picked for the first foray, muster at the boats. You will stay on shore for one day only and are tasked with securing the landing site. Pikes will be issued as you go and there will be a detachment of archers led by Geraint of Brycheniog. Once you are happy there is no threat, send the boats back to bring the rest of the first detachment and move further inland to check the area. If there are indeed any inhabitants, avoid conflict at all costs. We are sea weary and unlikely to put up any organised defence. Our priority is water and food, nothing more. We cannot afford to be distracted from our mission. In three days' time we sail again and the next time we step on land, will be in the footprints of Madoc.'

The deck broke into a frenzy of activity as both boats were made ready. Below decks, lancers stripped down to their breeches and stood alongside their horses as they waited to disembark. Each horse was fitted with a simple halter and Spider stood at the large hatch as the first lancer led his horse forward to face the ten-foot drop into the sea.

'He will be frightened,' said Spider, 'but you cannot afford to wait. As soon as he is in the door, we will push him straight out with these planks across his haunches. Be careful not to lose grip of his tether or he might swim in the wrong direction.'

The lancer nodded.

'I understand.'

'Then let's get you gone.'

Spider and Geraint picked up a plank and held it between them at the back of the horse.

'Ready?' asked Spider.

'Ready.'

'Go.'

The lancer pulled the horse forward and as it hesitated at the brink, Geraint and Spider pushed the board against the horse's rear, forcing it to jump into the sea along with the lancer. Within moments they were both swimming toward the land and due to the nearness of the shore they soon felt the sand beneath their feet.

A cheer rang out from the decks above where everyone watched with anticipation. The first feet of their expedition had reached the new world and within moments, splashes could be heard from all four ships as the other horses followed suit.

'Load the boats, Logger,' shouted Tarian, 'let's see what this new world has to offer.'

Chapter Nine

Brycheniog

'What's that noise?' asked Elspeth, sitting up straight in bed.

'It sounds like people outside,' said Garyn, 'yet the sun is still not up. Get dressed, it seems we have visitors.'

Garyn pulled on his breeches and climbed down the ladder from the sleeping loft. He threw a tunic over his head and peered through the shutters on the deep window alcove.

'Who is it?' asked Elspeth joining him at the window.

'I don't know,' said Garyn, 'but there are several horsemen outside.' A few seconds later, someone knocked loudly on the door.

'Garyn ap Thomas, open up in the name of the King.'

'It's the village constable,' said Garyn.

'What does he want?' asked Elspeth. 'We haven't done anything wrong.'

'I don't know, but I had better speak to him.' He walked to the door and removed the bars before opening it just enough to speak to the man outside.

'Are you Garyn ap Thomas?' asked the cloaked man.

'I am. What is this about?'

'Let me in,' said the man, 'we can discuss it inside.'

'I don't think that's a good idea,' said Garyn. 'How do I know you are who you say you are?'

'Look behind me, Garyn. What brigand comes supported by six armed lancers?'

'I suppose so,' said Garyn and opened the door wide to let him in.

'What do you want?' asked Elspeth as he entered the room.

'Garyn ap Thomas,' said the constable, 'do you have in your protection a woman of eastern descent?'

'He means Misha,' said Elspeth.

'I understand she goes by that name,' said the constable.

'We do,' said Garyn, 'but her presence is well known and she has been accepted by the village. She poses no threat to anyone and is as honest as the day is long.'

'That remains to be seen,' said the constable. 'Where is she?'

'I assume she is asleep. What is it that demands a visit by the King's constable?'

'Cold blooded murder, Master Thomas, and I am here to see she pays the price.'

'That is an untruth,' said Elspeth. 'Misha is a gentle soul and not capable of killing anything, let alone a man.'

'On the contrary, lady,' said the constable, 'she is more than capable and has actually killed two men.'

'I don't believe it,' said Garyn. 'There must be a mistake.'

'No mistake, Garyn. Not only do we have a witness but also a confession from her accomplice. You may know of him: he is known as Thomas Thatcher.'

Elspeth's hand flew to her mouth and stifled a gasp.

'I don't understand,' said Garyn. 'When is this supposed to have happened?'

'A couple of months ago they murdered a man called Guy of Lambourne and his fellow in a village near Caerleon.'

'But why would they do that?'

'That's why I am here,' said the constable, 'to take her into the Crown's custody and try her for murder. When she is found guilty, as she will be, then she will be hung as the criminal she is.'

'I don't believe it,' said Garyn again. 'She would have told us.'

'Lucky for you she didn't,' said the constable, 'or you could have been implicated as an accomplice.'

Elspeth stared at Garyn and he saw the doubt in her eyes.

'Perhaps this is the burden she spoke of,' she said.

'If it is,' said Garyn, 'then she must have had good reason. Perhaps she was attacked?'

'Enough talk,' said the constable, 'where is she?'

'Through here,' said Garyn and led the way through the forge to the back room where Misha made her bed. They entered the room but immediately saw it was empty. The constable ran to the open window shutter and peered outside.

'There she is,' he shouted, seeing a running figure disappearing into the darkness. 'Alert the guards. Get after her.'

Elspeth stared in disbelief.

'Why is she running, Garyn?' she cried. 'Surely it can't be true?'

'Of course it's true,' shouted the constable, 'now get out of my way.' He ran from the forge and mounted his horse before following his men into the forest.

'Oh Garyn,' said Elspeth, 'tell me it isn't true. Surely we haven't had a murderer in our house all this time.'

'I don't know, Elspeth. I hope not, though I worry her flight would suggest otherwise.' He closed the door again before setting the bars on all the shutters. 'You go back to bed, Elspeth; I will stay up and fire up the forge. Tomorrow I will go into the village and see if I can find out anything more.'

--

The following morning Garyn walked into the village and headed for the market. News travelled fast in Brycheniog and if there were rumours to be heard, the market was the place to hear them. Within minutes he could see by the sidelong glances that the news of the midnight visit had already spread.

'Garyn,' called a voice and he turned to see Elspeth's father walking quickly toward him.

'Fletcher,' said Garyn, 'good to see you.'

'Not as good as it is to see you,' said Fletcher. 'I have just been told you had been arrested for murder. Where's Elspeth?'

'Worry not, Fletcher. Elspeth is fine.'

'So there is no truth in the rumour?'

'There is a grain of truth though the tale changes with the telling.'

'What part is true?'

Garyn repeated the events of the previous night, finishing with the assurance that even if the girl was guilty, they were innocent of any involvement.

'Innocence is not a guarantee of freedom, Garyn. It depends on who hears the accusation.'

'Fletcher, I don't know what is happening to be honest but by the look on the faces of those around us, we are already complicit.'

'Then it is important they hear the truth as soon as possible,' said Fletcher. 'They will be the first to lynch any murderer, but if justice is seen to fall short then the view of the people can sway judgement. Leave that to me, I will put them right. You just make sure my daughter is safe; the rest is out of our hands, at least for the moment.'

'What do you think will happen?'

'Well, first of all they will try Tom Thatcher. If he is found guilty, he will be hanged, no question about it. With regards to the girl, they will send out search parties. If they fail to find her, she will be outlawed and word passed to all villages. With the colour of her skin, it is only a matter of time before she turns up.'

'I still don't believe it is true,' said Garyn, 'but if it is, then there must be a reason. Where is Tom Thatcher being held?'

'Normally it would be in the gaol of the courthouse but last months' fire damage still hasn't been repaired so the constable has asked the abbey to provide a cell until a jury can be assembled.'

'I must go and speak to him,' said Garyn. 'He will be able to explain what happened.'

'Garyn, wait, there is something you must know,' said Fletcher. 'I meant to tell you a few days ago but the opportunity did not arise.'

'You looked concerned,' said Garyn. 'What worries you so?'

'Garyn, what I am about to say needs to be heard with a calm mood.'

'What is it?' asked Garyn quietly. 'Tell me for my mind is running in circles.'

'Father Williams has returned from Rome. He has resumed his place as abbot of the order.'

Garyn stared at Fletcher for an age as the news sunk in.

'When?' he asked quietly.

'Last month. I only found out a few days ago and didn't know how to tell you.'

Garyn turned and stared up at the hill where the abbey was located.

'Garyn,' said Fletcher, 'what are your thoughts?'

'I must go and confront him,' said Garyn, 'and lay before him the accusation of Brother Martin.'

'Why, Garyn?' asked Fletcher. 'There is no evidence that the monk's words were true. All that will happen is you will make an enemy of the abbot and trust me, he is not an enemy you want.'

Garyn turned to face Fletcher.

'That man arranged for my family to be killed,' said Garyn quietly. 'He burned down the forge and used his influence to have my brother jailed in Acre. He almost cost me everything, all in the name of obtaining some shiny trinket for his own treasury.'

'Garyn, you have no evidence,' said Fletcher. 'He is freshly returned from his pilgrimage and will not be going anywhere for a long time. Bury your anger within, even if only until this business with Misha is concluded. Without solid proof, no person can accuse a man of the cloth without fear of retribution. The abbot answers to God and the King alone and it will take an event of enormous proportion to deliver justice to his door.'

Garyn stared at Fletcher as his words sunk in.

'You are right,' he said eventually. 'I have enough worries without making an enemy of the Church but my time will come. I swear on the memory of my father that one day I will have retribution.'

'I understand,' said Fletcher. 'But for the moment, leave that day in the mists of the future and concentrate on today.'

Garyn nodded.

'So,' he said, 'I cannot go up to question Thomas Thatcher or the abbot may find out and rekindle his campaign against me. Where does that leave us?'

'It leaves you exactly where you were before,' said Fletcher, 'an innocent bystander in a situation not of your making. I suggest you go back to the forge and continue as normal. I will ensure any rumour of your involvement is corrected and share the truth amongst all who will listen.'

'Thank you, Fletcher,' said Garyn, 'I'll do that.' He turned and left the village to return to the forge. On the way he passed three horse-drawn carts laden with stone, being pulled along the road.

'Good day to you, Master Wendsworth,' he said, recognising one of the cart masters as it passed.

'Good day to you, Master Garyn,' came the reply.

'You have a heavy load there,' said Garyn. 'Is there a house being built?'

'I know not,' said Wendsworth, 'only that this is part of a much bigger load ordered by the manor.'

'Perhaps they are returning to normal after the death of Cadwallader. I hear there will soon be a new lord moved in.'

'Apparently so. Rumour has it that the Lady Suzette is betrothed to a knight from England, Gerald of Essex.'

'The name is new to me,' said Garyn. 'Do you know of him?'

'Only that he is from a landed family and struts with the arrogance of youth.'

'A dangerous mix methinks,' said Garyn. 'I wish you a good day, sir.' And with that he turned off the road to head home. Within ten minutes he was nearing the forge but a noise from the bracken made him stop and peer warily into the undergrowth.

'Who's there?' he asked. 'Show yourself.'

'Master Garyn,' said a voice it is me.

'Misha,' gasped Garyn looking around in fear. 'What are you doing here?'

'I fled from the horsemen all night,' said Misha, 'and doubled back as soon as I could.'

'There are people searching everywhere, Misha. They say you killed two men. Tell me it isn't true.'

'They speak the truth, Garyn, but I swear it was unavoidable. They lay in wait for Master Thatcher and would have killed him if it was not for my blade.'

Garyn stared at her in shock as the information sunk in.

'Master Garyn, surely you don't believe them. I was defending a comrade; is not that an honourable deed in your culture?'

'Of course I believe you, Misha, but I fear the peoples' court will not see it that way.'

'I had no choice, Garyn. If I had stayed my hand, Master Thatcher would now lie dead.'

'What's done is done,' said Garyn. 'What matters now is what we do next.'

'Can you not speak to your lawmakers and explain? Surely they will see the justice in my actions and free me from condemnation.'

'I fear it is too late for that, Misha. If you had reported it straightaway there may have been leniency but by hiding the fact for so long, you suggest guilt on your part and an intention to avoid justice. And besides, the fact that you are different to us makes it easier for the ignorant to condemn. You are already seen by many as an infidel and this will only fuel the fires of their hatred.'

'So what can I do, Garyn?'

'I don't know, Misha. I need time to think.'

'Shall I hide in the roof space and wait for your guidance?'

'No,' said Garyn quickly. 'It's the first place they will search. We have to hide you away from the forge. I will think of something, Misha, but for now, you have to find somewhere in the forest.'

'There is a woodsman's hut deep in the woods. I have seen it when walking with Geraint.'

'I know the one,' said Garyn. 'Again, it is an obvious choice but it will have to do for now. I can't risk being seen with you but promise I won't leave you alone in this dilemma. Go back amongst the bracken until the sun sets. When it is dark, come to the forge and search within the wood pile. I will place some things there to get you through a few nights. Until this is sorted, I will support you in this way; however, stay away unless your need is great and then only come at night and after you check the area is clear of watchers. In the meantime, I will make enquiries as to what can be done.' He looked into her large eyes. 'Worry not, Misha, we will think of something. We just need to gather our thoughts.'

'I do not worry for myself, Master Garyn, for such things are bedfellows in the life of Hashashin. I only worry that you and Mistress Elspeth may suffer my fate.'

'If we are careful, that won't happen,' said Garyn. 'Now, disappear into the woods before you are seen. The provisions will be ready for you tonight.'

'Thank you, Master Garyn,' said Misha and retreated into the undergrowth.

Garyn swallowed heavily before continuing to the forge. His life had taken a dangerous turn and for the moment, he could see no way out.

–

For several nights Misha collected her food as instructed. She had found a deep cleft in a nearby crag and made a cramped but dry hideaway. The approach was through dense undergrowth and she covered up the entrance with a fallen tree. It was adequate for her purposes but both she and Garyn knew it was not sustainable. Finally Garyn came up with a plan and waited for her to turn up at the wood pile. For an age he waited and was about to give up when he heard her say his name.

'Master Garyn,' she whispered and he jumped in fright, realising she was immediately behind him.

'Misha,' he gasped, 'you gave me a scare.'

'My apologies, Master Garyn, my old skills are needed these days more than ever.'

'I understand,' said Garyn. 'Come into the forge, I have news.'

'Is it safe to do so?'

'I will take the chance this time but be quiet, I don't want to wake Elspeth.'

They walked quietly into the forge and Misha headed straight for the hearth to warm herself at the embers.

'It is cold out there,' she said, 'and your fire is most welcome.'

'Are you able to keep a fire where you hide?' asked Garyn.

'No. I wrap up and lay still until dark.'

'It is not good, Misha, and you will not survive the coming winter like this. I have made enquiries and found there are regular trading ships that ply between Bristol and France each month. They take paying passengers and as long as the purse is heavy, no questions are asked. It leaves you a thousand miles away from your home but I feel there is no other choice. If you stay here, you will either be killed by the constable's men or die of cold in the forest. At least in France you won't be known and you may be able to join a supply train going south.'

'It is the best we can do,' said Misha, 'and I appreciate your help. How do I pay for this passage?'

'I will raise the money,' said Garyn. 'It will take a few weeks so you must be patient a little longer. I will give you warmer blankets and leave whatever food we can spare but we have to continue to be careful.'

'I understand,' said Misha. 'Garyn,' she continued, 'what of Master Thatcher?'

'He is set to be judged two days hence by public trial,' said Garyn. 'With the death of Lord Cadwallader, the King's court has appointed the abbot as the hearing judge. He is not known for his fairness but luckily, Tom Thatcher is well liked in the village and the twelve jurors will be appointed from the population. Hopefully he will receive a fair hearing.'

'He killed nobody,' said Misha. 'It was my hand that wielded the blades and it would be an injustice for him to suffer in my place.'

'Hopefully it won't come to that,' said Garyn. 'Anyway, you go back into hiding and I will tell you what happens the night after the morrow.'

Misha held her hands out to the glowing embers once more before heading for the door.

'Your God will thank you for this, Master Garyn. You of all people are a just man.'

'Save your praise, Misha,' he answered, 'there is a long path ahead of us with many pitfalls.'

'The effort alone blesses you, Master Garyn,' she said, 'and I will not forget it.' With that she left the forge and closed the door behind her.

–

Two days later, Garyn and Elspeth made their way to the village to attend the trial of Tom Thatcher. The guild hall stood in the centre of the town and stood elevated above the market square on a stout oak frame. Despite the earliness of the hour, many people had already arrived and the hall was almost full. Garyn and Elspeth stood at the back amongst the rest of the traders privileged enough to get admittance.

As they waited the hall filled to capacity and news came that the market square was also filling with people keen to hear the outcome. Finally a crier entered and called the room to order.

'Pray silence for the abbot of the order of St Benedict, officiating on behalf of the King in the matter of the murderer, Thomas ap Iestyn of Brycheniog. All stand.'

Those crowded onto the few benches got to their feet and watched as a jury of twelve men entered and took their place, closely followed by the abbot. Everyone stayed on their feet as he blessed the gathered crowd.

Garyn stared at the man who had arranged the death of his family, yet kept control of his anger. The abbot remained unaware of him and talked quietly with the constable at his side.

'Bring in the prisoner,' announced the constable and a few minutes later, the crowd gasped as the forlorn figure of Thomas Thatcher was led in chains to stand before the court.

'Silence,' shouted the constable as voices were raised. He turned to Tom.

'You are Thomas ap Iestyn of Brycheniog, commonly known as Tom Thatcher?'

The prisoner mumbled a reply.

'Speak up for the court,' ordered the constable.

'Yes, my lord,' said Tom.

'Thomas ap Iestyn, you are accused as follows: on an unknown date, in the hills above Caerleon, you and a named accomplice of Misha ain Alsabar, a foreigner from lands afar, did deliberately do unto death two men of Gwent, whereby you undertook to spy upon them, ambush them and cut their throats before robbing them of all possessions and hiding their bodies in the undergrowth, leaving Christian souls to rot in unconsecrated ground. How plead you?'

'It wasn't like that, my lord,' gasped Tom.

'How do you plead?' asked the constable again.

'Not guilty,' he whimpered.

'Bring in the witnesses,' said the constable.

All heads turned to stare as a man entered the room. Tom recognised him as the attacker who had escaped from the hillside many weeks earlier.

'State your name and trade,' said the constable.

'John of Gwent, farmhand.'

'And you witnessed the attack we speak of?'

'I did, my lord, three of us were walking home from the tavern, looking after our own business with not a feeling of angst amongst us when this man and a screaming heathen fell upon us as brigands and murdered my comrades before we had chance to defend ourselves. I fought like a demon but was lucky to escape with my life.'

'No,' gasped Tom, 'it was not so, they attacked us.'

'Silence,' said the constable, 'you will have the chance to speak.' He turned back to the man and asked him to explain further.

John of Gwent went on in detail, all of which painted Tom in a murderous light. After he was dismissed, three whores from the tavern including Sian Buckley were called and gave sworn statements that Tom had been jealous of another customer, Guy Lambourne, and pressed their view that the murder had been in a fit of jealousy. Finally Tom was allowed to give his version of affairs and though he spoke the truth, his manner was weak and he knew he was as good as condemned.

'So you maintain it was the hand of the missing woman who killed the men,' said the constable.

'I do.'

'I understand this infidel is but a young woman of short stature and you expect these good people to believe she killed two men, a farmhand and a farm overseer, both of whom were strong and in good health.'

'She handled a knife like none I have seen before,' said Tom.

'I suggest it was you who wielded the knife and, in her absence, seek to lay the blame at her feet,' said the constable.

'I tell the truth before God,' said Tom. 'It was her hand, yet I do not condemn her. She saved me from certain death at the hands of brigands.'

'I say again, an unsupported claim from a desperate man.'

The hearing went on and heard all sides before the abbot called a break. Nobody left the room in fear of losing their position and soon the court reconvened for the verdict.

'Men of the jury,' said the constable. 'You have heard the testimony of all involved. You are charged before God to deliver a verdict. How say you?'

One by one each man stood and delivered his verdict. The results fell both ways and ended equal with six on either side. The crowd broke into argument at the outcome until once more the constable restored order. Eventually the abbot stood up and addressed the room.

'The jury is split,' he said, 'and by the laws of the land, it falls to me, in the name of the King to cast the final verdict.' He turned to face the prisoner.

'Thomas ap Iestyn. I have heard the evidence of these good people and find no reason to disbelieve such law-abiding citizens. I believe you and your accomplice set out that night to rob any innocent you could find and you now seek to save your neck by apportioning blame on the missing woman. Therefore, before the eyes of God and according to the laws of the land, you are found guilty of murder most foul and sentenced to be hung by the neck from the town gibbet, such sentence to be carried out immediately.'

The room broke into shouting at the verdict and the constable's men had to form a line to hold them back.

'This court is closed,' said the abbot and left quickly by the rear stair. Elspeth and Garyn joined the crowd flowing from the room and joined the hundreds outside. Thomas Thatcher was thrown onto the back of a cart and driven toward the outskirts of the village. Everyone followed the cart, some hurling abuse while others proclaimed his innocence. Finally they reached the crossroads and a soldier ran to the gibbet to cut down the rotting corpse of a brigand who had been hung weeks earlier.

'A new rope,' shouted the soldier and willing hands formed a hangman's noose before passing it up. Within minutes the gibbet was ready and as the crowd gathered around in a large circle, the cart was manoeuvred beneath the noose. The constable secured the rope around Tom's neck and took up the slack before securing the loose end to the gibbet post. Father Williams stepped forward and made the sign of the cross.

'Thomas ap Iestyn, you go before your maker a wicked man. Admit your crime before God and gain forgiveness for your sins. By doing so you will surely find yourself in the arms of our Lord Jesus Christ.'

'I am innocent,' sobbed Tom. 'I beg you believe me; I have not taken any life.'

The abbot shook his head in disappointment.

'May the Lord have mercy on your soul,' he said and nodded toward the constable.

'Wait,' shouted a voice and everyone turned to see a girl standing at the edge of the wood.

'*Misha*,' gasped Garyn. 'What is she doing?'

'Something we are incapable doing ourselves, it seems,' said Elspeth, 'seeing justice is served.'

'Who is it?' asked a voice.

'It's the girl,' shouted another, 'his accomplice.'

'Seize her,' shouted the constable.

Rather than run away, Misha submitted to the guards and they tied her hands before dragging her up onto the wagon.

'Misha,' said Tom. 'I thought you had long gone.'

'I had,' said Misha, 'but I will not see you die in my name.'

'But you will die in my place.'

'If that is Allah's will, so be it,' she said.

The crowd was getting rowdy and arguments broke out amongst the people.

'Silence,' shouted the constable as Father Williams stepped forward and faced the girl.

'Are you the Muslim girl they call Misha?' he asked.

'I am.'

'Then you have been accused of helping this man murder two men of Gwent. Is this true?'

'It is not,' said Misha to a gasp from the crowd but as Tom turned to face her in confusion, she went on to explain. 'It is not true because I did not help him kill them; they died by my hands only. Tom Thatcher had no part in their deaths.'

Another gasp echoed from the crowd.

'And how was this done?' asked the abbot.

'With my knife.'

'And you expect these good people to believe you killed two strong men with no help?'

'My people learn the skills of the blade as soon as they are able to walk. It is our way of life and no other people are as expert as the Hashashin in the way of administering death.'

'Did you say you are an assassin?'

'Hashashin,' said Misha, 'though in your language they are the same.'

'She is an assassin,' gasped a voice in the crowd.

'She condemns herself,' cried another.

'I killed them only to defend my comrade. Surely this is acceptable, even in this country?'

'It is,' shouted another voice, 'it was self-defence.'

'Tell me,' said Father Williams as soon as the noise had fallen away, 'is it true you cut the throat of a wounded man?'

The crowd fell silent in anticipation.

Misha looked over at Garyn before returning her gaze to the abbot.

'It is true,' she said and the crowd erupted in anger.

'Misha ain Alsabar,' shouted the abbot over the noise, 'by your own words you have admitted murder and condemned yourself. You are hereby sentenced to be hung by the neck until dead, such sentence to be carried out immediately.'

Two soldiers grabbed her and dragged her up to the gibbet. They took the noose from around Tom's neck and placed it around hers before turning to face the abbot.

'I know little of your faith, Misha,' said the abbot, 'so cannot promise salvation. Whatever it is that gives you succour, I suggest you turn to that place now. I will pray for your soul.'

'Garyn do something,' cried Elspeth.

'Stop it,' shouted Garyn pushing toward the cart. 'She fought in self-defence. Surely she is deserving of leniency.'

Father Williams looked over and his eyes widened in recognition.

'Stay out of this, blacksmith,' he snarled. 'You interfere with the law of the land.'

'She is but a girl,' shouted Garyn. 'In the name of the Lord I beg mercy in God's name.'

'She is a heathen murderer spawned from the land of the infidel,' shouted the abbot, 'and has condemned herself by her own words. Constable, continue.'

The horses were urged forward and the crowd cried out as the girl fell from the cart to hang with her feet only inches from the floor. Elspeth screamed and buried her face into Garyn's chest to avoid the scene, sobbing violently as the girl struggled at the end of the rope.

For several moments Misha's eyes bulged and her bound hands clutched uselessly at her throat. Her body twitched violently in its death throes but finally she hung limp, slain by people of a different faith in a land a thousand miles from home.

'That poor, poor girl,' sobbed Elspeth.

Garyn didn't answer. He was too busy staring into the eyes of the abbot with mutual hatred until a voice from the crowd broke the tension.

'What about the Thatcher?'

'Release him,' shouted another, 'he is innocent.'

'Quiet,' shouted the abbot and climbed up onto the cart. The constable's men formed a perimeter around the cart and drew their swords.

'The confession of this girl changes nothing,' shouted the abbot. 'Even if she told the truth, it is still a fact that he was present at the crime and failed to turn her in to the constable. This makes him complicit in murder and subject to the court's sentence.' He paused and looked around the crowd. 'My judgement stands; he is sentenced to death.'

'No,' screamed the crowd and surged forward, being held back only by the steel of the guards.

'Free him,' shouted a man. 'In the name of God, you cannot kill a man for no reason.'

'I have no choice,' roared the abbot. 'He is clearly guilty of aiding a murderer and our laws demand retribution. I am duty bound by the laws of this land. There is no other option.'

'There is,' shouted a voice.

The abbot turned to stare at the man who had spoken.

Garyn also turned and was shocked as Elspeth's father stepped from the crowd.

'There is another way,' repeated Fletcher, 'one that meets the law of the land and will decide whether he is to die or not.'

'What lies are these?' asked the abbot. 'The law is clear, death begets death.'

'Yes but where guilt is unproven then there can be trial by ordeal.'

A murmur rippled around the crowd.

'Trial by ordeal has been replaced by a jury of fellow men,' said the abbot. 'We are not barbarians.'

'I agree but in the case of unproven guilt, parishes are allowed to resort to trial by ordeal if the people so require.'

'I know of no such law,' said the abbot. 'You are wrong.'

'The fact that it is not written down does not make it wrong; the practice is common law and is the right of the people.'

'And who has poisoned your mind with such nonsense?'

'A monk once told me so,' said Fletcher, 'a learned man whom I respected greatly.'

'Then I suggest that he too was mistaken,' said Father Williams. 'The judgement is mine alone to administer in the King's name.'

'If he was mistaken,' shouted Fletcher, 'then I doubt your words also. The monk was Brother Martin and he died on his journey home from the Holy Land. He spent many years studying the ways of the law and did so under the roof of your own abbey.'

Again the crowd gasped in astonishment. Not only for the explanation of the little-known law but also for the fact that Fletcher was openly defying the abbot. Father Williams scowled but turned to face the crowd again.

'I am not aware of this law as I am mere man of God passing judgement in the name of the Crown. However, I am also humble enough to yield to the way of the people. This man, Thomas ap Iestyn, is guilty of helping a murder. I still maintain his fate lies at the end of a rope but will take your counsel. The choice is this: hang him now for the murderer he is, or subject him to trial by ordeal. Those who say hanging, let your will be known now.'

'Aye,' shouted a dozen or so voices.

'And those for trial by ordeal?'

'Aye,' shouted a hundred more and the abbot held up his hand.

'So be it,' he said and turned to face the accused. 'Thomas ap Iestyn, you are hereby committed to trial by ordeal. Sentence will be carried out three days hence in the village square. Select your trial.'

'Fire,' shouted Fletcher before Tom could answer, 'he chooses fire.'

'The choice is his alone,' roared the abbot over his shoulder, 'hold your tongue lest I hold you in contempt.'

Tom Thatcher stared at Fletcher, trying to understand the reason for the man's intervention but though Fletcher held his silence, the look in his eyes was clear. He was urging Tom to back up his choice.

'Fire,' said Tom quietly without taking his eyes off Fletcher, 'I choose trial by fire.'

Chapter Ten

The New World

Geraint stood on a hill looking down into a small yet lush valley. The horses grazed quietly while all around the hills, men sat in groups enjoying the sunshine and relaxing after their arduous journey. Two small wagons had also been brought ashore and while one contained weapons, chain-mail armour and gambesons, the other contained the day-to-day items needed for basic living, waterproof cloaks, cooking utensils and basic rations. Water was provided by two barrels on each wagon and though they were small, the men knew the lushness of the landscape meant water would be in good supply.

They had been on land for ten days and followed the shoreline south, taking their time to allow the horses to feed on the sweet green grass as they went. Slowly the animals regained their strength and while they grazed, the men took the opportunity to venture inland to see what game could be found to supplement their dried rations. At first, they had limited success but some had come from hunting backgrounds and soon the air was alive with laughter as a hunting party returned with a dead animal suspended from a pole carried between two men.

'Fresh meat for the first time in three months,' shouted one and the party gathered around to see what sort of animals lived in this strange place.

Spider came from behind the wagon and peered at the carcass. Now the horses had been handed back to their owners, his job aboard the *Coronet* was done and he had been allocated cooking duties to those on shore.

'It looks a deer,' he said.

'Of course it's a deer,' laughed one of the hunting party. 'What did you expect?'

'I don't know what to expect,' said Spider. 'Beasts change in every place. Have you ever seen a camel?'

'Can't say I have.' said the man, 'but have heard enough about them to say I wouldn't want to eat one.'

'Never a truer word,' said Geraint quietly.

The hunting party handed the deer to Spider and as he contemplated the best way to butcher the animal, those still on duty returned to their stations. They still hadn't seen any evidence of human occupation but didn't want to take any risks with the horses. They were by far the most important asset they had.

'Any news from the ship?' asked a hunter as he took off his pack.

'A messenger came ashore yesterday,' said Geraint, 'Sir Robert is taking the fleet five days south and will wait for us at the first bay he comes across. Tarian has also come ashore and will take command of the land force.'

'Where is he?'

'He's taken a scouting party to check the lay of the land.'

'Have you talked to him?'

'Only briefly. He seems to be a sound man with uncommonly good sense.'

'Good,' said the hunter and left to see to his needs.

Geraint climbed the hill again and joined Marcus, the archer he had befriended on board the *Coronet*. For the next few hours they watched over the plains for any sign of danger until finally the smell of hot food made their heads turn in anticipation.

'That deer meat smells wonderful,' said Marcus. 'I can't remember the last time I had roast venison.'

'And it will be a while yet,' said Geraint. 'I fear the deer is too small to allow us anything but the tiniest of tastes so have no doubt it is headed for the pot, at least that way we will all benefit.'

'More broth,' moaned Marcus. 'My stomach aches for a slab of burnt meat on a grease covered trencher.'

'Once our hunting parties know the ways of this place, I'm sure there will be meat aplenty. The signs show there is plenty of wildlife but their ways are strange to us.'

'A deer is a deer,' said Marcus, 'and an arrow is an arrow. What is so difficult?'

Geraint laughed.

'Shall I convey your criticism to those who seek our food or should I keep your comments between us?'

'For your ears only,' said Marcus. 'There are some surly looking men amongst that lot.'

The men continued to watch until another two climbed the hill to relieve them.

'Go and get some food,' said one, 'while it is yet hot.'

'Have you left any for us?' asked Marcus.

'Alas very little,' taunted the second man, 'and what is left is but gristle but that is good enough for men of Builth.'

'It is a shame your humour is not as big as your girth, sir, for I would surely be pained with laughter as you speak.'

'I am only this big because I have just eaten your share,' he answered. 'Now be gone quickly lest you are left with nought but bones.'

Geraint and Marcus descended to the valley floor and approached the pot hanging over the fire. Surprisingly there was healthy amount left and they filled their wooden tankards with rich broth before sitting amongst the other men. They made another two visits to the pot before sitting back and joining in the conversation.

'At least we have learned one thing,' said a voice.

'And what is that?'

'Deer tastes the same the world over.'

Murmurs of approval came from the men.

'So what's next?' asked Marcus. 'When do we strike inland?'

'I think this man may be able to tell us,' said Geraint and indicated a group of men descending the far hill.

'Is that Tarian?'

'It is.'

The resting men watched as the scouting party returned and helped themselves to the contents of the pot. Finally they too were sated and talk once more returned to the business of the day.

'My lord,' said Geraint, 'how lies the land?'

'Fair ground,' said Tarian, 'with two small rivers to cross but nothing we can't handle.'

'Any sign of life?'

'None,' said Tarian. 'These lands seem un-trodden by men but that is to be expected. Our destination is still many days south.'

'How do you know where we are headed?' asked Marcus.

'We have the journals of Madoc,' said Tarian, 'and they tell of a great river that turns the sea brown. Our ships seek the mouth of that river and once there, will row ten days upstream as did our predecessors. After that it is a case of sending out search parties for any sign of civilisation.'

'What if there is no sign?'

'There must be,' said Tarian. 'Madoc led two expeditions and carried hundreds of people seeking a new start. The landing place is clearly documented and though a hundred years have passed, that amount of people will have left a trail. We may even be lucky and find they have set up a town near to where they landed.'

'Let us hope so,' said Marcus.

'Do you tire already from the quest?' asked Tarian.

'Not at all, my lord, but a town means taverns and ladies. What more can a man want?'

Tarian laughed along with the other men.

'You may be right, soldier, though I fear we must tread carefully. A hundred years have passed since they conversed with outsiders and they may find our ways strange to them. We are here to seek Madoc's heirs only and hopefully persuade at least one to return to unite our country.'

'There was talk of bounty,' said Marcus.

'And there will be,' said Tarian, 'though not obtained by conflict. It is hoped this bountiful land has been able to give up its treasures to the settlers and we will trade what we can, but even if there is little of value, you will be rewarded from the treasuries of men like me when we return. Now, I suggest we get some rest. Tomorrow we strike south until we meet the fleet once more. Once there, I will talk with Robert of Shrewsbury and discuss the next stage.' He stood up and walked to the shelter of a small copse as the other men dispersed.

Geraint got two waterproof cloaks from the wagon and he and Marcus found themselves a sheltered place to try and sleep.

–

For five days the column headed south, always keeping the coast in sight. Day by day the horses grew stronger and the hunters became more successful. Foraging parties were sent out and often returned with baskets of fish or strange fruits the likes of which they had never seen before, but by far, the most popular was the large bird that looked like a giant guinea fowl. Its plumage was black and it had a long red crop hanging from its neck but most importantly, it was easily caught and heavy with meat.

For the first time in weeks, the men enjoyed the taste of cooked meat and by the time they set eyes on the anchored fleet, their morale was high. They set up camp near the shore and watched as boats were despatched from the ships.

'Do you think we'll all be sent back aboard for the next leg?' asked Marcus.

'I can't see how,' said Geraint. 'The horses cannot board unless the ship is alongside a dock. No doubt some men will rotate but let's just hope we are not of them. All this walking is tiring but it beats the darkness of those shitty holds.'

'I agree,' said Marcus.

Down on the shore, a table had been set up and Geraint could see the four captains as well as Tarian and Shrewsbury deep in conversation around a set of journals. Though he couldn't hear them talk, their manner suggested there was disagreement between them with much gesturing and pointing inland. A chart lay before them and Geraint guessed it was the cause of the problem. Finally the meeting broke up and after the boats had been filled with barrels of fresh water, the captains returned to the ships.

'It seems we stay on dry land,' said Geraint.

An hour later, Tarian called the men together for a briefing.

'Gentlemen, the situation has changed,' he announced. 'Our destination is still far to the south in a sea that is said to be blessed with constant sunshine. To get there we need to sail around a headland bigger than our homeland before heading west to search for the mouth of the great river. As you know, we have been shadowing the fleet along the coast. This was to allow the horses to regain their strength and the ships have been travelling slowly to offer support if so needed. However, the captains have expressed concern about the speed of progress. It would seem that if we continue like this, the journey to the river will take many months and could extend this quest far beyond that which had been envisaged.'

'We are travelling as fast as we dare,' said Geraint.

'Indeed we are,' said Tarian, 'but with fair winds, the ships can travel ten times as fast and can be at the river within weeks.'

'Why don't we just re-board?' asked Marcus.

'The horses need level platform to safely board and the chances of finding a natural dock alongside deep water are very small. We have searched for such a place since arrival but lost valuable time.'

'So what is the answer?' asked a voice in the ranks.

'I have met with Shrewsbury and have made a plan. Over the next few hours we will spread our forces between the land and the ships with equal strength. More stores will be landed and we will be equipped to be as self-sufficient as possible. Once done, the ships will head at full speed down the coast and sail around the headland into the warmer sea. Once there they will locate the river and travel upstream as originally planned. We estimate this journey will take no more than three weeks.'

'But if they do that,' said Marcus, 'they will leave us far behind and it will take many months to catch them up.'

'If we stay within sight of the coastline, we will indeed fall too far behind. That is why we will head inland and head directly for the river.' The men gasped in astonishment at the news and many voices of concern were raised.

'My lord,' asked a man, 'if I understand this correctly, you intend marching the column due west across an unknown land to an unknown destination, not knowing what terrain or enemy forces lie between us.'

'That is exactly what I intend,' said Tarian. 'With regard to enemy forces, I have seen nothing that suggests these lands are inhabited. The terrain I can do nothing about except trust in God and the dedication of you men.'

'We know not the way, my lord.' said a voice. 'How will we know the route if the clouds are in and cover the sky.'

'We will use an instrument from one of the ships,' said Shrewsbury. 'It has the ability to point north at all times and in any weather. By doing so, our direction will be clear.'

'How long will it take?' asked Geraint.

'Though the distance will be far shorter, our speed will be slower and we estimate we will reach the river about the same time as the ships.'

'How will we find the ship?'

'We will aim to reach the river upstream of the meeting place. Once there, we just have to follow it south until we meet the ships coming the other way.'

'How will we know it is the right river?' asked Geraint.

'Because Madoc has recorded it is the biggest river he had ever seen. We have calculated that at normal marching speed it will take three weeks, though not allowing for mountain ranges. By keeping careful records and with Madoc's descriptions we are confident the river will reveal itself to us as described in the journals.' When the questions died out, Tarian outlined the order of march.

'There will be outriders to the fore and to either flank, each staying within sight of the main column. Their role will be to guard our flanks from any surprise attack. Similarly an armed guard will bring up the rear.'

'Did you not say there was no sign of other people?'

'Just because there is no sign doesn't mean they don't exist. I can show you shoreline in Wales as unpopulated as this coast yet within half a day's ride of a cathedral. To the fore,' he continued, 'a party of riders will scout the easiest route and leave signs for us to follow. The foot soldiers and archers will flank the carts and be ready to support any resistance we may find.' He paused before continuing. 'You have just come from a great sea journey and your sword arms will be fatigued from little use. However, every one of you has had experience in the armies of Henry, Llewellyn or even just your local lords. Take what opportunity you can to become battle ready for though I do not expect any trouble, if something happens, we will not be found wanting. Spider, double the meat portion in tonight's broth and thicken it with dried fruit. You will ensure every man gets at least one hot meal a day on pain of flogging. The rest of you, see to your kit and get a night's sleep. We set out at dawn and while the pace will be achievable, it will also be relentless. Our aim is to do ten miles a day for twenty days. If we can meet that pace then we will hit the river with time to spare. Gentlemen, the real adventure starts here. I have spoken, disperse to your duties.'

The following morning saw the column formed up ready for the march inland. The ships had already sailed but not before furnishing those on shore with extra men and provisions. Another four carts had been floated on to the beach and attached to the pairs of donkeys, brought especially for the purpose. Outriders sat upon their horses in the morning mist, and the animals pawed at the ground as if impatient to get started. Many archers wore their gambesons as extra protection from the cold but the quilted jackets meant to provide protection from arrows or knives were cumbersome and many would be back in the carts before a mile had passed.

Tarian looked over the column of almost two hundred men, satisfied that they had done all they could to prepare. He looked inland to the far blue mountains, using his vast experience to estimate the distance. Nightfall should see them at least halfway to the slopes and if it did, he would be a happy man.

'Scouts,' shouted Tarian, 'lead out. The rest of the column, upon my command, step out with heads high and hearts full. We march for the unity of our country. Men of Wales, *advance*.'

The column lurched forward toward the distant hills and as Tarian looked back toward the sea, he couldn't help but wonder if he would see his home again.

Chapter Eleven

Brycheniog

The morning of the trial arrived and Garyn joined the rest of the townsfolk in the village square. Thomas was already there and sat chained in a cart as the preparations were made. One of the constable's men stoked a brazier while another laid out two pieces of rope on the ground, ten paces apart. The constable called for order and the crowd fell silent as Tom Thatcher was dragged from the cart and his chains removed. Tom looked over at Garyn who stared back, emotionless.

'Good citizens of Brycheniog,' shouted the constable, 'the will of the people has decreed that Thomas ap Iestyn is subject to trial by ordeal and having chosen fire, presents himself here for judgement.'

'Where's the abbot?' whispered Elspeth to Garyn.

'The actual trial is beneath the likes of him,' said Garyn, 'and the constable stands in his place. I suspect he will reappear in three days to announce the outcome.'

'Thomas ap Iestyn,' announced the constable, 'upon my mark you will grasp an iron heated in this brazier and walk between the markers before you. At the far end there is a barrel of water and you may plunge your hand therein. Know ye well that should you fail to reach the far marker, or drop the bar at any time, you will be found guilty as charged and will hang before the sun sets on this day. Do you understand?'

'I do,' said Tom.

'However, complete the trial and you will be granted three days in which you can beseech God to heal your wounds. If they still fester at that time, you will be guilty as charged but if God grants a miracle and you are healed then you will be freed as an innocent man. Do you understand?'

'I do,' said Tom again.

'Then let the trial begin.'

Tom was dragged to the first rope and stared at the water barrel at the far end. Though it was only ten paces away he knew it may as well be a mile for the chances of him reaching the barrel without collapsing was virtually nil. The crowd was silent as one of the constable's men reached into the brazier with a tongs and withdrew a twelve-inch bar, glowing red through heat. He approached Tom and held up the tongs so the bar was in front of him.

'Open your hand,' ordered the constable but Tom's fist remained clenched at his side.

'I can't,' stuttered Tom, his face recoiling from the glowing heat.

'Open your hand,' said the constable again, 'and face your trial.'

'I can't,' said Tom again. 'Don't make me do this.'

'Thomas ap Iestyn,' said the constable, 'if you refuse a third time it will be seen as an admission of guilt and you will be hanged this day.'

Tom looked up as a voice called out across the square.

'You can do it, Tom. Have faith in God.'

Another voice joined the first.

'We are with you, Tom. Be strong.'

The crowd broke into shouting and Tom looked around at the surrounding villagers, surprised at the support.

'Tom,' shouted Fletcher from alongside the water barrel, 'look at me. You can do this. Take the first step as you grasp the bar and run as fast as you can. Ten steps, Tom, that's all it is. You are a strong man; you can do this.'

Tom nodded and looked at the constable.

'Thomas ap Iestyn,' said the constable, 'for the last time, hold out your hand.'

Slowly Tom's arm came up and he unclenched his fist.

'Ready?' asked the constable.

Thomas nodded.

'Then let the trial commence.'

The man holding the tongs dropped the bar into the open palm and as Tom took the first step forward, the crowd's shouting was drowned out by his first scream of pain.

–

Up in the abbey Father Williams was sharing a jug of wine with Gerald of Essex. They were in the abbot's private rooms and a fire roared in the hearth.

'So,' said Father Williams, 'I hear your wedding has been agreed.'

'It is,' said Gerald, 'the ceremony will be held at my family's chapel in Essex but we will return here soon after to manage my new estate.'

'I look forward to it,' said the abbot. 'I have to say that having a like-minded person in a position of power so close at hand has the potential to present many opportunities.'

'I'm sure our mutual understandings will benefit us both,' said Gerald.

'And our arrangement?'

'Has already been set in motion. You should start to see the results within days.'

'Good,' said the abbot.

'So,' said Gerald, 'did you manage to arrange that other little matter?'

'I did,' sighed the abbot, 'though it wasn't easy as I had to go out of the area. Luckily circumstance provided the ideal candidate.' He stood up and led Gerald through a side door. The room was sparse and in the corner was a single bed. On top of the bed a forlorn figure lay curled in a foetal position.

'Stand up,' said the abbot quietly.

The unkempt woman stood but clutched the horsehair blanket about her to cover her nakedness.

Gerald smirked at the bruises on her face and the cut lip.

'I assume you have already sampled the goods?' asked Gerald.

'Let's just say she was a bit spirited,' said the abbot. 'I think you will find her more than willing now.'

'She will do,' said Gerald. 'What is your name, woman?'

'Sian Buckley, sir,' she answered quietly. 'Please, don't hurt me anymore; I will do whatever you ask.'

'Yes, Sian Buckley, you will,' said Gerald, 'though I can't promise not to hurt you.'

Father Williams left them alone and closed the door before stepping out into the corridor. It was no business of his and besides, it was almost time for morning prayers.

Despite the pain the first four steps seemed strong but then the agony kicked in and Thomas stumbled. The crowd gasped but he kept his feet and staggered forward.

'Look at me,' screamed Fletcher. 'Keep going; you can do it.'

Tom stumbled forward and fell to his knees in agony just before the line.

'Get up,' screamed the crowd and with one hand on the edge of the barrel, he hauled himself up and plunged the hand holding the bar into the water. Clouds of steam billowed from the barrel and Tom screamed again as the cold water was just as much a shock to his system as the heat had been. Fletcher grabbed him as he collapsed again and held him upright.

'Well done, Tom,' he said quietly, as the crowd cheered. 'Well done.'

'Let me see,' said Elspeth and gently pulled his arm from the water.

Tom gasped as his hand came out and Elspeth looked over at Garyn, trying desperately to conceal the horror on her face. The skin on his palm and fingers were burnt beyond all recognition and in places, the bones were exposed where chunks of flesh had come away when he dropped the bar. The smell of burnt meat was overpowering but despite the severe injuries, there was no bleeding as the heat had cauterised any damaged veins. Giant blisters were already starting to form all over the wound and the hand was deformed into the shape of a bird's claw. Elspeth put it back in the water.

'Keep it there as long as possible, Tom,' she said. 'The water needs to cool the injury. I will bring bandages.'

The constable stepped forward.

'You have earned my respect, Tom,' he said, 'I have seen this done three times when I was a young man and every time the accused failed to end his run. Get your hand bandaged and I'll take you back to the abbey.' He turned and started to disperse the crowd as Garyn turned to Fletcher.

'Why?' he asked. 'Why did you make him choose fire?'

'It was the only sensible option,' whispered Fletcher. 'Trial by water demanded he drown to prove his innocence while trial by combat would have seen him put against any champion Father Williams chose. He would have stood no chance against a knight. At least this way he gains three more days.'

'To what end?' asked Garyn. 'You saw his hand; there is no way it will heal in three days. All you have succeeded in doing is prolonging his death but in the meantime administering suffering beyond belief.'

'A lot can happen in three days,' said Fletcher before walking over to speak to Tom now curled up on the back of the cart. 'Where are they keeping you, Tom?'

'In one of the monk's cells in the abbey, he groaned.'

'Which part?'

'I know not the names of these places but I can see a courtyard through the bars on the door.'

'You must be near the cloisters. Are you guarded?'

'No, but the door is locked.'

'Who holds the keys?'

'There is a servant who mans the gates. It is he who opens the door on each occasion I have been let out.'

Fletcher looked around as the constable approached once more.

'I know it hurts, Thomas,' he said, 'but dig deep inside, there are things afoot.'

'What things?' asked Tom.

'Things I cannot share with you,' said Fletcher, 'but I will say this: I am tired of the injustice of this so-called man of God and will not stand by while he takes another innocent life.'

'Make haste,' shouted the constable, 'I need to get him back to his cell.'

'Stay strong, Tom,' said Fletcher as Elspeth returned with the bandages, 'I will not fail you.'

–

The remaining crowd looked on in concern as the cart rolled away to return to the abbey. Tom sat in the back, a picture of abject despair as the pain of his hand seared through his entire body.

'Come,' said Garyn, 'there is no more we can do here. I have a commission to finish at the forge and then some business to attend.' As they walked out of the village, they could see men working on an old house that had long fallen into disrepair. The faces were new to him and though Garyn would normally have walked by, he could see an anvil waiting to be unloaded from a cart.

'What are they doing?' asked Elspeth. 'It seems the cart is laden with tools of a forge.'

'I don't know,' said Garyn, 'but I will find out.' He walked over and hailed a man who was working on patching the roof.

'A very good morning to you, sir,' he said. 'I beg a few moments of your time.'

The man looked down and though he mumbled a few curses to himself, courtesy demanded he grant the request. He climbed down the ladder and faced the couple.

'Good morning to you too, sir, and indeed to you, my lady. What is it I can do for you?'

'I am just interested in your task, sir. I haven't seen you here before and would make your acquaintance.'

'My name is Iolo ap Hywel,' said the man, 'and hail from Senni not ten miles hence.'

'I know of Senni,' said Garyn, 'and know a man called Hywel. He holds the role of blacksmith to the village there.'

'Indeed he does,' said Iolo. 'He is my father and I share his trade.'

Garyn's brow lowered in concern and looked again at the blacksmith tools on the cart.

'You confuse me, sir,' he said. 'I see you are restoring the old mill but if I am correct, look set to start the business of blacksmith within the walls.'

'I am indeed,' said Iolo. 'The village is without a black-smith within its boundary and whilst this was indeed a surprise to me, it was an opportunity I eagerly seized upon when chance was presented. I will have my forge fired within the week so if there is anything you need, please call around.'

'We already have a blacksmith here,' snapped Elspeth. 'It is situated not half a mile hence on the approach road from Builth. Why would we need another?'

'I am an honest man, my lady, and know not the politics of the Cadwallader estate. All I know is they sent invitation to my father to set up his business within the village boundary and it is a rare opportunity too good to miss.'

'There is hardly enough work for one forge, let alone two,' said Elspeth. 'You will be taking the bread from another man's table.'

'My apologies,' said Iolo, turning to Garyn as realisation dawned. 'Are you Garyn ap Thomas, son of Thomas Ruthin the blacksmith?'

'He is,' said Elspeth, 'and it is our business you will be stealing.'

'My apologies, Garyn,' said Iolo. 'My father respected your father very much and we would not have dared step foot in Brycheniog had we known you were still trading, but we were informed you were about to go out of business and there was an opportunity here to be filled.'

'Well, you were told wrong,' shouted Elspeth. 'So pack up your cart and return to Senni. We run the blacksmith's forge and will continue to do so. There is no place for you here.'

'Elspeth, hold your tongue,' said Garyn. 'The fault does not lay with this man, for he too has mouths to feed. The question must be asked of those who made the decision.'

'You are right,' said Iolo, 'and while I squirm with embarrassment, I regret I cannot return for I have sold all my assets to make the move. There is no way back for me and I have to make this a success.'

'The blame lies with others,' said Garyn, 'and I do not hold you responsible. There may yet be room for two as most of my trade comes from the Builth road and those I grew up alongside will no doubt still give me their trade.'

Iolo stared at Garyn silently.

'Your gaze concerns me, Iolo,' said Garyn. 'What other news adds to this burden?'

'Do you not know of the new road, Garyn?'

'What new road?'

'The estate of Cadwallader has opened up land for travellers from Builth to head straight to the town. When done it will cut two miles off the journey.'

Garyn's eyes narrowed.

'But that's impossible; they would have to cross the river and there is no ford.'

'They create a new ford as we speak,' said Iolo, 'and it nears completion. Within weeks, the old road will be fenced off and returned to grazing with all new traffic directed via the new route.'

Elspeth's hand flew to her mouth as she realised the implications. With a shorter route from Builth, not only would they have no passing trade but they would be isolated in the centre of their own lands with no public road anywhere near. Their business was doomed to failure.

'Thank you for your honesty, Iolo,' said Garyn eventually. 'I wish you well.' He turned to Elspeth. 'Come,' he said, 'there are things that need to be done.'

–

The rest of the walk home was travelled in silence as Garyn struggled with his thoughts. Finally they sat across their own table and Elspeth poured him a tankard of ale.

'Do you think he speaks the truth?' asked Elspeth eventually.

'I see no reason for him to lie,' said Garyn. 'Besides, I have seen the carts of stones being taken onto the manor fields with my own eyes. Obviously, they are meant for the ford and to pave the wet parts of the approach. I fear my time as a blacksmith nears an end, Elspeth, and our future looks uncertain.'

'Can we not set up elsewhere?'

'With what? We have no money and most villages will already have a blacksmith.'

'We have enough land; can we not turn to farming?'

'I am no farmer, Elspeth, and without funds, how am I to buy stock?'

'What are we to do?' asked Elspeth.

'I don't know but I think we need to seek audience with the Cadwalladers and press our concerns.'

'And we will but first we will close the shutters on this cursed day. Tomorrow will be a new dawn and after a good night's sleep, nothing will seem so bad.' Together they sealed the house and locked the world outside but Garyn knew he would get little sleep that night.

—

Tom Thatcher lay on a bunk in his cell, his hand still heavily bandaged. The monks changed the dressing several times a day but if anything it was getting worse, and Tom knew there was no way it was going to heal. The pain was excruciating despite the potions given to him by the monks, and he lay on his back with his hand elevated and tied to a board.

The abbot hadn't visited him at all but he was allowed out three times a day to pray for salvation at the foot of the crucifix in the abbey itself. No visitors had come to see him and as it was the third night since the trial, he knew he had but a few hours left and would be hung as a murderer as soon as the sun rose.

Outside in the night, a storm battered the abbey and lightning flashes illuminated the grey stone walls for seconds at a time. Though he was tired he stood up and walked to the door, looking through the barred window at the sky above, determined to experience every last sensation he could before his life ended. Finally he returned to his bed and lay down, exhausted yet unable to sleep.

–

Within the perimeter walls of the abbey grounds, a monk sat at a candlelit desk writing laboriously in a journal. In a corner, a servant lay snoring loudly on his cot. The thunder outside was loud but the monk looked up as sound of the hand bell echoed through the night.

'Evans, wake up,' said the monk and the servant sat up, instantly awake.

'I wasn't sleeping, Brother Oliver,' he said, 'just resting.'

'Of course,' said the monk. 'Put on your cloak; it seems there are travellers at the gate.'

'In this weather?' said the servant. 'What fool would be abroad in such a storm?'

'All the more reason to find out,' said Brother Oliver. 'They may need our help. Come, we will see to their needs.' The two men left the room and crouching against the rain, ran the few yards along the wall to the barred gate. Evans opened a small hatch in the door and peered outside.

'Who goes there?' he asked.

'We seek sanctuary,' came a voice, 'shelter from the storm. Our horses bolted at the thunder and we find ourselves lost in the forest. The walls of God's house were a welcome sight and we seek a roof until it passes.'

'Who are you?' asked Evans.

'Simon of Builth,' said the voice, 'and my brother, Carwyn. We are traders with goods for Brycheniog but one of the horses fell lame and the night was upon us too soon. Can you shelter us we pray, if only for a few hours?'

'How do I know you are not brigands?' asked Evans.

'I have no way of proving we are not, sir,' said the voice, 'except my word as a gentleman.'

Evans closed the hatch and turned to the monk.

'What say you?' he asked.

'Let them in,' said Brother Oliver. 'We will turn away no man. Open the gate.'

Evans pulled back the bar and allowed the two hooded men through. As soon as they were in, one fell upon the monk and forced him to the floor, holding a knife to his throat. Evans spun around and was about to call out the alarm when a fist smashed into his face, knocking him back against the wall. Within seconds he too had a knife held to his throat.

'Silence,' hissed the cloaked man, 'and listen well. You will take me to the cell of Tom Thatcher immediately or that monk will have his throat opened. Do you understand?'

Evans stared at his attacker. All he could see was the eyes as a hood covered the man's head and a band of linen enveloped his mouth and nose.

'Do you understand?' said the man again punching the servant in the stomach.

'Yes,' gasped Evans, 'I understand.'

'And don't go getting any fancy ideas,' said the attacker, 'because if anything happens to me, or if you call out in any way, this monk will die and you will go to hell as having caused the death of a holy man. You wouldn't want that on your conscience, would you?'

Evans shook his head.

'Good,' said the attacker. 'Now let's go.'

Evans led the man through the garden and unlocked one of the doors before heading down a corridor and out into the cloisters. Within minutes he unlocked a cell and the attacker whispered into the darkness.

'Tom Thatcher, are you here?'

'I am,' said Tom. 'Who is it?'

'A friend,' said the man. 'Come with me if you value your life.'

Tom needed no further invitation and followed the two men back across the cloisters and into the grounds. The first hooded man had tied and gagged the monk and soon did the same to Evans.

'Let's go,' he said and they quickly left the abbey behind them as they disappeared into the forest. Five minutes later they stopped in a clearing and turned to face Tom.

'There is a horse tied to a tree a few yards further on. In the pack there is food, a waterproof cape and a few coins. Ride north, Tom, for there is no longer any future for you here. As soon as they find those two, they will raise the alarm and seek you out. You have to ride hard and do not stop until your horse can take no more.'

'Who are you?' asked Tom. 'And why are you doing this?'

'It matters not,' said the man. 'Let's just say we have mutual friends.'

'You talk of the fletcher?'

'Say no names ever again, Tom, for innocent men may be accused. Just be thankful you have a chance. Now, be gone and never look back.'

'Thank you,' said Tom, 'and whoever it is that put you up to this, thank them also.'

'We will,' said the man and together the two rescuers walked into the forest leaving Tom alone with the horse.

Two weeks later Garyn stood outside the manor house waiting to be seen along with many others of the village who had issues to air. Some were petty squabbles, some had requests for work, and there were even those asking permission to marry outside of the parish, but all had something in common: they needed the lord or lady of the manor to resolve their issues.

Eventually they had permission to enter and were shown into the hall where three seats stood empty behind a long table. A rope was draped between two statues of hunting dogs limiting how far each person could approach. Rumour passed around the audience that Lady Elisabeth was bedridden and that her daughter would judge in her name. Everyone waited nervously until three people entered the hall and silence fell as they made themselves comfortable in the chairs.

'Citizens of Brycheniog,' announced an usher, 'pray silence for audience with her ladyship, Suzette Cadwallader, daughter of Elisabeth Cadwallader, lady of this manor, esteemed knight, Sir Gerald of Essex and the honourable abbot of the order of St Benedict, Father Williams. This audience is now in session.'

'Bring the first case,' said Gerald and one of the ushers brought forward two elderly men.

'My lady,' said the usher, 'there is an argument between these two plaintiffs about the ownership of a pig.' He turned and pointed out each in turn. 'A deal was made to my lord, this man's sow with this man's boar. The coupling was successful with thirteen piglets born. Each man has had six piglets but dispute the ownership of the thirteenth, claiming their own animal was the most important in the union. They respectfully seek judgement.'

Suzette looked at Gerald nervously, unsure how to proceed. He leaned forward to whisper in her ear and she nodded quietly before clearing her throat.

'My finding is this,' she said, 'each man will look after the pig for six months, at the end of which, the pig will be slaughtered and cut down the middle with each plaintiff receiving one half.'

The two men mumbled but bowed their heads in acceptance before leaving the hall. One by one the ushers brought cases before the panel until eventually Garyn stood at the rope.

'My lady,' said the usher, 'Garyn ap Thomas is the village blacksmith and brings complaint that his business has been unfairly curtailed by the laying of a new ford.'

Again Suzette turned to Gerald but the young man's eyes never left those of Garyn.

'My lady,' said Gerald, 'I know of this situation and beg permission to judge in your name.'

'Granted,' said Suzette.

'Garyn ap Thomas,' said Gerald, 'your concerns are recognised but the needs of one man cannot be put before the needs of the many. The new road will shorten travel distance for traders and travellers alike. Indeed, those seeking pilgrimage to our abbey will find the journey that much easier as soon as the ford is finished and the village will benefit from better trade. The Lady Elisabeth signed the order herself.'

'I can see the benefit, my lord,' said Garyn, 'but question why a family of long standing within the village must be made destitute without recourse to the law of the land.'

'Are you saying she acted illegally?' asked Gerald, a dangerous smile playing about his lips.

'My lord, I am sure the Lady Elisabeth acted in good faith with the needs of many in mind, but my father was held in high esteem by Lord Cadwallader himself and I don't think this situation would have been allowed to happen if Robert Cadwallader was alive today.'

'Perhaps not,' said Gerald, 'but he is dead and I would advise you not to besmirch his name. The ford is going ahead and the decision will not be reversed.'

'My lord,' continued Garyn, 'the new road isolates my land and prevents trading. My family will become destitute and I respectfully request recompense for the loss of our livelihood.'

'Recompense,' said Gerald with a quizzical look on his face. 'Young man, I think you misunderstand the situation. The land upon which the new road is being laid belongs to the manor, as does the location of the new ford. The old way which is to be fenced off also belongs to the estate and as such, the law does not require us to pay any recompense. The fact that your father chose such a stupid place to build his forge is of no consequence.'

'He chose the existing ford to take advantage of the existing traffic,' said Garyn.

'Then he was a fool with no vision,' said Gerald. 'Anyone of sense could see there was a better route to the village, it just needed someone such as I to make it happen. There will be no compensation.'

Suzette leaned forward and spoke into Gerald's ear and after a whispered conversation, Gerald turned to face Garyn again.

'Garyn ap Thomas,' he said, 'my whim is to have you thrown out and whipped for insolence however, Lady Suzette is of a kinder disposition. Out of the kindness of her heart she has authorised me to offer you a deal which will help you settle your family elsewhere.'

'What sort of deal?' asked Garyn.

'We will buy the land from you at a fair rate,' said Gerald, 'and turn it over for grazing the manor's flocks.'

'How much?' asked Garyn.

Gerald turned and talked quietly to Father Williams before facing Garyn once again.

'We will pay ten pounds,' said Gerald, 'a generous price I think you will agree.'

'Ten pounds,' said Garyn in disbelief, 'it's worth ten times that.'

'With full access, I would agree but as you have said yourself, it will soon be isolated and no use to any man.'

'That is not a fair price,' said Garyn and turned to face Suzette. 'My lady, I beseech you to intervene and pay a fair price.'

'The lady has authorised me to act on her behalf,' said Gerald loudly, 'and I would thank you not to offend her ears with your begging. The price will be ten pounds and no more, take it or leave it.'

'This is brigandry,' shouted Garyn. 'You cannot do this; I won't allow you to.'

The hall gasped in shock at the outburst and silence fell as Gerald got to his feet.

'Your outburst is an insult to this manor, blacksmith, and I will not let it go unpunished. With immediate effect your lands are hereby confiscated in the name of the King and will be administered by the Lady Suzette of the Cadwallader estate.'

'You can't do this,' shouted Garyn.

'Furthermore,' shouted Gerald, 'you are condemned to a week in the village stocks with no succour from man or shelter. The rest of you, take notice. Before this month is out, I will be wed to the Lady Suzette and will reside permanently in this house. Let this be a lesson to all, for when I become master of this estate, I will countenance no insolence of nobility or station, whether it be lord or king. Guards, seize this man and take him to the stocks; this audience is concluded.'

The armed men around the hall ushered the remaining people out as two guards dragged Garyn through a different door. Suzette left the room and when the hall was empty, Gerald turned to Father Williams.

'I expect you are happy with the outcome?' he asked.

'More than happy,' said the monk. 'He unwittingly played his role perfectly and the result is exactly as I hoped.'

'So,' said Gerald, 'I get the land and you get to see him humiliated before his village. What exactly did he do to you that was so bad?'

'He humiliated me before Longshanks himself,' said abbot, 'and denied me possession of the holiest of relics. His death will be a gift like no other.'

'Death?' asked Gerald. 'He is going to the stocks, not the gibbet.'

'Anything can happen over five days,' said the abbot. 'Who knows what assassins or brigands may take advantage of his predicament.'

'You are a vicious man, father,' said Gerald. 'I'll have to remind myself not to cross you.'

'You do that, Gerald,' said the abbot. 'It may be the best decision you ever make.'

Chapter Twelve

The New World

For weeks the column headed westward through the forests and into the rolling plains beyond. At first the going was tough but eventually it got easier and the routine soon settled into one of ease and shared adventure. Those allocated to hunting parties roamed far afield and started to learn the habits of the indigenous animals. Deer and the black feathered birds made up their staple diet and after each day's march ended, the evenings were taken with setting up camp and eating the meaty broth that Spider made in the giant cooking pots. Fruit and berries were eaten straight from the bush and strange plants were tried carefully to check if they were poisonous before adding to the quickly growing range of food they were gathering.

After a particularly difficult day, Tarian called a halt and the men fell gratefully to the ground to rest. Some of them were tasked with building the fire and Spider hung the communal pot on an iron frame while others butchered the large deer the hunting party had brought back that day.

'I should have the choicest steak,' shouted Marcus for all to hear. 'It was my arrow that brought him down.'

'I hear the animal threw itself at you,' laughed Geraint, 'and any man could have had the same success. You were in the right place at the right time, no more.'

'But is that not a skill in itself?' asked Marcus. 'It is true the beast did not flee but my arrow still needed to be true and it pierced the heart as good as any tournament winner. Perhaps my future lies in winning prizes around the castles of England.'

The men groaned at his words for he had been boasting since he returned with the deer.

'My lord,' cried Geraint, 'allow this man a steak I beseech thee, for all our sakes.'

'If it stops him crowing,' said the knight, 'he can have the choicest slice.'

The men laughed and continued to set up the camp as the food cooked. Night fell and they started to gather around the fire, their mouths watering at the smell of the pot contents. Finally Spider shouted the words they were all longing to hear.

'Food's done!'

Everyone gathered around and filled their tankards with the potage and each was allowed to spike a piece of meat with their knives before they returned to their sleeping space.

'Where's my steak?' roared Marcus, much to the mirth of all present.

'Alas, beneath the heavy hide your beast was but a scrawny one,' said Spider, 'and there was not enough meat to spare a steak. However, there is meat aplenty on this.' He reached into the pot and withdrew the thigh bone of the deer.

Marcus mumbled in disappointment but took the leg nevertheless. There seemed to be quite a bit of meat still attached and besides, he knew the bone would be full of marrow. He walked over to sit alongside Geraint and both ate in silence, relishing the hearty meal at the end of an arduous day.

'I feel I will sleep like the dead tonight,' said Geraint. 'My body is exhausted.'

'Me also', said Marcus, draining the tankard and reaching for the leg bone, 'do you want some of this?'

'No, you can take it,' said Geraint. 'It is your kill. I'm going to get more cawl.' He returned to the pot and nagged Spider to issue a refill before returning to sit alongside Marcus but as he approached, he could see his friend was holding his mouth in pain.

'What ails you?' asked Geraint.

'I've broken a cursed tooth,' said Marcus.

'How did you do that?'

'I don't know,' snapped Marcus, 'probably on a bit of detached bone.'

Geraint picked up the leg bone and examined it, his fingers probing into the flesh where something was lodged.

'No wonder you broke your tooth,' he said eventually, 'you bit into an arrowhead. That's why the animal didn't run; it was already wounded.'

'Impossible,' said Marcus, 'besides, my arrow found the heart and I extracted it intact. I will have no other man claiming a share of my kill.'

'I don't think there is any chance of that,' said Geraint quietly, opening his hand for Marcus to see. 'This arrowhead is made of flint.'

–

Within five minutes the camp was a hive of activity as Tarian marched about, issuing his orders.

'I want every man to form a perimeter,' he shouted. 'Form a circle around the carts at twenty paces distance. You will lie in pairs with weapons to hand. Each will take it in turns to rest and may God help any I find sleeping who should be awake. Spider, refill the pot and stoke the fire, I want tomorrow's food done and the fire extinguished before it turns dark.'

He turned to face some of the lancers.

'Place two men on each hill but do not expose yourselves to prying eyes. As it gets dark, bring the horses inside the cordon and take your place in the defences. We have no idea who these people are. They may be friendly or they may be hostile but when we encounter them, we will not be found wanting.'

Men formed a line at the wagons and retrieved their weapons. Archers donned their gambesons while lancers pulled on their chainmail shirts. Pikes were handed out to the foot soldiers while an extra bundle of arrows was issued to every bowman. Finally they were in place and as it fell dark, the horses were tied to the wagons, the fire extinguished and the camp fell silent.

Geraint lay alongside Marcus and both faced outward toward the treeline.

'Do you think this is a bit much?' asked Geraint.

'I don't know,' said Marcus, 'but it doesn't hurt to be wary. For all we know there is a huge army out there with cavalry untold, just waiting to run us down with lances.'

'We would have surely seen something by now,' said Geraint.

'Perhaps they are laying up inside their fortresses.'

'Perhaps,' said Geraint, 'though I have my doubts.'

'Why?'

'That arrowhead was made of flint,' said Geraint. 'Only the poorest of peasants back home resort to such things; iron has been used for as long as anyone knows.'

'Perhaps there is a shortage of iron ore in these lands.'

'If that is so, then we can hope to meet an inferior force, for no weapons of wood or flint can compete with those of iron. Tarian displays caution and that is good, but I think he fears unduly.'

'Geraint,' said Marcus, 'you have forgotten one thing. We are but two hundred men in a strange land. Who knows how many there are and if their numbers are great, it matters not if they attack us with flint-tipped arrows or just their bare hands, eventually we will be overwhelmed. Tarian has taken fair precaution.'

'It is a point well made,' said Geraint. 'You get some sleep, Marcus, I will take the first watch.'

—

The night passed uneventful, as indeed did the next few days. Rations were cut as the hunting parties stayed close to the main force and often came back empty-handed. Eventually Spider approached Tarian and voiced his concerns about the food stocks.

'My lord, the barrels of meat are three parts empty. We need to bring in some game lest we will be eating grass within the week.'

'I understand,' said Tarian. 'I will send out a strong force on the morrow. We have to be careful of those who use the flint arrows, but hunger is no less a foe. Leave it to me.'

The following morning, Tarian assembled a foraging group consisting of ten lancers and ten archers. Only bowmen able to ride were selected and they too were issued with horses, a situation usually unheard of but it was essential the group were able to range far if they were going to be successful. Geraint had been given command of the hunting party and sat upon one of the animals as did Marcus but all declined their gambesons as it was essential they were as unencumbered as possible when they started tracking.

'We are going to hunt, not fight,' Geraint had said, 'and if we are close enough to be struck by arrows, I feel we will have bigger problems to worry about.'

The group set out making good ground as they headed into the unknown territory. Soon they were amongst tall forests and though there was plenty of spoor, their efforts were unsuccessful and noon passed without anything being caught.

'Our luck is cursed,' moaned Marcus as they rode, 'It seems this forest laughs at our efforts.'

'The deer certainly seem more wary,' said Geraint, 'and that is a concern. Perhaps they have encountered men before.'

They crossed a small stream and Geraint called a halt to rest and water the horses.

'I'll carry on a while longer,' said Marcus, 'and see what lies beyond this hill.'

'Take David of Caerleon with you,' said Geraint, 'no man should ride alone out here.'

Marcus summoned the young man and together they rode ahead beneath the widely spaced trees. The rest of the men dismounted and gave their horses the bundles of grass they had collected whilst crossing a valley earlier that day. Each man had a small portion of salted beef and they chewed quietly while taking advantage of the fresh water supply.

'We will give the horses a chance to rest,' said Geraint, 'and then we will make the return journey. Perhaps our luck will change on the way back.' Before he could continue, a noise made them stand in alarm and within moments, Marcus and David came crashing back through the undergrowth.

'Marcus, hold your gallop,' shouted Geraint, 'your horse will break a leg in this brush.'

Marcus reined in his horse and caught his breath.

'Geraint,' he said, 'get the men mounted and follow me back. There is something you must see.'

'What is it?' asked Geraint. 'Are we in danger?'

'In a way,' said Marcus, 'but my words will not do this justice. You need to see for yourself.'

The men mounted quickly and within moments were following Marcus through the forest. As they approached the ridge, Marcus dismounted and tied his horse to a tree before indicating the rest to follow him. Finally he dropped to his knees and Geraint joined him as he crawled forward to peer through the undergrowth at the unbelievable sight before him.

—

At first Geraint couldn't quite understand what he was seeing but then his eyes widened in shock as realisation dawned. Below him the forests had disappeared and, in its place, the landscape opened up into enormous rolling plains as far as the distant horizon. Swathes of healthy green grass stood knee high, blowing gently in the wind but what was most astonishing of all were the thousands of enormous animals grazing on the luscious growth at their feet.

Geraint had never seen such animals in his life and his first thoughts were that they looked like the cattle at home but were much, much bigger. In addition, these animals had a heavy fur coat on the front of their bodies only and the rear end seemed small in comparison with the heavily muscled front. Their heads hung low from the enormous shoulders and were draped in heavy fur manes. The noise of rutting males reached the watching men and they stared in amazement as the biggest animals crashed into each other in clouds of dust and roars of defiance as each fought for the right to mate.

'What are they?' asked Geraint to anyone in earshot.

'I don't know,' answered Marcus, 'but they look a lot like cows to me.'

'Yet twice the size,' said another man.

'Twice the size means twice the meat,' said Geraint, 'I think our food problems have just become far less a worry.'

'I have never seen so many animals in one place,' said Marcus. 'We could kill one a day for every man for the rest of our lives and their numbers would still be more than stars in the sky.'

For an age they stared at the enormous herd until finally Geraint instructed them to withdraw from the ridge and return to the horses.

'So what now?' asked Marcus.

'Now we return to Tarian and let him know what we have found.'

'Why don't we just go out there and take one down?' asked one of the men, 'many are within arrowshot of the forest edge and a few well-placed arrows would bring down even the largest.'

'And then what?' asked Geraint. 'We came expecting to bring back a deer or a couple of birds, not the biggest cow I have ever set eyes on. No, we need the wagons and the butchering skills of Spider. Come, if we ride hard, we can be back here by morning.'

The men mounted up and headed back the way they had come leaving the forest silent once more. A few minutes later, a nearby bush moved and a man clad in deer skin emerged. Slowly he unstrung his bow and slipped it into the pouch on his back before crouching to examine the tracks left by the horses. Finally he stood up and without a backward glance, started following the strangers back through the forest.

–

The following morning Geraint and his comrades were once more at the forest edge, though this time their bows were strung and other preparations had been made to help with the hunt. At first the rest of the expedition didn't believe them but as soon as they saw the numbers involved, Tarian put things into place to ensure they were as successful as possible.

Geraint gave the signal and six archers crept forward through the grass, selecting a nearby animal seemingly smaller than the others. The men made sure they stayed downwind and the smell of the herd was almost over-powering but they continued to crawl forward until the animal was well within an arrow's flight. Finally each man notched an arrow onto his bowstring and waited for the final command.

'Now,' hissed Geraint and as one, the archers got to one knee and took aim at the grazing animal. For a few seconds the beast didn't realise the danger but as the first arrow embedded itself into its haunches, it gave out a bellow and spun to escape the pain.

Three more arrows thudded into its side but despite its pain, the animal charged across the plain causing the herd to scatter.

'Four hits,' shouted Marcus, 'it won't get far.'

'Our job is done,' said Geraint. 'The rest is up to Tarian.'

They looked further along the tree line and as expected, a line of horses galloped out onto the plain. Tarian led the charge and each man carried a lance usually used for jousting or lethal battle with enemy knights.

'There they go,' shouted Geraint, 'come on, after them.'

Out on the plains the horses chased down the wounded animal, easily catching it up as it lumbered through the herd. Within minutes it slowed to a walk but stayed upright and turned to meet its tormentors.

Tarian slowed his horse to a halt, and rather than charging in with the lance, he dismounted and walked slowly toward the magnificent beast. He held his lance parallel to the ground facing the animal and the rest of the riders formed a circle around both man and beast.

For a few moments Tarian and the buffalo stared at each other until finally the animal grunted and lumbered toward him. Tarian gripped his lance tighter and using his full strength, thrust the weapon deep between the animal's forelegs and into its chest. The animal kept coming but Tarian jumped to one side. The rest of the men joined in the attack and within moments the animal lay gasping its last breaths. They all stood around as it died and Tarian looked at the rest of the herd. Though they had scattered, they were still only a few hundred paces away and were already acting as if nothing at happened.

'I don't believe this,' said Tarian, 'this is a hunter's paradise.' As he talked, Geraint and the archers caught them up.

'Well, that was easy enough,' said Marcus, looking at the enormous corpse.

'It was,' said Tarian, 'almost too easy. Geraint, send for the wagons. The rest of you, back to the wood line, we may as well kill what we can while they are here. Who knows when they may move on?'

The rest of the day they repeated the process until they had ten animals, dead on the plain. Spider brought up the wagons and they set about butchering the carcasses. For the first time in months, each man was allowed a thick slab of flesh to roast over their own fires and they set up camp out amongst the herds. The rest of the meat was salted and placed in barrels and they spent the next few days travelling through the plains, killing more animals as they went. Finally they reached another set of hills and left the plains behind them. The wagons were full of meat and spirits were high as they climbed the heavily wooded slopes.

'How much further?' asked Marcus as he walked alongside Geraint.

'Tarian reckons we should find the river within two days,' said Geraint. 'All we have to do then is join the ships and seek any sign of Madoc.'

'This is a bountiful land,' said Marcus. 'No wonder Madoc returned to find more settlers. A man could raise a family out here with ease.'

'Thinking of staying, Marcus?'

'I might,' said Marcus, 'let's see the standard of their taverns first.'

They continued uphill but gradually came to a halt as the column in front slowed to a stop.

'What's going on?' asked Marcus.

'I don't know' said Geraint, 'but I will find out.' He walked past the men who had dropped to the floor to rest and joined Tarian at the front of the column. Slowly they walked forward, not sure what they were looking at. All around them, man-made frames had been erected supporting latticework platforms. At the base of each structure, piles of pots and clothes lay neatly bundled along with unstrung bows and mounds of flint headed arrows. Geraint looked up at the bundle of rags on top of one of the platforms and realised what they had found.

'They are bodies,' he said quietly, 'this is a graveyard.'

'I fear you are right,' said Tarian, 'but what sort of heathen leave their dead to rot in the open air? It goes against the will of God.'

They looked around them and realised there were hundreds of similar frames as far as the eye could see. Some had collapsed with age and the remains had obviously been destroyed by scavenging animals but many were still intact and the heavily wrapped bodies lay exposed to the sky above. One of them was obviously only a recent addition and crows squabbled around the body's head as they stripped away the rotting flesh.

'We need to get out of here,' said Tarian quietly.

'I agree,' said Geraint, 'I will find a way around.'

'No,' said Tarian, 'we go straight through. Our direction is still west and we will lose time going around. Who knows how wide this cursed place is?'

They rallied the men and forged ahead. It took almost half a day to get through the graveyard and by the time they were out, their spirits were low. Despite the lateness of the day they continued on as hard as they could, determined to put as much distance between them and the silent world of the dead they had left behind. Camp was set up in almost darkness and the perimeter formed as usual, though not many men enjoyed the release of dream-free sleep.

The following morning saw them on their way again, keen to reach their destination and get away from the unknown people who treated their dead so strangely. Marcus had been tasked to lead the day's scout patrol and they were already miles in front when they crested a ridge and saw the sight they had been longing to see for so long.

Before them was a slow-moving river, bigger than anything they had seen before. The far bank was shrouded in mist, but the mountains which rose beyond the water were at least ten leagues away.

'I think this must be it,' said Marcus.

'I have never seen the like,' said William Blessed, one of the lancers. 'Surely there is not enough water in all the world to feed such a river.'

For a while they watched the waters flow lazily by before Marcus roused them from their reverie.

'Enough,' he said sharply. 'We need to get back. Tarian should know we have arrived unharmed.'

'There is no sign of the ships,' started William, 'and I can't…'

The sentence went unfinished as his body jerked forward. He looked down in shock and was confused to see the bloody stone tip of a primitive lance sticking out of his chest. Looking up he tried to say something but as blood oozed from his mouth, he fell to one side and slipped from his horse.

'To arms,' shouted one of his comrades, 'stand to your weapons.' He tried to turn his horse but as he did, an axe flew through the air and though it was only the haft that hit his head, the impact made him lose control of the horse and it reared up in fear, throwing him to the floor. Within seconds a man ran from the undergrowth and fell upon him. The native wore only deerskin leggings and his naked torso was heavily daubed with ash and coloured paints. Before the fallen man could defend himself, the attacker smashed a stone axe across his head.

All around, the undergrowth burst into life as the native war party descended on the panicking scouts. The men tried to defend themselves as best they could but to no avail, and those not immediately killed were knocked to the ground before being bound as prisoners. One of the lancers tried to gallop away, and though he burst through the first line of attackers, he hadn't gone far before his horse was brought down by a dozen arrows and he landed on the floor, pinned by the dying animal.

A warrior walked over with knife drawn as the boy tried desperately to free his leg. The native's head was completely bald and he was dressed in only flaps of leather around his waist. More leather strips were tied tightly around his upper arms and his face was scarred through previous encounters with flint blades. One eye was half closed where a wound had healed badly.

He stared at the injured man for a few seconds before issuing a command in his strange language. Two of the other warriors dragged the lancer screaming from under the horse.

'Please,' whimpered the wounded man, 'don't hurt me.'

The native looked down at the man's leg where the bloodied end of a broken bone protruded through his leggings. For a few moment's both stared into each other's eyes before the native stepped forward and silently ground his heel into the jagged end of the bone.

The forest echoed with the sound of the lancer's screams but was soon silent again as he fell into unconsciousness.

A few miles away the main column ploughed onward through the forest, unaware of the drama unfolding before them. Due to the denseness of the trees, they marched in close order and the going was slow. Eventually they reached the river and broke into cheering as they realised another part of the journey had been successfully completed.

'There it is,' said Tarian, 'the river Madoc was so impressed with.'

'And little wonder,' said Geraint, 'it is huge, but where are the scouts?'

'They're probably around somewhere,' said Tarian, 'and if we have missed each other, they have been instructed to rendezvous downstream.' A noise echoed through the forest and many of the men stopped their celebrating to stare at each other nervously.

'What's that?' asked Geraint.

Again the sound reverberated through the trees.

'Unless I'm very much mistaken,' said Tarian, 'it's a screaming man.' He turned to shout at the men. 'To arms,' he roared, 'form a perimeter.'

Within moments the patrol made an outward facing line of armed men, each holding their weapons nervously.

'Help me,' screamed the voice again and many faces turned to Tarian.

'My lord,' shouted Geraint, 'it is one of the patrol; we have to do something.'

'Knights, don mail and helms,' shouted Tarian. 'Geraint ap Thomas, get ten men into gambesons and follow the knights along with ten pikemen. It sounds like they are no more than a few hundred paces away. The rest of you, close up and present a wall of steel.'

As they got ready, the man's cries escalated in ferocity until suddenly they stopped and the forest fell silent.

'Knights, follow me,' shouted Tarian and rode in the direction of the now silenced screams. The rest of the men ran behind as fast as they dared but fell behind the horses.

'What's that smell?' shouted Geraint as they ran but as they bust through into a clearing, the source became clear. It was burning flesh... human flesh.

In front of them, a lancer's naked body was stretched between two trees, with his arms and legs spread eagled. His hands were tied high so his body was held upright and on the ground between his legs was a small fire.

The tortured man's legs were blackened through the heat and all his bodily hair was burnt away, leaving his flesh blistering horribly as his head lolled forward onto his chest.

'Get him down,' screamed Tarian and Geraint ran forward to kick away the remains of the fire. He laid him on the grass but it was too late: the lancer was dead.

'What sort of people do this?' gasped Geraint.

'I have seen men burn before,' said Tarian, 'but not like this. The fire was kept small to inflict as much pain as possible and draw out the death. Get him back to the

164

column; I will take the knights and seek out those who did this.'

'I fear you will be unsuccessful,' said Geraint. 'Their tracks are light in the soil and lightly armed men are too fleet of foot to be run down by horses in forests as dense as these.'

'I suspect you are right,' said Tarian, 'but we have to try.'

–

Just before night fell, the mounted knights returned to the main column and dismounted.

'Any luck, my lord?' asked Geraint.

'None,' said Tarian removing his helm. 'We followed their sign for many hours but they have disappeared as easily as mist. What is more confusing is that we saw no evidence of any horses. No tracks, no dung, no hairs on the thorn bushes, nothing.'

'Perhaps their mounts were hidden far away?'

'We circled for many miles,' said Tarian. 'There was nothing. Unless I am mistaken, I believe these heathen, whoever they may be, do not have the use of horses.'

'Every culture I have ever heard of has horses,' said Geraint. 'How would they otherwise survive?'

'I know not,' said Tarian, 'yet strange as it sounds, this group at least were on foot.'

'My lord, there is something that adds weight to your words,' said Geraint. 'While you were gone, we found the rest of the scouts. Most are dead but three are missing. What is stranger, is that every horse was slaughtered and it seems one was butchered for the meat. We couldn't understand why they weren't just taken for their own use but if what you suspect is true and they are not familiar with the animals, then they would seem little more than an easy source of food.'

'It makes sense,' said Tarian, 'and if this is proved to be true, it gives us a huge advantage.' He stopped and thought for a few moments.

'Who is our best tracker?'

'Well, believe it or not, it is the cook, Spider. He was once a poacher and knows the ways of the forest animals as good as any man.'

'We seek men not animals.'

'They are but the same, my lord,' said Geraint. 'If anyone can follow their spoor, he can.'

'Tell him his services will be required to the fore at first light. We will spend the rest of this day finding a position that is easy to defend and go to ground with the wagons. Tomorrow, we will take as many men as we can spare and follow those who murdered our comrades.'

'I thought our focus was on the quest.'

'It is but we will spare two days. If by then we have not found them, then we will return and leave their fate in the hands of God.'

'So be it,' said Geraint leaving to make the arrangements. Within a few hours they had found a rocky ridge where their backs were protected and a clear approach meant anyone coming close would be seen long before any were in arrow range.

'We will go firm here,' said Tarian. 'Get the men to cut small trees from the forest and erect a wall. We may not have time to make a strong stockade but it will give some protection from arrows. Put out markers in case of assault and place guards in the forest edge. If anyone approaches, they are to retire immediately and take their place at the stockade.'

By the time night fell, the wagons were secured amongst the rocks and a wall of saplings stretched between boulders at the base of the cliff. Bundles of arrows lay along the palisade and the men spread out along the defences, each able to leap into position within seconds.

'It will have to do,' said Tarian. 'At first light I will seek out these killers and exact my revenge upon them.'

–

Dawn saw the whole camp wide awake and a column of forty riders stood alongside their horses. Each man had dried food for two days and wore their chainmail armour as protection. The horses were draped with their caparisons, blanketed drapes of heavy cloth that were efficient against most arrow shots and much lighter than the heavier metal barding preferred when going into battle against other knights.

'Your orders are clear,' said Tarian to the remaining defenders. 'You will wait here for two full days, not a minute more. If we do not return by then, continue as planned and follow the river south to meet the ships. They are surely making their way upstream by now. If we still survive, we will follow you as soon as we can. Geraint ap Thomas, you will command the palisade and I hold you responsible. The rest of you, his word is my command and you will do as he says.'

The column mounted up as Spider rode his horse from behind the wagons. He wore no armour or even a gambeson.

'You ride light, soldier,' said Tarian.

'I am no soldier, my lord, and do not intend to fight these savages. I will lead you to them and then withdraw to see you do what it is you do.'

'We are all soldiers, Spider,' said Tarian, 'and your sword arm may yet wield a blade before this day is out. Lead us out and do not spare your horse; our time is limited.'

Chapter Thirteen

Brycheniog

Garyn stared down at the floor. His back hurt and his wrists were red raw from the chafing of the wood. He had been detained for three days, kneeling on the small patch of mud that counted as a village green, his hands and head sticking through the wooden stocks. By order of the constable, anyone offering any comfort apart from basic food or water was turned away.

The nights were long and despite Elspeth demanding she be allowed to stay at his side, Garyn was adamant she returned to her father's house and the safety therein. It was deep into the third night when he heard a noise behind him and his eyes opened in fear.

'Who's there?' he asked. 'Elspeth, is that you?' No reply came but he was aware someone had walked up behind him. 'Who is it?' he asked again. 'What do you want?'

'Nothing from you,' said a quiet voice, 'except the blood of your throat on my blade.' Before Garyn could cry out, a hand covered his mouth and a knife was placed between his chin and the lower half of the stocks.

'Nothing personal,' said the voice, 'it's just business.'

Garyn tried to call out but it was no use, he was completely in the control of the unseen assassin. His eyes closed as he anticipated the killing stroke but it never came. The sound of an arrow flying through the air was followed by a thud and the man fell away with an arrow in his back. Garyn gasped in relief and strained his neck to see who had come to his aid.

'Who's there?' he gasped. 'What's happening?' Within moments a man knelt at his side and placed an iron bar through the shackles securing the stocks.

'Fletcher,' gasped Garyn, recognising the man, 'what are you doing here?'

'I'm getting you out,' said Elspeth's father. 'There were rumours that you were to be killed within the stocks so we have been watching over you these past few nights. Obviously, the rumours are true.' He paused to strain against the bar until the shackle snapped. A few moments later the second shackle followed suit and Fletcher lifted the upper half of the stocks from around the young man's neck. Garyn stood up and moaned as his back straightened for the first time in days. He looked down at the would-be assassin.

'He's dead,' said Garyn.

'He is,' said Fletcher retrieving the arrow.

'If anyone finds out you will hang for murder.'

'I know but that is a risk we have to take.'

'We?'

Fletcher stared at the young man.

'Garyn, I didn't enjoy what I have just done but my daughter loves you and I only have her happiness at heart. For some reason you have raised the ire of both the manor and the abbey and that makes you a marked man.'

'I have done nothing wrong.'

'Since when has that made any difference to those who seek to further their own position? No, you have to leave here right now.'

'Leave?! But what about Elspeth?'

'You have to forget about Elspeth,' said Fletcher. 'I know you love her but if you stay, you will be dead within weeks. How is that going to make her happy?'

'But…'

'There is no other option, Garyn. Yes, she will be upset but rather that than she has to visit your grave.'

'But where will I go?'

'There is a rider at the bridge waiting for you with Silverlight. Ride north and seek out those loyal to Llewellyn. There is no love lost between him and those nobles loyal to the English Crown, you can seek out a new life amongst the ranks of his army.'

'For how long?'

'It has to be permanent, Garyn. When the stocks are found empty you will be outlawed and a bounty placed on your head. If you return, there are those who will turn you in and I will not be able to help.'

'But why would Llewellyn accept an outlaw into his ranks?'

'Llewellyn offers an amnesty to petty criminals who agree to serve his cause. Your crime is nothing but standing up against Gerald of Essex, a staunch supporter of the dead King.'

'What about him?' asked Garyn, pointing at the dead man at his feet.

'He is nothing but an assassin in the pay of the Crown,' said Fletcher. 'Leave him to me; his body will not be found.'

'Can I not even say goodbye to Elspeth?'

'No, it is too risky. If you are seen, she will be implicated and labelled as an accomplice. As it is, she knows nothing and will be seen as nothing more than an innocent victim of your cowardice.'

'What cowardice?'

'Don't forget, there will be no assassin's corpse so nobody will know what has gone on here this night. Everyone will think you arranged an accomplice to free you and have run to escape your punishment.'

'But that's not true.'

'I know, but it must be so. That is the only way Elspeth will be allowed to live as a free woman. I know it is hard, Garyn, but there is no other option. At least this way you will both have lives to live.'

Garyn shook his head slowly.

'My wife, the only woman I have ever loved will think me as a coward who ran to save his own skin.'

'Garyn,' snapped Fletcher, 'what other way is there? If you stay here, she will be a widow within weeks. If we tell her the truth and someone finds out, she will be labelled an accomplice to an outlaw and at the very least be sent into a lifetime of servitude in a convent. This way she will be completely innocent of any complicity and allowed to get on with her life. If you love her, Garyn, you will let her go.'

Garyn nodded silently as the reality of the situation sunk in.

'It is true,' he said eventually, 'and I will not have her suffer over me.'

'Then make haste and get to the bridge before we are seen,' said Fletcher.

'Tell her…' started Garyn but realised that there could be no words passed without compromising her safety.

'I'm sorry, Garyn,' said Fletcher, 'I will look after her, I promise, but now you must go, before it's too late.'

Garyn stared at the man but realising there was no other option, walked backwards a few steps before turning and running into the darkness. Fletcher watched him go before reaching down to grab the dead man by the shoulders. Another man stepped from the shadows to help.

'How was he?' asked the newcomer.

'It took some time but he is convinced,' said Fletcher.

'And he didn't know my involvement in this?'

'He knew someone else was involved but never suspected you.'

'Good,' said the man, 'and for the moment, that is the way it must be. I suspect we will meet again, but for now our paths will remain separate.'

'He owes you his life,' said Fletcher.

'Then a debt has been paid,' said the man and bent to help Fletcher drag the body to a nearby cart.

—

Garyn ran through the darkness until he neared the bridge. A horse snorted in the shadows and a rider came out to greet him.

'Master Garyn,' said the man, 'thank the Lord above. I feared we might have been too late.'

'Tom Thatcher,' said Garyn in surprise. 'What are you doing here? I thought you were long gone.'

'A family in Senni heard of my plight,' said Tom, 'and lucky for me they did. My hand was infected and would have festered if they had not taken me in. The old lady of the house applied poultices from the plants of the forest and though I came close to death, the infection passed and I live to tell the tale. My hand is useless but luckily God graced me with two.'

'But if you are caught, both you and they will hang.'

'You are right and I was about to flee north but when I learned of your plight there was no way I would leave you to your fate.'

'But how did you know?'

'There are many who hate the way this manor kneels to the English kings, Garyn, and though they hold their counsel, they silently oppose them in whatever way they can. That may be very little but times like these find hidden allies amongst the masses. There are those who dwell within the confines of the Cadwallader estate who hate their masters as much as any and when the whispers came of a plot to kill you, word spread quickly.'

'So you came to help?'

'Not just I, Garyn. There are many who hold this grudge and oft meet to condemn the way of the manor.'

'How come I wasn't aware of this?'

'Garyn, you forget you rode alongside Longshanks to the Holy Land, and in times of war men form strong allegiances. We did not know which way your loyalties lay.'

'Who else is in this allegiance?'

'I cannot tell you,' said Tom.

'So I am still not trusted?'

'No one is trusted,' said Tom. 'Each man knows only two or three others who share his views; that way the risk of discovery is small. We carry out no great movement against the authorities for most are village men and have families to support. Yet should Llewellyn ever ride south, then we will take up arms alongside him.'

'I fear that day is a long way off,' said Garyn.

'Perhaps so,' said Tom, 'but whether it is our hands that wield the weapons or those of our sons, the day will come.

Now mount up and prepare for a long ride, we will not rest until it next gets dark.'

Garyn walked over to Silverlight and received a quiet whinny of recognition.

'Come on, boy,' said Garyn quietly, 'it seems I will be relying on your strength yet again.' He mounted his horse and after a nod to Tom, rode across the bridge and up the track into the hills.

—

The following morning a crowd gathered around the stocks, talking quietly amongst themselves. A large man barged his way through and stared at the broken shackles.

'What has happened here?' shouted the constable. 'Where is the prisoner?'

'It looks like he has escaped,' said a voice.

The constable turned around and stared at the fletcher, who stood amongst the crowd.

'And what do you know of this?'

'Nothing,' lied Fletcher, 'but the evidence is before your very eyes. The man has gone and good riddance I say.'

The constable stared at him.

'The man is wed to your daughter,' he said quietly. 'Why do you now slight him so?'

'He was no choice of mine,' said Fletcher, 'and was only welcomed into my home as it pleased my only daughter. I always thought he was a rogue and as everyone around here knows, most of my business is sent through the armouries of Cadwallader. The continued presence of this boy threatened my living and my daughter's happiness is a minor wound to see the boy gone. In truth, I hope he is captured quickly and pays the price of his treason so we can all get back to normal.'

The constable grunted, happy with the explanation.

'Well,' he said, 'Sir Gerald will hear of this soon enough and will arrange his capture. Your daughter is well rid, Fletcher, but make sure she knows that if he comes back, she needs to tell us as soon as possible. Harbourers of outlaws share the same fate as those they aid.'

'But is he an outlaw?'

'Not yet perhaps but it is a formality. He has absconded from a legal punishment and as such is outside of the law. His days are limited, Fletcher, and you and your family would do well to remember it.' Without another word the constable marched away toward the manor and the crowd dispersed.

'I can hardly believe it,' said a woman as Fletcher passed. 'He was always such a nice young man.'

'It just goes to show,' said Fletcher, 'you just never can tell.'

–

'What do you mean escaped?' shouted the abbot. 'The man was held within the stocks; there was no way he could have got out.'

Gerald didn't react to the abbot's raised voice but continued to pour wine into the goblet. He had come to the abbey to relate the news himself and had been taken straight through into the abbot's private quarters.

'He had aid,' said the knight. 'Someone broke the shackles.'

'Then you must ride them down and put them to the blade,' snapped Father Williams. 'Why haven't you got men out there already?'

'There are men on their trail but they have a half day's advantage and as you know the Welsh hills are easy to disappear into.' Gerald took a drink from the tankard and turned to face the abbot.

'Tell me,' he said, 'what is it about this peasant that drives you so? We have ruined his reputation and confiscated his lands. Why do you pursue such a small man even unto death?'

'I have already told you,' came the answer, 'he humiliated me before Longshanks himself and was instrumental in me returning the most precious artefact in Christendom to the Pope.'

'But as a man of the Church surely that was your obligation?'

'Of course, and I would have taken it willingly, but as a gift given by my own hands, not as a mere messenger of the king. Longshanks himself now bears the Pope's blessing and history will tell the return of the cross was his doing, not mine.'

'So you seek retribution?'

'I seek his death,' said Father Williams, 'and will not stop until his rotting corpse lies beneath my feet.'

'If that is so, why have you waited so long?'

'I wanted him to witness the collapse of everything he holds dear before he leaves this life. Now that has been achieved there is no reason to delay. I want him dead.'

'I will see what I can do,' said Gerald, 'but don't hold much hope. He is probably deep into Llewellyn's territory by now and will soon be beyond even my influence.'

'Then find someone who has a longer reach,' said Father Williams.

'And where will I find such a man?'

'That is your problem. I have kept all my parts of our bargain and you are a considerably richer man for it. All I ask in return is the death of one man and for someone such as you, I suggest that is an easy task.'

Gerald drank back the last of the wine and replaced the tankard on the table.

'I will do what I can,' he said, 'but there will be a price to pay.'

'What price?' asked the monk. 'You already have the forge and the boy's lands.'

'Fear not,' said Gerald, 'the task is easy for a learned man such as you. The Lady Elisabeth is a lingering thorn in my side.'

'I hear she is very ill.'

'Indeed she is but hangs on to life like none I have seen before. Her daughter dotes upon her and takes her counsel on everything, even so far as to defy my wishes. Of course I will continue to act the dutiful son-in-law until such time as she leaves for purgatory, but my patience wears thin. As long as she lives my bride-to-be pays me scant attention and exhibits a will that raises my ire.'

'Is this not a situation you would normally take a great pleasure in? The woman is bedridden so what stays your hand?'

'Her family surround her like a bad smell and I cannot be seen to be an accomplice to her death. If Suzette was to even suspect my involvement, she would refuse our union and bring shame on my house. No, I need the old woman to die a natural death, or at least one that seems natural.'

'What are you saying?'

'Make a draft,' said Gerald, 'a medicine to ease her pain but one that will also end her life.'

'You want to poison her?'

'Call it what you will. I understand you monks are learned men and have access to tomes that list such things.'

'We do,' said Father Williams, 'and there are plants in the forest that induce the sleeping death without any visible effects.'

'Then seek them out and bring the liquid yourself.'

'You want me to administer the poison with my own hand?'

'I do. You are a man of God and as such are above suspicion.'

'No,' said the abbot, 'it is too risky.'

'Do this and I will bring you this boy's head on a pike, even if I have to get it myself.'

The abbot stared in silence.

'When do you want it done?'

'The quicker she is cold, the quicker I can sort out your own petty grudge.'

'And you promise you will kill the blacksmith?'

'I may be a ruthless man, Father, but my word is still my bond.'

Father Williams nodded in reply.

'I will gather the plants and brew what is needed with my own hands. Expect me before the sun sets tomorrow.'

'Good,' said Gerald standing up. 'As usual, it is good doing business with you, Father.' He left the abbot's quarters and made his way out of the abbey.

Chapter Fourteen

The New World

Spider dismounted from his horse and crouched on the ground, examining the slightest of marks in the leaf litter. Behind him, Tarian sat astride his charger at the head of his ten knights and another thirty horsemen. They had ridden hard the whole day and crossed a wide plain before reaching another wooded hill. Each time Spider checked the trail he was confident they were getting closer to their quarry.

'Well?' said Tarian. 'Surely they can't be much further in front.'

'They move fast for foot soldiers,' said Spider, 'but I feel we are almost upon them.' He looked up at the ridge. 'Perhaps it would be prudent to keep the men here while we check the ground in front. If they know we are following, we could be walking into a trap.'

'Good idea,' said Tarian dismounting from his horse. 'Lead the way, Spider, I will accompany you. The rest, wait here but be prepared to disperse onto the plain should it be a trap. I don't care how fleet of foot they are; they cannot compete with chargers.'

The two men left the patrol and walked up the hill. Slowly they picked their way through the undergrowth and as they neared the top, Spider dropped to all fours and signalled Tarian to do the same.

'What is it?' whispered Tarian.

'I smell wood smoke.'

Carefully they crawled over the ridge and peered down into the valley below. Before them was a village like they had never seen before. Small huts covered with painted animal skins filled the valley and dozens of fires sent their wispy smoke up into the tree-filled slopes. Children played in the dust and skins of various animals were stretched on frames in the sun to dry. Women sat on the banks of the river running through the centre of the valley and rubbed wet clothes against the rocks to rid them of the dust of the day. However, what caught the eye of Tarian was the group of men at the far edge of the valley.

About one hundred armed warriors stood in a circle, surrounding a smaller group of twelve sitting cross legged on the floor. The standing men were mostly dressed in deerskin leggings whilst some wore only loin cloths. Their upper bodies were painted in various designs and their faces smeared with ash from the fires. Every warrior carried spears and some had bows slung across their backs.

The men sitting on the ground were obviously much older and wore brightly coloured beads and feathers in their hair. A young man stood before them and was shouting something in his own language, gesturing in the direction of the unseen watchers.

'There they are,' whispered Tarian.

'What do you think is happening?' answered Spider.

'I don't know but I would wager the men sitting down are the leaders. The bald one must be a warlord and perhaps relates news of our presence in their lands. Can you see any sign of our men?'

Spider shook his head but then grabbed Tarian's arm as two of the warriors left the group and headed toward a nearby hut.

'Look,' he said.

The two warriors ducked inside and pulled a tied man outside, dragging him into the circle of warriors.

'That's Owens from one of the other ships,' said Tarian quietly.

'What are they going to do with him?'

Tarian didn't answer but watched with growing horror as events unfolded. The archer was thrown into the dust near the fire and then forced back up to his knees. One of the older warriors got to his feet and walked over to inspect the prisoner. He held a short stick in one hand, decorated with feathers and the skulls of small birds. Though weaker than the younger warrior, his voice still reached Tarian's hiding place and from the tone of his words, the watching men guessed he was shouting questions at the bound man.

Over and over the man circled the prisoner, screaming his questions and striking him with the stick. The prisoner stared at his tormentor defiantly until finally the old man struck him hard across the face and he fell sideways into the dust. Two of the younger warriors stepped forward and dragged the prisoner to his feet before throwing him face first into the flames.

Spider gasped and turned his face away as the tortured man's screams echoed through the valley. The watching warriors shouted their approval until the screams died with the man.

'I have seen enough,' said Tarian. 'We must make our move now before it is too late.' The two men crawled back down the hill until they were once more sheltered from view. 'Spider, we have to move fast and I need your support.'

'What would you have me do?'

'Return to the slope above the village and crawl down as near as you dare without being seen. I will return to the men and lead them to the other end of the valley before driving into the very heart of them.'

'They number by the hundred, my lord, our numbers are but forty.'

'Agreed, but I saw no sign of any horses and truly believe they do not use such beasts. This means if they are not used to mounted warfare, they will not know how to defend against a charge. We will probably have but one pass and need to take the opportunity. While the front ranks engage the enemy, your task will be to enter the hut with the prisoners and use your knife to cut their binds. I will task the last six riders to look for you and pick up any survivors.'

'But we don't know if there are any more survivors.'

'We do not, but there is no other option. If there are no prisoners left, we will head straight back to the wagons and make haste to leave these lands as soon as we can.'

'But what if...'

'Enough,' snapped Tarian, 'my mind is set. We came here to save our comrades and whilst we may be too late, I will not leave until we have tried. Now make haste, for the village will thunder to the sounds of our hooves within a thousand heartbeats.'

'Of course, my lord.' said Spider and started back up the hill as Tarian ran down toward the horses.

'Mount up,' shouted Tarian as he approached, 'and prepare for assault.' Within moments Tarian led the men around the hill and toward the valley entrance. As they galloped, a young woman with a woven basket strapped to her waist stepped from a thicket and stared in horror at the approaching horses.

'Keep going,' shouted Tarian and the riders galloped on, trampling the poor girl beneath them.

Across the other side of the hill, Spider pushed his body as close as he could to the ground and crawled slowly down toward the village. He reached the bottom and moved opposite the hut containing the prisoners, waiting for the arrival of his comrades. As he waited, another prisoner was dragged from the hut and Spider stared in horror as his throat was sliced open before he too was thrown to the flames.

Spider's heart raced but within minutes, the sound of shouting echoed around the village and the warriors turned to stare toward the far end of the valley. Spider followed their gaze and saw a line of mounted lancers trotting into view. Before the warriors could understand what was happening, he heard Tarian's voice roaring above the babble and Spider knew the time was upon him.

The horses broke into a canter and were halfway through the village when their leader called out again.

'Front and second ranks, present lances. On my command, advance!'

The front two ranks of horses started to gallop and the lancers lowered their weapons parallel to the ground. The warriors realised the danger but rather than form any structured defensive formation, reacted by drawing their knives and racing toward the attackers. As soon as they were in range, many of the natives paused to throw their spears but despite many finding their target, the flint tipped weapons were little use against the chainmail armour of the lancers and the heavy quilted caparisons draped over the horses. One animal fell to a spear through his eye but the rider rolled away as he hit the ground and was on his feet in seconds, drawing his sword to defend himself against the oncoming hoard. Within seconds the natives at the front of the counter-charge were speared on the lances of the front two ranks and many of those behind were bowled over by the enormous military horses as they galloped through.

Those warriors still standing threw themselves against the horses with little effect and within seconds, two more ranks of riders came storming into the village with swords drawn.

Spider saw his chance, and jumping from his hiding place sprinted across the open space between him and the prisoner hut. He used his knife to cut through the skins on the back of the structure and climbed into the gloom.

At first, he struggled to see in the dark interior but soon realised there were several bodies strewn around the floor.

'Men of Tarian,' he hissed, 'make yourselves known.'

'Over here,' groaned a voice and Spider ran to cut the binds of a man propped against a supporting pole.

'Marcus,' said Spider as he recognised the captive, 'good to see you alive, my friend.'

'I thought I had seen my last sunrise,' said Marcus. 'Thank God you came in time.'

'Thank not the Almighty, Marcus, thank Tarian, thirty lancers and ten of the best Welsh knights.'

'Whoever is responsible, I will be forever in their debt,' said Marcus as his binds were cut.

'Are there any others?' asked Spider.

'I am the last,' said Marcus. 'Everyone else has been taken.'

'Then who are these?' asked Spider indicating the rest of the prisoners.

'I don't know,' said Marcus, 'but I suspect they are enemies of those who took us captive.'

'Then we are done here,' said Spider.

'What about these other men?' asked Marcus looking around at the expectant faces.

'They are none of our business,' said Spider. 'We need to go.'

'I will not leave them to die,' said Marcus. 'Give me your knife.'

Spider handed over the blade and watched as his comrade cut the rest of the prisoners free. Most ran from the hut immediately and made their escape but one remained and stood slowly, rubbing his wrists as he stared at his rescuer. He was also dressed in deer skins but unlike his captors, his hair was thick and fell loose around his shoulders.

'What are you waiting for?' snapped Spider. 'Get out of here.'

The native stared at the two men before speaking quietly.

'What tribe are you,' asked the native, 'who speak the old words.'

Marcus was shocked. Though the sentence was fragmented, the meaning was clear.

'You speak our language,' he gasped. 'How can that be?'

The man just shook his head and stared in reply.

'Tell me,' said Marcus again, 'how do you speak our words?'

'Come on,' said Spider, 'we have no time for this; we have to get out of here.'

'Wait,' snapped Marcus, 'this is important. The only way he can possibly speak our language is if he has been taught by others before us.'

'Then bring him if you must,' said Spider, 'but decide quickly.'

Marcus turned to the native.

'Do you have a name?' he asked.

The man stared back, uncomprehending.

'A name?' repeated Marcus. 'What are you called?'

'I am known as Achak,' said the man.

'Good,' said Marcus. 'Achak, I don't have time to explain but I want you to come with us. Do you understand?'

'Where is it you go?'

'Some of our people are not far from here and we would talk with you. Will you come with us?'

Achak paused but finally answered.

'Achak will come.'

'About bloody time,' said Spider, 'let's get out of here.' He led the way out of the hut and ran across to where a lancer was holding a spare horse. All around, men were dying as Tarian's knights wreaked havoc amongst the unprotected natives.

'You two, mount up,' shouted Spider, 'I will ride behind my comrade.'

Marcus ran over and grabbed the saddle but Achak stayed where he was.

'Come on,' screamed Spider, 'what are you waiting for?'

'He has never seen a horse,' shouted Marcus, 'come, help me get him up.'

'Knights, remount,' roared Tarian. 'Unhorsed men, mount behind your comrades, prepare to withdraw.'

Within minutes Marcus and Spider were galloping out of the village. Achak sat behind Marcus with his hands wrapped tightly around the archer's chest, a look of terror on his face. Many natives ran after them but were soon left behind as the horses cleared the valley. They rode hard for five minutes before slowing to a walk and Tarian rode up alongside Marcus.

'Good to see you again, Marcus.'

'And you, Tarian, though I wish my fellows were here to share my relief.'

'And who is this?' asked the leader, indicating his riding companion.

'His name is Achak and I think he will greatly aid our cause.'

'In what way?'

'He speaks our language, Tarian, and that can mean only one thing: he must know the ancestors of Madoc.'

Tarian stared at Achak in disbelief.

'Is this true?' he asked.

Achak stared back at the impressive knight before answering.

'I am Achak of the Mandan,' he said, 'and I speak the old words.'

'Well, Achak,' said Tarian, 'I have a great many questions but we have a long way to go.'

Without warning, Achak slid from the horse and stood to one side.

'What are you doing?' asked Marcus, 'remount.'

'Achak will run,' came the answer from the native.

'It's a long way,' said Marcus. 'It's easier on horseback.'

'Achak will run,' repeated the native.

Marcus looked at Tarian.

'What do you think?'

'His choice,' said Tarian.

Before they could start again, a distant sound made all the men look around them nervously.

'What's that noise?' asked Marcus.

'Drums,' said Achak, 'the spirits of Apalach sing of war. We must go.'

—

The patrol rode south once again and though the pace was steady, Achak followed close behind, scorning the numerous offers to share a horse. Finally darkness fell and Tarian paused to order a night camp but Achak walked over and stood before him.

'We must go on,' he said.

'Not in the dark, Achak it is too dangerous and the horses need rest.'

'The Apalach will not rest,' said Achak.

'That may be so but we have struck a severe blow to their numbers so they may not be so keen to take us on.'

'Apalach villages are many,' said Achak, 'and spirit drums call them to war.'

'How many?' asked Tarian.

Achak looked up at the sky and waved his hand across the expanse of stars.

'This many.'

Tarian looked at him in disbelief and Marcus stepped forward.

'That can't be,' he said, 'we haven't seen anyone before they attacked our men. How can so many people not leave a sign?'

Achak waved his hand again.

'This many?' he repeated.

'Do you believe him?' asked Marcus.

'He believes it,' said Tarian, 'and that's what worries me. Even if his estimates are wrong, it is obvious they have great strength. Perhaps he is right and we should keep going.' He turned to Achak. 'Can you take us back to the great river in the dark?'

'Achak will lead you back the way you came,' he answered.

'But how do you know which way?' asked Marcus.

'Your animals left a trail as wide as a storm,' said Achak. 'I see the way, but the Apalach will also see. We must go.'

'We have no choice,' said Tarian. 'Give the horses water from your skins, we ride again as soon as we can.'

Within ten minutes they started out once more though this time at a much slower pace. Achak trotted in front, closely followed by Spider and the rest of the patrol. Several hours later, Achak stopped and waited for Spider to catch him up.

'Your people are there,' he said pointing into the darkness.

'How far?' asked Spider screwing up his eyes but seeing nothing.

'Two arrows,' said Achak.

Tarian rode up.

'What's the problem?' he asked.

'He reckons we are back,' said Spider, 'and the wagons lay ahead.'

'Only one way to find out,' said Tarian and kicked his horse to go forward. Within seconds, a voice rang out of the darkness.

'Hold there, rider, on pain of death. Declare yourself!'

'Hold your weapons, soldier,' answered Tarian. 'It is your leader returned from campaign.' He rode forward into to the defensive position.

'My lord,' said Geraint from a rock above, 'your return is welcome.'

'It is good to be back,' said Tarian, 'but my command are exhausted. Task men to take care of our horses and arrange some food. As soon as they are within the boundary, double the guard and stand to the defences. We may be followed.'

'Were you successful in your task?'

'We have brought back two men,' said Tarian, 'one of whom is your fellow.'

'Marcus is alive?'

'He is, but lucky to be so.'

'And the other?'

'A native of this land but not one of the attackers. He also speaks our language.'

Geraint paused as the information sank in.

'A fortuitous outcome,' he said eventually, 'does he have news of Madoc?'

'I don't know but as soon as the patrol is bedded down, I intend to find out.'

—

Within the hour all horses were rubbed down and covered with heavy blankets to protect their sweating bodies from the night mist. Tired lancers sat around sheltered fires and roasted pieces of meat on the hot stones whilst others immediately rolled in their blankets, exhausted after the two-day campaign.

Some of the knights sat around a central fire talking quietly amongst themselves and were eventually joined by

Tarian and Geraint. Behind them came Marcus and Achak who took their place amongst the knights.

'Sit,' said Tarian indicating a vacant rock. One of the knights handed Achak a piece of raw meat and they watched with fascination as the native barely warmed it up before eating it almost raw. When he was done, he drank deeply from a leather flask and looked around the men as each fulfilled their need to eat. Finally they fell silent and all eyes turned to the native.

'Achak,' said Tarian, breaking the silence, 'I understand you speak our language. Is this true?'

'Some,' said Achak.

'Good,' said Tarian. 'Can you tell us who you are and how it was you were held prisoner in that village?'

'I am Achak of the Mandan,' he replied. 'I live across the great river with my people. I was taken by the Apalach to die on their fires.'

'These Apalach, are they the people we fought?'

'Yes.'

'And they are your enemy?'

'Apalach are enemy to many. They carry the war bow easily.'

'You say they are many.'

'Like buffalo on the plain.'

'What are buffalo?' asked Tarian.

'This,' said Achak, picking up what was left of his meat.

'Achak,' said Tarian, broaching the subject they were all waiting for, 'how is it you speak our language?'

'They are the old words' said Achak. 'Our children learn them before they learn to speak as a Mandan.'

'What do you mean the old words?'

'They were spoken by those who came before.'

'A murmur circled the fire and men sat straighter as they waited for him to continue.

'Achak,' said Tarian, 'we would share your story. Would you tell us about those who came before?'

The native looked around the fire as each bearded face stared back in expectation. Finally he took a breath and related his story.

'At first the Mandan were a people that were not a people,' he said. 'Our ancestors came from a land afar and the old men talked of the days when spirits with heavy coats ruled these lands. Mandan served the spirits and grew strong in their shadow. They were days of plenty and Mandan were feared by all. But then the spirits were angered for they left our lands and our people were as ghosts upon the plains. Other tribes saw the Mandan were weakened and they grew strong. They preyed upon my people as the wolf upon the buffalo. Our women were taken to bear children and the men burned upon the fires. Yet the Mandan stayed loyal to the spirits and walked the plains without a home for the wind had sung that one day the spirits would return.'

'When was that?' asked Tarian.

'More seasons have passed than fish in the streams' said Achak, 'but then the spirits forgave us for the huge war canoes of the ancestors sailed up the great river once more and brought those who spoke the old words. This time they brought their women and settled amongst our people to live alongside our ancestors. They shared our food and in return they taught us many things. We learned their words and together the spirits and the Mandan grew into a strong people. But the other tribes again grew angry and carried the war bow against us. Though we were strong, the others were many and our ancestors fled up the great river, seeking a place of peace but always the others came. The spirit people built villages protected by walls of trees but fire arrows of the Apalach burned them down. My ancestors showed the spirit people where the ancients had built villages of stone and they were greatly pleased for the walls were like those of their homeland. War parties fell against them many times but they were now safe. Finally the Apalach returned across the great river.

'That was in the days of my father's grandfather and as the years passed like the wind, the last of the spirit people died out. Their children joined with our children and became Mandan. Now there are no more spirit people but we teach our young the old words for the spirits still sing that they will return and become as many as the buffalo. When they do, the Mandan will be waiting.'

The men stared at him in silence, astonished at the story they had been told.

'Achak,' said Tarian, 'these spirit people who came in the time of your grandfathers, did they have a leader?'

'The stories tell of a great man as strong as a buffalo and as tall as a tree.' said Achak.

'What was his name?'

'He was known as Madoc.'

The men around the fire looked at each other as the implications sunk in. Finally Geraint broke the silence and said what was on all their minds.

'I don't believe it,' he said in astonishment. 'We have found it, Tarian, the link to Prince Madoc.'

Chapter Fifteen

Brycheniog

Garyn and Tom Thatcher rode hard through the night and well into the next day, keeping off the well-trodden roads and finding their way along the smaller paths over the mountains of mid-Wales. Finally they saw an abandoned shepherd's hut and stopped to seek shelter from the afternoon rain. Both horses were taken into a side room and wiped down. The two men returned to the main room and removed their wet cloaks and jerkins before wrapping their riding blankets around their shoulders and sitting against the walls. Tom produced bread and fruit from his pack and they ate in silence as they listened to the rain outside.

'We could do with a fire,' said Garyn.

'There's some kindling there,' said Tom, 'but no firewood.'

'How's your hand?' asked Garyn, looking at the way Tom held his heavily bandaged injury.

'It's painful,' said Tom, 'but gets better each day. I am told that as long as I can avoid infection it should heal, though I am unlikely to ever get full use again.'

'That abbot has a lot to answer for,' said Garyn quietly.

'He does,' said Tom, 'and you have suffered more than most.'

'I have,' said Garyn, 'and I believe he was responsible for the fire that killed my family.'

'Do you have any evidence?'

'If I did, I would present it before the court and seek justice. As it is, I only have the word of a dead monk.'

'Then there is no proof.'

'Perhaps not for the court but it is enough for me and one day he will feel my blade between his ribs.'

'You would kill a man of the Church?' asked Tom.

'Any man who kills to achieve his aims is no more holy than you or me, Tom, no matter what cloth he wears. Justice demands I settle the account. The only reason I have stayed my hand this long is because I had to think of Elspeth and would not put her at risk. Now he has even taken her from me and there is nothing to stop my blade. I will seek refuge in the north for now but one day he will see my face again.'

'If you kill him, then you are no better than he.'

'He has already made me an outlaw; I have nothing else to lose.'

'You have your life.'

'A thing of little value,' said Garyn. 'I have lost everything, and only the fact that Geraint fights on distant shores keeps me from riding back right now.'

'Have you heard from him?'

'No, nor am I likely to. The fleet upon which he sailed was shrouded in secrecy and their destination was unknown. All I know is he expects to be back within three years. I will wait that long and then seek my retribution.'

The two men fell silent and listened to the rain outside. Finally they wrapped themselves in their blankets and lay upon the floor to sleep.

Garyn wasn't sure what woke him but the room was dark and the rain had stopped. Tom Thatcher snored lightly beside him but apart from that, the silence was total. He lay motionless for several seconds, listening intently in the dark and was about to accept that he had been dreaming when the noise came again. It was a cough. Garyn rolled over and shook Tom's shoulder.

'What?' started Tom, waking instantly but Garyn's hand covered his mouth.

'Shhh, there's someone outside.' Both men got slowly to their feet and walked over to the barred doorway. Garyn peered out between the slats.

'Can you see anything?'

'Riders coming up the path.'

'We have to get out of here,' hissed Tom.

'I don't think there's enough time,' said Garyn, 'but get the horses anyway. We will have to bluff our way out.'

The riders came closer, and though Garyn couldn't see their faces he could hear them talking amongst themselves.

'There it is,' said a voice outside. 'We will spend the night here.'

Garyn cursed quietly and turned to face Tom.

'Hurry up,' he hissed.

'I'm done,' said Tom and handed Garyn the reins of his horse.

'I fear the chase is over before it has begun,' said Garyn, 'but I won't give up without a fight.'

'Then let us go out and meet them head on, Garyn,' said Tom. 'There is no room to fight in here, at least outside we may have a chance to take some of them with us. I would rather die with a blade in my gut than a rope around my neck. Open the door.'

Garyn nodded quietly and after lifting the bar on the door, led his horse out into the night. High above, the moon shone down between the passing clouds and immediately Garyn could see there were at least ten men before the hut, each seeing to his own horse.

'It seems we have company,' said a voice and all the men turned to face Garyn and Tom.

For a few seconds, nobody moved but eventually a man stepped forward and stood before them.

'Well, what do we have here?' he asked sarcastically. 'Two sweethearts emerging from their love nest?' The men behind him laughed but the big man's gaze did not waiver.

'Who are you?' he continued, 'And what are you doing in my hut?'

'Our names are unimportant,' said Garyn, 'and we thought the hut was abandoned. We only sought shelter from the rain. Now it has stopped, we will move on.'

'Well, it's not quite as simple as that,' said the man. 'You are in my territory without invitation and whilst you are keen to keep your identities secret, I am also keen to know who it is roaming the countryside expecting free lodgings.'

'We are just travellers,' said Tom, 'and seek no trouble. Let us be on our way and we can all get on with our lives.'

'The more you speak, the more you raise my curiosity,' said the man. 'If you were simple travellers, why would you keep your names shielded? For all we know, you could be outlaws with a price on your heads and what sort of good citizen would I be if I was to allow you to roam free? Why, it would be my civil duty to take you to the nearest village and hand you over to the constable.'

Tom's hand went around his back and he drew his knife.

'I will die first,' he said.

The man's smile slowly disappeared but he remained unflustered.

'Now, that is a mistake, stranger,' he said. 'I will ask you once only. Put the blade away before I am forced to make you bleed on your own steel.'

'At least I will take you with me,' said Tom.

'Tom,' snapped Garyn, 'do as he says.'

'I will not go back, Garyn.'

'Put the blade way,' said Garyn again.

Slowly Tom put his knife back in the scabbard but kept staring at the leader of the group.

'I have a suggestion for you,' said the man eventually, 'if ever again you grace the threshold of a tavern, buy your friend here a tankard for he just saved your life. Now, let's start again and this time, no more heroics. My name is Goddeff and I am master of these men. Who are you and what are you doing in my territory?'

'If this is your territory then can I assume you do not serve the constable of Brycheniog?'

'The constable?' laughed Goddeff, 'I promise you, stranger, you can safely assume I am not one of his men. Now answer my question.'

'My name is Garyn ap Thomas,' sighed Garyn, 'and this is Thomas Thatcher. We hail from Brycheniog in the south.'

'And what business do you have around here?'

'None, if truth be told,' said Garyn, 'we only pass through to reach the lands of Llewellyn.'

'To what end?'

'We seek to join with him and serve in his armies.'

'Have you been outlawed?'

'What makes you think that?' asked Tom.

'You fear the constable and flee north to serve in a conflict that doesn't affect your home. Either you are outlaws or you are stupid.'

'The answer is we don't know if we are outlawed,' said Garyn before Tom could answer. 'Things were moving too fast and we escaped while we had the chance.'

'And your crimes?'

'I escaped the stocks, sent there for standing up to an arrogant English knight.'

'And you?' asked Goddeff, looking at Tom.

'It's complicated,' said Tom but said no more.

Goddeff looked down at Tom's bandages.

'What happened to your hand?'

'Trial by fire,' said Tom.

Goddeff nodded silently and turned to look around his men.

'What do you think, brothers?' he said. 'Shall we let them go on their way or bury their bodies behind the hut.'

Tom's hand went again to his knife.

'Let them be,' said a voice. 'Anyone who stands up to the English is a friend to me and the cripple has guts.'

'Aye,' said a few of the men and Goddeff turned to face Garyn and Tom once more.

'Ease your minds, men of Brycheniog,' he said. 'Every man here has reason to avoid the law and you have found kindred spirits. Secure your horses and stay this night amongst us. We have food and firewood. You are welcome to share.'

'Why would you do that?' asked Garyn. 'You don't know us.'

'The storm has not yet abated and the night is long before us. I know not if your tale is true but you have an honest manner. Stay or go, the choice is yours.'

Garyn looked at Tom who shrugged his shoulders in silent reply.

'We will stay,' said Garyn, 'and leave with the dawn. Perhaps you could give advice as to the road ahead.'

'So be it,' said Goddeff and turned to his men. 'See to your mounts and go firm here. No need to post a lookout for the coming storm will be our guard this night.'

Within the hour the men were sitting inside the hut enjoying the heat from a roaring fire. Garyn looked around warily, still unsure exactly how to take them as each man ate whatever food they had in their pack. One of the riders took out a dead rat, skinning it before removing the guts and skewering the carcass on the end of a stick.

'The meat is just as good as rabbit as long as you cook it properly,' he said, turning the makeshift spit in the flames.

'Disgusting,' said Tom.

'Says a man who has never seen true hunger,' came the answer.

'I have been hungry,' said Tom, 'on many occasions.'

'Really?' answered the man turning to face the thatcher. 'How hungry have you been, stranger? Ever eaten rotten dog carcass, or the innards of a rancid horse? Ever eaten the flesh of a man?'

'A man,' gasped Tom, 'that is truly against the very laws of God. Surely you haven't lowered yourself to the level of the devil himself?'

'I didn't say I have,' said the man poking the wood in the fire. 'I just asked if you have.'

'Why would you ask such a question?' asked Garyn.

'To silence the wittering of one who knows nothing,' replied the man.

'I could say the same of you,' said Tom.

'Eric is a well-travelled man,' said Goddeff, 'and has seen things most see only in their nightmares.'

'And what makes you think he is the only man to witness such things?' asked Garyn.

'I don't,' said Eric, turning around to face him, 'but it raises the bile within me when men of inexperience comment on things they don't understand.'

'You know nothing about us,' said Garyn quietly.

'What is there to know?' asked Eric. 'The cripple is fat around the waist from too much ale and you are a mere babe fresh off his mother's breast. You have probably never been outside the borders of Wales, let alone seen hardship.'

'You are quick to criticise,' said Tom, 'yet could not be further from the mark. Yes, I am known to frequent the taverns of Brycheniog, but my friend here has probably been closer to death than all of you put together.'

'Tom,' snapped Garyn, 'that's enough.'

'No,' retorted Tom, 'I will not sit and see your character besmirched.' He turned to face Eric. 'Yes, he is young but in the past few years, he has seen Crusade, infiltrated an enemy castle, been pursued across the Holy Land by a hoard of infidels and retrieved a relic that contained a piece of the cross that once touched the flesh of Christ himself.'

All eyes turned to face Garyn.

'Is this true?' asked Goddeff.

Garyn stared in annoyance at Tom but eventually answered.

'It is,' he said, 'but it was not through choice. My path was forced upon me.'

'Still, it is an impressive list for one so young. There is a long night before us, Garyn. Perhaps you would make it shorter by sharing your tale?'

'It is not one I have repeated since my return,' said Garyn, 'and the telling will bring back memories unwelcome.'

'You are amongst men of common mind,' said Goddeff, 'for most here have tales of similar vein. Humour us and share the story.'

Garyn paused and looked around the room. The firelight cast its dancing light amongst those gathered and he knew they were the faces of hardened men. Finally he agreed and for the next hour, retold the story of how he retrieved the True Cross from the tomb of Sinan in Syria. Throughout the telling not one voice interrupted him as all were enthralled with the tale and despite his nervousness, he found the opportunity to share his story with similarly minded men very satisfying. When he was finished there were a few murmurs of admiration and even Eric nodded toward him in recognition of his feat.

'If you speak true then you have my respect,' he said. 'You should ride with us, Garyn of Brycheniog, for there is always a place amongst us for a man of your ilk.'

'I am yet unaware of your calling in this life,' said Garyn. 'For all I know you could be brigands.'

'I will share that we are a band that lives outside of the binds of feudal living,' said Goddeff, 'but brigands we are not. We travel between those who seek a fist to deal with inequality, yet call no man master.'

'I would say that makes you mercenaries,' said Tom.

'Call it what you will,' said Goddeff, 'but it is honest work for honest pay.'

'And are you in the pay of anyone as we speak?'

'We have just finished a commission,' said Goddeff, 'but there is no shortage of takers. It is often cheaper and easier for the rich to hire expertise rather than maintain their own garrison. So, what say you, Garyn? Does Eric's proposal stoke a fire within? Does a life of valour appeal to your inner bear or is it the path of a lamb before you?'

'I am no warrior, Goddeff,' said Garyn. 'Yes, I can hold my own in a fight but I feel I would be the weakest of your band.'

'Yet you seek to serve in the armies of Llewellyn?'

'I suspect a mercenary life demands a far higher standard than one in the lines of an army.'

'Whether soldier or mercenary, death's scythe strikes equally across all men.'

'I am honoured with your offer, my lord, but my path lies elsewhere.'

'So be it,' said Goddeff. 'In the morn we will go our separate ways, but until then I will retire to the warmth of my blanket. Sleep well, Garyn.'

Each man made himself as comfortable as possible in the little space available and before long Garyn fell into a dreamless sleep, warmed by the embers of the fire.

–

The following morning, Garyn and Tom watched as the men readied their horses but before they left, Goddeff approached Garyn.

'May your path be fair, Garyn of Brycheniog, and perhaps one day we will ride together.'

'Perhaps so,' said Garyn, 'but I fear my sword arm is not strong enough for your needs.'

'Then as a teller of tales,' laughed Goddeff, 'for your story was well told even if it was made bigger than the truth.'

'I don't know what you are saying,' said Garyn. 'My tale was true.'

'I have no doubt that in the main it was,' said Goddeff, as he mounted his horse, 'but I know you held back on the final destination of the True Cross.' He looked down from his saddle at the young man. 'I don't blame you, Garyn, for it makes a good end to the tale but in my trade, I hear a lot of things and I know the relic lies in the hands of Llewellyn. I suspect that is why you head north.'

'You are wrong,' said Garyn. 'The cross is in Rome and we ride to seek only a future with the Welsh Prince. Your knowledge falls far from the truth.'

'Whatever you say, Garyn,' laughed Goddeff, 'it is no business of mine. Follow the paths northward and seek out the village of Mynydd-Du. They are fiercely loyal to Llewellyn and may be able to supply the information you seek. Fair ye well, young man, and live long for I hear it is far better than the alternative.' With that Goddeff spurred his horse and galloped after his men, leaving Garyn to stare after him in confusion.

'What was all that about?' asked Tom walking up alongside him.

'I'm not sure,' said Garyn. 'Something about the cross being in the hands of Llewellyn, but I know that to be wrong for it was sent to Rome.'

'Perhaps it never got there,' said Tom. 'Perhaps the bearer got greedy and veered away from his task.'

'It was guarded by a unit of Hospitallers,' said Garyn, 'and more devout knights I have never seen. No, I have no doubt it would have reached Rome intact so Goddeff must be mistaken.'

'Perhaps,' said Tom, 'but we will never know either way. Come, it is time to go; we have a prince to find.'

Chapter Sixteen

The New World

'My lord, the men tire,' said Geraint, 'and beg rest.'

'Not yet, Geraint,' replied Tarian, 'we need to find a place we can defend. Achak says we are at risk as soon as we stop and as he is the only one who knows anything about this place, we have to heed his advice.'

'Of course,' said Geraint and turned to relay the message.

They had been marching for two days, following the banks of the great river downstream, always on the lookout for the fleet. The banks had become swampy and the undergrowth increasingly tangled the further south they travelled. The going was tough but Achak had insisted they stay away from the easier going on the grass plains a mile inland explaining that the Apalach preferred to fight in the open. The wagons had been discarded and the mounted men stayed inland with orders to avoid conflict and return to meet the main column as soon as conditions allowed. The provisions were shared out and both parties went their separate ways.

Tarian learned from Achak that the Apalach had no horses so the knight was happy his lancers could stay out of trouble but his foot soldiers were another matter. The harder the path became, the more he worried about the state of his men. Not only did they tire quickly from the difficult terrain but the heat was taking its toll and their heavy packs weighed them down. On top of that, the air was filled with the sound of distant drums and Achak had explained it was the way the different villages of the Apalach communicated.

'They string the war bows and sharpen their blades,' he had said. 'Your hair will look good on the lodge walls.'

'What do you mean?' Tarian had asked.

Using the edge of his hand to mimic the action of a knife, Achak demonstrated how many men would be scalped.

'But why?' asked Tarian. 'What use is it to them?'

'Scalps make warriors strong,' said Achak.

Since then the men had set to the march with renewed vigour but Tarian knew they had to stop soon. Finally they came across a small island in the midst of the mangroves and whilst there was little in the way of natural defences, the dirty water provided a moat of sorts.

'This is good,' said Achak. 'We will be safe here.'

Tarian looked around.

'I cannot defend this place,' he said. 'It is too open.'

'Apalach will stay away from here,' said Achak. 'It is a place of demons.'

'What demons?'

'Sulagi live here,' said Achak, 'so we must light fires to keep them away.'

'Whatever you say, Achak,' said Tarian turning to face the men behind him. 'Spread out and see to your kit. We will go firm here tonight.'

The men were glad of the rest and sought what shelter they could on the tiny island. Search parties were sent out for firewood with instructions not to go far as they could easily get lost in the dense undergrowth. As they waded across the waist deep channels Achak approached Tarian and pointed toward the outgoing patrols.

'Tell them to stay together,' he said, 'or Sulagi will seek their spirits.'

'They are well armed, Achak,' said Tarian, 'and where we come from, we pay little respect to spirits.'

Achak nodded and returned to his space alongside Spider. Soon there were dozens of small fires burning around the island and men sought the heat against the chill of the evening. Dried meat was handed out and while some chewed it raw, others were more patient, using their rations to flavour a shared broth. One young man waded slowly in the water, staring into the depths for any sign of fish to add to the pot. Gradually the light faded and the mood was quiet, when a terrifying sound echoed across the water.

'Aaarrgh, help me,' screamed a voice, 'in the name of Christ help me.'

As one the men jumped to their feet and ran to the riverbank. A few paces out they could see the young boy who had gone fishing but it seemed he was struggling with someone in the water. He thrashed in panic, screaming in fear and pain as he struggled violently against the unseen attacker.

'What's happening?' roared Tarian, 'are we under attack?'

'No, it is Sulagi,' said Achak, 'a beast of the water. There is nothing to be done.'

'Help me,' screamed the boy again and though the churning waters were rapidly turning red, Tarian grabbed a lance and waded in to help.

'What are you waiting for?' screamed Tarian. 'Our comrade needs us.'

Within seconds the river was full of armed men, lunging at the submerged beast that was attacking the boy. Over and over again they attacked with their weapons until finally the struggle ended and they dragged the boy back to the island. Those on shore stared in disgust at the dismembered body.

'It is too late,' gasped Tarian. 'He is dead.'

'What sort of animal does this?' gasped Geraint, staring at the place where the boy's leg had once been.

'We are about to find out,' said Tarian and looked along the shore to where his men were hauling something up onto the land. They walked over and stared down in horror. The beast was similar to the lizards that crawled amongst the grasses of home but the size was something from their nightmares. It lay as long as two horses end to end and as high as a man's knees. The mouth was enormous and lined with vicious teeth, still stained by the bloody flesh of the unfortunate fisherman.

'It's a dragon,' said a voice in awe.

'It is Sulagi,' said Achak. 'The river is their home.'

'A beast of the devil himself,' said Geraint.

'It is no devil's animal, sacred spirit or dragon,' shouted Tarian, 'so there will be no more such talk. This is a strange land with stranger animals and this is no more than that. It fell to our steel as will any others that venture near but the danger is clear. Let no man go anywhere near the water without a comrade or weapon. We will not lose anyone else through ignorance. Achak, you will lead us from here on in and will warn us of anything we need to know. Now get this man buried and get some sleep.

We will strike out with the dawn and hope the day brings sight of the fleet.'

Some of the men bent to pick up the body while the others went back to their fires. Spider lingered alongside Tarian as he stared down at the alligator.

'My lord.' he said quietly, 'the stores are running low and we need to hunt.'

'Hunt what?' asked Tarian lifting his gaze toward the tangled undergrowth, 'even if we caught sight of a deer, there is no way we could run it down.'

'What about this?' said Spider kicking the corpse of the dead animal.

'What about it?'

'I agree with your view that it is no more than an animal and all animals can be eaten. Perhaps it holds enough meat fill a pot.'

Tarian looked over to Achak who was on his knees in the sand with arms outstretched and head tilted back as he sang a song of respect to the Sulagi spirit.

'Is there no other way?' he asked quietly.

'We need the meat,' said Spider. 'The men already hunger.'

'Do it,' said Tarian eventually and walked back to the camp as Spider drew his knife.

Achak looked up and his eyes narrowed as he realised what Spider had in mind.

'It is forbidden to eat Sulagi,' he said quietly.

'You may be forbidden,' said Spider examining the animal's scales for the best place to insert his knife, 'but we suffer no such rules. Now, how do I cut this thing up?'

Achak didn't answer but turned away and walked through the water into the darkness. Spider shrugged his shoulders and called out to some nearby soldiers.

'You men, help me turn this thing over.'

–

The following morning the men once more set out on their trek. Behind them they left a shallow grave and the stripped carcass of a giant alligator. Geraint paused to look back at the scene and thought for the hundredth time, this was indeed a strange land.

–

The rest of the day passed without incident and Geraint walked alongside Tarian.

'Any sign of Achak?' asked Tarian without breaking stride.

'None, my lord, I suspect he has returned to his people.'

'So be it,' said Tarian, 'at least we know Madoc passed this way and we need to cross this river.'

'Without the ships, I can't see how it can be done,' said Geraint.

'Nor can I,' said Tarian, 'so our future lies in the hands of Robert of Shrewsbury.'

Both men looked up as the sound of drums started up once again.

'They sound closer,' said Geraint.

'They do,' said Tarian, 'pass the word back, we need to increase the pace.'

The column pressed on but as they went, strange calls echoed amongst the trees, causing the men to look about them in fear and tighten the ties of their gambesons. Finally one of the scouts returned to meet Tarian.

'My lord, the ground opens up before us and there is a rocky hill at the far side. It looks like a good place to go firm.'

'Good,' said Tarian, 'pass the message: one last push and we will make a stand.'

Within half an hour they left the claustrophobic cover of the swamps and emerged onto a grassy plain. To their front, an escarpment reached skyward and Tarian knew it would be as safe a place as he could hope for. The rest of the column left the tree line and stared before them.

'There is no cover between us and the mountain,' said Geraint quietly.

'Perhaps not,' said Tarian, 'but we either risk the crossing or stay in the swamp. We will take our chances.' He turned to face the exhausted column. 'Men of Wales, I know you tire but we cannot stay here. Rest and safety lie but a mile away and we need one more effort to find shelter. Increase your step and hasten to the hill yonder.'

The column headed into the open, pushing as hard as they could to cross the plain. Within minutes the sound of the drums changed and Tarian sensed that the situation was about to get a lot more serious.

'Archers break ranks,' he shouted, 'and form a rear guard. The rest of the column, make for the crags as fast as you are able. Geraint, have your archers form two lines. I feel we will have need of them before this is played out.'

'Archers, string your bows,' roared Geraint. 'Double line, ten paces between ranks.'

The men formed up quickly as the cries from the swamp edge grew louder.

'Notch arrows,' shouted Geraint, 'take aim at the forward edge of the treeline.'

'Geraint,' shouted Tarian, 'drop any man that comes forth and follow us to the rocks as soon as you can.'

'Arrows, my lord,' roared a voice and every man turned to see dozens of arrows fly through the air from the forest edge but though there were many, every one fell well short.

'I don't understand,' said Tarian. 'We are well within range of a bowman.'

'Not necessarily,' said Geraint, stringing his own bow. 'Don't forget these people haven't even seen a horse so the chances are they haven't yet learned the benefits of the longbow.'

'What do you mean?'

'I mean I suspect their weapons are too small,' said Geraint, 'with a tension too slack to add any range. If this is the case, then they are doomed for my men can drop them at two hundred paces.'

Another flight of arrows flew from the trees but again fell well short.

'I think you are right,' said Tarian. 'Make the most of this advantage, Geraint, but sacrifice none of our men on unseen folly.'

'Yes, my lord.' said Geraint.

'Here they come,' shouted a voice and everyone looked at the men leaving the treeline. Across the entire front of the forest, lines of Apalach warriors walked carefully from the cover. Each was bare-chested and clad only in loin cloths or buckskin leggings. Their naked torsos were daubed in red dye and their long hair tied back. Necklaces of bird skulls and feathers hung around their necks and many had feathers hanging from their hair. More arrows followed uselessly behind those already fired but within moments the bows were discarded and they could be seen drawing knives and axes from their waistbands.

'Front rank, notch arrows,' shouted Geraint, 'take aim, upon my mark.'

The line of bowmen raised their bows skyward and drew back the drawstrings.

'Loose arrows,' shouted Geraint and he watched with satisfaction as a line of steel tipped arrows flew through the air toward the enemy. Within seconds, they found their mark and many Apalach warriors fell to the ground.

'First rank, withdraw ten paces,' shouted Geraint. 'Second rank notch arrows, upon my mark…'

Again the order was given and again, dozens of warriors fell to the onslaught but instead of causing fear amongst their number, the devastating hail of arrows only served to raise the ire of the natives. A wail rose from amongst them and within seconds, they started to run toward the archers, brandishing their flint bladed weapons. Behind them, more and more warriors emerged from the tree line to add to the hundreds already charging the archers.

'By Jesus,' shouted a man, 'there are thousands of them.'

'Keep firing,' shouted Geraint, 'each rank loose two arrows before withdrawing twenty paces behind the other. Keep moving backward.'

'We'll never make it,' shouted Marcus. 'There are too many of them.'

'Another half a minute,' shouted Geraint. 'Cut down their front ranks; it will give our men time to form a line amongst the rocks.'

The archers drew their bows as fast as they were able but despite the rapid rate of fire, the native lines kept coming, screaming their war cries as they swarmed to the conflict. Finally Geraint gave the command to withdraw.

'Break off,' he roared, 'and get to the rocks.'

As one, the archers turned to follow their comrades to the safety of the escarpment but they hadn't reached halfway when it became obvious they would be easily outrun by the lightly clad natives.

'It's no good,' shouted Geraint, 'we'll never make it, turn and stand.' Each man drew their blades and turned to face the inevitable. For a few seconds, their manic pursuers increased their pace, sensing an easy victory but as each archer prepared for his own death, the tables were suddenly turned by the sound of thundering hooves.

From the eastern flank, ten fully armoured knights galloped headlong into the fray, their lances levelled before them. Behind them the supporting lines of thirty lancers spread out in support and within seconds, the screams of skewered men echoed around the killing field. As lances snapped, the mounted men drew their swords and steel hewed flesh apart in a frenzy of undefended slaughter.

The native rush faltered as they stared in disbelief at the unfamiliar sight of large armoured men riding giant beasts of war. Many froze to the spot and were trampled beneath the wide-eyed horses as they tore through the transfixed enemy, and many warriors were hacked apart by the knights' swords before they realised the danger.

The braver amongst the Apalach attacked the horses with their knives and axes but the animals were protected by their heavy caparisons and the mounted knights soon felled the attackers with swift thrusts of their blades.

'Get to the rocks,' shouted Geraint, 'while they are distracted.' The archers took the opportunity to flee as the mounted men slaughtered the attacking natives behind them. Within minutes they ran through the lower lines of boulders and between the lines of pikemen who had formed steeled lines of defence.

'Get your archers onto the higher boulders,' shouted Tarian. 'The enemy are reforming and the lancers have lost the element of surprise. Prepare to cover them as they return.'

Out on the field the sound of a horn signalled the retreat and the cavalry galloped to join the rest of the patrol. Behind them they left two dead horses and one dead lancer. Tarian strode amongst the defenders, issuing orders to strengthen the defences. As they approached, the riders dismounted and led their mounts up into the rocks.

'Your arrival was perfectly timed, Sir Crispin,' said Tarian.

'We have been here since yesterday,' said the leader of the horsemen, 'and patrolled outward in anticipation of your arrival. It would seem God was with you today.'

'Whatever the reason, your intervention was most opportune and saved the lives of many men. Now get your mounts up amongst the rocks; we can handle it from here.'

'Are you sure? Their numbers are many.'

'Yet undisciplined,' said Tarian. 'If they attack us head on, they will find a wall of Welsh pikes waiting, each wielded with stout heart. The odds have balanced some-what and whilst the day is young, it will not find us wanting.'

For the next hour or so, Tarian took the opportunity of organising the defences. Rows of archers proved the first line of defence from their high positions, able to drop any attackers at a range of two hundred paces. Down below at a natural choke point in the approach, pikemen stood in lines, while behind them, men at arms bearing a range of weapons from swords to clubs formed the last line of defence.

Deep amongst the rocks, the squires looked after the horses while the lancers supported the pikemen. The knights separated into two groups as a reaction force and positioned themselves centrally, ready to respond to any breaches of the defences. Finally, Tarian sent Marcus of Builth and a small command of six men up to the top of the hill with orders to protect the rear.

'My lord, the men are ready,' said Geraint, joining Tarian amongst the lancers.

'Good,' said Tarian. 'All we can do now is wait.'

They looked out onto the plain where the natives were recovering their dead.

'It's a shame we didn't have chance to recover the arrows,' said Geraint.

'How many do you have left?' asked Tarian.

'About twenty for each man,' said Geraint. 'We brought enough only for hunting and skirmishes, not for full battle. I am told there are more on the ships.'

'If I recall correctly there are over twenty barrels of arrow heads on the ships but that doesn't help us here. Tell the men to make every one count.'

'Yes, my lord.' said Geraint and returned to his men.

–

Marcus led Spider and five other men to the top of the escarpment and looked back down at the plain below as they caught their breath. The number of Apalach was growing by the minute and the sound of drums reverberated through the air. Many of the warriors had formed lines across the whole front and made false charges toward the rocks, chanting their war cries and brandishing their weapons, yet retreating before they came within range of Geraint's archers.

'What are they doing?' asked Spider.

'I don't know,' said Marcus, 'but one thing's for sure, if they all attack at the same time then there is no way we can kill them all. We have to find a way out of here.'

'But we were sent only to cover the rear?'

'Achak said there are thousands of these people,' said Marcus. 'What will happen if the same number comes from behind? It will be slaughter. No, we will venture a little further and see what lies beyond that hill. At least we will know one way or the other.' They set out again, heading for a further slope less than a mile distant. At the top they encountered another wooded area but within minutes they broke free to stare down at the sight before them.

'I don't believe it,' gasped Marcus.

At the edge of the treeline, the ground cleared and sloped down before levelling out onto a thinly wooded plain. A mile away they could see the silver glint of the mighty river as it snaked its way toward the sea, but it was not the water that grabbed their attention, it was the welcome sight of four magnificent cogs anchored at the water's edge.

'Thank the Lord,' gasped Spider, 'it's the fleet.'

'I can't believe our good fortune,' said Marcus quietly, 'Spider, take three men and get to those ships as fast as you can, tell them we are on our way. The rest of you, follow me, we need to tell Tarian that relief is at hand.' The group split up to their tasks and while some scrambled down the slope toward the river, the rest ran as fast as they could back to the column.

Within ten minutes Marcus stood gasping at the top of the escarpment and looked in dismay at the scene below them.

The false attacks had ended and the real assault had started. Thousands of arrows rained down upon the defensive position and though they were poorly aimed, many were finding their mark. Though chainmail coifs and padded gambesons were very effective against the flint arrowheads of the Apalach not everyone had such armour and many defenders fell to the arrows.

'Why aren't our men firing back?' asked one of the men.

Marcus pointed out dozens of dead savages on the plain.

'It looks like they have,' he answered. 'They must be out of arrows.'

'Then it is only a matter of time,' said the soldier. 'Once that hoard attacks, our men have no chance.'

'We are not done yet,' snapped Marcus. 'Come on.' He leaped off the rock and scrambled down the crag as fast as he could.

—

'Archers, support the front line,' screamed Tarian. 'Use your blades.'

The archers discarded their redundant bows and ran to add their strength to the narrow defending lines. The few shields amongst the lancers were pushed to the fore and Apalach warriors fell against the wall of wood and steel. At first the line staggered backward but the archers added their weight and pushed back against the enemy. Within seconds the tide turned and the defenders forced their way forward step by step until they had regained the ground lost. Half-naked warriors hung bleeding from many of the pikes, their bodies still impaled on the long and deadly shafts. For a while the pressure eased as the natives withdrew in disarray but as they walked backward, one warrior remained, facing the defenders with a murderous look in his eye.

'What's he doing?' asked Geraint as the Apalach warrior withdrew a flint bladed knife from his waist band.

'I have no idea,' answered Tarian, 'but it looks like we are about to find out.'

As he spoke the native started to run forward alone.

'Madness,' gasped Geraint, 'what does he expect to achieve?'

Tarian didn't answer but watched as the wall of shields braced for the impact.

The warrior ran faster but just as it seemed he would run straight onto the blade of a pike, he launched himself into the air and using the body of an impaled comrade as a platform, cleared the defences and landed amongst the shocked archers behind. The unexpected action took the defenders by surprise and before anyone could react, the warrior's blade pierced the hearts of two men without retribution. A defender kicked the blade from his hands but the warrior knocked him to the floor and ripped open the boy's throat with his teeth before he was overpowered and fell to the cuts of a dozen knives. A lancer ran forward and plunged his weapon down through the man's chest, pinning him to the floor before someone finished him off with a sword.

'Look to your fronts,' screamed Tarian as the Apalach renewed the attack, having seen the success of their comrade's actions and within moments many more warriors came over the defensive wall to battle hand to hand with the men at the rear.

'They are using their own dead as platforms,' shouted Geraint. 'We have to drop the pikes.'

'I will not surrender weapons to the enemy,' shouted Tarian.

'My lord, we will be overwhelmed in minutes,' answered Geraint.

Tarian looked around frantically, looking for a solution.

'Front rank,' he screamed suddenly, 'drop your pikes and advance ten paces. Rear ranks, clear the blades. Lancers present your weapons over the shields.'

The men did as they were told and though the platform of bleeding flesh was rapidly denied the attackers, many had already breached the defence and the archers were being overwhelmed by the native assault.

'Clear the way,' shouted a voice and within seconds, the ten fully armoured knights waded into the fray, using their heavy swords to cut through the attackers like a scythe through corn. The Apalach were no match for the trained soldiers and the threat was eliminated within minutes.

Once again, the attack faltered but there was no sign of any permanent withdrawal. Geraint pointed to one side of the killing field where several hundred men were running up to join the attack but these men didn't carry bows, they had spears.

'We can't defend against spears, my lord,' said Geraint, 'even those tipped with stone. Any finding their mark will breach a gambeson.'

'I agree,' said Tarian, 'but am out of ideas.'

Suddenly a voice echoed around the rocks.

'My lord, the patrol has returned.'

Tarian turned to see Marcus scrambling down the steep slope.

'What is it?' shouted Tarian. 'Are we under attack from the rear?'

'No, my lord,' gasped Marcus trying to get his breath back, 'it's good news. The fleet are beyond this hill, anchored against the bank not two miles hence. If we retreat, safety is within reach.'

'Excellent news,' exclaimed Tarian and looked around at the expectant looks on the faces of the men around him.

'Geraint,' he said, 'get your men up the slopes and back to the ships immediately. They have no more use here. Take whatever surplus men you can. I will lead a rear defence with the lancers and the knights.'

'But, my lord…'

'Do as you are ordered,' shouted Tarian, 'before the assault is renewed. It is pointless men dying for no reason. The rest of us will hold out as long as we can before withdrawing. Now get out of here.' He turned to the rest of the men. 'I want every shield to the fore and every knight in support. We need at least ten minutes to give the rest of them a chance to reach the ships. Now, stand to your positions quickly before the battle is rejoined.'

'My lord, a word,' said a quiet voice and Tarian turned to see Sir Crispin nearby.

'What is it, Crispin?' asked Tarian.

'My lord, your words are brave but we both know that the men who remain in the wall are doomed to die where they stand.'

'Perhaps so,' said Tarian, 'but my options are few. At least this way, half the patrol will live to continue the quest.'

'And you?'

'I will not be found wanting, Crispin. I will remain with my men.'

'My lord, this quest is of your making and we can't come this far to fall short. It is essential you stay alive to lead us onward.'

'I will not condemn my men to die while I flee, Crispin. You of all men know this.'

'And nor do I expect you to, my lord, but there is another way.'

'Explain.'

'My lord, my men are from the best blood in Wales and are fearless knights. There is no way we can climb this crag in our armour and even if it is discarded, we won't leave our mounts to be slaughtered for meat.'

'What are you suggesting?'

'Use us as we are meant to be used,' said Crispin. 'Unleash us in the face of the enemy and use the time to lead the rest of the column to safety.'

'What about the lancers?'

'They have no obligation to the code and are free to join you in your flight.'

Tarian stared at the knight he had known most of his life.

'Crispin, there is no doubt in my mind that you are the bravest man I know and I am sure you will strike fear amongst the very heart of them but even you know you cannot prevail against such numbers.'

'Perhaps not, but I swear there will be a lot of Apalach widows before the last of my men fall.'

'I will not sacrifice you for my own safety.'

'Then sacrifice us for the success of this mission and the ultimate freedom of Wales,' said Crispin. 'Before this day is out I will either kneel before my Lord in heaven alongside my fellows knowing the quest continues, or I will kneel before Him alongside a hundred comrades knowing we died in vain. Grant me the former, I beseech thee.'

Tarian stayed quiet before realising the knight was correct.

'Crispin,' he said eventually, 'if this mission achieves the success God demands, I will ensure the memory of you and your men is enshrined for eternity.'

'Then I can ask no more,' said Crispin and turned to organise his men.

Tarian returned to the men providing the shield wall.

'Gentlemen,' he said, 'in a few moments, Sir Crispin will lead his command to glory. As soon as they clear our lines, you will discard your equipment and follow the archers up the cliff. Do not hesitate or pause to look back. They are giving their lives so you may live. Honour them by seizing the opportunity.'

Within minutes the sound of horses' hooves came from behind the boulders and Sir Crispin came into site aboard his magnificent charger, accompanied by his knights and the full complement of lancers. To a man, they had volunteered to support the knights in their task. Crispin had donned a tabard emblazoned with his house emblem over his armour and the visor was lifted on his pointed helm. He looked down at his leader.

'We are ready, Tarian,' he said.

'Then I pray God go with you, Sir Crispin,' came the answer. He paused a moment more before giving the order. 'Open the lines.'

The wall of shields swung back against the rocks and Sir Crispin stood up in his stirrups to address his men.

'Knights of Cymru,' he shouted, 'it has been my privilege to serve alongside you but the day for which we were born lies before us. Honour now your name, your code and almighty God.'

He drew his sword from its scabbard and held it high above his head.

'For honour, for country, for freedom,' he roared and as forty armoured horsemen echoed his cry, he galloped his charger through the defensive line to meet his destiny.

Chapter Seventeen

North Wales

Garyn and Tom took longer than expected to travel through mid-Wales, taking the lesser-known paths through the hills rather than the better travelled routes preferred by patrols of the King's men. The weather was breaking at last and they knew they were approaching the lands of Gwyneth, the stronghold of Llewellyn. Finally they rode down from a rain lashed hill and headed toward a tiny village at the side of a river. An aged man shepherded a small flock of sheep toward a walled fold and Garyn called out as he passed.

'Hail friend,' he said, 'what village lies before us?'

'Mynydd-du,' said the shepherd.

'Is it a friendly place?' asked Garyn.

'That depends,' said the shepherd.

'On what?'

'On which side of the Marches your loyalty lies, Llewellyn's or Henry's son.'

'Our fealty lies with the Welsh Prince,' said Garyn.

'Then you will find a warm welcome,' said the shepherd.

'Is there somewhere we can get a dry night's sleep and perhaps a crust to eat?'

'You will find a small tavern next to the bridge,' said the shepherd. 'They do not have rooms but their stable is dry.'

'Many thanks,' said Garyn and the men rode onward into the village. Within moments they found the tiny tavern with a rail outside. After tying up their horses they ducked under the low lintel and into a darkened room lit only by a fire and a few candles. At the far end two old men sat close to the hearth and an older woman stirred an enormous iron pot, a utensil blackened by generations of cooking on open fires. Sitting to one side was another man, a tankard of ale upon an upturned barrel before him.

'Good day,' said Garyn, 'I am told this is a tavern.'

'You have been told right,' said the woman holding her back as she got to her feet. 'You will find ale and cawl for the weariest of travellers.'

'We would be grateful for both,' said Garyn, 'but first would have our horses seen to.'

'What coin do you have?' asked the woman.

Garyn withdrew his purse and after undoing the leather laces, poured out the last of his money.

'Three copper coins,' he said. 'It is the last of my purse.'

'Three coins hardly pays for fodder for your horses,' said the woman. 'How will you pay for your ale?'

Garyn glanced at Tom who shook his head, indicating he had no money to add.

'It seems we are at your mercy,' said Garyn.

'For the three coins I will give you cawl and ale,' said the woman. 'The horses can be let out into the field to graze. It is the best I can do.'

'They have eaten nought but grass for days,' said Garyn. 'They need grain and hay.'

'Then make your choice,' said the woman, 'for though I feel your plight, many such as you pass this way and if I gave free grain to every traveller suffering hard times, I would soon starve.'

'I understand,' said Garyn. 'Think upon it no more.'

'So do you want the cawl?'

'No,' said Garyn, 'we will have the grain for our horses. Their need is greater than ours.' He handed over the three coins.

'Take the animals around to the stable,' said the woman, 'and I will have them taken care of. Perhaps I can find a crust of bread to ease your hunger.'

'That would be good,' said Garyn and the two men turned to leave but a voice made them stop in their tracks.

'Wait,' said the man sat alone in the corner.

They turned toward him but his face was hidden in the shadows.

'Do you address us, sir?' asked Tom.

'I do,' said the man. 'Woman, give these men a bowl of cawl each and make sure your ladle is heavy with meat.'

'You have our gratitude, sir,' said Garyn.

'Any man who puts the needs of his horse before his own is worth a bowl of cawl,' he said. 'See to your animals and return when you are done. The food will be waiting.'

'Thank you,' said Garyn as they left the tavern. Half an hour later they returned. The horses were in the stable and had been rubbed down with dry straw before being given a leather bucket of oats, as well as a net of hay and a bucket of fresh water. Garyn looked around the room. The two old men were still there but the mysterious benefactor had gone.

'Ah, you are back,' said the woman. 'Sit yourself down, I will bring your food.'

'Where has he gone?' asked Garyn.

'Who knows the mind of Meirion?' said the woman. 'He comes and goes as he sees fit. It is no business of mine or indeed yours. Just be thankful he has left enough coins for your food, some ale and a dry blanket in the stable.'

'Why would he do that? We are not known to him.'

'Really?' asked the woman. 'What if I was to say your name is Garyn and your fellow there has a crippled hand from the fire trial?'

'What witchcraft is this?' asked Tom, his eyes narrowing with suspicion.

'No witchcraft,' said one of the old men near the fire without looking up. 'Word travels fast in these parts and many people pass this way.'

'It must have been Goddeff or one of his men,' said Garyn.

'It matters not the name,' said the man, 'and you will need to learn not to drop names into conversations. Such habits get men killed.'

The woman brought two wooden bowls over to an upturned barrel. Each was piled with meat and root vegetables in a thick juice.

'Food fit for kings,' said Tom and drew his eating knife to spear the contents. The woman returned with two tankards of ale and a hard-crusted loaf, still smeared with ashes from the village oven. For several minutes nobody spoke as the two men pushed gravy-soaked bread into their mouths, interspersed with chunks of meat and vegetables. Finally they drained the bowls before using the last of the bread to wipe out the gravy and swilling it down with mouthfuls of bitter tasting ale. Garyn wiped the froth from around his mouth and waited for Tom to finish before speaking.

'Probably the best meal I have ever had,' he said.

'Hunger does that to a man,' said Tom, using his knife to pick meat from between his teeth.

One of the old men got up and walked over to them at their makeshift table.

'Can I join you?' he asked.

'Be our guest,' said Garyn.

'Woman, more ale,' said the old man and within a minute, the old woman brought a jug to replenish the tankards.

Garyn nodded in gratitude and lifted the tankard, draining half the contents before placing it down.

'So,' said the man, resting his own drink, 'you are from Brycheniog.'

'We are,' said Garyn.

'And you seek service in the army of Llewellyn?'

'Whoever it was who gave you the information was well informed,' said Garyn. 'What else do you know of us?'

'Not much,' said the man, 'I know you upset an English lord and fled the stocks; I also know that your friend here suffered trial by fire but ran to escape justice. That probably makes you outlaws.'

'We are no outlaws,' said Tom.

'Perhaps not,' said the man, 'but if that's all I have to go on, you would forgive me for thinking otherwise.'

'You do not know the details,' said Garyn.

'I don't,' said the man, 'so why don't you fill in the gaps.'

'Why would we do that?' asked Tom. 'We are grateful for the ale but I see no need to tell a stranger our business.'

'I'll tell you why,' said the old man, 'because I can give you direct access to Llewellyn. Now start talking.'

231

A hundred miles south, a group of four horsemen gathered outside of the abbey in Brycheniog. Amongst their number was Sir Gibson of Glamorgan, an ageing knight whose tournament days were behind him but though his face was wrinkled with age, he was still held in high esteem around the circuit for contests won and battles fought. They waited patiently until finally the man they had been expecting walked out of the abbey gates: Gerald of Essex.

'Well met,' said Gerald. 'As you know, a few weeks ago, two men escaped the authority of this manor and rode northward. One is charged as an accomplice to a cold-blooded murder, whilst the other has escaped a legal punishment passed down by his betters. By doing so they have placed themselves outside of the law of our land and each now has a price on his head. As we speak, they probably think they have escaped their punishment but I can assure you they have not. You men are tasked with pursuing these brigands wherever they may flee and take them back into custody. Bring them back here to hang and you will be handsomely rewarded by the abbot of this town, a God-fearing man who values honesty amongst the best virtues of Christianity. If you cannot take them alive, then their heads will suffice as evidence and you will collect half the bounty.'

One of the men spoke up.

'My lord, it is a massive country and we are but four men. With respect, they could be anywhere.'

'Possibly,' said Gerald. 'However, you will be furnished with letters for every church from here to Conwy. They will pass the message to their congregations and the word will soon spread. Eventually the outlaws will have no place to hide.'

'But even if we find them, they are unlikely to be handed over. The northerners hate the men of the South when they interfere with their business.'

'We anticipate this,' said Gerald, 'so I have here a scroll under the seal of the Crown of England, demanding any man hands over the outlaws. Present this to any offering succour on pain of death.'

'My lord,' said Sir Gibson, 'I understand they may be seeking to join forces with Llewellyn. If this proves to be true then our opportunities will be limited.'

'Any nobleman worth his salt will recognise a royal seal, even if it goes against their better judgement. Why risk the ire of a king for the lives of two commoners?'

'This is Llewellyn we are talking about,' said Sir Gibson. 'Since when does the Welsh Prince bend his knee at the sight of a wax seal?'

'If he doesn't then it will add to the list of crimes against the Crown he will one day answer for; however, I accept this doesn't help you so we have trickery on our side. This man here fought alongside the one called Garyn in the Holy Land. He is trusted by the blacksmith and when you find him, as you will, he will lure him to a place where he can be overwhelmed.'

'Why are these men so important that they demand this level of attention?' asked Gibson.

'Let's just say there is honour at stake and the situation has become personal,' answered Gerald.

'So be it,' said Gibson. 'If there is nothing else, we will be on our way.'

233

'Make haste, Gibson,' said Gerald, 'and when you bring them back, we will feast in your name, as we did in days gone by.'

'A distant memory,' said Gibson.

'Yet easily relived,' replied Gerald as he turned to walk away.

'And if we fail?'

Gerald paused but did not turn around. Instead he spoke just loud enough for the riders to hear and understand his manner.

'Do not fail,' he said quietly. 'Now be gone.'

The riders turned their horses and rode away from the abbey as Gerald stepped inside the walls. Father Williams waited for him having listened to the meeting through the wooden gate.

'Do you think they will succeed?'

'I do,' said Gerald. 'Gibson may be old but he is a formidable knight. At least, he was. Since the death of his wife he has withered as an apple in autumn and he yearns for one more quest before he dies. I have granted him the opportunity and he will move mountains to once more have his name lauded.'

'I see you have included the squire from the estate. I have had dealings with him in the past and know he was once a comrade of the man we seek. Is this a wise move?'

'He was a squire to Cadwallader,' said Gerald. 'I learned about him from Elisabeth. Apparently, he committed some indiscretion in the Holy Land and missed out on knighthood. She gave him a place back amongst the squires on the understanding that if her husband absolved him of blame on his return, he could once more take up the code. As we are aware, that cannot now happen as Cadwallader is dead so he had no place to go. When

I found out he was once a comrade of the blacksmith I grasped the opportunity. He helps us catch his friend and in return I will become his sponsor and see to it that Longshanks himself bestows knighthood upon him.'

'You can do that?'

Gerald shrugged.

'It matters not,' he said. 'I have no intention of bestowing knighthood on any man who defied an order from his betters.'

'But he will surely proclaim that Gerald of Essex goes back on his word.'

'Possibly,' said Gerald, 'but luckily there is another amongst them who has the morals of a rat and will ensure he doesn't return to besmirch my name.'

'And this man can be trusted?'

'He can and has carried out several such acts on my behalf in the past.'

'You never cease to amaze me,' said Father Williams, 'the depths of your deceit and lack of morality are surely unequalled across this kingdom.'

'On the contrary,' said Gerald, 'I stand before a man who surpasses me in all things corrupt. Now, let's go back inside; I know you still have that bitch from Caerleon somewhere and I would once more sample her wares.'

Father Williams shook his head yet laughed at the demand.

'You are an evil man, Gerald,' he said, 'yet I find your company agreeable.'

'That's because we are cut from the same cloth,' said Gerald. 'Now lead the way.'

As the riders reached the road out of Brycheniog, Sir Gibson called a halt and turned his horse to face the others.

'Fellow riders,' he said, 'before we travel one league further, I suggest we take a moment to learn of each other. I am Sir Gibson of Glamorgan. Introduce yourselves I pray so our journey is easier.'

'I am Brother Maynard,' said the monk amongst them, 'and am here to protect your souls from the devil's temptation. In addition I carry the message for the houses of God proclaiming the guilt of the outlaws.'

'And as the eyes of the abbot,' sneered one of the men.

'That as well,' said the monk.

'And you are?' asked the knight turning to the smaller man.

'I am known as Buckler,' said the man, 'and am a representative of Gerald himself.'

'And you?' asked the knight turning to the last man.

'I am Dafydd,' came the answer, 'and hail from the estate of Cadwallader.'

'You mean the estate of Gerald,' corrected Buckler.

'Of course,' said Dafydd, 'I stand corrected. Forgive me, the familiarity and allegiance of a lifetime is not easy to forget overnight.'

'Nevertheless, you would do well to remember your new master.'

'Of course,' said Dafydd.

'Tell me, Dafydd,' said Sir Gibson, 'you are equipped in the manner of a squire and I wonder why Gerald would send a man of inexperience on such a quest.'

'My training is complete, my lord.' said Dafydd, 'and I only need a sponsor to bequeath my title. When Cadwallader died I was left without route to knighthood but

236

Gerald has picked up that role. However, he demands I prove myself on this task as evidence of competence. Should we succeed, he promises he will arrange the honour from Edward himself.'

'I understand you know our quarry?'

'I do.'

'And are you a comrade of his?'

'I rode alongside him on Crusade but have not shared conversation for more than two years.'

'And you are comfortable in your role?'

'Sir Gibson,' said Dafydd, 'as long as I can remember I have craved the honour of knighthood and worked hard to achieve the dream. I was first amongst my peers and rode on Crusade alongside Cadwallader himself. While there I allowed myself to be distracted from my quest for moments only, yet that lapse cost me my dream. I have learned my lesson and am now focused completely. No more will I take my eyes off a quest accepted and I am committed to bringing this to a successful conclusion, whatever that may be.'

'Even unto the death of your friend?'

'If necessary,' said Dafydd.

'Then so be it,' said Gibson. 'Gentlemen, we have a hard ride before us and know not how long this quest may take. It could be weeks; it could be years but we will not return until it is fulfilled or we lay dead. This is my oath. Make no mistake, I lead this group and will suffer neither fool nor coward. Cross me, and you will feel my wrath and let not my age confuse you: I could easily defeat any one of you on equal terms. Now, take a moment to tighten your straps for there will be little rest. I will not slow the pace nor wait for the lost. So, if there are no more questions, our quest starts here.'

In the tavern of Mynydd-Du, Garyn and Thomas Thatcher told their story to the old man. When they were done, he sat back and sipped on his ale as he stared at the two men before him.

'Tell me,' he said, 'what makes you think Llewellyn will allow southerners into his ranks?'

'Why wouldn't he?'

'It is well known the people of the south are inclined to follow the English Crown. Indeed, many of the lords have pledged their allegiance to Longshanks, even though he has yet to return from Crusade. You may be spies or worse still, assassins.'

'I have no way of proving otherwise,' said Garyn, 'except my word. I am an outcast from my village and have left the woman I love to save her from persecution. I can offer no evidence except for my blade against Llewellyn's enemies and in that, I am willing to prove my loyalty.'

'And you?' asked the man turning to Tom.

'I doubt my sword arm is of much use,' said Tom lifting his clawed hand, 'but I'm sure there are other tasks that need attending.'

The man nodded before retrieving a leather purse from within his tunic. He placed seven coins on the table and looked up at them.

'In the morning, there will be a column passing through heading for Conwy. I will make arrangements for you to join them. The first six coins will get you food and drink for three days.'

Garyn picked up the coins and looked at the seventh. It had the head of a prince on one side and Llewellyn's coat of arms on the reverse.

'And this one?'

'On route to Conwy you will travel through a pass guarded by Dolwyddelan Castle. Present it to any guard at the gates and it will get you audience with the sergeant at arms.'

'You are suggesting I try to pay a bribe to a soldier of Llewellyn. Surely my head would be forfeit.'

'That coin will buy neither ale nor bread. It has no value to anyone except to send a message to Llewellyn that the bearer has been recruited by a trusted man. So, do you want it or not?'

Garyn stared for a moment before placing the coin within his purse.

'I thought so,' said the man. 'Now, I suggest you finish your ale and join your horses in the stable. The column rides at dawn.'

'Thank you,' said Garyn and both men stood up.

'I wish you well,' said the old man, 'for there are uncertain times before us all.'

'Has it ever been any different?' asked Tom. They left the tavern and within the hour, were fast asleep upon the hay bales of the stable.

A hundred miles away, four horsemen rode hard through the night, oblivious of the weather.

Chapter Eighteen

The New World

'My lord.' shouted a voice, 'there are men approaching.'

Sir Robert of Shrewsbury ran across the deck and leaned against the rail.

'Where?' he demanded.

'On the slopes of the hill.'

Robert spotted the men and tried to make out the detail.

'Are they our fellows?' he demanded.

'I'm not sure,' said the voice, 'but if they are, they are in a hurry.'

All eyes turned to stare at the running men.

'I think they are,' said Robert, 'but where are the rest of the column?'

The Captain came up beside him.

'Perhaps they are just over the hill,' he said, 'and these have been sent forward to make contact.'

'No,' said Robert, 'if anyone was sent forward it would be mounted scouts. Those men seem frantic and carry no armour. Something is wrong. Captain, secure the ships for sailing.'

'But we haven't refilled all the water barrels yet.'

'Secure what we have. Until we know there is no danger, we will not be found unprepared.'

The captain shouted out the orders and mariners ran to their tasks. The men from the column closed in fast and were soon alongside the ships, walking the final few yards surrounded by the comrades they had not seen for weeks. Sir Robert strode down the gangplank and forced his way through the growing crowd. Finally he stood before them and waited patiently as they gathered their breath and drank their fill from offered water skins.

'Well met,' he said eventually, 'I trust you have come with news of the column.'

'We have, my lord.' said the archer, 'though the news may not be what you expect.'

'Then tell your tale, man,' said Robert, 'and waste no time in flowery language.'

'My lord, the rest of the column are just over that hill but are currently embattled with an army ten times their size and more.'

There was an audible gasp around the gathered men but Robert raised his hand for silence.

'Tell me more,' he said. 'What manner of foe do they face? Are they armoured? Do they have siege engines? What is the strength of their cavalry?'

'None of these, my lord. The enemy seem to be savages and wield weapons tipped with stone.'

'They have no knights?'

'No, my lord.'

'Then surely Tarian will make short work of them despite their strength?'

'You would think so, my lord, but as quick as we kill them their numbers swell threefold. They know no fear and our archers are out of arrows.'

'Then we will send support.'

'My lord, with respect you would be sending even more men to their death.'

'I will not leave them to die, soldier. Are they not brothers in arms?'

'Their numbers are uncountable, my lord; we cannot defeat them.'

'What are numbers when weighed against valour?'

'Forgive me, my lord, but valour is of little use when facing an entire nation.'

'You suggest leaving them to their fate?'

'No, my lord, other runners have been sent to tell them you are here. I suspect there will be survivors and the best you can do is prepare defences. Do not deem to face this enemy, my lord, at least not yet. Prepare to sail as soon as the last man is aboard and we can lick our wounds while we decide what to do.'

The knight stared at the archer. Every bone in his body demanded he led his men in support but he knew there was merit in the soldier's words.

'The ships will be ready for them,' he said eventually, 'but I will not stand by and see them slaughtered. If you speak true, there is something we can do to help, something the enemy will never see coming.' He turned to his second in command. 'Owain, how long will it take to assemble your equipment?'

'We trained with it this very morning, my lord; the opportunities have been limited these last few months.'

'Then fortune shines on us. Man the forecastles and prepare to offer support. The rest of you, don your armour and see to your weapons. We may not be able to fight a nation but we will do what we can. Take your men aboard; you look spent.'

'My lord, we beg not rest but bows. They are still our comrades and though it may be a fool's errand, I would rather fall aiding my fellows than hiding behind oaken planks.'

'Well spoken,' said Sir Robert. 'Meet back here not five minutes hence and harness what strength you have. If what you say is true, it will be needed before this situation is resolved.'

—

Tarian scrambled up the rock face as fast as he could. Ahead of him, the rest of the column cleared the summit and ran toward the next, knowing full well that relief lay on the other side. An arm reached down and helped Tarian over the top and he looked up to see Geraint standing before him.

'Why are you waiting?' he said.

Geraint didn't answer but just stared past Tarian down to the plain. Tarian turned and followed his gaze. What he saw made his heart sink. All across the plain, groups of lancers stood together fighting furiously against overwhelming numbers. Any still aboard their mounts were quickly pulled down and disappeared beneath a sea of screaming warriors. Within minutes the last few knights fell to the Apalach until only one was left standing.

Sir Crispin stood upon a rock wielding his two-handed blade manically around him, cutting down men as if they were sun ripened corn and his deathly blade a farmer's scythe. The enemy gradually stopped hurling themselves at this lone survivor and slowly the noise of their battle cries died out.

'Come on,' screamed Crispin, 'what are you waiting for?'

A warrior with a full feathered headdress stepped out of the encircling enemy and stared up at the knight. He held up a spear and chanted something in his strange language, shaking the weapon toward the exhausted man on the rock.

'What's happening?' asked Geraint.

'I think their leader is paying him respect as a fellow warrior,' said Tarian.

'Do you think they will let him go?'

Tarian shook his head and pointed toward more men with spears, making their way through to the front of the circle.

As if knowing he was being watched from above, Sir Crispin turned and gazed toward Tarian on the escarpment edge. Tarian stepped up onto a nearby rock so his profile could be seen against the sky. He drew his sword and after kissing the hilt, raised the weapon high above his head. Down below, Crispin lifted his helm from his head and threw it to the floor. Slowly he mirrored Tarian's salute and as he lifted his own weapon to the skies, Tarian's voice echoed across the plain.

'To the glory of God,' roared Tarian.

'For freedom,' roared Crispin but before any more words could leave his mouth, a spear sailed through the air and thudded into his throat. The knight fell to his knees and his sword dropped to the ground. A few seconds later, Tarian and Geraint watched the Apalach swarm over the mortally wounded man, each warrior keen to claim the scalp of the magnificent knight.

The Apalach chief bent over and picked up the fallen sword, examining its bloody sheen with interest. Finally he turned and looked up at Tarian upon the ridge. Around him his warriors looked toward the chief, waiting for his command until finally he raised the knight's sword and pointed it toward the rocks.

His own command echoed across the plain and as the drums started up once more, thousands of warriors raced toward the escarpment.

'We should go, my lord.' said Geraint. 'This day is done.'

Tarian stared at the now visible body of Crispin far below before jumping from the rock and joining Geraint to flee the killing fields.

—

'Here they come,' shouted the lookout and all eyes turned to see the remains of the column racing down the slopes toward the ships. The fleeing men had no structure but just ran headlong from the certain death they knew pursued them. Sir Robert turned to face the ships.

'*Owain*,' he roared, 'ready your men.'

'We await your command, my lord.' shouted the soldier.

'Then heed me closely,' answered Robert, 'for many lives lie in your hands.'

'My lord,' shouted the lookout, 'the enemy are on their heels.'

Sir Robert stared up at the slopes again and saw hundreds of half-naked warriors streaming in the wake of the retreating men.

'Men at arms,' shouted Sir Robert, 'form lines, archers to the rear. Pikemen, upon our retreat you will form a wall of steel.'

'Aye, sir,' shouted the men in acknowledgement.

'Form up,' shouted Robert, 'line abreast. Advance!'

The remaining men took their places and advanced across the plain toward their oncoming comrades. Within moments the first of the exhausted runners ran through the defensive lines, gasping for breath as they headed for the safety of the ships. Less than five hundred paces separated the first and last man and within minutes there were only a few stragglers, left limping across the grass, one being supported by Tarian himself. Behind them, hordes of warriors chased them down.

'Archers ready,' shouted Sir Robert, 'release arrows, volley fire.'

The air filled with of arrows and before the first fell amongst the Apalach, the second volley was already airborne. For a few seconds the enemy faltered but soon regrouped to continue the pursuit.

'Keep firing,' shouted Sir Robert before turning to an archer at his side.

'Send the signal, soldier,' he said. 'Let's show these heathen something they have never seen before.'

The archer dipped his arrow into a fire pot and a few seconds later a flaming trail sliced through the clear sky.

—

Back on the ships, Owain saw the signal and turned to his command.

'There it is, men,' he shouted, 'bend your backs and send them to hell.'

Seconds later, the timber boards of the ship's fore-castles shuddered from the release of stored energy as powerful mangonels loosed their lethal missiles to soar into the afternoon sky. Seconds later, clay fire pots smashed amongst the advancing enemy, showering the warriors with sticky burning oil.

Each ship had two mangonels and after the first volley caused havoc amongst the attackers, the speed and training of the operators ensured the hail of burning death was maintained at a deadly rate. The effect on the Apalach was instantaneous and panic reined as they sought escape from the unforeseen threat.

'Archers, up your rate,' screamed Robert. 'Pikemen forward, allow no respite.'

Lines of men ran up to use their weapons against the panicking enemy. Apalach warriors fell by the dozen but Sir Robert could see hundreds more coming to their aid.

'Withdraw,' he roared and the men turned to run back to the ships. The last line of pikemen presented a line of solid steel as a final defence but despite the carnage many natives threw themselves against them and as men fell, gaps inevitably appeared. At close quarters the fight was more even and though the axes used by natives had stone heads, they still dealt crushing blows and many of Robert's men fell beneath the onslaught.

'Men at arms, steady retreat,' shouted Sir Robert and the wall of defence walked backward toward the ships. Above their head, the air filled with fire balls and kept the main enemy force at bay. Individual battles continued and though the lightly armed Apalach sustained heavy casualties, the men of Wales suffered no less grievous losses with over half falling before reaching safety. Finally the survivors reached the ships and as exhausted men raced up the gangplanks, archers already aboard rained their arrows down upon the pressing enemy. Within minutes the pikemen finally boarded the ships and the gangplanks raised as every available man continued the murderous onslaught from the rails along the side.

Despite their horrendous casualties, the Apalach continued the pressure and even as the ships eased away from the banks, their retribution fell amongst the fleeing fleet. Burning arrows rained about the decks and soon the furled sails caught light, the flames roaring up the wind dried fabric as frantic mariners climbed the rigging with leather buckets of water. Slowly the fleet pulled away and eventually they were mid-stream, being carried south by the current but the danger wasn't over. All four ships were alight and one in particular was ablaze from stem to stern.

'Tarian, we have to get back to land,' shouted Sir Robert. 'We cannot fight the fires out here.'

'We will be going back to our deaths,' answered Tarian. 'We have to get away.'

'If we stay out here the ships will burn and we will surely drown,' shouted Sir Robert. 'There is no other option.'

'Yes, there is,' shouted Tarian. 'Send signal to the other ships; head for the far bank. At least we will have a river between us.'

'We will never make it.'

'We will take our chances,' roared Tarian, 'but the longer we argue the less chance we have. Now give the order.'

Sir Robert turned to his men.

'You heard him,' he screamed, 'every man to the oars. Either we will reach that far shore or we will die trying, now move!'

Within minutes the ship changed direction and headed across the river. Signal was sent to the fleet and all the ships changed course to follow their lead, but Tarian was horrified to see the other three ships also in flames. Soldiers and mariners alike fought against the fires, but cloying smoke mixed with the burning tar of the caulking meant they struggled to make any headway.

'My lord,' shouted a voice, 'the Swan is sinking.'

Tarian watched hopelessly as one of the ships was engulfed. The burning mast fell crashing to the deck and the sounds of screaming men reached them across the water. Sparks must have reached the hay stores in the hold for roaring flames could be seen bursting from the deck hatches.

'They are doomed,' said Robert as they watched panicking men hurling themselves from the burning deck into the river and men stared helplessly as many of their comrades sank beneath the waters. Those few who could swim struck out toward the nearest ship as though it too had suffered fires, it was relatively undamaged. Ropes were thrown from the side and those managing to reach the cog were hauled to safety though most were swept past by the current, out of reach to any would-be rescuer.

Behind them, hundreds of warriors lined the banks, screaming their war cries and waving their weapons at the retreating fleet while many more ran alongside the river edge, seeking the scalps of any survivors who managed to swim to shore.

Tarian shook his head in dismay as he watched his men die. Over the past few months he had grown close to many and though he had watched some fall in battle, that was a risk that all men of war took. In the eyes of most soldiers, drowning was a fearful death.

'Tarian, we approach the bank,' shouted the captain, 'what area do you favour?'

'Just beach her,' shouted Tarian, 'and get us off this thing.'

The captain moved the rudder to aim his ship at a low part of the bank.

'Increase the speed,' he shouted and below decks the order was passed to the rowers. Within minutes the prow drove up onto the bank and mariners leapt from the side to secure the ship to nearby trees. 'Every man to the buckets,' shouted the captain, 'we need to save what we can.'

For an hour, the men formed a chain as bucket after bucket of water was thrown on the flames and though they were eventually extinguished, what was left was hardly recognisable as a vessel. A hundred yards downstream, the second crew fought a similar battle to save their own ship and by the time evening fell, two smouldering wrecks lay motionless against the riverbank while the one surviving ship lay anchored a hundred yards offshore. All around the bank, men lay exhausted while others tended to wounds suffered in the battle. Tarian and Sir Robert walked amongst them, checking on each one.

'Our losses are substantial,' said Robert, 'an unacceptable outcome.'

'Battles are won and battles are lost, Robert. What is important is how we regroup.'

'The enemy are but savages, my lord, and we should have done better. Are we not experienced soldiers?'

'We were well prepared for any warfare familiar to us, Robert. Nobody could have expected such a strong enemy with so little regard for their own lives.'

'Nevertheless the men are crushed, my lord. It will be difficult to raise their spirits.'

'What they need is direction, Robert. Give them leadership and they will remould into the unit we know they can be. Find the fittest amongst them and post a picket.

Let the rest sleep but in the morning form them up and we will see what we have left.'

Sir Robert looked out at the single ship moored offshore.

'At least we have one cog left,' he said. 'The captain of the *Dragon* has sent word the damage is minimal and will take only weeks to repair. Once she is seaworthy there should be room enough for all those left.'

'To what end?'

'To sail home, of course,' said Sir Robert. 'We can't stay here.'

'On the contrary,' said Tarian, 'I have no intention of returning yet. We came here to find Madoc's heir and that aim has not changed.'

'But our forces are decimated, my lord; of those who survived, many are wounded. Most of the spare weapons were on the Swan, our fellow knights have fallen and we have no horses. How can we continue in such a state?'

'We have come across half the world, Robert, sailed unknown seas and lived off a land totally strange to us. We have fought an enemy unlike any we have faced before and though we have suffered casualties, we can still field a force of over a hundred foot soldiers. We haven't gone through all this to turn and run now. No, we will lick our wounds and regroup. Tomorrow we will salvage what we can from the ships and take stock. Once we know our strengths, we will continue our quest.'

Sir Robert remained quiet but the look in his eyes told Tarian he doubted the sense in his leader's words.

'Is there anything else?' asked Tarian.

'No, my lord.' said Robert.

'Then sort the guards and get some sleep. There are arduous days ahead of us.'

The following morning the men formed up in loose ranks. The mood was quiet and they had already buried three comrades who had succumbed to their injuries overnight. The remaining wounded had been sent out to the *Dragon* while the able-bodied had salvaged what they could from the still smouldering hulks. Men talked quietly as Tarian walked amongst them, checking what weapons they had and what stores they had managed to accumulate.

'It's not much,' said Sir Robert, 'but the rest is spoiled.'

'It will be enough,' said Tarian.

'There is hardly enough for ten days.'

'If we halve the rations and forage off the land we can last for a month.'

'And then what? We have no horses.'

'Neither do these natives and they seem to manage alright. Are we no better than them? What we will do is this...' He stopped talking and looked at Sir Robert who had fallen silent and was staring in horror over Tarian's shoulder.

'What's the matter?' asked Tarian but turned to follow the knight's stare.

'Mother of Christ have mercy,' whispered Sir Robert and made the sign of the cross on his chest.

Up above them on the hill, the edge of the forest seemed to come alive as hundreds of men emerged from the undergrowth. Even though they were half a mile distant, Tarian could see they were natives and his heart sank as he realised his remaining force was vastly outnumbered. The enemy walked slowly down the slopes and Tarian addressed Sir Robert over his shoulder.

'Get the men into defensive lines,' he said quietly, 'pikemen to the fore.'

'What's the point?' asked Sir Robert, 'their numbers are as many as bees in a swarm.'

'Do it,' said Tarian. 'This may be our last stand, my friend, but too many have died for us to simply lay down as beaten dogs. We will sell our lives dearly.'

'My lord,' said a voice behind them, 'I don't think that will be necessary.'

Tarian turned and saw Geraint behind him.

'What do you mean?'

'Look,' said Geraint and pointed to a man walking a few yards in front of the main body of natives. 'Is that Achak?'

'I believe it is,' said Tarian, 'and unless I am mistaken, there are also women and children amongst them.'

'What difference does it make?' asked Sir Robert. 'If they are like their brothers on the far side of the river then our lives can be measured in minutes.'

'On the contrary,' said Tarian. 'If Geraint is right, and I believe he is, these people do not intend to kill us, but welcome us with open arms.'

'Why would they do that?' asked Robert.

'Because they are not Apalach, my friend; they are Mandan.'

'And that means what?'

'It means we have reached our goal,' said Tarian. 'We did it, Robert, we have found the descendants of Madoc.'

Chapter Nineteen

Dolwyddelan Castle

Garyn stood waiting amongst a line of recruits. All had spent the last few days sleeping in a cold stone hall with nothing but thin potage for food. The Prince's coin had gained him entrance but any thoughts of being recruited to a position close to Llewellyn were short lived as he saw he was just one amongst hundreds hoping to gain employment in the Welsh army. Finally the sergeant at arms called them to stand in line in the castle courtyard. A knight in full colours sat behind a trestle table along with an administrator writing on a vellum scroll. As the line shuffled forward, Garyn could see men being sent in different directions and forming into separate groups around the courtyard. Finally he reached the table and the administrator looked up to greet him.

'Name?' he said.

'Garyn ap Thomas.'

'Birthplace?'

'Brycheniog.'

'You are from the south?'

'I am.'

'What brings you north to fight alongside the Prince?'

'Circumstance.'

'Are you outlawed?'

'On minor charges only.'

'What are your skills?'

'Horsemanship, lance and sword.'

'Have you seen combat?'

'I have been on Crusade but saw little conflict.' At that the knight's head turned toward Garyn for the first time.

'With whom did you crusade?' he asked.

'Sir Robert Cadwallader,' said Garyn.

'I know of Cadwallader; he died in service.'

'He did, my lord.'

'So how have you lived yet your lord and master perished?'

'It is a long tale, my lord, but the truth is I was released from service.'

'Are you a coward?'

'I am not, my lord. If I was, I would not be here.'

'We will see,' said the knight. 'I will hear more of your story, Garyn ap Thomas, but now is not the time.' He turned to the administrator. 'Put him with Lewis of Conwy.'

'My lord, he is yet untried,' answered the clerk.

'If he is found wanting, Lewis will sort him out,' said the knight.

'Place your mark here,' said the administrator and indicated a place on the vellum. Garyn took the quill and signed his name beneath a column of simple marks made by others before him. The administrator nodded in quiet admiration.

'The boy can write,' he said.

'I am my father's son,' said Garyn.

'Name your sire, Garyn,' said the knight, 'for there is a familiarity about you.'

'My father was Thomas Ruthin of Brycheniog.'

The knight nodded as his suspicions were confirmed.

'I thought so,' he said. 'Head over to the main tower and await instruction.'

Garyn walked away and sat at the base of the huge fortification.

'Did you know his father?' asked the administrator.

'Oh, I knew him,' said the knight. 'I fought alongside him for three years.'

—

Garyn sat against the base of the tower walls as the rest of the recruits filtered through the process. Eventually Thomas Thatcher signed his name and walked across the courtyard.

'Tom,' shouted Garyn as his friend walked toward him, 'what is your posting?'

'Kitchens,' said Thomas. 'The best I could have hoped for in the circumstances.'

Garyn glanced at the withered hand.

'It may get better,' he said.

'I don't think so,' said Tom. 'Anyway, at least I now have a future which is a lot more than other cripples.'

'You are no cripple, Tom.'

'Nor can I ever be a thatcher again,' said Tom. 'Anyway, I hear the wenches in the kitchens can be very friendly. Fret not, Garyn, my life has taken an upturn. I may not be destined for glory but I will settle for a warm bed, female company and a full belly. What man could ask for more?'

'If you are satisfied, Thomas Thatcher, then I am happy for you.' Garyn stood up and held out his hand in friendship. 'You have my gratitude, Tom. Thank you for being a friend when I needed one most.'

'You get ahead of yourself, Master Garyn,' said Tom. 'You don't get rid of me that easily. While you are training it seems you will be getting fed from the castle's kitchens. No doubt you will face me across a table with an empty bowl and a hopeful look in your eyes.'

'Ha,' laughed Garyn, 'then I should take care not to upset you, for a very wise monk once told me a soldier's best friend is the camp cook. Hopefully that piece of advice will bear fruit.'

'Who knows?' said Tom. 'I cannot have favourites, Garyn, but my hand is weak and if the ladle slips while pouring potage into a man's bowl then surely I cannot be held responsible.'

'Good luck, my friend,' said Garyn with a smile.

'And you,' said Tom and after grasping Garyn's arm in friendship, continued across the courtyard toward the kitchens.

—

'You men,' shouted a squire, 'follow me.'

Garyn and a dozen others followed the boy into the main hall and gathered together, talking quietly amongst themselves. Finally another knight entered and strode over to face them.

'My name is Lewis,' he said, 'and I am a knight of Llewellyn's guard. You men have been selected to join the lower ranks of the guard and will support your betters with lance and shield. In the morning you will be allocated mounts and weapons. There will be a period of training and those who reach the standard will be deployed within weeks.'

'Deployed where, my lord,' asked a voice.

'Wherever it is that Llewellyn deems fit,' said Lewis. 'There is rumour of an attempted coup from within and we are working hard to find the conspirators. That could be in any manor from here to Anglesey and as far south as Builth. Prepare to train hard and campaign even harder for we will not rest until we face these traitors or hunt them down as the dogs they are. You are about to go to the armoury for chainmail and helms. Take time to ensure your equipment fits well for you will live in little else for weeks on end. Now, before we go, who is the one known as Garyn ap Thomas?'

'That's me, my lord,' said Garyn.

'You will stay here,' said Lewis.

'But why?' asked Garyn.

'Curb your mouth,' said the knight, 'and do as I say. The rest of you, follow me.'

The rest of the group left the hall leaving Garyn alone with the squire. The young boy looked at him nervously as Garyn paced the slabbed floor. Finally, he stopped walking and faced the squire.

'What do you know of this?' he demanded.

'I know nothing, my lord,' said the boy.

'You must know something,' said Garyn. 'Why have I been left behind?'

'Because I requested it,' said a voice and Garyn turned to face a man who had entered the hall behind him. For a few seconds, he struggled to recognise the familiar face but then it came to him. It was the leader of the mercenaries he had met weeks earlier.

'Goddeff,' said Garyn, 'what are you doing here?'

'The same as you, I suspect,' said Goddeff, 'undertaking gainful employment in the name of Llewellyn.'

'But I thought you had a commission to fill?'

'I do indeed and here I am, fulfilling it.'

'You intended coming here all along?'

'It would seem so,' said Goddeff.

'But why didn't you say?'

'I knew you for hours only; why would I share such knowledge with a stranger?'

'A point well made,' said Garyn. 'So you now serve the Prince?'

'For the foreseeable future,' said Goddeff, 'or at least until his supply of coins dries up.'

'You fight for his money?'

'That's what mercenaries do. Anyway, don't you want to know why?'

'Why what?'

'Why I asked for you to remain behind when your fellows departed?'

'Enlighten me.'

'Because, Garyn of Brycheniog, my offer of a few weeks ago still stands. I want you to ride with me and my men.'

'But why? I am a far inferior soldier to those you call comrade.'

'At the moment perhaps, but you have a noble pedigree for one so young. Skill, I can teach; heart, I cannot.'

'What do you mean?'

'Your exploits in the Holy Land still ring in my ears and such a man will always be welcome to ride alongside me but there is something greater that influences my mind.'

'And that is?'

'Your lineage.'

'I don't understand,' said Garyn.

'You come from good stock, Garyn. Your father's name was well known across the country not only on the tournament fields but across the Holy Land as a feared knight.'

'He was a mercenary.'

'But a knight, nonetheless. Many men speak his name in awe and though you told me of his fate, I only made the connection when Sir Fredrick recognised you.'

'Sir Fredrick?'

'The recruiting knight.'

'He rode with my father?'

'He did,' said Goddeff, 'as did I.'

Garyn gasped in astonishment.

'I don't understand,' he said. 'We are a hundred miles away from my birth town yet my father's name is held in great esteem.'

'He was a local man, Garyn and his name borders on legend.'

'But I always thought he was from the south.'

'I would suggest that's what he wanted you to know. It is no secret he tired of war and sought the peace a family brings. There was no shame for he proved himself many times in battle. Where better to start a new life than at the other end of his country?'

'So how did you know him?'

'We joined forces in Syria and shaped a formidable alliance. A band of men feared across the Holy Land. Our names were spoken in awe by friend and foe alike and for three years we roamed Palestine at will, administering our wrath on the enemies of any man who could pay our price.'

'You mean any Christian who could pay our price.'

'I meant what I said.'

'But surely you didn't serve the infidels?'

'We fought for many paymasters of many faiths but I will say this: we only killed Christians when paid by other Christians.'

'That is unforgiveable.'

'Really, then why are you here?'

'I don't understand.'

'Do you not think you may have to kill a man, perhaps many?'

'Possibly.'

'And you are comfortable with that?'

'I am.'

'And of what faith do you think they will be?'

Garyn fell silent as the realisation sunk in.

'It's not the same,' he said eventually.

'It is exactly the same,' said Goddeff. 'Anyway, we waste time. My offer still stands, I want you to join me and my men. You will be well fed, well paid and have respect from men of note across Wales.'

'Even though I may fight on many sides?'

'Perhaps so, but I promise you this. I will never ask you to raise a fist against our own countrymen on behalf of the English Crown. If Welshmen want to kill Welshmen then that is their business, however, we will never accept English coins against our own kinsmen.'

'But I signed allegiance just this very morn.'

'I have already secured your release should you see fit to accept my offer.'

'I don't know,' said Garyn. 'There is much to consider.'

'Then let me tell you this: the days before us will be fraught with danger. You have already proven you are a man of bravery; you owe it to yourself not to become a man of stupidity. Llewellyn keeps his favoured knights close and though they are men of honour, he will not risk them in conflict unless there is a high chance of victory. To do that, the battle must first be one of pike and poleaxe and it is well known that many men die before knights are committed. Why do you think he recruits, Garyn? What sort of man do you think he sees you as?'

'As a fellow soldier in search of a common goal.'

'No, Garyn, you and all the rest of them out there are nought but cattle, a price worth paying to achieve the ultimate aim. It is nothing personal, just the ways of war. Wake up and take this opportunity, if not for your own sake, then in your father's name. The offer stands until nightfall only; after that, it will not be made again.'

'I will not need the time,' said Garyn. 'I accept your offer.'

'It is the right decision,' said Goddeff. 'Now, retrieve your horse from the stables and meet me at the gates at dusk.'

'Are we not staying here?'

'Walls are a boundary we do not countenance, Garyn. Like our namesakes we prefer the forests to the keep, the stars to the ceilings. We drink from rivers, not wells, and hunt the deer of the forest.'

'Your namesakes?'

'We have garnered a reputation amongst the nobles of Wales, Garyn. They see us as wolves amongst men and have named our group after those noble beasts. You may have heard of us.'

'You are the Blaidd?' said Garyn with incredulity.

'We are,' said Goddeff, 'and as of this moment, so are you.'

Chapter Twenty

The New World

Geraint walked alongside Achak as the Mandan led them through the hills of their land. The survivors of the Apalach attack were surrounded by happy, chattering natives and were astonished to find that most of their hosts spoke at least a smattering of Welsh. The Mandan talked about the spirit people and the ancestors who had come from across the sea in the times of their grandfathers. The landscape changed as they walked and they were soon walking through cultivated fields of corn being tended by Mandan women. Along the edge of the fields and on the ledges of the nearby cliffs, men armed with spears and bows watched them approach and Achak explained their role was to look out for Apalach raiding parties. Eventually they dropped down into a valley and the column could see smoke plumes rising into the afternoon air behind a wooden palisade stretching across the valley.

'Look at the walls,' said Tarian, 'the poles are bound with rope, a similar construction to back home.'

'I expect Madoc left them with many skills,' said Sir Robert, 'and it will be good to grasp the arm of his descendants.'

They walked through the gates and though the construction of the walls was familiar, what lay beyond was totally strange to them. As far as they could see, hundreds of domed huts lay semi sunken into the valley floor. The small parts of the walls that were visible were clad in mud and covered with painted images of the many animals hunted by the Mandan. The domed roofs were made from woven reeds and smoke came from holes in the apex, evidence of the cooking fires within. Naked children ran amongst the huts and skinny dogs snapped at the strangers' heels. In the distance, the glint of sun on open water signalled the location of a lake and they could see dozens of small round boats being used for fishing.

'Unless I am mistaken, they are coracles,' said Tarian quietly, referring to the traditional boats used across Wales. As they walked, the men took the opportunity to examine the Mandan more closely. All the natives were dressed in animal skin leggings with some having a decorated flap of worked buffalo hide attached around their waist. Their upper bodies were unclad though covered with painted designs of many colours, as indeed were their faces. Their heads were shaved at the sides and the remaining hair on the top hung down their backs, decorated with a mixture of coloured beads, ornate leather ties and the feathers of many strange and different birds. The women were dressed in calf length dresses made from similar skins and again they were decorated with multi-coloured designs of birds and animals.

Interest was high in the strangers and crowds gathered as they walked deeper into the village until they finally stopped in a central clearing.

'Look at that,' said Sir Robert. In the centre a large pole soared skyward adorned with strings of blue beads and the skulls of all sorts of animals. Coloured feathers blew in the wind and carved images of bearded men were sunk deep into the surface. Tarian and Sir Robert walked over for a closer look and Tarian dropped to his knees to wipe the dust off a brass plate fixed to the base of pole.

'Well,' he said eventually, 'if there was doubt before, there isn't any more.'

'What does it say?' asked Sir Robert.

'It says *Gwennan Corn*,' said Tarian. 'This was the main mast of Madoc's flagship.'

Throughout the day the men of the fleet were shown to various huts around the village and given food by their hosts. Tarian and Sir Robert were taken to a hut different to all the rest, a wooden building constructed on stilts. They climbed a ladder and entered a smoky room unlit by any apertures in the bark latticed walls.

Inside, their eyes became accustomed to the gloom and they could see it was one big room. In the centre a small fire smouldered on a flat stone while the walls were adorned with ornate native lances. Achak indicated the animal pelts stuffed with grass along the base of the walls and the two knights dropped their packs before looking around the room.

'Look,' said Tarian and they stared at the far wall. Amongst an array of feathered headdresses, they could see half a dozen rusting helms. They walked over and stood before them in awe. Tarian raised a hand and touched the most ornate helmet on display.

'I wonder if any of these were worn by the Prince,' he said.

'Machitaw will know the answer,' said Achak.

'Who is Machitaw?'

'Our medicine man. He sits with the elders of the Mandan.'

'Is he your leader?'

'We have many leaders.'

'Where are they?'

'They sit in counsel at the fires of another village.'

A Mandan woman climbed the ladder and brought them a maize porridge flavoured with berries.

'Eat the food of our people,' said Achak. 'Tonight we will feast on meat for it is the season of the buffalo, we will send for you when it is time.' He disappeared down the ladder and left the two men alone.

'I wonder how the *Dragon* fares,' said Robert.

'They have been tasked with staying midstream,' said Tarian, 'and to make what repairs they can. With luck we will be able to meet the Mandan chiefs and find out if any of their people are directly descended from Madoc. After that it's a case of being patient and persuading his lineage to return with us to Wales.'

'What if there are no descendants?'

'There has to be, Robert. God has seen fit to deliver us here. I am sure we would have perished if he did not see merit in this quest.'

'It is possible that any still of his line could be female.'

'It is something I have considered. Obviously, it would be better if it was a man but a woman can be no less a figurehead. Are we to forget the tale of Gwenllian, daughter of Prince Gruffudd, who in his absence led his army at the battle of Deheubarth?'

'That was a hundred and forty years ago.'

'Yet still fresh in the memory of our people. She wielded a sword as well as any man and though she died that day, her memory served as a beacon for many years.'

'Well,' said Robert, 'in a few more days we will know either way, and if it is God's will then we could be heading back within weeks.'

'Indeed, and if a figurehead is found, we will be returning to a new future for our country.'

'I suggest we get some rest,' said Robert, 'for these are indeed a strange people and I feel the days before us will be filled with new discoveries.'

'I agree,' said Tarian and retrieving his blanket from his pack, lay down on the straw stuffed deerskins to get some sleep.

–

When they awoke the air was reverberating with the sound of drums. They rose from their mats and climbed down the ladder before walking toward the centre of the village. Native women ran toward them and plied them with clay beakers full of a fermented fruit drink.

'It tastes similar to ale,' said Robert.

'Another legacy of Madoc, methinks,' said Tarian. They joined the crowd in the centre of the village and were pleased to see their men intermingling with their hosts. Three complete carcasses of giant buffalo were being roasted over the fires, and a large circle of painted warriors shuffled around the flames chanting songs in their native language.

Achak saw Tarian approach and walked over to address him.

'You are welcome here,' he said, 'and will sit with the elders.' He pointed over to the far side of the fire where ten aged men sat cross legged on reed mats.

'Are these your leaders?' asked Tarian.

'They are council only,' said Achak. 'Our chief is known as Pachua.'

'What does it mean?' asked Robert.

'It means snake of the water,' said Achak. 'Pachua will return tomorrow and will be glad to eat with the spirit people.'

'I think that's the man we need to speak to,' said Tarian.

Achak led them across the clearing to sit alongside the old men. Their skins were a mass of wrinkles from a lifetime in the sun and Tarian could see that at least two of them were blind. None of the elders made any effort to speak, yet all had bowls of burning leaves and bent forward regularly to breathe in the smoke.

'What is that?' asked Robert.

'It is the dream smoke,' said Achak. 'Our elders see the visions of the spirits and tell us which way to go.'

The two knights watched as the festivities unfolded. The drums were hypnotic and dancers formed fantastic shapes with their bodies as they acted out the history of the Mandan. An hour or so in, all the men of the fleet sat up with renewed interest as a group of natives ran into the circle wearing Welsh helms and the remains of rusty chainmail. Awkward parodies of sword fights followed and though it bore little similarity to the real thing, it was obvious that the Mandan saw the display as an important part of their heritage. As the night wore on, native girls carved slices of hot meat from the buffalo carcasses and handed them around on boards of wood. The native beer had an effect and Tarian was intoxicated, not only from the drink but from the unbelievable welcome they had experienced.

Finally the drums' beat became louder and the crowd opened for a line of women to form their own circle around the fires. As the men of Wales looked on, the women's dance got more and more suggestive until finally each woman walked forward and grabbed the hand of a soldier, leading them away into the darkness. Two beautiful young women approached Tarian and Robert, pulling them to their feet.

'What's all this about, Achak?' asked Tarian.

'They are a gift from the Mandan to you,' said Achak. 'Your beds will be warm as long as you are here.'

'I'm not sure this is honourable,' said Sir Robert. 'Why would you give us your women? Surely they have husbands?'

'They are the widows of those who have burned in the fires of the Apalach. This is not a burden to them. They would be insulted to be rejected.'

'I don't know,' said the knight. 'It seems to be behaviour unbecoming of a noble.'

'Robert,' slurred Tarian, 'feel free to be a slave to your morals but I for one will not insult our hosts.' He turned to the young woman. 'Lead the way, young lady,' he said, 'and we will cement the friendship between our nations.'

Robert watched him go before turning to stare at the beautiful native still holding his hand.

'She will be offended?' he asked.

'She has no man,' said Achak.

Robert sighed but gave in to temptation.

'Then I will be honoured to share the bed of such a beautiful woman.' The Mandan woman smiled and led him away toward her hut. Across the camp, many men were experiencing similar hospitality and as the last went to the huts of the widows, a native approached Achak from the shadows.

'They are truly a strange people,' he said.

'They are, Machitaw,' said Achak, 'but they have honour and are brave warriors.'

'Then set your heart upon it, Achak. The wind songs cannot be wrong and the spring sun will see the Apalach villages but ash upon the plains.'

'It will be so,' said Achak and walked away into the night.

–

The sun was already high in the sky when Achak came for them the following day.

'Pachua has returned,' he said, 'and grants you audience.'

'Excellent,' said Tarian and rose from the deerskin bed.

'I will join you,' said Sir Robert.

'No,' said Achak, 'Pachua will meet with your leader only.'

'Sir Robert is my second in command and I value his counsel.'

'Pachua will speak to you only.'

'Don't worry,' said Sir Robert, 'I will wait here and you can share the conversation when you return.'

Tarian nodded and followed Achak down the ladder. The Mandan took him across the camp until they reached a hut situated apart from the main village. As they drew near, Tarian could see many warriors guarding the area.

'Is there need for this?' asked Tarian.

'The Apalach value Pachua's scalp above all others and their young men seek it as a trophy of war. Those who come, die, but still they come.' He stopped before the doorway of the hut and spoke to one of the two warriors standing guard. Tarian couldn't understand the conversation as it was carried out in Mandan but it was obvious they would not be allowed in.

'What did he say?' asked Tarian.

'He said Pachua will see you when he is ready.'

'So what do we do now?'

'Now we wait,' said Achak and dropped to the ground to sit cross legged before the entrance. Tarian followed suit and sat beside him. For over an hour they waited and Tarian was getting impatient but Achak convinced him to stay.

'It would be a great insult to leave,' he said.

Another hour passed and finally there were signs of movement. First a young woman came out and tied the buffalo hide flap out of the way before placing four deerskins on the ground in front of Tarian. Another two young women came out and took their place on the outer two skins. One had a wooden plate of berries and buffalo strips while the other had a clay flask of water. Within minutes, two men left the hut and walked toward them. The first was an old man clad in heavy buckskin leggings and tunic. On his head he had a feathered headdress that hung down his back to his calves. In his hand he carried a lance draped in decorations of a different kind.

'Pachua is a great warrior,' said Achak, 'and his knife is dulled by Apalach scalps.'

The second man was much younger and wore only a loincloth. His headdress was no less impressive, being made from the entire hide of a grey timber wolf including the upper half of the animal's skull. His body was covered in the white tell-tale scars of hundreds of knife cuts.

'He is Machitaw,' said Achak.

'The medicine man?' said Tarian.

'His magic is strong,' said Achak. 'Every cut on his body comes from his own knife when he dances with the spirits.'

Tarian looked at Machitaw and though he knew little of the ways of these people, he could see the man had the look of a fighter. His body was strong and his sun-burned skin was tight over a muscular frame. Both men sat cross legged on the remaining two deerskins and stared at the man from across the sea.

'Pachua…' started Tarian but Achak grabbed his arm.

'Wait,' he said.

One of the women offered the wooden platter to Tarian.

'Take one,' said Achak quietly, 'he is welcoming you as a friend.'

Tarian took a piece of meat and passed the platter on. Achak and Machitaw each took a piece but again Achak told him to wait. Pachua didn't take any meat but waited as one of the women chewed a piece on his behalf. Finally she spat it out onto the plate and handed it back to the chief. Without pausing, Pachua picked up the chewed meat and placed it into his mouth. The platter was passed around several times, following the same routine until it was empty. Finally each man drank deeply from the beaker before the girls took the remains of the ritualistic meal away. Eventually Machitaw spoke in his native language and Achak translated as he talked.

'You are known as Tar-ian,' said Machitaw, 'and lead the strangers from across the big water.'

'I am,' said Tarian. 'We come from a country called Wales across the eastern sea.'

'We know of this place,' said Machitaw. 'Many have come before you and have built lodges amongst the Mandan.'

'I know,' said Tarian, 'and it is this that brings us here.'

'You seek your people?'

'In a way, yes.'

'Then look around you Tar-ian, for they are all around you. Many here bleed the blood of your country. Their father's grandfathers came in giant canoes many moons ago but their seed mixed with ours and their offspring are as Mandan as I.'

'And we are proud that our two peoples mix,' said Tarian. 'It is a strong allegiance.'

'It is said that you wish to take them back across the sea,' said Machitaw. 'Is there truth in this?'

'Not exactly,' said Tarian, 'we seek only one bloodline for their ancestor was a great leader in our country.'

'You speak of Madoc,' said Pachua in Welsh.

Tarian turned to face the chief. Up until now he hadn't spoken and Tarian was surprised to hear a strong voice coming from such a frail man.

'I do, great chief,' he said. 'Madoc was a great man and we seek his line to once more rule in our land as you do in yours.'

'There is no chief as great as Pachua,' said Machitaw.

'I'm sorry,' said Tarian, 'I did not mean to offend. I meant only that to our people Madoc's line would demand great respect.'

'And why should we give you this person?' asked Pachua.

'We ask that you identify his line,' said Tarian. 'If there is such a man, and Pachua agrees to send him with us, the chief's name will be spoken of in another land and his greatness celebrated.'

The chief's head nodded almost imperceptibly and Tarian knew he had struck the right tone.

'And what do you offer in return?' asked Machitaw.

'Much of our equipment sank with the ships,' said Tarian, 'but we will leave what we can. We have steel weapons and many bows. All are far superior to the weapons of the Apalach.'

'Achak tells of animals that bore you into battle with the Apalach,' said Machitaw.

'The horses were either killed or captured by the Apalach,' said Tarian.

'Do you have more?'

'No, all are gone.'

'We have eyes in the Apalach villages,' said Machitaw, 'and they say that some beasts still live.'

'How many?'

'As many as the fingers on two hands. We will make war on the Apalach and capture them. You will teach our people how to use them in war and in the hunt.'

Tarian nodded slowly but his mind was racing.

'We could,' he said, 'but we have little time. As soon as the *Dragon* is fixed, we have to set sail.'

'What is this *Dragon*?'

'Our remaining ship. It needs repairs and once done we have to leave. Our country is in turmoil and needs a leader.'

For a few moments both natives spoke in their native language before turning their heads to face Tarian once more.

'We will help in this task,' said Machitaw, 'but there is a price to pay.'

'Name it,' said Tarian.

'The Apalach are fearsome warriors. Our children go hungry when they raid our fields and our braves grow impatient to wield the war bow.'

'What stops you?'

'The wind songs told us that there will come a time when the spirit people come again. Now that you are here the time is right and our people gather their weapons.'

'Do you think you can defeat them?'

'With your help all Mandan enemies will sleep lightly in the huts.'

'What do you mean "our help"?'

'Our people saw beasts of wood roaring fire into the skies.'

'You speak of the mangonels,' said Tarian.

'Never have we seen such a thing,' said Machitaw, 'and Apalach warriors will burn in the beast's breath.'

'We have only two left on the *Dragon*,' said Tarian.

'Then you will make more.'

'We could,' said Tarian, 'but it will take time.'

Both Mandan stared at him but did not respond. Finally Tarian broke the silence.

'If we do this, will you take me to Madoc's descendants?'

'This will be discussed when the time is right.'

'What is that supposed to mean?'

'It is our way, Tar-ian,' said Machitaw and he summoned the two women to help the chief to his feet.

Tarian watched them go and walked back to the hut with Achak. He climbed the ladder to find Sir Robert waiting for him.

'Well?' said Sir Robert, 'how did it go?'

'A good start,' said Tarian. 'They will give us manpower to fix the ships but in return they want the mangonels.'

'A small price,' said Sir Robert, 'but what about Madoc's heirs?'

'They were reluctant to discuss the issue,' said Tarian, 'but it is early days yet. There is no rush while the *Dragon* is being repaired.'

–

For the next few weeks Tarian and his men enjoyed the hospitality of the Mandans and each day he asked Achak if Pachua would discuss the descendants of Madoc. Acha counselled patience but Tarian knew they had to move soon or they would be stuck there for the oncoming winter. Finally he decided to go back to the chief's hut himself and despite Achak's protestations, he strode through the village determined to get an answer. Sir Robert walked alongside him and as they walked, a crowd of Mandan warriors followed in their trail, keen to see the outcome of the confrontation. Pachua was renowned for his short temper.

'Tarian, wait!' shouted a voice and the leader paused to see who had called. Behind him he could see Geraint running through the village.

'What is it, Geraint?' said Tarian, 'for I have business to attend.'

'My lord, there is news from the *Dragon*.'

'What news?' asked Tarian.

'It is not good,' said Geraint. 'There was another fire and the carpenter reports the lower hull was severely damaged.'

'What fire?' roared Tarian, 'how can this be?'

'One of the Mandan saw fit to light a fire against the cold, my lord, and it got out of hand.'

'How bad is it damaged?'

'The planks were severely burned and are now less than half the thickness that they were.'

'Can they be fixed?'

'He has tried, my lord, but many need replacing and we have no timber suitable.'

'Can any be salvaged from the two wrecks?'

'They have gone, my lord, the river rose in the night and washed them away. The Mandan say there was a storm in the hills last night and the river often rises higher than a man's head.'

'What are you saying, Geraint? Can the *Dragon* be fixed or not?'

'It can, my lord, but will take many months. Our tools are few and we need to find a source of suitable trees from which to draw planks.'

Tarian stared at Geraint, struggling to contain his anger.

'Is there no other way?'

'My lord, the carpenter says if we risk the open sea without repairing the hull, she will sink in the first storm we encounter.'

'Then surely our path is clear, Tarian,' said Sir Robert. 'We have to make the repairs needed or we will never get home. A few more months are nothing to ensure the success of our quest.'

'Months, Robert? I fear it will be more than that. The winds already get cold and winter is around the corner.'

'I hear they do not have winters as we do in Wales.'

'Perhaps not, though it is not snow or ice I fear but the storms. Achak tells of winds that uproot trees and throw them as if they were nothing. We cannot risk coming this far and having our future ripped from us due to bad weather.'

He stopped talking and stared up toward the chief's hut a few hundred paces away. Outside the hut he could see Machitaw waiting along with six armed warriors. Finally he turned back to Geraint.

'Go back to the ship,' he said. 'Tell them to beach the *Dragon* and secure her for the winter, I will arrange manpower from Achak to get her ashore. Task the carpenter to effect what repairs he has to. We will speak to the Mandan and find what trees we can before the winter sets in. After that I want every capable man working on the repairs. By the time spring comes I want that ship stronger than when we first sailed from Caerleon.'

'What about the men at arms, my lord?' said Sir Robert, 'they know nothing of ships and I fear they will only get in the way.'

'They will help find the desired trees,' said Tarian. 'After that, task them with building the mangonels the chief desires so much.'

'Tarian, what about Pachua? I thought we were going to ask him about Madoc's descendants?'

'There's no rush now, Robert. Let the chief play his games. We will concentrate on repairing the *Dragon*, but until he deems fit to deliver his promise, hold back on the mangonels. They are our only bargaining point and we should use it well.'

'So what now?'

'Go amongst the village and gather the men. We will meet at the ship at dawn and bring her further ashore, we may be stuck here for a while but we will not have idle hands.'

'So be it,' said Sir Robert and strode away to his task.

'What about the men, my lord? Do you want them camped at the river?'

'I am not a cruel man, Geraint, and the Mandan are generous hosts. Let the men sleep in comfort amongst the native huts, but make it known that any who do not report for duty each morning will be flogged in front of the village. Comfort is one thing; laziness I will not countenance.'

'Yes, my lord,' said Geraint.

'One more thing,' said Tarian. 'Speak of our situation in a positive manner. They will be missing their homes and we do not need despondency. The task has been extended by a few months, nothing more.'

'Of course, my lord,' said Geraint and headed back to the village.

Tarian watched him go before looking back at the chief's hut.

'There is still a resolution to be had,' he said quietly to himself, 'and this quest has not ended.'

Chapter Twenty-one

The New World

The following winter was hard for Tarian and the surviving members of his fleet. The *Dragon* was damaged far worse than had been thought and ended up being hauled far from the river to avoid the floods the winter rains brought. Many weeks were spent trying to find the right sort of timber to make the repairs and when a suitable forest was found, it was so far away it often took days to bring the trunks back to the edge of the river. Samuels the carpenter rejected some of those found as not suitable, often resulting in vicious arguments between him and the men doing the hauling. Finally Tarian had to intervene and went to the temporary dry dock to confront him.

'Samuels,' he called as he neared the grounded ship, 'attend me.'

The carpenter threw down his adze and walked over to where Tarian waited.

'My lord?'

'Samuels,' said Tarian with barely veiled anger, 'I am sick to my gut of hearing about you and your temper. This winter has been hard enough but I am aware how hard this work is and have deliberately stayed out of the argument. However, this can't continue. Our men bring you the best they can find and travel days to find suitable wood, yet I hear you reject eight from ten. Tempers wear thin and if you don't ease your unreasonable demands, I fear it is only a matter of time before someone breaks and you find a blade between your shoulders. Now, I accept you want to do a good job but I demand your manner is eased before tempers break and I lose my only carpenter.'

Samuels stared at Tarian without speaking.

'Well?' said Tarian.

'Well what?' asked Samuels.

'Will you curb your manner and ease your demands of the men?'

'I will not, my lord.'

Tarian was taken aback and stared at the carpenter with narrowed eyes.

'Explain yourself, Samuels, before it is my temper that snaps this day.'

'My lord, do you remember the day I first took your coin back in Caerleon?'

'I do.'

'Then you will remember what you said that day?'

'Remind me?'

'You told me you wanted the best carpenter in Wales and that man had one role only: to return the fleet safely from distant shores across seas unknown.'

'I did and that is still what I expect.'

'Then I will make no apology for my manner or what seems like unreasonable demands of the ignorant.'

'The ignorant?'

'Ignorant in the ways of my trade. Would I dare to show an archer how to string a bow or instruct a knight the art of swordsmanship? Of course not, but by similar standard I will not countenance being judged by those who know not one tree from another.' He looked around and picked up a nearby piece of planed wood. 'Give me your dagger,' he said.

Despite the carpenter's impertinence, Tarian handed over his knife.

Samuels inserted the blade into the end grain until there was a gap big enough for his fingers.

'This is typical of what they bring,' he said and throwing the knife to one side, tore the log in two with his bare hands. Tarian was astonished.

'The grain is as loose as a linen weave,' said Samuels, 'and would last but days in the hammering of the waves.' He looked around and picked up another log. 'This sucks up water like a woollen cloth and that pile over there is as tough as iron and will not take working by a blade. We have one ship left, my lord, and you have tasked me with getting it back to Wales in one piece. Given the right timber I will do that but I will do it in my time and to my standards.'

'And how long will this take?'

'It may take weeks or it may take a year, I know not but I do know is this: if I use the rubbish brought so far then the *Dragon* will be little more than splinters on the open sea. I am but one man, Tarian, and though I can make the *Dragon* seaworthy again, there are not enough hours in the day to do it all alone. Get me the right timber and it will be all the quicker.'

'The men travel for days seeking the right wood.'

'Then double the distance if need be. Tell them not to return unless they have found trees similar to the oak of home. I will furnish them with samples of suitably grained wood so they can judge the match. The trees are out there, Tarian, for I have already received some but they are few and far between. The search parties must be more diligent and curb their keenness to return to the fires of the native huts and the flesh of their women.'

'You think their priorities are becoming fogged?'

'As are yours, Tarian. We have been here for six months and I see flab about the bellies of the men. Some of their women are with child and I fear we are all at risk of adopting these people as our own. The men are not solely at fault for they have found a comfortable life of plenty. To stay would be the easiest option and I fear they do not pay the task as much attention as they could.'

'You are right,' said Tarian picking up his knife. 'The men have become soft and the fault lies with me.' He paused before continuing. 'Sharpen your tools, Samuels, and set out your trestles. You will have the timber you need for I will lead the search myself.'

'It is the right decision, my lord,' said Samuels and watched as Tarian walked back toward the native village.

—

Geraint lay under a heavy buffalo blanket in the hut he shared with Kamoi, the Mandan woman he had met on the first night. He was suffering from a fever and she sat alongside him bathing his head with cool water as they waited for his strength to return. The medicine man had spent many hours chanting his strange words and making foul smelling smoke from the flames of the fire. Finally the worst was over but when Tarian ducked into the hut, Geraint was still too weak to get up.

'Tarian,' said Geraint weakly, 'it is good to see you.'

'And you, Geraint. I see your recovery is delayed.'

'The worst is over, but I would struggle to fight a babe such is my weakness.'

'Then you will stay here,' said Tarian, 'and in my absence, assume my authority.'

'Your absence, my lord? Where are you going?'

'We need timber for the *Dragon*, Geraint. I am taking the men out on an expedition to find a suitable source. We could be gone for quite a while but it is important we reignite the flame of the quest.'

'Then I will come with you,' said Geraint, struggling to rise.

'No, you will stay,' said Tarian. 'I am leaving a group of ten to help the carpenter and there are others who are afflicted with the same ague as you. Stay here and when you are strong, see that they are gainfully employed either by helping Samuels or with weapon training. Our muscles have become soft and our blades rust through lack of use. The carpenter says he need two dozen trunks to finish the repairs and that is what he will get. We have lingered long enough, Geraint. It is time to finish what we started.'

The following day Tarian led a column of foot soldiers up into the hills alongside a hundred Mandan warriors. Geraint watched them go through the doorway of the hut until Kamoi insisted he returned to the fire. For a week he grew steadily stronger until finally he was able to walk around the village without getting out of breath.

—

Tarian had been gone for ten days and Geraint took advantage of a mild evening to walk up a nearby hill with Kamoi until finally he sat on a ridge and stared down at the scene before him. Directly below, the village sprawled out along the valley floor between the lake edge and the palisade wall that stretched across the valley. Smoke tendrils stretched from hundreds of Mandan huts and the smell of roasting meat rolled up the slopes to tease their hunger.

'You have a good life here, Kamoi,' said Geraint.

'It is our way,' said Kamoi. 'When it is good, it is good, but when the Apalach carry the war bow, many tears are shed.'

'Why they haven't bothered us since the battle at the river?'

'Winter is a bad time to make war and all people stay at their campfires. When the sun warms the earth, then they will come.'

'Are you worried?'

'It is the way it is,' said Kamoi.

'Kamoi,' said Geraint, 'you know that when the spring comes, I will have to leave this place.'

'You could stay with us.'

'It is very tempting,' said Geraint, 'but there are greater things before us. The fate of a nation may rest on us finding the man we seek.'

'You seek the sons of Madoc?'

'We do and your chief keeps his counsel until we make him the weapons he demands.'

'The fire throwers will kill many Apalach.'

'Don't pin your hopes on the mangonels, Kamoi. They are best used against fortifications not foot soldiers and though you may kill many with the first volley, a determined attack can overwhelm a battery of mangonels within minutes.'

'Then why does your leader not say this to Pachua?'

'They play the games of men,' said Geraint. 'Tarian won't tell Pachua the folly of such weapons whilst the ship is being repaired and Pachua won't reveal the location of

Madoc's people. But soon, both men must talk sense or all will suffer.'

'Geraint,' said Kamoi, 'there is something you should know.'

'What is it?'

'Pachua too holds secrets to his chest.'

'What sort of secrets?'

'About the descendants of Madoc.'

'What of them?'

'You speak as if there are many and you would take a young man as a leader?'

'Not quite a leader, but yes, a descendant of Madoc could help my country unite against our oppressor.'

'Pachua gives you false hope, Geraint. The last of Madoc's line died out many winters ago and now only his son's wife lives to tell the stories of the days of our grandfathers.'

Geraint stared in disbelief.

'No,' he said, 'you must be wrong.'

'I am not wrong,' said Kamoi, 'for I take food to the old woman when her baskets are low. She tells me the stories of the old days when your kinsmen reached these lands.'

'You know where she lives?'

'She stays in the Welsh cave with the body of Madoc's son.'

'What is the Welsh cave?'

'It is a place where the son of Madoc fell to the Apalach many years ago. He lived as a Mandan and fought alongside us against the Apalach but they hated the white skinned and vowed to rid our lands. They brought a great war party and many Mandan fell. Madoc's son hid in the Welsh cave but died beneath an Apalach axe. His body lies there still.'

'Then our quest has been in vain,' said Geraint.

'No,' said Kamoi, 'it has just led you to a different path. Now there is no need to return to your lands and you can stay here with the Mandan. Live alongside us as one and join with our people. Together we can fight the Apalach and become the masters of these mountains.'

'I don't know, Kamoi,' said Geraint. 'This news is too great to make a decision such as this. Tarian needs to know. There are men who crave to see the sea cliffs of Wales again and have families they have not seen for a long time.'

'Do you have sons?' asked Kamoi.

Geraint paused and looked at her without speaking.

'Do you have sons, Geraint of Wales?' she asked again.

'No, but there is a woman.'

'What is her name?'

'She is called Misha ain Alsabar and she comes from the Holy Lands.'

'The Holy Lands?'

'A place far, far away where people kill each other in the names of their Gods.'

'Are the Apalach there also?'

'No,' smiled Geraint, 'but there are other people who are just as warlike. This world is a big place, Kamoi, and it seems there is no place of peace.'

'If you stay and fight the Apalach, perhaps we can make these mountains a place of peace. We can build a hut and raise strong sons together.'

'You are a good woman, Kamoi, but my place is at home alongside Misha. I have never kept my wish to go home from you.'

'I know this,' said Kamoi, 'but hoped you would change your mind.'

'So what of this old woman,' asked Geraint. 'You say she knows of the time of Madoc.'

'She was the woman of Madoc's son,' said Kamoi. 'Her mother watched Madoc's ships sail up the rivers for the first time and passed down the stories to our children.'

'Can you take me to her?'

'Why would you want this?'

'We have sailed across a vast sea and it seems our quest has been in vain but at the very least, it would be good to hear of the man himself. If you will take me there, I can ask her of how it was and what became of him.'

Kamoi nodded and stood up.

'Come,' she said, 'we must get some sleep and when the sun rises, I will take you there.'

Geraint stood and together they walked down the hill.

-

The following day they took a path through the mountains carrying a woven bag of dried fruit and smoked fish for the old woman. For most of the day the path wound through forests of tall trees until finally they reached a small river. Kamoi led them upstream until they reached a waterfall where she pointed to a cave entrance high in the cliff face.

'This is the Welsh cave,' said Kamoi, 'Angenni lives within.'

'Is that her name?'

'Yes, it means "little spirit". Wait here and I will ask if she will see you.'

Geraint watched her climb the rocks and disappear into the cave. For hours he waited until finally Kamoi emerged and called down.

'Angenni will see you now.'

Geraint climbed the rocks and crouched low to get into the cave. The inner space stank of smoke, which had blackened the low ceiling. A few logs burned against a far wall and Geraint could see a frail form wrapped in a deerskin blanket. Kamoi sat cross legged at the fire and told Geraint to join her.

Geraint stared across the flames at the woman. Her head was bent forward and her tangled white hair hung down onto her lap. Slowly her head rose and though the light was poor, he could see she was older than any person he had ever seen before. Her eyes were sunk deep into her face and as she spoke for the first time, he could see there was not a single tooth left in her mouth.

'Ger-aint,' she said slowly, carefully forming the Welsh words, 'you seek the seed of Madoc.'

'It is true, Angenni,' said Geraint. 'His father once ruled the lands of my birth. We came seeking his descendants and hoped to lead them home.'

'Madoc is long dead, Ger-aint. His sons fed these lands with their blood and his line died out many years ago.'

'Kamoi told me of this,' said Geraint.

'So why do you still search?'

'I want to know what they were like, Angenni. They may be dead but still have a tale to tell. Show me who they were and how they lived. You saw them with your own eyes and I would learn about men who venture across unknown seas without knowing if any land exists. Such men truly have no fear in my eyes.'

'I never shared food with Madoc,' said Angenni, 'so can't tell of the man himself. My time was with his son and I was his woman until he was killed by an Apalach war axe. His body lies deeper in the dark.'

Geraint glanced toward the back of the cave.

'I thought your way was to leave your dead to the winds and the rains?' said Geraint.

'It is,' said Angenni, 'but before he died, he asked that his body be placed beneath the soil. I honour his wish but by doing this, his spirit is not free to return to the winds. This is why I stay.'

'It must have been a strange time when they first arrived,' said Geraint.

'My mother told of great joy amongst the elders,' said Angenni, 'for Madoc's ships were not the first. Many such men have come to our lands for many generations and all have shared food with the Mandan. Many stayed and built great villages of stone to protect them from the Apalach.'

'You talk of castles?'

'This is the word they used. Many were built but they now lay fallen amongst the tree roots, nothing more than lairs for the beasts that crawl.'

'Castles take a long time to build, Angenni, and take hundreds of men.'

'They were built over the time of many grandfathers,' said Angenni. 'At first they were places of strength but the Apalach kept coming. Now they turn to dust.'

'But that means there must have been ships travelling between our lands for hundreds of years.'

'Madoc was the greatest of them all. His name will be spoken around Mandan fires until we are no more.'

'If so many came, surely their descendants would still be here.'

'We are their seed, Ger-aint. We keep alive the old words in their memory. Many Mandan have eyes of blue and light hair. These are the line of Madoc. Look to the warriors for many grow hair upon their face as do you;

this is not a Mandan thing and is brought by the blood of their Welsh grandfathers. Our people call you Gods, Ger-aint, but I know you are only men. You tread the same paths of many predecessors yet like all before you, you too will die and the winds will still blow.'

'I have no intention of dying yet, Angenni.'

'Death is but a heartbeat away, Ger-aint. Whether by Apalach axe or passage of time, the span is thinner than an insect's wing. You will die and others will come, the circle will continue. But I see a change coming, Ger-aint. My people are innocent to your ways and will become buffalo to your strength. Each time you come, your ships are bigger, your lances longer and your bowstrings tighter. The Apalach are strong and the keepers of these lands but even they will soon fall to your strength. When this happens, all tribes will fall to the invader. Mandan, Apalach, Seminole or Miccosukee, all will fall. It may not be by your hand or even the hand of your sons' sons but eventually men will come and swat away the Apalach as I swat away a fly. On that day, the earth will cry.'

'Surely this will be good. The Apalach are your enemies.'

'The mountain lion is the enemy of the deer yet they exist side by side. Take away one and the spirits cry at the imbalance.'

'You don't know this will truly happen,' said Geraint.

'Madoc's people told of great things,' said Angenni, 'of huge places where people live with no air. They said countries fight each other for more space and brother fights brother for land and honour. When the land is not enough, they will look toward the Mandan plains as did Madoc and soon the ships will number as the birds in the sky. It is the way of your people.'

For hours Geraint talked to Angenni and learned what he could about Madoc and finally stood to leave.

'Angenni,' he said, 'I would pay respect to Madoc's son and beg leave to pray at his grave. Do you consent?'

'It is your way,' she said and nodded at Kamoi. 'Take him.'

Kamoi picked up a burning branch from the fire and led Geraint to the back of the cave. The roof swept down until Geraint had to duck but eventually, they stood in a small side cavern. Kamoi left him alone and returned to the old woman. Geraint held up the torch to see the cave properly. Piled at the back was a mound of rusting armour but in the centre, an elongated circle of rocks outlined where the man was buried.

Geraint knelt alongside the grave and prayed silently in the darkness. When he was finished, he sat for a while, alone with his thoughts. His mind was awash with what this man's father and his men had gone through in this new world. They had found a strange country with stranger cultures and no doubt their days were spent full of uncertainty and fear, knowing they would never return to their homes. They had to make it work or die; it was as simple as that.

With a sigh he stood up, knowing that his own journey had come to an end. As soon as Tarian returned, he would let him know what Angenni had said and they could focus all their energies on repairing the ship. It was a sad realisation but one that Geraint welcomed with all his heart.

Out in the main cave, the two women watched him return.

'Are you done, Ger-aint?'

'I am done,' he said, 'and would leave you alone with your memories.'

'I am not alone, Ger-aint; the spirits are with me.'

Geraint nodded.

'One more thing, Angenni,' he said, 'the grave is of Madoc's son. Do you know where Madoc himself lays?'

'Nobody knows,' said Angenni, 'for he was not in the lands of the Mandan when he went to the spirits.'

'Had he gone inland?'

'No, Ger-aint, he went back to his own lands.'

'You are mistaken,' said Geraint. 'Thrice, Madoc sailed to your lands but after the third time, he never returned to Wales.'

'You are right that his fleet came three times,' said Angenni, 'but the third time it arrived without him. He stayed in his homeland.'

Geraint stared at the woman in disbelief.

'This cannot be,' he said. 'The man buried back there is his son; he must have been here.'

'His son was born on his second visit,' said Angenni. 'When he went back the last time, he never returned.'

'But I saw the mast of the ship in the village. It must have made it back.'

'The ship did, as did the others, but Madoc was not aboard. He stayed at home to nurse his sick woman and newborn son. The tale was told to us by the new people who came on the ships.'

Geraint sat back down.

'Can you tell me the tale, Angenni?' he asked. 'It could make all the difference.'

'I tire,' said Angenni, 'but will speak when I awake. Come back at dawn and I will tell you the tales of my forefathers.'

Kamoi and Geraint left the cave and set up a small camp near the river below. Kamoi lit a fire and after sharing a meagre meal, they settled down to sleep.

–

The following morning, Kamoi woke to find Geraint had gone. She checked the signs but soon realised he had gone back to the cave. She climbed the rocks and went inside. Angenni still slept but there was no sign of Geraint. Kamoi made her way to the rear of the cave and found Geraint sitting at the foot of the grave he had visited the day before. The room was illuminated by the flames from a fire pot Geraint had brought with him.

'What are you doing here?' she asked.

'I couldn't sleep,' he said.

'Angenni may be offended.'

'I only pay my respects,' said Geraint. 'This man was a Christian and it disturbs me that his final resting place is marked by nothing more than stones.'

'It is our way,' said Kamoi.

'But not ours,' said Geraint. 'There are no stones large enough for a headstone so I made this.' He picked up a simple cross he had fashioned from two branches. It stood half the size of a grown man.

'It's not much,' he said, standing up, 'but every man should have a marker.' He walked to the far end of the grave and pushed the cross into the soil before removing a crucifix from around his neck and hanging it over the upright part of the cross. The chain glistened in the dim light of the fire pot as the tiny figure of Christ span slowly above the grave.

'It is fitting,' said Kamoi quietly.

'What are you doing here?' asked a voice and they turned to see Angenni standing in the dark.

'Old mother,' said Kamoi, 'we meant no harm. Geraint has made offering to his own Gods in honour of a fellow warrior. No offence was intended.'

Angenni shuffled forward and lifted the crucifix in the palm of her hand.

'He wore one such as this,' she said, 'but it was taken by the Apalach when he died.' She turned away and returned to her fire, closely followed by Kamoi and Geraint.

After eating a porridge of maize, Angenni sat back and stared at Geraint.

'Ask your questions, Ger-aint,' she said, 'and I will tell you what I know.'

For the next few hours, Geraint heard the history of how Madoc arrived in the lands of the Mandan only to find they were not the first. Tales abounded of men from across the sea who had visited these shores for many generations. Some had come in peace while some had come to conquer but Madoc was the first to settle amongst the Mandan and it was for this reason they had become embedded in the local culture.

He heard of how Madoc came first with four ships and was made so welcome by the Mandan he returned home to gather more volunteers to form a colony. Once again, he returned having lost only one ship but soon left again to bring the rest of his family and though he left his son behind with the Mandan to oversee the growing colony, his wife travelled with him back to Wales. During the voyage, Madoc's wife had fallen pregnant and though they reached Wales safely, the birth was difficult and the baby very weak. Despite this, plans were made to sail another fleet and eventually Madoc's seconds managed to raise enough funds for another six ships. Commoners begged for inclusion on the exodus to the new world but as the time approached, Madoc's wife got worse and he refused to leave her side. As the winter approached the fleet was under pressure to leave and finally, he made a decision. The ships would sail without him and he would travel the following spring when the weather was good and his family strong. That was the last they ever saw of him in the new world.

'I assume he did sail eventually,' said Geraint when Angenni finished her tale, 'but was lost at sea.'

'Perhaps,' said Angenni. 'The last of his people arrived and told us the tale. For many years they lived amongst the Mandan but many died at the hands of the Apalach. Those who survived walked upriver to seek a new life inland.'

'Did they survive?'

'Many tribes live inland who do not welcome strangers. We heard of many battles and when we traded with the peoples of the north, they offered spears decorated with the scalps of white men. No more was ever heard.'

'So that's it,' said Geraint. 'It ends here. Thank you, Angenni, your counsel has opened my eyes. I will convey your words to our leader and we will return home as soon as our ship has been fixed.'

'Before you go, I would give you a gift,' said Angenni and removed a pendant from around her neck. On the end was an oval flat stone inscribed with a strange diagram resembling a letter 'V' overlaid with another 'V' though this time inverted.

'Madoc was a great man, Ger-aint,' she said, 'and our elders honoured him with his own mark. This charm belonged to him and then his son; now it belongs to you.'

'Why?' asked Geraint.

'You replaced the sign of your own God on the grave of Madoc's son,' she said. 'This is powerful medicine and I know his spirit can finally rest. Now I too can leave and sing the wind songs at the campfires of the ancients.'

'What do you mean?' asked Geraint taking the pendant.

'After this day, my songs will join the winds. It is a good thing. Go home, Welsh man, and let the medicine of Madoc's charm take you safely across the seas.' With that, Angenni closed her eyes and sat back against the wall.

'But…'

'Geraint,' interrupted Kamoi, 'there is nothing more to be heard, it is time to go.'

'Goodbye, Angenni,' said Geraint but when no answer came, he stood up and followed Kamoi out of the cave.

'Kamoi,' he said as they walked, 'what did Angenni mean when she said she can visit the fires of her ancestors?'

'It means that she will die this day,' said Kamoi.

'But how does she know?'

'It is her choice, Geraint,' she said. 'It is our way.'

Geraint said no more but as he walked, he fingered the pendant of Madoc hanging around his neck. The quest may be over but he had a tangible memory of the man himself.

Chapter Twenty-two

Gwynedd

For months, Garyn rode with the Blaidd, riding as mounted guards and protecting Llewellyn's supply wagons from brigands as they passed through the hills. At first, he played a small part but whenever possible, Goddeff took the time to train him in the art of warfare. Every evening they traded blows with dulled practice swords, until Geraint was comfortable in handling a blade as well as any of them.

'Always remember,' Goddeff had said, 'try everything to settle an argument without conflict, but should it be unavoidable, draw your sword for one purpose only, to kill your opponent. A man who enters a fight with the intention of sword play is doomed to failure. Go for the death blow immediately and always suspect a second assailant in the shadows. A man is at his most vulnerable when he stares down at another drawing his last breath.'

Over the months Goddeff added lance work to Garyn's skills, not as a favoured method of combat but so Garyn would know how to react should he be attacked by a lancer. At first Garyn was shocked at the methods, but he soon realised Goddeff was more concerned with success in combat, no matter what it took, and any unnecessary drills or tactics already learned in his past, no matter how chivalrous, were soon forgotten as he learned how to fight dirty.

'I have to admit,' said Garyn one evening after a session on how to hamstring a charging horse, 'your methods stray far from those learned in the service of Cadwallader.'

'I make no apology, Garyn,' said Goddeff. 'Cadwallader was a good knight and few could better him in his day, but I would have put any man here against him and wagered my life on the outcome.'

'How so?'

'Cadwallader was a good man, but like many others he was blinkered by tradition and chivalry. When it comes to keeping your life, I would prefer skulduggery and trickery.'

'And my father?'

'What of him?'

'What sort of knight was he?'

'One that survived the wars. That's all you need to know.'

'A mercenary.'

'That fact you already knew and by using the techniques that I am teaching you, he survived long enough to start a family. If nothing else, remember that one fact.'

Garyn sat in silence as he remembered his father but his reverie was short-lived when Goddeff stood up once more.

'Enough talk,' said Goddeff, 'we have work to do. From now on we will concentrate on the knife.'

Garyn's training continued for many weeks until finally the day came when his skills were put into practice. The Blaidd were riding as escorts to a supply column when one of Goddeff's forward scouts rode back to speak to the leader. Goddeff called the Blaidd in and explained the situation.

'There is sign that horses passed this way no more than a few hours ago,' he said. 'These mountains are famed for brigands in the pay of an English lord called Ridgeway. Ridgeway lives across the border but allows these brigands license. They are led by a man called Edmund Burke who holds a grudge against Llewellyn and it seems his men make camp not far from here.'

'How do you know it is him?' asked Garyn.

'There have been rumours of his presence for over a month and he was seen less than ten miles away as recently as yesterday morning.'

'Do you think we have the beating of this man?'

'One to one there is no contest but his numbers are tenfold and we are far from reinforcements. If, as I suspect, he intends setting a trap, then we have little chance and will have to leave the supply train.'

'Desert our posts?' asked Garyn incredulously.

'Llewellyn has no use for chivalrous dead men,' said Goddeff. 'Grain he can buy, experienced men at arms are harder to find.'

'But as mercenaries, surely our role is to defend the supplies?'

'Not at the cost of our lives.'

'Then what has all this training been about?' snapped Garyn, 'if at the first test we are to run away.'

'Run away?' said Goddeff. 'Who said anything about running away?' He turned to the scout. 'You know what to do,' he said. 'We will meet you at the cleft above the river junction at last light. Garyn, look to your weapons; it is time you earned your keep.'

-

Four hours later, Garyn led his horse along a narrow path that wound its way through a dense forest. The Blaidd had ridden hard and though the evening was cold, the sweat ran in rivulets as they climbed the wooded slopes. Finally the single file halted and Garyn peered through the gloom as Goddeff once more met his scout. The message was passed down to tie the horses to the trees and assemble at the forest edge.

Minutes later Garyn joined Goddeff and along with the rest of the Blaidd, he crawled up the last of the slope to peer into the valley below. Along the banks of a river he could see a band of men setting up camp. Waterproof cloaks were stretched between trees providing makeshift shelter from the rain and dozens of men crouched at their campfires against the chill evening air.

'Are they Burke's men?' whispered Garyn.

'They are,' said Goddeff quietly. He pointed over to a man urinating into the stream, 'And there's the man himself.'

Garyn stared in silence. Despite the distance he could see the man was large in stature. His leggings and sleeveless tunic were of black leather and his full black beard was complimented by the black patch over one eye. In his hand he held a pike almost twice his size, tipped with a long slicing blade with a serrated back edge. The point was a four-pointed barb and even this far away, Garyn could see it was a monstrous weapon.

When he was done, Burke returned to the makeshift camp and Garyn watched as he snatched a flask from one of his men to drink deeply.

'A formidable foe,' said Garyn.

'Indeed,' said Goddeff, 'and he holds no fear. That pike can pierce the hardest armour and the blade has removed more heads than the King's executioner.'

'Is he your equal?'

'Perhaps. His strength is formidable, but, in his hands, he holds the one thing that will bring his downfall.'

'His pike?'

'No, the flask. He has a thirst for wine like no other and only when his senses are dulled is he likely to be bettered.'

'So what's the plan?'

'This man has been a thorn in my side for years,' said Goddeff, 'and it's about time he was dealt with. This is what we are going to do.'

For the next few minutes Goddeff outlines his plans. Some men disappeared back down the path with their horses while others retrieved their weapons from the horses' packs. Garyn listened to his part in the scheme and sat in silence as they waited for darkness to fall.

–

Hours later, Garyn and Goddeff made their way down the steep slope taking care not to slip and alert the men below. All along the hill, other members of the Blaidd took up position in the undergrowth in case their support was needed. Finally the two men reached the forest floor and keeping low, crept toward the nearest tent.

At the river's edge, many of Burke's men had congregated around a large fire and were raucously singing the songs of soldiers as they quaffed whatever wine and ale they had managed to steal from the monasteries and taverns in the area. Many were already intoxicated and lay where they had fallen, ignored by their comrades who seemed hell bent on joining them as soon as possible.

'There are no guards,' whispered Garyn.

'Everyone fears Burke,' said Goddeff, 'and in his arrogance, he feels he has little use for defences but make no mistake, there will be men on watch.'

As if to prove his point, a shadowy shape approached from the gloom and Goddeff dragged Garyn back into the shadows.

'That was close,' whispered Goddeff. 'We must take more care.'

'There's another,' said Garyn, pointing across the camp to a man standing near a fire.

'We have to get rid of them,' said Goddeff.

'How?' asked Garyn.

'You are a better bowman than me, Garyn. Do you think you can make a killing shot from here?'

'I'm not sure,' started Garyn.

'Wrong answer,' said Goddeff. 'To succeed, you must have confidence in your own skills or you are as good as dead. Now, I have seen you take a bird from the air with an arrow so surely a target as big as he is but a training shot.'

'I can drop him but I cannot wager on finding his heart.'

'His heart is not the target, Garyn. I need you to pierce his throat.'

Garyn nodded and unslung his bow, selected an arrow and carefully notched it into the drawstring. He took a deep breath and turned to Goddeff.

'I am ready,' he said.

'Wait until the other guard returns,' said Goddeff, 'and as soon I give the signal, drop the man at the fire. If your aim is true, he will not cry out and his fall will be shielded from the eyes of those who celebrate.'

Garyn nodded and watched as the other man circled the camp. Finally the guard approached the hidden men's position and Garyn saw Goddeff draw his knife.

Slowly the leader of the Blaidd raised his hand and Garyn took aim with his bow.

Suddenly Goddeff's hand dropped and Garyn drew a deep breath before steadying his arm and loosing his arrow. The muted thud of the released bowstring made the nearest guard turn and for a second, his eyes widened as he saw Garyn standing in the shadows. Instinctively he reached for his sword but before he could call out, Goddeff's hand clamped over his victim's mouth as his other hand plunged a knife into his victim's throat. Goddeff clung on tightly as the man thrashed out his final death throes but finally lowered him to the ground, lifeless.

'Was your aim true?' gasped Goddeff.

'I'm not sure,' said Garyn. 'My attention was drawn by your kill.'

Goddeff looked toward the fire where the other guard once stood.

'There is no sign,' he said with satisfaction. 'It must have been a good kill.'

'What now?' asked Garyn.

'Burke isn't with the rest of them,' said Goddeff. 'That's not like him. I was hoping he would be silhouetted against the fire and an easy target but his absence concerns me.'

'So what do we do?'

'We haven't come this far to fall back now, Garyn, so now we go and find him.'

'Where?'

'If I know Burke, he will probably be in that big tent with one of his whores.'

Garyn looked over and saw the shape of an old tent in the dark.

'He campaigns with women?'

'All brigands have camp followers, Garyn. They are as essential as bread and wine to these people and give freely of their charms in return for a share of the spoils. If you should be confronted by one, waste no time in cutting her down for their allegiance is with Burke. They will not hesitate to open your throat given a chance. Now, enough talk, follow me.'

Goddeff crouched down and made his way through the darkness to the tent. Within moments they lay alongside the damp linen walls listening for any sounds within.

'I don't hear anything?' whispered Garyn.

Goddeff slowly moved a few of the rocks pinning down the tent walls and indicated to Garyn to crawl inside. Garyn did as he was told and after looking around one more time, Goddeff followed him in.

The interior wasn't as dark as Garyn had expected and was lit from the glow of a small fire at the centre. He looked around, checking for danger but the only man within was snoring quietly under a deerskin cover.

Goddeff looked at Garyn and nodded silently. He had guessed correctly. Not only was their quarry within but he was also fast asleep and would offer no resistance.

Garyn swallowed hard. He knew what they were about to do and he wasn't sure he could go through with it. Killing an enemy with an arrow at a hundred paces was one thing but cutting a sleeping man's throat was quite another. Slowly he shook his head and despite the gloom, he could see the anger in Goddeff's eyes.

The leader of the Blaidd got to his feet and drew his knife before walking slowly across the tent. With one final glance at Garyn, he lowered himself to his knees and after a final pause, grabbed a handful of the deerskin blanket and rammed it onto the sleeping man's face before plunging his knife into his heart. The wounded man struggled briefly but Goddeff pushed his victim's head down firmly as he twisted his knife. Within moment's the man was dead and Goddeff knelt up to gather his breath. He removed the deerskin and stared in confusion at the dead man.

'Garyn, bring a light,' he said.

Garyn picked a burning brand from the fire and carried it across the tent. The two men looked down into the victim's face. The mouth was still open from his muffled attempts at a scream and the dead eyes stared coldly upward to the tent roof.

'I thought Burke had just one eye,' said Garyn quietly.

'He does,' snapped Goddeff, 'this is not him. Come on, we have to get out of here.'

Before they could move a noise to one side made both men spin around in fear. For a few seconds Garyn wasn't sure what he was looking at but soon made out another figure in the darkness. Far from being asleep, this one was wide awake and staring at the men with fear in their eyes. For what seemed an age no one moved and Garyn held his breath, waiting for the shout of alarm that would surely follow.

Seconds passed and still no cry came. Garyn held up the brand and could see the figure was bound and gagged against one of the wall posts.

'It's a prisoner,' he said.

'Cut his bonds,' said Goddeff. 'He can ride with us.'

Garyn ran over but was surprised to see the captive was a woman.

'Goddeff, it's a girl,' he hissed.

'Shit,' answered Goddeff, before adding, 'leave her, Garyn, we can't carry stragglers.'

'But won't they kill her when they find the body?'

'They have no reason to; she was bound the whole time and played no part. Anyway, she's probably one of his whores who got a bit disobedient.'

The girl shook her head wildly and tried to say something through her gag. Garyn reached down and untied the knot.

'No,' she gasped immediately, 'please, set me free. I will be no burden to you I swear.'

'We can't,' said Goddeff. 'When Burke finds what we have done here, he will scour this area for days. We have to move fast and you will only slow us down.'

'Please,' begged the girl, 'don't leave me here with these animals. Just cut my bonds and as soon as we are clear of this place, I will take my chances alone in the hills.'

'I'm sorry,' said Goddeff, 'it's too risky.'

'Then kill me now,' begged the girl through quiet sobs. 'Pierce my heart as you did his, I beseech thee.'

'We will not kill an innocent woman,' answered Garyn, 'so banish that thought.'

'Why not?' cried the girl. 'Death is by far preferable than the torment they put me through. Just give me a knife and I will do it myself.'

'Those who take their own lives are sent to hell,' said Garyn.

'I am already in hell,' she whispered and looked up at him with tears streaming down her face.

Goddeff drew his knife and strode over before Garyn realised what he was doing.

'Goddeff, wait,' he hissed, thinking the girl was about to be killed.

'Fret not, blacksmith,' said Goddeff, 'I may be a mercenary but I have the remains of a heart.' With that he cut the girl's binds and pulled her to her feet. 'Know this, woman,' he said, 'if you don't keep up, we will not wait. Understood?'

'Understood,' she whispered.

Moments later they had left the tent and all three scrambled up the slopes. Halfway up they met one of Goddeff's men.

'Did you get him?' the man asked.

'No,' said Goddeff. 'That man is as elusive as a fox. Withdraw our men and ride from here with all haste. When those bodies are found no doubt there will be hell raised.'

By dawn the Blaidd had returned to the supply column and arranged a different route. Though the attempt on Burke's life had failed, they now knew the whereabouts of his men and could avoid the riskier paths. Goddeff spent the morning talking to the woman and left her with the supply wagon to get some rest and food. Garyn was sitting against a tree when the leader walked over to stand above him.

'I couldn't do it,' said Garyn without looking up.

'Couldn't do what?'

'I couldn't murder the man in the tent.'

'Murder?'

'Isn't that what it was? Cold blooded murder?'

'Why was that so different to dropping that guard with your arrow?'

'I don't know, it just was. The guard was armed and had a role to play. If I had been seen, it could have been me with an arrow in my throat but the man in the tent was sleeping and had no chance. It just feels different.'

'It is the way it is, Garyn. Sometimes you have to do things that go against your innermost beliefs. If that man had been Burke then his death would have avenged many others and stopped the suffering of more in the future.'

'But it wasn't him. It was an innocent man.'

'None of Burke's men are innocent, Garyn, and the fact there are three less to breathe God's air is a blessing to all.'

Garyn looked up as the drivers of the wagon teams urged the horses into action and the supply train creaked into motion.

'So what now?' he asked.

'Now we will continue as normal and escort these supplies to Llewellyn's army. Our route will take us well wide of Burke and I foresee few problems.'

'Then let's get to it,' said Garyn standing up.

'No,' said Goddeff, 'not you, Garyn, your path lies elsewhere.'

Garyn stared at the man in confusion until realisation dawned.

'Oh, I see,' he said eventually. 'I have failed to live up to your murderous expectations so you discard me like a rotten apple core.'

'No, Garyn,' said Goddeff, 'that's not the case. I took you under my wing as you are the son of a friend. In the ranks of Llewellyn you would have been just one more head of cattle waiting to be sacrificed on the battlefield. I could not let that happen. These past few months I have taught you what I can and though the time has been brief, you have all the skills to survive in these challenging times. What I can't teach you is cynicism and brutality; only life has those skills. From here on in you have to find your own way. Choose your own path whether it's that of the Welsh Prince or even the English Crown. Obviously, I would prefer the former but it is your life and the decision is yours. What I will say is this: be your own man and do not enlist into the ranks of any man's army, that way only lies pointless death.'

'Where would I go?'

'Just follow your instincts, Garyn. I will furnish you with a heavy purse and supplies for one month but from here you must control your own destiny.'

'I will not accept your money, Goddeff.'

'It is not a gift but a payment.'

'For what?'

'I want you to do one task for me. I want you to take the girl to Conwy in the north. It turns out her father is the sheriff of Conwy and is a favoured man of Llewellyn. The girl was kidnapped a few weeks ago and subject to Burke's whim. I expect the sheriff will pay a pretty purse for her safe return.'

'Why can't you do it?' asked Garyn.

'Llewellyn needs these supplies. Word has it his brother has turned against him and a battle looms between the two factions. He needs these wagons intact and with Burke on the rampage, I cannot risk leaving them unguarded. Our path lies eastward while Conwy is on the north coast. I will have one of the men show you a little used route that will take you safely through the mountains and you can be there in days. Take the girl to safety and claim what reward you can.'

Garyn nodded silently and caught the leather purse that Goddeff tossed toward him.

'You are a good man, Garyn,' continued Goddeff, 'and can match any man with most weapons. Avoid conflict where you can but where it is inevitable, don't stand with ceremony or noble intent. Deal your blows with one aim only: a quick kill. For it is what you can expect from any opponent, worthy or otherwise.'

'So it ends here?' said Garyn, staring at his friend.

'Oh no, Garyn ap Thomas,' said Goddeff, grasping the young man's forearm, 'for you, this is just the beginning. Take this opportunity to choose your own path and if it leads you back to us, then so be it.'

Garyn watched him walk over to his horse and then ride after the last wagon. Within moments they had disappeared into the treeline and Garyn turned to see the rescued girl talking to Eric, the mercenary he had first met many months earlier.

'Hello again,' said the girl as he approached.

'I am Garyn,' he said 'and have been tasked with returning you to your father.'

'So I am told,' she said, 'and the sooner we go the better.'

'Why the urgency?'

'It is a tale for later, Garyn,' she said, 'but suffice to say, I yearn to see my home again.'

'Understandable,' said Garyn and turned to Eric.

'Are you to show us the route?'

'I will ride alongside you today only,' said Eric, 'and be gone by dawn. By then your path will be clear. Now, as the lady says, look to your equipment and let's get out of here.'

Chapter Twenty-three

The mountains of north Wales

Garyn and the girl rode up into the mountains. They took the little-known paths and were soon deep amongst the huge rocky monoliths that separated north Wales from the rest of the country. Eric had left them earlier in the evening and they had one more night to spend above the snowline before they descended into Conwy. Garyn made a small fire and warmed some meat in the flames before sitting beside the girl.

'Are you warm enough?' he asked.

The girl pulled her woollen cape tighter around her.

'I will be fine,' she said, 'though truth be told, my stomach aches for a taste of that mutton.'

'It won't be long,' he said. 'So, we haven't had a chance to talk much, why don't you tell me something about yourself.'

'Not much to say,' she said.

'You could start by telling me your name.'

'My name is Bethan Roberts and I am the daughter of the sheriff of Conwy.'

'The daughter of a sheriff,' said Garyn. 'Why does that raise concern within me?'

'Not all such men are corrupt, Garyn; my father is a good man.'

'How did you come to be a prisoner of Burke?'

'I was visiting my family in the mountains when he attacked the farm. He killed everyone but my face was recognised and he ordered me taken alive.'

'Did he… I mean, has he hurt you?'

Bethan stared at Garyn with a cold, intense stare.

'If you mean did he force himself on me, then yes, he did, over and over again. Not just him, Garyn but also his men.'

'I'm sorry, I didn't mean…'

'Don't be sorry,' she said, 'it was not you. Yes, they treated me like a common whore, but I do not judge all men by their actions. They are filth who deserve to die, but I will not allow them to ruin my life further.'

'You are very strong,' said Garyn. 'Many women would crumble at such treatment.'

'Well, this one won't. I will go home and recover my strength. After that, I will engage the best men I can to find this pig and cut out his eyes. I may not fall apart, Garyn, but neither will I forget. Whether it is this year or next, he will feel my wrath.'

'Back in the valley you said you needed to return as soon as possible. Is it to embark on this path of retribution?'

'That is one reason, but there is another. During my time in Burke's tent he talked freely before me. I suppose he thought it was no risk as he intended to kill me anyway. He talked with other men of a mission from Lord Ridgeway to steal an artefact from under Llewellyn's very nose.'

'What artefact?'

'The True Cross.'

Garyn paused and looked at Bethan.

'That's impossible,' he said.

'Why?'

'Because... well, it just is.'

'You are making no sense.'

'The True Cross lies elsewhere in a safe place.'

'You are wrong, Garyn. It lays in the abbey at Conwy. I have seen it myself.'

'You may have seen something, Bethan, but I promise you it wasn't the True Cross.'

'You decry my statement quickly enough but offer no explanation. Why should I countenance your words?'

'Because they are true,' said Garyn. 'The golden cross was sent from Acre to Rome by Longshanks himself.'

'How do you know this?'

'Because I was there when he made the decree.'

'Even if you are right, who is to say that the cross ever made it? Perhaps a switch was made en-route? Perhaps the one in the hands of the Pope is fake and ours is the real one.'

'It matters not,' said Garyn. 'Whichever lies within the abbey at Conwy, it will not contain the true wood of Christ.'

'You make no sense, Garyn. Back up your words or we will change the nature of this conversation.'

'I cannot, Bethan for I have already said too much. Let the matter lay and we will say no more about it.'

'You are a strange one, Garyn,' said Bethan. 'You are a young man yet your eyes are already old. Methinks you have seen many hardships already in your life.'

'The mutton is done, Bethan,' said Garyn leaning forward. 'Let's eat.'

Two days later they rode into Conwy and headed to the town centre. Within moments crowds gathered around the horses as Bethan was recognised by many of the passers-by. Messages were sent to find the sheriff and within half an hour, a band of riders galloped into the village, led by a giant of a man clad in black chainmail. He slid effortlessly from his horse and Garyn watched as Bethan threw herself into her father's arms.

'Bethan,' gasped the man, 'are you in good health?'

'I am a little tired but nothing worse,' she answered.

'Where have you been? We thought you were dead.'

'And I would soon have been if it wasn't for this man and his comrades,' said Bethan indicating Garyn. 'They rescued me from the clutches of a man called Burke.'

'I feared as much,' said the sheriff and turned to face Garyn.

'What is your name, sir?' he asked.

'My name is Garyn ap Thomas and I hail from Brycheniog. I am no knight, sheriff, but a foot soldier who has ridden with the Blaidd these past few months.'

'The Blaidd are mercenaries,' said the sheriff.

'They are, sir.'

'And you count yourself amongst their number?'

'I did, but no more. Is that a problem?'

'Not really. I have never had cause to cross swords with them, yet I find the idea of a roving band of mercenaries distasteful. There is a fine line between Goddeff's men and those of Burke.'

'Apart from the fact that one band abducted your daughter while the other saved her.'

'A point well made, Garyn of Brycheniog. I know not the strength of your sword but your tongue is as fast as a rapier. Come, you will accompany us to our home and feast with my family. We owe her life to you.'

'My lord, before we go, I would beg a favour.'

'Name it.'

'I would go to the abbey and lay hands on the True Cross.'

'The True Cross?'

'Aye. I assume it is still there?'

'It is, Garyn, but you can see it any other day. Come and get rested after your exertions. The abbey can wait until the morrow.'

'No,' said Garyn a little too quickly, 'I need to see it now. I need to put my mind at rest.'

'From what?'

'He will not say, father,' said Bethan, 'but I add my support to his plea. He saved my life; grant him this small boon.'

'Very well,' said the sheriff, 'we will accompany you but hurry before the rain sets in.'

The group walked across the square and through the gloomy streets darkened by the overhanging facades of the wooden buildings. Within five minutes the abbey's tower appeared above the ridgeline and the claustrophobic streets opened up to reveal the magnificent place of worship. They walked inside and Garyn was immediately struck by the profound silence within.

'Where is it?' whispered Garyn.

'Over there,' said Bethan, pointing at a line of people waiting to gain access to the relic. A Cistercian monk held out a leather bag to collect the pennies required for the privilege of praying before the artefact and above them, a golden cross over a cubit in length was fixed against the wall illuminated by dozens of burning candles. Garyn walked over and stared up in wonder. The others joined him and followed his gaze.

'Now, do you believe me?' asked Bethan.

'I need to get closer,' he said.

'But why? It is there before your very eyes.'

'I can't tell you, Bethan but I have to see it close up.'

'Bring the abbot,' said the sheriff to a nearby monk. 'I would bring this to conclusion.'

A few moments later, the abbot joined them at the cross and welcomed the sheriff as an old friend before turning to face the young woman.

'Bethan,' he gasped, 'I have just been told the news but hardly dared believe you are safe. Thank the Lord himself. Are you well?'

'I am fine, Father Carter,' said Bethan.

'What happened to you?'

'It is a long story,' said Bethan, 'and with your grace, perhaps I can share it another time.'

'Of course,' he said and kissed her hands before turning back to her father.

'It is good to see you, Sheriff Roberts, you must be so thankful for the return of your daughter.'

'I am, Father Carter, and we will return to thank the Lord in the proper manner but in the meantime, I have a favour to ask.'

'Name it,' said the abbot.

'We need to let this man touch the cross.'

Father Carter turned to look at Garyn.

'Does he seek a miracle?'

'On the contrary, father,' said Garyn, 'I need to see if a miracle has already happened.'

'I know we ask a lot,' said the sheriff, 'but there will be a significant donation to your funds in return.'

The abbot paused before turning to the nearby monk. 'Clear the abbey,' he said.

A few minutes later, the large doors slammed shut and the monk returned with a ladder. He climbed up to unfasten the iron clasps before passing the cross down to two other monks who placed it carefully on the floor.

'It is even more beautiful close up,' said Bethan.

'The gold is dull compared with its true glory,' said the abbot and knelt beside the cross. 'You are very lucky, young man, for it is soon to be moved from here and placed in a cathedral where its glory will be displayed to the masses.'

Garyn knelt down beside him.

'Where is it?' he asked.

'Where's what?'

'The wood of Calvary,' said Garyn.

The abbot leaned forward and opened a panel in the centre of the golden cross to reveal a glass pane. Everyone leaned forward to see a small piece of aged wood nestled on a red velvet cushion.

'Do you want to hold it?' asked the Sheriff.

'No man can touch it,' said Father Carter, 'for none are worthy.'

'Where did you get it from?' asked Garyn.

'From a friend in the south. He brought it back from the Holy Land. Do you wish some time alone to pray?'

'It's not necessary,' said Garyn with a sigh, 'I have seen enough.'

He stood up and walked away, alone with his thoughts. The sheriff and Bethan watched the monks replace the cross before talking quietly with the abbot. Garyn walked around the walls of the abbey, looking at the many tombs of the nobles who had been laid to rest there over the years. His mind was troubled for what he had just seen was impossible.

'Garyn, we are done here,' called Bethan. 'Will you join us?'

'Of course,' said Garyn and crossed the abbey. He said his goodbyes and left with Bethan and her father. Outside, the storm clouds had gathered and the rain started to fall.

'Are you happy now?' asked Bethan.

'No, not really,' said Garyn.

'You still think it's fake?'

'On the contrary,' said Garyn, 'I believe the cross is true.'

'Then why the concern?'

'Because it means I have been betrayed by one I called a friend.'

'I don't understand,' said Bethan.

'It matters not,' said Garyn. 'There is nothing I can do about it, at least, not yet. Come, your father beckons.'

–

Garyn stayed for several days in the house of the sheriff and was made welcome by the family. In particular, he enjoyed the company of Bethan and found himself drawn closer to her. A week went by and one evening, he was sitting at the family table sharing a meal of chicken and pork. The freshly cooked roasts were a welcome change from the dried meat he was used to and he relished every mouthful. Finally he sat back drinking his ale, enjoying the fact he was warm, comfortable and had a full belly. He made small talk with the family until a knock came at the door and the sheriff apologised as he was summoned to business in the town. A few hours later, he returned and Garyn could see his mind was heavy with concerns.

'Are you alright, Father?' asked Bethan.

'I am fine, girl,' he answered, 'but would have word with this young man. Garyn, can you come with me?' Garyn glanced at Bethan and answered the unspoken question with a shrug of his shoulders before following her father into a smaller room. A roaring fire burned in the hearth and Garyn turned to see the sheriff lock the door behind them. They were alone.

'Please sit,' said the sheriff.

Garyn did as he was bid and found the chair extraordinarily comfortable.

'More ale?' asked the sheriff walking over with a jug.

Garyn nodded and waited silently as the man filled his tankard before replacing the jug on the table and taking his place in the other seat.

'So,' said the sheriff, 'why don't you tell me what's going on?'

'I don't know what you mean,' said Garyn.

Roberts put down his own ale and stared at Garyn.

'What I mean,' he said, 'is what was all that about in the abbey a few days ago?'

'It's nothing to worry about,' said Garyn. 'Forget about it.'

'On the contrary,' said the sheriff, 'there is everything to worry about.'

'Why?'

'Listen, Garyn,' said the sheriff, 'my daughter is kidnapped by the biggest band of brigands in Wales and then rescued by notorious mercenaries. She then returns to tell me one of the holiest relics in the possession of the church is being lined up to be stolen and subsequently, the man who rescued her, who admits to being part of a group with dubious reputation at best, asks to see the relic close up. Now, how do I know that you are not in league with these brigands and just wanted to see the cross to find out the abbey's security measures?'

'That's ridiculous,' said Garyn, 'you spoke to your daughter. She was a captive and we released her.'

'It could have been a situation arranged between you and Burke for this very reason.'

'I can assure you; I am my own man and have no links with Burke or have any plans to take the cross.'

'It's not enough,' said Roberts.

'It's all I have,' said Garyn.

'In that case we have a problem,' said the Sheriff sitting back. 'You see, I have just been to see Father Carter. A few days after we visited the abbey, he received a delegation from his counterpart in Brycheniog. They brought gifts and matters of the clergy but amongst them was a communique regarding a wanted man thought to be headed this way. Apparently, it warned of an outlaw with a grudge against the Church. He even went as far as to name this man, and guess what, that very man shares my house. Now, you dare to sit before me, enjoy my hospitality and tell me I have nothing to worry about?'

'It is not what you think,' said Garyn.

'Then tell me the truth, Garyn, for I am under pressure to arrest you right now and have you returned to Brycheniog to be tried as a thief and a murderer. You would be hanged within days.'

'Sheriff Roberts,' said Garyn, 'the man you mention in Brycheniog is as corrupt a man as ever walked this earth. He killed my family, blackmailed me to obtain a relic from the Holy Land and tried to have my brother murdered. Since then he has stolen my family's lands and sought to discredit my name. Subsequently he forced me to run but I promise you this, I am no brigand.'

'You seem to be a likeable young man, Garyn, and the fact that you saved my daughter means I am forever in your debt but surely even you can see the position I am in? Tell me your tale in its entirety and if I see even the tiniest piece of truth in your words, I promise to do all I can to clear your name.'

'And if I refuse?'

'Why would you refuse to tell the truth?'

'For there is a profound act within my conscience that may yet condemn me.'

'And was this act criminal?'

'It was done with clear conscience and I do not regret it.'

'Talk to me, Garyn,' said the sheriff, 'for at this moment, I am the only hope you have.'

The next few hours, Garyn told the Sheriff of everything he had been through over the previous few years. He left nothing out from the day his family had been murdered right up to the day he rescued Bethan from the clutches of Burke and his men.

'That's it,' he said finally. 'You know everything.'

'Not quite, Garyn,' said Roberts. 'You mentioned something earlier about one act that weighs upon your conscience.'

Garyn nodded slowly. He had wanted to keep it to himself but it was obvious that his life was on the line. For a few moments he hesitated and thought of his old friend from the Holy Land. By filling in this last piece of story he would be doing his friend's memory a disservice but he knew it had to be done and that if Brother Martin was looking down from heaven, he hoped he would forgive him.

'Well?' said Roberts.

'I desecrated the one True Cross,' said Garyn. 'While I was in my cell in the headquarters of the Hospitallers in Acre, I tore apart the artefact and removed the sliver of wood that once touched Christ's bloody flesh.'

Sheriff Roberts stared in astonishment and stayed silent for a while before finding the right words.

'I did not know what to expect, Garyn, but I did not expect that. Are you certain?'

'As certain as I sit here.'

'If this is true, what did you do with it?'

'I hid it about my person and replaced it with a piece of wood from a cheap stool.'

'But why?'

'I was sick of the pain and suffering such false imagery could cause and thought that if I removed the holy fragment, then its draw would diminish and men could live in peace, a foolish ideal in the circumstances.'

'And what did you do with the real fragment?' asked the Sheriff.

Garyn paused before answering.

'I placed it in the dying hands of a great man before he went to his grave.'

'And you saw him buried?'

'I did.'

'So you are sure the fragment lies with him?'

'I dug his grave with my own hands,' said Garyn.

'But in the abbey, I heard you say the fragment was real, if that is so, how can it be in two places at one time.'

'It can't,' said Garyn, 'and that is what is so confusing.'

'Who else knows of this?' asked Roberts.

'Only one other,' said Garyn. 'One whom I once called friend.'

In the abbey at Conwy, Father Carter shared warmed wine with four men in his rooms. They had been there all day and one of the men paced back and forth nervously.

'We should go and get him,' snapped the nervous man. 'After all this time our quarry is within touching distance and we wait like frightened lambs.'

'Be patient, Buckler,' said Brother Maynard. 'We have not come this far to fall at the final hurdle. Let the law take its course and we can take him back alive.'

'Gerald will accept his head as evidence,' said Buckler. 'Why wait for someone else to make a decision? We can get in there, kill him and be back on the road south within hours.'

'Alive he is worth twice as much,' said Sir Gibson, 'and besides, I will not be party to the murder of a man without trial. Curb your impatience, Buckler, a few more hours matters not.'

The abbot spoke up, interrupting the conversation.

'What I don't understand,' he said, 'is what act can be so vile that Sir Gerald demands this boy should die?'

'It matters not, father,' said Sir Gibson, 'just be comfortable in the knowledge he is a brigand and as such lies outside of the law. When the sheriff hands him over, he will be returned to justice in Brycheniog.'

'I just think we should give him the chance to explain his story,' said the abbot. 'After all, he saved an innocent's life just days ago and, as such, may deserve a little mercy himself.'

'We have been on the road for over a year,' said Buckler, 'and the only mercy he can expect from me is a quick death.' The abbot was about to argue but the sound of door slamming made them all look at each other.

'What's that?' asked Dafydd who up till now had remained quiet.

'It is the main door of the abbey,' said the abbot. 'It seems we have company.'

'About time,' said Buckler, 'let's get this over with.'

The five men walked out into the main hall and stopped before the altar. At the far end, they could see the sheriff of Conwy and Garyn walking down the aisle toward them. Nobody spoke but as they grew closer, Garyn's eyes locked on those of Dafydd, the friend he had rode alongside on his journey to Acre many years previously. Finally they all stood opposite each other and waited in the silence.

'Sheriff Roberts,' said the abbot, 'thank you for coming. I am sure we can resolve this sorry state of affairs in an amicable manner.'

'Forget the meaningless talk,' demanded Buckler. 'Hand him over.'

'Buckler, hold your tongue,' said Sir Gibson, 'I am in charge here and this will be done in the proper manner.' He turned to face the sheriff and Garyn. 'Sheriff,' he said, 'I have here a communique authorising the release of this criminal into my custody. On behalf of Sir Gerald of Essex, I am grateful to you for doing your duty and I will ensure suitable reward is sent back as soon as we return.'

'My lord,' said the sheriff, 'I understand you are keen to carry out your task but I question your authority here and would seek more information from the abbot.'

'And why would you do that?'

'Because all may not be as it seems and there is a possibility this man is innocent of all charges.'

'Horseshit,' shouted Buckler. 'The man is as guilty as sin itself and you have no right to challenge our authority. We demand you hand him over immediately or face the consequences.'

Sir Gibson grabbed the arm of Buckler as he reached for his sword.

'Be still,' he said. 'The man has asked for further evidence and there is always merit in such an action.' He turned to face the sheriff. 'We would not see an innocent man die, sir, so what is it you need to know?'

'I would question the honour of Father Williams of Brycheniog Abbey,' said Roberts.

'What has he got to do with anything?' asked Buckler.

'He has everything to do with this,' said Roberts, 'and I hear worrying tales about his integrity not only as a man but as a servant of God.'

'Sheriff,' said Father Carter quietly, 'you besmirch the name of a man I hold in great esteem. I refuse to accept he is of low morals and request you withdraw that statement.'

'He is the sponsor of these men,' shouted Garyn, 'and has personally paid them to ensure my death.'

'Sir Gerald of Essex paid our fee,' said Sir Gibson, 'not the abbot of Brycheniog.'

'Gerald may have passed you the purse,' said Garyn, 'but I am telling you, Father Williams is the paymaster.'

'Young man,' said Brother Maynard, speaking for the first time, 'I can assure you that no servant of the cloth would pay for the death of another man, no matter how heavy the evidence to his guilt. That is the role of the law, who in this case is Sir Gerald of Essex.'

'On the contrary, brother,' said Garyn, 'the man we speak of is not only capable of doing such things but has already sent many to their graves.'

'Nonsense.'

'Is it?' sneered Garyn. 'He arranged the murder of my family as well as blackmailing me to steal an artefact from the Holy Land so he could further his own name.'

'I don't believe you.'

'I don't expect you do,' said Garyn, 'but take not my word for it.' He turned to face Dafydd, 'ask him!'

Everyone turned to Dafydd and could see the strain on the young man's face.

'What is he saying, Dafydd?' asked Sir Gibson. 'Do you know anything of these accusations?'

'I…' started Dafydd.

'Tell them the truth, Dafydd,' said Garyn. 'You know full well my story; tell them of my persecution from that so-called man of God.'

'I'm not sure, Garyn,' said Dafydd. 'They were stories only. I have no way of knowing what was true and what was false.'

'I told you the truth,' hissed Garyn. 'Be true to yourself and speak honestly.'

Everyone stared at Dafydd as a bead of sweat ran down his brow.

'Well?' said Sir Gibson.

Dafydd looked around the group. Every pair of eyes was upon him until finally he took a deep breath and spoke out.

'Like I said, I heard his stories only. I have no knowledge if they were true.'

'Dafydd,' shouted Garyn, 'don't do this.'

'I am sorry,' said Dafydd quietly, 'but I stand by my words.'

'Well,' said Sir Gibson, 'It seems your accusations are no more than the ramblings of a condemned man. Sheriff, I hope your doubts have been answered and I ask again, will you release this man into our custody?'

Sheriff Roberts turned to face Garyn. 'I am sorry, Garyn,' he said. 'There is nothing more I can do.'

'Wait,' shouted Garyn and turned once more to face Dafydd.

'You were once a man of honour, Dafydd. Where is that man who rode against the infidel?'

'Garyn, I have never witnessed any matter to doubt Father Williams. If I did, then perhaps my actions would be different.'

'Then ask yourself this: what about the cross?'

'What cross?'

'The one True Cross, Dafydd. What part did Father Williams play in persuading you to dig up the poor corpse of Brother Martin?'

A gasp of horror escaped Brother Maynard and all heads turned to face Dafydd.

'I know not of what you speak,' said Dafydd.

'Yes, you do, Dafydd, for apart from me, only one other man knew the location of his grave and that man is you. I accuse you of digging up the grave of a man of God and stealing the fragment of the cross.'

'You speak false, Garyn. Retract your accusation.'

'I will not. You dug up the body on the orders of Father Williams and delivered the cross fragment to him.'

'Why would I do that?'

'Only you know the detail but I assume in return to finance the rest of your training.'

'You have no proof of that.'

'What did he tell you, Dafydd? Did he say it was for the glory of God? Did he say it would be displayed in the abbey at Brycheniog? What price is enough to rob the grave of a friend?'

'I say again, Garyn,' said Dafydd drawing his sword. 'Retract your accusation or I will demand redress.'

'Garyn, your wild accusations help you not,' said the sheriff quietly. 'Unless you have proof, let it go. The law must be allowed to take its course.'

'I have proof,' said Garyn, 'and it lies in this very room. Look to the cross of gold upon the wall, Dafydd. What do you think lies within?'

Dafydd shook his head nervously but did not speak.

'I'll tell you what lies within, Dafydd, a piece of wood from Christ's cross, the same wood that soaked up his blood in Calvary,' he paused before adding, 'and the same fragment that I placed in the hands of Brother Martin before I buried him.'

'That's impossible…' said Dafydd.

'You would think so, Dafydd, but I have seen it with my own eyes and it still bears the marks of my knife where I prised it from its housing in that cell in Acre. It is exactly the same piece.'

'This is going nowhere,' said Sir Gibson. 'You weave tales of trickery but all aimed at deceit. There is no purpose in pursuing this further.'

'Then let me give you purpose, sir knight,' said Garyn. 'My life lies in the hands of four men sent on the whim of an evil man. To prove my case I accuse Father Williams of Brycheniog of paying this man to dig up the grave of Brother Martin to retrieve the fragment of the True Cross for his own end. Once in his possession he aimed to sell it to the highest bidder and line his own coffers with the proceeds.'

'That is a serious accusation, Garyn,' said the sheriff.

'It is but I will add meat to the bones. I think that as he was known to have recently returned from the Holy Land and professed to taking the cross to Rome, he couldn't then declare the artefact without casting suspicion on his own name. He had to conceal his new-found bounty and seek an alternative method to realise its value. What better way than to conceal it within another golden cross and have it sold via a different route?'

'Utter nonsense,' said Brother Maynard.

'Is it? Ask Father Carter where he got the cross from.'

All heads turned to the abbot.

'Well?' asked Garyn.

'It is true we received it from Father Williams,' he stuttered, 'but it has been in their possession for many years.'

'How do you know?' asked Garyn.

'His envoys told us so,' said the abbot and the room fell silent as he realised the weakness of the argument.

Garyn finally broke the silence.

'The fragment within that cross is the same piece I brought back from the Holy Land and the only way that can be is if it was stolen from a dead man's grave. If Father Williams sent that cross to you, then he is an accomplice.'

Silence fell in the room again as the implications sunk in.

'Show me,' said Dafydd.

'Show you what?'

'Show me the fragment.'

'Enough of this trickery,' shouted Buckler and before anyone could move, he drew his knife and lunged toward Garyn.

Garyn reacted slowly but Sheriff Roberts saw the move coming and hurled himself at the would-be assassin. Both men fell to the floor but before Garyn could help, Dafydd drew his sword and held it to Garyn's throat.

'Leave it, Garyn,' he said. 'This will play out as it will. Move and I will slice your throat from ear to ear.'

'Why are you doing this, Dafydd?' gasped Garyn. 'We were comrades in arms.'

'You know why,' said Dafydd quietly. 'My future has been snatched from me yet again. I have no sponsor and without knighthood, I have nothing.'

'Is this the course of a true knight, Dafydd?' asked Garyn. 'Where is the honour in this?'

'All I am doing is apprehending an outlaw,' said Dafydd. 'Old friendships do not come into it.'

Behind them the two men fought on the cold slabs of the abbey but within moments Sheriff Roberts disarmed Buckler and pinned him against a column.

'How dare you try to kill a man in a place of worship,' he hissed. 'I will see you hang for this.'

'Unhand him,' said a voice. 'I will decide who dies and who lives in this abbey.'

The sheriff felt a cold blade on the back of his neck and turned slowly to see the abbot bearing a blade.

'Father Carter,' gasped the sheriff, 'what is going on. What do you think you are doing?'

'I am sorry, sheriff,' said the abbot, 'this wasn't supposed to happen but you leave me with no other choice.'

'What are you talking about?'

'The path of a monk is a hard one, sheriff, and after a life of prayer, the nights are no less cold and life is no less short. I grow old, sheriff, and have doubted my faith for a long time. I would see my last few years lived in earthly comfort and the wealth promised by Father Williams would see me a rich man.'

'You are in league with Father Williams,' gasped Garyn, 'I should have known.'

Buckler pulled free from the sheriff's grip and picked up his blade.

'Enough talk,' he said. 'Now they know the truth, they cannot be allowed to live. They have to be killed.'

'Over my cold corpse,' shouted Sir Gibson and drew his sword but it was hardly out of the scabbard before Brother Maynard reached around from behind the knight and dragged a blade across the old man's throat.

Sir Gibson dropped to his knees clutching at the wound, his eyes wide with fear and confusion as blood poured through his fingers.

'He was always the one that was likely to give us trouble,' said Brother Maynard as the old man died. 'Now let's bring this to conclusion.'

Before he could move, Dafydd pushed Garyn to one side and with a mighty swing, drove his blade down through the neck of the monk.

'Garyn, what are you waiting for?' he roared. 'Arm yourself.'

Garyn needed no more invitation and bent to pick up the dead knight's sword. Sheriff Roberts also took advantage of the confusion and with a twist of his body, turned away from the blade of the abbot and knocked him to the floor. Buckler saw the danger immediately and before Dafydd could defend himself, he drove his

332

dagger into the young man's stomach before turning to run through the abbey.

'Stop him,' roared the sheriff but it was too late, he was already out of the door and headed toward the maze of houses outside the abbey.

Garyn turned to Dafydd and saw the blood pouring through the man's hands as he clutched uselessly at his wound. Slowly Dafydd dropped to his knees and Garyn ran to his side.

'Dafydd,' he said, as he laid the young man onto the cold slabs, 'let me see the wound. Perhaps I can stem the blood.'

'It's too late,' Garyn said Dafydd. 'My time is done.'

'Fight it,' Dafydd, 'I will send for a surgeon.'

'No, listen to me for I need to confess. You were right, I did betray you, Garyn. I sold the location of the grave for money but I swear I did not dig up the monk. That was the work of Father Williams and his henchmen. I have regretted it ever since.'

'But why?' asked Garyn gently.

'I was desperate, Garyn. In a moment of ale-fuelled bravado I boasted of our time in Acre and my loosened tongue let slip the story of the cross. Father Williams heard the tale and his men threatened me with public humiliation and starvation in the stocks if I did not reveal its whereabouts. I could not do it, Garyn, I could not face the shame of the stocks so I told them everything. After that... well, you know the rest.'

'Worry not, Dafydd,' said Garyn. 'The truth is now known and I do not hold you responsible.'

'There is one other thing, Garyn,' said Dafydd weakly. 'I did not forsake you completely. That night you were released from the stocks in Brycheniog...'

'What about it?'

'I was there, Garyn, I was hidden in the bushes.'

'To what end?'

'It was I who passed word to Fletcher about your intended murder. I could not reveal myself as I was a trusted man of Gerald. Luckily Fletcher and I got there in time.'

'You saved my life,' said Garyn slowly.

'As you once saved mine,' said Dafydd and gasped as pain racked his body. 'I think my time is close, Garyn,' he said. 'Say a prayer for me when I go. Pray for a misguided soul who only ever wanted to be a knight.'

'You are a good man, Dafydd,' said Garyn gently, 'and in my eyes, will always be the most honourable knight I have ever met.'

Dafydd smiled weakly and his eyes half closed.

'Sir Dafydd of Brycheniog,' he whispered weakly. 'It would have been a wonderful title.'

'It would,' whispered Garyn with tears in his eyes and as Dafydd slipped away, he laid his old friend down on the abbey slabs.

–

A few weeks later, Garyn broke his fast with Bethan one last time as they sat together outside her home enjoying the weak morning sun. A page brought Garyn's saddled horse around from the stable and waited patiently as the young man said his goodbyes.

'So what happens now?' asked Bethan.

'I will return to the Blaidd,' he said, 'and seek a life with Goddeff's men.'

'But why can't you stay here with me? The abbot awaits trial and father has arranged the cross to be taken to

Llewellyn for safe keeping. Surely your name is now clear and you can live in peace?'

'Alas no, Bethan, for I have admitted taking the fragment from the True Cross in Acre and in the eyes of the Church, I will always be a condemned man. The Blaidd pour scorn on such indiscretions and within their number, I will have a life of relative freedom.'

'Will we ever see you again?'

'Possibly, for who knows where dwells the man with the higher price?'

'Then travel well, Garyn, and one day I hope you find the peace you seek.'

Garyn stood up.

'There will never be peace for me, Bethan, not while a certain abbot in the south draws breath. But I swear before God, before I die there will be a reckoning.'

Bethan kissed him on the cheek and watched as he walked his horse toward the distant hills and the uncertain life of a mercenary.

Chapter Twenty-four

The village of Dolwyddelan, north Wales – 1280

Two men ducked under the low lintel of a tavern doorway and paused to take in the welcome smell of ale and cawl, an aroma they hadn't smelled for many years. Both wore beards down to their chests and their hair was tied back out of their eyes, eyes that spoke of hardship and pain. Some of the men in the tavern stared at the unkempt strangers but soon turned away when their gaze was returned with a cold stare. For the last eighteen months Tarian and Geraint had travelled from the new world in their last remaining ship along with fifty of the original crew. The rest had elected to stay with the Mandan.

The need for provisions and repairs had delayed them longer than they had wanted but finally the *Dragon* had sailed from the lands of the Mandan and though the cruel seas had pounded the battered ship relentlessly, it had finally grounded on the shores of Ireland and many of the remaining crew had cried at the feel of solid ground beneath their feet. On the way home they had lost many to disease including Sir Robert of Shrewsbury, Spider and Logger, while others had taken the first opportunity to head in different directions, keen to see their families and forget the ill-fated quest in search of Madoc.

Tarian and Geraint had spent a long time together on the *Dragon* and had become close friends despite the difference in station. In addition they shared a fascination for Madoc and by the time they landed they had made a pact to bring the story of the Prince full circle.

'What can I get you?' asked the inn keeper.

'Four tankards of ale,' said Tarian.

The innkeeper looked over the shoulder of the two men to see if there were any other customers behind them.

'Four?' he asked.

'You heard him,' said Geraint, 'and two large bowls of the cawl in that pot.'

The innkeeper scuttled away and the two men sat on a bench in the corner to wait for their meal.

'Breathe it in, Geraint,' said Tarian, looking around the busy tavern. 'I have dreamed of this day for many years.'

'It has to be said: there is no comparison to a Mandan sweat lodge,' answered Geraint.

The ale was brought over and the innkeeper was told to keep them coming. The cawl soon followed but despite their best efforts, they failed to finish the meal and the bowls were left half full, a consequence of shrunken stomachs from the tiny rations on the trip home.

The innkeeper took away the remnants and poured it back into the pot. As the ale flowed, Tarian opened his purse and fished out his last silver coin.

'Innkeeper,' he said, 'this is the last coin I own in this world. We have been away a long time so what will it get a man in these troubled times?'

'What is it you want?' asked the innkeeper.

'A couple of horses perhaps and two warm beds for the night.'

'Is it real silver?' asked the innkeeper.

'Check it,' said Tarian and tossed it over.

The innkeeper and another man inspected it closely and then looked over in agreement.

'I will give you two horses,' said the second man, 'and my barn is good for a dry night's sleep.'

'What about a couple of women?' asked Tarian.

'You push the value,' said the man, 'but I will give you a copper coin back. At least that way you will eat tomorrow.'

'It was worth a try,' laughed Tarian. 'Include two more ales and we have an agreement.'

Two more tankards landed on the table and the innkeeper placed a copper coin alongside them.

'The horses will be outside in an hour,' he said, 'and I will have a boy show you the way to the barn.'

As he walked away, Tarian drank half his tankard in one draught and wiped the froth from his beard before turning to face Geraint.

'A couple of horses, a good night's sleep and an aching head,' he said. 'Tomorrow should be a good day. What say you, Geraint?'

Geraint didn't answer but slowly reached out and picked up the copper coin.

'Geraint, you fall silent on me,' said Tarian. 'Has the ale muddled your brain already?'

Geraint stared at the coin without answering before standing up and marching over to the innkeeper. He grabbed the man's arm and spun him around.

'Where did you get this?' he asked.

'What?' asked the man.

'This coin,' said Geraint, 'where did you get it from?'

'Unhand me, sir,' shouted the innkeeper. 'It was a fair deal and that coin is genuine.'

'I don't care if it is genuine or not,' snapped Geraint. 'Where did you get it from?'

Two men stood up from their table and walked over to aid the innkeeper. Tarian intercepted them with his hand on the hilt of his sword.

'Stay where you are, gentlemen,' he warned. 'I am as perplexed as you but we will see how this unfolds.'

'I do not mean you any harm,' said Geraint to the innkeeper. 'I just want to know where it is from.'

'I'm not sure,' said the man. 'Many coins pass through these walls; it could be from anywhere.'

'This mark on the back,' said Geraint, 'who makes such a coin?'

'I don't know,' shouted the man. 'Now unhand me.'

'It is the mark of Dolwyddelan,' said the horse seller as he slammed a matching coin on the table. 'It is nothing special, stranger. Now leave him be.'

Geraint let the innkeeper go and the tense atmosphere visible eased.

'Happy now?' asked Tarian.

'Let's get out of here,' said Geraint.

'Why?' asked Tarian. 'We have nowhere to go and I haven't finished my ale yet.'

'On the contrary,' said Geraint, 'our destination is clear to me.'

'And where would that be?'

'Look at the mark on the coin, Tarian.'

Tarian stared at the strange symbol and shrugged his shoulders.

'It means nothing to me.'

'It does to me,' said Geraint and withdrew the stone pendant from beneath his shirt. 'Look at the etching on this. Does it look familiar?'

'They have the same designs,' said Tarian quietly.

'They do,' said Geraint, 'and what interests me is why does a small Welsh village mint coins with a Mandan mark upon them.'

'I have no idea.'

'Perhaps they were influenced by someone many years ago, someone who must have lived amongst the Mandan.'

'Madoc?' said Tarian.

'Exactly.'

'Then you are right, Geraint. Let's get our horses.'

—

The following day they rode through the outskirts of a village and paused at a crossroads. One path led up to the castle while the other wound down to the thatched houses. Geraint looked up at the castle.

'It all makes sense,' he said. 'Madoc was born in that castle and would have returned to die there.'

'I'm not sure,' said Tarian. 'I have had reason to visit that castle many times in the past and even prayed in the chapel but never have I seen any tomb of Madoc. Surely a prince such as he would have had a tomb there?'

'Perhaps not,' said Geraint. 'Remember when he left, his brothers were divided and fought amongst themselves for his father's legacy. Perhaps the victor did not welcome him back so he sought a humbler resting place, yet close to the place he grew up.'

'Such as?'

Geraint stared over Tarian's shoulders.

'Perhaps a place such as this.'

Tarian followed his gaze and saw a small stone church down a nearby foot path.

'It is worth looking,' said Tarian and together they rode down the track and dismounted before the entrance. The door was open and they walked in to find the quiet space empty except for a solitary priest, praying before the altar. At the sound of their approach the priest turned and his face fell at their appearance.

'Bring peace, brothers,' he said. 'We are a humble church with nothing worth stealing.'

'We are not brigands, father,' said Tarian, 'and seek only information.'

'Then I hope I can help,' answered the priest. 'What do you want to know?'

'We wondered if your church held the tombs of any princes,' said Tarian.

'This little church?' said the priest. 'Unfortunately not. All nobility lie in the grounds of the castle.'

'Are you sure?' asked Tarian.

'I know all the named tombs,' said the priest, 'and all the names on the headstones in the graveyard. The rest are all paupers in unmarked graves.'

'I'm sorry, father,' said Geraint. 'We must have been mistaken.'

'Of course, there is one strange stone,' said the priest suddenly remembering. 'It lays in the corner of the grave-yard but is unnamed.'

'Can we see it?'

'Of course,' said the priest, 'but don't expect much. No nobility lie there and it is visited once a year only by his descendants to pay their respects.' He led them out and pointed over to the far corner.

'Thank you,' said Geraint and they walked over. The grave was unkempt and the stone was covered with moss. Geraint knelt down and scraped away the growth before getting back up to stand alongside Tarian. For two minutes, neither said a word until Tarian said what was on both their minds.

'A lot of men have given their lives to find this man,' he said quietly, 'and he was within an arrow's flight of where this quest was first proposed.'

Geraint stared at the stone. No name was engraved within its weathered surface, instead there was a simple symbol: the one given to Madoc by the Mandans.

—

An hour later, the priest left the church and was surprised to see Geraint and Tarian still sitting alongside the unmarked grave. He walked over to address them.

'Still here, gentlemen?'

'We had a lot of talking to do,' said Tarian standing up.

'Do you know who he was?' asked the priest, indicating the grave.

'Possibly, but we thought you would be able to tell us more,' said Tarian.

'I'm sorry,' said the priest, 'I know very little except this. Once a year, a woman comes to lay a posy on his grave. She doesn't say much but I am aware she travels from Anglesey and I am pretty sure this man was her grandfather.'

'Really? That is a dangerous trip for a woman in these trying times.'

'It is,' said the priest, 'though she does travel with an armed guard. A sensible step, especially with a small child.'

'She has a child?' asked Tarian.

'She does.'

'And it is hers?'

'I believe so. Is that important?'

'It may be,' said Geraint standing up beside Tarian. 'Tell me, father, is this child a boy or a girl?'

'A boy,' said the priest, 'and though they hail from Anglesey, coincidentally he is named after an old prince that once lived in the castle.'

'What's his name?' whispered Geraint, hardly daring to breath.

'His name is Madog,' said the priest, 'Madog ap Llewellyn.'

For a few moments nobody spoke until Geraint finally turned to face Tarian.

'He had a grandson,' he said. 'All this time, the man had a grandson under our very noses.'

'Fret not for the past, Geraint,' said Tarian, 'for the dream is now reborn.'

'What dream?' asked the priest.

'But he is yet a boy,' said Geraint, ignoring the priest, 'and would be unprepared in the way of the world.'

'Prepare who?' asked the priest. 'What is all this about?'

'Then we should protect him until he is of an age to understand,' said Tarian.

'Agreed?'

'Agreed,' said Geraint and both men walked back toward their horses.

'Understand what?' shouted the priest, running after them. 'Who are you talking about?'

The men ignored him again and mounted their horses.

'Who lies in that grave?' asked the priest standing beside them. 'Where are you going?'

'We are going to Anglesey, father,' said Geraint.

'I don't understand,' said the priest. 'To what end?'

'To fulfil a quest,' said Tarian, 'and change the destiny of Wales.'

With that they turned their horses and galloped back the way they had come, their hearts filled with joy yet unaware that less than a hundred miles away, for the second time in four years, Edward Longshank's army were gathering for an invasion and this time, they were coming to stay.

Author's Note

Whilst the storyline is obviously fiction, during the research I came across many fascinating events or references claiming trade between Europe and America took place long before the arrival of Columbus. Whether they are true or not I will leave the reader to decide but whichever way your decision falls, I hope you find them as interesting as I did.

The True Cross

There was indeed a relic kept in the abbey of Aberconway for many years that was known as the True Cross. The Cross of Neith was said to have contained a fragment of the cross that held Christ at his crucifixion. It was brought to Wales by King Hywel Dda after his pilgrimage to Rome in 928 AD.

The Discovery of America

History would have us believe that Christopher Columbus discovered America in 1492 and whilst his four voyages were very historic in recording the new world, many experts now acknowledge that he was probably not the first. There is certainly proof that the Vikings founded a settlement in Newfoundland long before that and some archaeologists are confident that it is only a matter of time before more southerly settlements will be found. Indeed, archaeological evidence suggests that the ancestors of the Native Americans walked across the ice land bridge thousands of years earlier and if that is possible, others may also have made the journey.

Pre-Columbus Trade

There is a strong argument from many quarters that not only did medieval ships reach America prior to Columbus, but there is also evidence of these visits across the eastern edge of the continent. Traditionalists scoff at this idea but the arguments are growing stronger by the day, and those people not afraid to challenge conventional thinking work hard to prove their theories. Records are available that show graves have been found in the south-east of North America containing 'iron clad' warriors in stone lined graves, a type of burial common in early medieval Europe. There are even suggestions emerging that trade existed long before that with Roman artefacts being found along the eastern coast and whilst these are commonly dismissed as 'mislaid artefacts' from careless collectors, it is extremely interesting that no such carelessness exists along the west coast where no such artefacts have ever been found.

Prince Madoc

The stories of a Welsh Prince sailing to America in the eleventh century are well known, not only across Wales but across the world and especially in America. It is claimed that Prince Madoc sailed across the Atlantic on his flagship, the *Gwennan Corn*, not just once but returned for more settlers on two more occasions before leaving for the last time, never to return. The legend claims he landed in Mobile Bay in Alabama and made his way up the Missouri river, fighting battles with local tribes along the way. It is claimed that his descendants eventually merged with the Mandan Indians leaving stories of 'white Indians' with blue eyes and fair hair. In 1782, the first governor of Tennessee, John Sevier met with the chief of the Cherokee nation, Oconostota, and asked him about the many stone fortifications along the rivers. The chief told him that they had been built by a people from beyond the great water in great ships and were called 'The Welsh'. Sevier recorded this conversation in his writings in 1810. Oconostota also told of a story where many of these settlers died in a great battle with the indigenous tribes.

The Welsh Cave

In Desoto state park in Northeast Alabama there are a series of five caverns known locally as the Welsh caves. Nearby there are also the ruins of what seems to be a defensive structure, built using European techniques not known by the native Americans at the times.

Earliest reference to Madoc

In 1584, Dr David Powel published a document called, the history of Cambria. The following is an excerpt.

> Madoc left the land in contention betwixt
> his brethren and prepared certain shipps with

men and munitions and sought adventures by seas, sailing west. He came to a land unknown where he saw manie strange things. Of the viage and returne of this Madoc there be manie fables faimed, as the common people do use in distance of place and length of time, rather to augment than diminish but sure it is that there he was. And after he had returned home, and declared the pleasant and fruitfulle countries that he had seen without inhabitants, and upon the contrarie part, for what barren and wilde ground his brethern and nepheues did murther one another, he prepared a number of shipps, and got with him such men and women as were desirous to live in quietnesse, and taking leave of his freends tooke his journie thitherward againe. This Madoc arriving in the countrie, into which he came in the yeare 1170, left most of his people there, and returning back for more of his own nation, acquaintance, and friends, to inhabit that fayre and large countrie, went thither againe.

The Mandan Indians

The Mandan Indians themselves claim to be descended from the Welsh Prince and later travellers found the tribe had many traits similar to the Welsh. Many were light skinned, had fair hair and blue eyes, traits that were not shared by any other Native American tribes. In addition, where other tribes used dug-out or hide covered canoes, the Mandans used coracles, circular boats used across Wales at the time. Even the method of steering the coracles with single paddles was the same, itself an unlikely coincidence. Finally and the most telling evidence was the fact that these Mandans and their descendants are reported to have spoken Welsh.

Evidence of medieval occupation in America

There are many stone-built fortifications in the area but it is unlikely that Madoc had either the time or the resources to build castles during his lifetime. However, evidence exists of several stone fortifications that not only predate Columbus, but are totally alien to any methods of construction used by any Native American tribes. Locations include, Lookout Mountain in Alabama, Ft Mountain State Park in north Georgia and Manchester in modern day Tennessee. Many archaeologists agree that these forts predate Columbus by hundreds of years and are unlike any structure ever built by Native Americans. It has also been found that the construction and designs are closely similar to construction methods used in Europe at the time.

Capability of medieval sailors

Although commonly known as the dark ages, historians increasingly believe the period of time between the Romans leaving Britain in the fourth century and the Norman invasion, was an era of culture and interaction with many other countries. The Welsh were famed for their sea going capabilities and even as far as back as Julius

Caesar in the first century AD they were renowned for having a far superior fleet to the Romans. Therefore it is not too great a stretch of the imagination to think that medieval sailors were capable of transatlantic crossings.

The Martyrdom of St Edmund

And finally, in England there is a village called Stoke Dry. In the church, there is a mural on the wall that dates from the 10th century and is labelled as the Martyrdom of St Edmund, which is supposedly the killing of St Edmund by Danish soldiers. Though this is accepted by many, experts remain unsure due to the specific dress of the attackers. Some say the designs have been influenced by the voyages of the Vikings who may have encountered similarly dressed people in Newfoundland hundreds of years earlier but nobody is actually sure who the drawings depict. If any curious readers are passing the church, I will leave it for you to decide.

More from the author

The Blood of Kings
A Land Divided
A Wounded Realm
Rebellion's Forge
Warrior Princess
The Blade Bearer

The Brotherhood
Templar Steel
Templar Stone
Templar Blood
Templar Fury

Novels
Savage Eden
The Last Citadel
Vampire

Audiobooks
Blood of the Cross
The Last Citadel
A Land Divided
A Wounded Realm
Rebellion's Forge
Warrior Princess